Stop the Sirens:
Sirens of the Zombie Apocalypse, Book 3

E.E. ISHERWOOD

ISBN: 0692717188
ISBN-13: 978-0692717189 (Isherwood Media, LLC)

Fiction / Science Fiction / Apocalyptic & Post-Apocalyptic

For Grandma. May your journey never end.

*A world built on the certainty God exists would be indistinguishable
from a world built on the certainty God did not.
Without doubt, there is no faith. Without faith, there is no humanity.*

PROLOGUE: SHUSH!

Marty awakened lying in a clean bed, inside a well-lit room. She was on her back, and felt rested for the first time in a long time. She crawled out without her usual fear of falling. A clean change of clothes waited for her; a fuchsia pantsuit. What she really needed was a bath, but she wasn't going to turn anything down.

The outside sky caught her attention as she considered changing; she was high up in a skyscraper. The room seemed clinical, like a hospital, but she couldn't be sure. She wasn't even sure what city was outside. The "North Star" of her hometown of St. Louis was the Gateway Arch. The famous landmark would at least give away the city, though it was nowhere to be seen.

She only saw the upper portions of other buildings and lots of smoke near the ground below. A blur of light remained on the western horizon. Whatever clues she could find outside might help her identify her location. She spent twenty minutes looking, but saw absolutely nothing which gave her the all-important answer.

Where am I?

Resigned to her ignorance, she took a seat in a little chair next to her bed. While rubbing her legs she happened to look down at the bed's foundation. The words "Riverside Hotel and Casino" were stamped on the side. That made it much easier. Not a hospital after all.

She laughed despite her fear.

So I'm still in St. Louis.

She had no idea what day it was. How long she'd been there. If any tests had been done. The last thing she remembered was getting on the helicopter after Liam said goodbye, waving to him, and then—

—nothing.

I'm old. I must have zoned out.

She stood up again. She felt good. Getting up from a chair was normally a laborious process. Even her back wasn't bothering her at the moment.

"Al, am I dreaming right now?"

Her late husband/guardian angel did not respond.

"OK, I'm not dreaming."

She found a mirror over the sink in her room, and was happy to see herself for a change. Rather than the usual drooping eye sockets, her eyes looked bright. Even her skin seemed a little more firm on her face.

Maybe it was all that exercise.

She laughed out loud at the notion. She hadn't had so much exertion in decades.

"Hmm, exercise really is the best medicine."

She winked at herself in the mirror, then returned to the large window. The world outside was as dark as pitch on the ground and in the sky. No other lights were visible. The entire city appeared devoid of it. She had an inspiration to turn off the lights in her room so she could get a better look at the stars. She allowed some time for her eyes to adjust and beamed when she finally saw the stars.

She put her hand into the pockets of her pants, fighting a chill. Her hand brushed against something foreign. It was small, boxy, smooth, and about the length of her hand. She pulled it out to get a good look at it in the glow of the stars.

She inadvertently hit a button which turned it on.

Marty didn't know what a lock screen was, but she could appreciate the picture on it. Staring up at her, with a conspiratorial grin on his face —and a few tears in his eyes—was her great-grandson Liam. He had one hand in front of his mouth, with one finger up in the traditional "shush" symbol. Behind him she could just make out part of her own head, and the rotors of the helicopter. After a few seconds the screen went blank and she pocketed the device without audible comment.

He must have snapped the picture while giving me that big hug. Clever boy indeed.

Marty lay back down in her bed. Content for the time being. Somewhere out there people were thinking about her. Trying to get to her. Drawn by her siren song. A song she continually tried to mute.

Normally she prayed for others. Health for the sick. Luck for the out-of-work. Help passing a school test. Some prayers were epic in scale, others a simple show of affection. Always for someone else. But in a rare moment of spiritual weakness she requested something for herself.

Lord, if they come to save me—

Liam couldn't help himself. He would find a way. It was already written.

—please, I don't want anyone to die.

She admitted that wasn't how siren songs end...

3

EXODUS

Eight days since the sirens.

Fifteen-year-old Liam Peters looked up from the muddy water. He and several of his companions had escaped the bombs dropped on his neighborhood by jumping into a shallow creek at the far end of the shopping center parking lot they'd just sprinted across. First the A-10's swept his block of modest ranch-style homes—their deadly Gatling guns announced themselves like the horns of the Four Horsemen the Apocalypse. They were spot on for the actual apocalypse. And then something came down from high in the sky—the colonel he'd met at the government medical camp called them bunker busters—and moved the Earth just as they reached the creek for protection. Smaller bombs chased their big brother. He wasn't brave enough to look up over the bank of the creek to see the remains of his neighborhood yet. For now it was enough to be alive.

He studied the line of survivors, searching for his parents, his friends, and his recently-mistaken-for-dead girlfriend. He saw most of them from his patch of mud. He definitely saw *her*. Victoria! She was his apocalyptic girlfriend. A girl he met during the zombie plague. An older woman too. She was seventeen.

They'd met less than a week ago, but they'd been through a lifetime's worth of adventures in that time. They walked up the Gateway Arch together to help the St. Louis police department defend the park below from zombies and from waves of desperate looters. She went back up alone a second time as a diversion to save Grandma. That was the first time he thought she was as good as dead. After that, they teamed up for the impossible task of helping 104-year-old Grandma Marty escape the collapsing city of St. Louis to reach Liam's home in the suburbs. They pushed her in a wheelchair to escape zombies. They rode a freight train through hordes of the undead. They broke a blockade across a river set up by the Arnold, Missouri police department. Then they teamed up with an officer of the same department as they all watched the little town implode with the arrival of the refugees from the metropolis next door. And if that wasn't enough excitement, they reached Liam's home only to find his parents had left to go to retrieve Liam from Grandma's house. He had made it all the way home only to find he had switched houses with Mom and Dad. It was enough stress to drive anyone crazy.

But Victoria was there. She provided a quality he couldn't describe. A stability. A peace. Liam knew he tried harder when she was around, and because she was as smart as any girl he'd ever known, she was able to see things from a different perspective and give him ideas he otherwise would never have considered. He had actually started to believe things were going to be OK, even with a zombie plague unloading itself all over the world.

But then she was shot.

Throughout all their adventures they were being watched, and then pursued, by a guy named Douglas Hayes. He said he was a truck driver for the CDC—a man with no job once the medical unit effectively ceased to exist—but it became clear he was more than that. He eventually showed up at Liam's parents' house to collect Grandma. He requested Liam bring her to his military truck, but when he refused— well, Victoria got shot. That was the second time Liam thought she was as good as dead. By all rights she probably would have been, but the single gunshot hit the small but durable travel Bible Liam had procured for her earlier in their travels. The force of the bullet knocked her back and she hit her head on the ground when she fell, but she emerged relatively unscathed. Liam and Grandma were whisked away before they knew her fate, so Liam had several days to lament her passing.

Now, in the brackish creek, she was very much alive. Minutes earlier she had been wearing a clean and bright white shirt and blue jeans, with her brown hair tight in a ponytail. She reminded him of a perfect angel, returned from the dead. That angel was now covered in mud and filth. Her top was ruined. Her hair was soaked and sprinkled with debris. And her face...

Her face was a wreck. In the last week she'd been beat up violently by looters at the top of the Arch. Her face was graced with two black eyes, and more abrasions than Liam could count. Her nose might have been broken, though he couldn't say. Neither would she. In short, her face had seen some rough treatment of late. The water washed off the heavy makeup she'd applied to hide her wounds; he could see her face as it really was. He could only think of how much pain she suffered, and how it made him angry someone would have done that to her. It made his thoughts turn dark.

That is, until he saw her emerald green eyes look at him with a twinkle of mirth. Her demeanor suggested she was happy. He guessed she had a big smile on her face too, though her hand was over her mouth.

"What's so funny?"

She moved—sloshed—to be closer before she answered. "I think I broke a tooth jumping in here." She removed her hand, and sure enough blood was dribbling down her lower lip, mixing with the muddy water already there. A large cut graced her top lip. She removed her hand completely and gave Liam a genuine smile, a big one. She had lost one of the sharp top teeth. The visage was both horrible and comical. Liam couldn't help but laugh.

"Good Lord, Victoria, you need to start wearing a face mask."

His parents chose that moment to slither along into the conversation. Victoria smiled for them as well. Their faces reflected a more serious analysis than Liam's, but his sense of humor tended to activate under high-stress situations.

"Mom, Dad, I'd like to take this opportunity to introduce you to my wonderful and elegant girlfriend, Victoria. Victoria, this is my mom, Lana, and my dad, Jerry."

She played along, even though she'd already spent time with them. "Very pleased to meet you. Forgive me for not curtseying." They looked at her like she was crazy, but noticed Liam was laughing hysterically and decided it was just too silly not to laugh.

Across the parking lot their entire lives burned to cinders in the aftermath of the bombing.

Laughter took the edge off.

2

The group crawled out of the water, but stayed along the slope of the creek bank so they could observe the fires. It had been twenty minutes since the big one went off, and no more A-10's flew by. The attack appeared to be over.

Liam's dad wondered, "Who are we missing?"

Everyone scanned the area to take stock of any survivors. Liam saw all the people in his core group, including his parents. He could see Phil, the ex-police officer way down on the end. He was next to Melissa, a shoe saleswoman and apparently a military veteran of some kind. Liam didn't really know her yet.

The only person he didn't see was Drew, the boy who helped him get Grandma from the Boy Scout camp to Liam's house. He was last seen lying on the street after Hayes had punched him to commandeer his bicycle—with Grandma trapped in the bike trailer behind. The street corner where Drew was last seen was well within the impact zone.

In the end they accepted many of their neighbors were undoubtedly dead. When Liam's crew chased after Hayes in the direction of his waiting helicopter, they all escaped the potential blast zone. The neighbors remained in their homes or on their lawns, celebrating the fact they had defeated a small contingent of Hayes' soldiers in their Humvees. That celebration lead to their deaths.

The humor of the situation ebbed away as everyone realized the gravity of the loss.

"What do we do now, Dad?"

Liam had been waiting eight hellish days to ask that question. Ever since he and Grandma left her house in the city, he'd been trying to get home and find his parents. Yes, he wanted to be sure they were safe, but he also wanted to effectively hand over the responsibility of caring for Grandma so he didn't have to worry about her. Mom and Dad were always there when he needed them, even if he didn't agree with all their methods—such as sending him to Grandma's for the summer after a particularly trying period of family conflict. Now, his question rang hollow. Mom and Dad, he realized, didn't have all the answers.

They couldn't wrap up all his problems into neat solutions for him. Grandma had been taken by Hayes to do medical testing, despite his best efforts to protect her. Even his father wasn't going to have an answer to counterbalance that loss. His excitement at seeing them was quashed by the circumstances of the reunion.

His dad was lying face down in the weeds. His arms were spread out in front of him, and his hands were tucked back so they were on his face, as if he were using them as pillows. His mom was lying next to him, on her back, looking straight up at the sky. They had just lost their house. It was effectively destroyed days ago when a big military truck tore the whole thing to shreds with its top-mounted Gatling gun, but Liam wasn't bothering with the details. That was a previous run-in with Hayes. But now even the perforated frame of the house was gone; wiped off the Earth forever.

But it was more than that. Liam's dad had spent years diligently stockpiling supplies he would need in the event there were catastrophes —man-made or natural. He knew about the secret room in their basement where Dad stored all his goodies, including lots of guns. Liam suspected that was what really had him upset, above and beyond the loss of friends and neighbors. That was supposed to be their life raft in these chaotic times.

Jerry popped his head up to look at him. "I don't know Liam. I guess we wait for the fires to die out and then see if there's anything we can salvage. I'm sure our house is wrecked, but from here I can't see if it's a crater. We'll see."

Liam knew it was their only viable option. Wait and see. So they waited. The morning dragged by. As noon approached everyone was getting antsy. Melissa and Phil had been talking, and Melissa came over to Liam's parents.

"I know we all want to check it out, but we should wait a little longer. I have a bad feeling about going back to the scene of a crime, if you catch my drift. What if they're watching for us to return? There could be drones high above. It's what I'd do if I were running this operation."

Melissa was a forty-something woman Liam met several nights before as she walked up the street toward his house as a refugee. By almost any definition Liam figured she would be described as physically pretty. A little taller than most women, but shapely and well-proportioned. She kept her long blond hair in a ponytail, though now her hair was a mess, just like Victoria's. Though initially reluctant to accept the hospitality of Phil and Liam, Victoria convinced her to give up some of her fears. By her own account she had been sexually assaulted by her former boss, then harassed by the sickos of the refugee crowds as they all fled the city. She was in no mood to accept the hospitality of a couple men, until Victoria brought her in.

She then went on to organize some men and women around Liam's house, and together they got the drop on a group of hostile men intent on taking the house by force. The ensuing firefight was brief but intense. She proved her worth, though she ended up killing some of the wounded hostile men. She said it was to prevent them from coming back to harm them when they healed up. In his brief interludes of quiet thought of late, he'd wondered how Phil and his parents had agreed to keep her around after what were essentially battlefield executions. She was still with them, and going strong it seemed. Victoria said she helped organize the resistance on his whole street earlier today. She was probably very familiar with the people now dead up there. Liam was inclined to listen to her. Apparently everyone else agreed. They waited.

They were rewarded for their patience less than twenty minutes later when the sound of propeller-driven aircraft approached from south of them.

"Everyone down!" Mel cried.

The trees near the creek offered some protection from above, as did the mute color of all their clothes after being in the muddy water, but they didn't want to take any chances of being seen.

The two big planes drifted menacingly over their heads and tilted their wings so their propellers faced straight up. The ungainly-looking planes descended like helicopters to touch down on the large parking lot where Hayes' copter had departed hours earlier. Liam was so enamored with the planes he almost forgot why they were there. The back ramps dropped and Army men poured out. He could see about twenty per plane.

"What are Army men doing here?" Liam asked.

Melissa watched the drama with everyone else. "Not Army. The planes are V-22 Ospreys. Troop carriers. Those are US Marines."

Marines. Great.

"Liam, you must have made quite an impression on someone," Mel quipped.

He could only wonder. Were they sent by Hayes to clean up his mess? If he had them on speed-dial, why not send them first if he really wanted to capture Grandma without incident?

The Marines spread out in careful formations, alternating with each other to various positions until they were up in the ruins. It became difficult to see what they were doing; there was a lot of smoke wafting around from smoldering fires. They didn't appear to be searching any specific piece of the street.

"We should leave. They have to be looking for us." As his dad would say, sometimes they really *are* trying to get you. His instinct said run.

Phil was quick to agree. "Any competent police sweep we ever did would investigate any nearby hiding areas for survivors. This ditch will be high on their lists once they start fanning out."

Liam's parents seemed most reluctant to leave, but they were pragmatic about it in the end. They slid away with everyone else.

The creek provided an easy way to stay hidden. They followed it to a wider branch which went underneath a nearby roadway. Soon they had the entire road between them and the Marines. They kept going into a thick woodland beyond, then took stock.

Melissa gave her assessment. "We're probably safe over here, but I'd vote we go deeper into these woods just to be sure."

Jerry agreed but added one important request. "Once those guys leave, we have to go back and grab our stuff."

Liam looked at him like he was crazy. "Dad, our house is gone. There's no way your supplies survived that inferno. I'm sorry but it's true. We should never go back if we think all is lost. It would be a big risk. Right?"

Phil and Melissa glanced sideways at each other, each with big smiles on their faces. Melissa seemed to be bursting to share her secret. "Liam, I know your house is a smoldering ruin. I'm sorry about the loss of your friends and neighbors, and sorry your grandmother got captured by Hayes. But we've been busy beavers while you've been away."

Dad added, "We have a prepper, a US Army veteran, a police officer, and two whip-smart women on our team. Do you really think we'd leave our most important treasures sitting in our basement for anyone to take if we thought government agents were coming to our house to capture you?"

Liam thought about it for a few seconds, and grasped the implications. "No, I guess I don't think that at all."

For a brief time, the laughter returned.

3

The Marines weren't there long. The lumbering Ospreys were impossible to miss as they left. The group waited a suitable time and then returned to observe their street from a different vantage point.

"You think they would keep someone behind as a lookout?" Liam asked as he crouched behind a tree.

"Doubtful, I don't think any agency has the resources to fly aircraft in and out more than the absolute minimum. Marines are used when they want to kill someone or lots of someones. Special Forces are used when they want to observe undetected. Or assassinate you."

"Thanks, you're a real pick-me-up!" he responded.

The spirits of the group had simmered back to a disheartened baseline after the rush of dodging bombs, dragging themselves through creeks, and hiding in forests. Now they headed home—to see if anything more than splinters was left of the Peters' residence. Liam wasn't hopeful.

The remains of the street itself could be seen here or there, sometimes in remarkably undisturbed stretches of flat surface, but several bombs found purchase smack dab on the road. The resultant craters were impressive. Those big bombs had flattened all the houses in their immediate area, and the follow-up fire bombing had burned everything in the area to ash. Even the cars and trucks were empty hulks of fire-bathed steel. No one knew what kind of explosives had been used; Melissa said many of the most destructive types of ordnance had been outlawed against civilians, though there was no consensus on what constituted "civilians" when half the population was technically dead.

Liam's father tried to be pragmatic. "All we know for certain is that this street was considered such a high value target the military was able to task several planes, unload a significant amount of bombs, and send a couple platoons of Marines to make sure it was erased. All those resources would probably have been more useful fighting the zombies right now."

Liam and his father hadn't had time to catch up on all that had happened to them both since the sirens, but Liam took the opportunity to share the most salient bits of his struggle. "Hayes gave me a warning as he was taking Grandma away in the helicopter. He told me the planes were coming, which gave me time to escape. He said it was a detail he couldn't overlook, since I'd spared his life and the lives of his men. But he said nothing about why he needed to bomb us clean off the map. A colonel I met in the government medical camp said he was responsible for deploying the strikes on other camps when containment failed. The planes were designed to erase all threats posed by the plague."

All threats.

Liam's memory was jogged by his own statement. Several days ago he stood on a riverbank and wondered if his father knew the collapse was coming. He sent Liam to live with Grandma a few weeks prior to the outbreak of the plague, and she turned out to be an important objective to the CDC. Just a coincidence?

Liam pulled his father aside as they sifted through the ruins. "Dad, did you know the outbreak was coming? Is that why you sent me to live with Grandma when you did?"

His dad looked at him like he had grown a second head. "I sent you to live with Grandma because your attitude this spring was getting so bad both mom and I were arguing over which one of us would get to kick you out of the house when you turned eighteen. Your mom won that argument by the way." He gave a slight smile, continuing. "We decided we couldn't take a full summer of the yelling and screaming, so we asked Grandma if she'd mind having an extra helper around. We figured if nothing else she wouldn't be as affected by your attitude, and because she couldn't hear well we didn't have to worry about you being too loud around her with all your yelling."

That made a lot of sense. It was exactly the kind of statement he'd expect from his father. He also appreciated his dad hadn't exactly said no. Instead of pushing the issue, he moved on to a pain he knew they both shared. "I'm sorry I let Grandma get away. She said to tell you and Mom she loved you."

His father put his arm over Liam's shoulders. "I'm sorry you both got you mixed up in all this intrigue. It's bad enough escaping from the infected, but you were tough enough to get Grandma to safety even with all these other people trying to catch her. I'm real proud of you. In the end it was just bad luck that ruined your plan."

Liam had no doubt in his mind his father was on the up and up about loving him and wanting him to be safe, but there was something in his tone of voice that told him something more was on his mind.

"Here it is!" Liam's mother found the stake in the ground, signifying the location of the cache of weapons and material they had stashed in the woods. It was near a small fir tree which still had a lot of branches on fire.

"Behold, the burning bush."

Victoria's exclamation startled him. The small fir was the only such tree burning in the entire area. Other trees were smoldering, but this one still had flames on it. He watched it with rapt attention.

Victoria continued, in a distant voice. "The burning bush from the Bible was where Moses was given the task of leading the Israelites out of Egypt."

"OK, so who is Moses here? And where is the promised land?" Liam wondered.

They all stopped what they were doing and looked around at each other. It suddenly felt like a legitimate question. Was it Liam? He seemed most likely after leading Grandma and the others to this place. But at fifteen he had a long way to grow. Was it Jerry? Liam's father was capable and had also made a trip into and out of the fallen city. Or was it Grandma? She seemed to be a solid candidate given her age and her devotion to religion—if she were there to lead. Liam would be happy if it were anyone but him. He didn't judge himself a capable leader.

Nothing was clear cut in the real Apocalypse.

Phil finally spoke up. He pointed straight down.

"Right now these weapons are our Moses. They're going to lead us out of this wretched place, maybe not to the promised land, but to somewhere safer than this."

Almost in unison, they all replied with a hearty "Amen!"

4

The day ended with everyone huddled in the woods for protection. A small pile of supplies had been exhumed, including guns, ammo, and even Liam's backpack.

The bombing did its job and cleansed a wide area around the neighborhood of everything—including zombies—but more had stumbled in after the fact. It upset him they took their sweet time and didn't come until *after* the Marines departed.

He shared what he'd learned in the Boy Scout Camp, especially how they whittled stout sticks into nasty spears and how they used them to puncture the skulls of the zombies. "The key is to kill them with the minimal amount of noise so we don't keep bringing in more. A spear isn't as sexy as a gun, but it's free, it's plentiful, and it works. It also keeps the zombies at arms-length while you do your thing."

As they all tried their hands at making adequate spears, and dispatch the odd wandering zombie, they were pleased to learn a few neighbors did survive the assault. One of them was a man who lived several houses up the hill from Liam. He was old and gray, and had a serious demeanor almost all the time. Liam remembered him from his youth as the guy you never wanted to tangle with.

His name was Paul.

"Me and the Wright's from across the way were standing on my lawn when those birds first came through with their cannons. It was a sound of pure evil. We got lucky they was shooting right up the middle of the street instead of in the lawns and houses. Well I guess unlucky if you were in the street. I saw one man—I didn't recognize him—standing in the street one second, and then he evaporated. Just poof!"

The stern man almost showed emotion at that, but continued. "Well you can bet your ass we started running. Everyone scattered into the woods. My old legs wouldn't carry me faster n' a wounded dog but I never looked back. Them bombs hit the bottom of the street and worked their way up, so I had a little extra time. Others were in the woods too, running much faster. Most haven't come back. Maybe they ran into the dead walking toward the sounds of destruction..."

Paul explained he came back because he had nowhere else to go. No family. No friends. Nothing. Not even a pet.

No wonder he's a sour man.

It made Liam feel slightly better to know there were some survivors. Even crusty ones. He felt bad enough for being responsible for Drew's death. He'd given up hoping his friend survived once he saw the area he'd last been standing. There wasn't even a body to bury.

They didn't light a campfire for fear of being seen. They salvaged some stout patio chairs which had survived everything, and used those as a base camp of sorts. It at least gave them some place to sit besides the ground. For the first time in a long while Liam could relax in the company of his family. The whole group was engaged in hushed conversation around him.

Victoria sat in the chair next to his. Perhaps it was coincidence, but they were given extra room by the others. When she noticed him looking her way, she leaned forward to quietly talk, "We have to do something to get Grandma back. I feel horrible all this happened because of me."

"Because of you? This all happened because *I* brought her back here. If I would have kept her away she might still be with me." He knew that wasn't exactly true. Hayes had been looking for them the whole time. It was bound to happen sooner or later. He had a lot of resources apparently. But he wasn't going to let her take the blame for the end result. It was bad luck, as Dad said.

She was about to argue, but Liam moved on. "We can't worry about what's happened. We have to worry about what's next. Where do we even start looking for her? How can we rescue her? Is it even possible?"

Victoria sat back in her chair, thinking. The soft light from the moon made her bruises and abrasions disappear. Even her swollen lip was difficult to see. He was happy to be in her presence again, despite all the destruction it had brought. He was happy Victoria wanted to find Grandma too. It would be so easy to write her off as a loss and instead tackle the not inconsequential matter of survival day-to-day.

"You're always talking about the end-of-the-world books you loved to read. Did any of them give any clues on how we can get through this? Do you and I storm the city ourselves to rescue her, like they do in the movies?" She laughed.

He was put on the spot. He *was* always drawing parallels to the stories he'd read. Books about zombies were all over the place in subject matter, and of varying usefulness to the real life zombie apocalypse as he'd found out many times. Fictional stories always had clues. That was the big difference from reality. When it mattered in his own ongoing life saga, he saw no such convenient clues.

He felt in his pockets, thinking he was overlooking something. His pocketknife was in one, and the family picture given to him by Colonel McMurphy was in the other. He pulled it out and thought about the man he watched shoot himself in the head back at Elk Meadow—after he was bitten by a zombie test subject. In the dim light he could only see the outline of the man's wife and teenaged son. He had asked Liam to find them and tell them he loved them. It was his final request. Liam felt a lump in his throat as he relived those last moments. He turned the photograph over to see the address on the back. It was some town in Colorado.

Some clue!

He didn't think it likely they'd be going to Colorado anytime soon. Although...

"Didn't you say you are from Colorado?"

"Uh huh. Denver. Why?"

"The colonel. He gave me this picture of his family and said if I should ever be in their neighborhood, I should stop in and give them his last words. But the address is in Colorado. Some place called Grand Junction."

"I see the city name all the time on the interstate signs driving around Denver, but I've never actually been there that I know."

"It doesn't matter. We aren't going out-of-state anytime soon. We'd never make it." Liam recognized he was in delicate territory now. He didn't want to discount *ever* going to Colorado. Her parents were there. But clue or no clue, there was no way to safely cross 1,000 miles of the unknown. Certainly not for a flimsy clue. Not even for her parents.

Uh oh. Bad Liam!

He realized the irony pouring off his declaration. He'd travel any distance to find his own parents, but hers, not so much. At least, he was afraid that was how he sounded to her.

Victoria made a sound Liam couldn't interpret.

"I didn't mean anything by it. Someday we'll try to get there after this is over. I'd like to meet your parents." He tried to be cheery, and she even reached over and touched him on the arm, but he knew it was perilous to hope anyone could survive whatever *this* was. The end of the world. The Zombie Apocalypse. End Times. Take your pick. "Let's focus on one rescue at a time. Grandma first because we owe her. Then let's talk about getting you home to your parents. Deal?"

She was silent for a long time. He tried to play it cool. Did he say the wrong thing? The right thing? He chanced a look in her direction. She was silently crying.

He stood up, then drew her out of her chair. They held each other in the soft ambiance of moonlight.

Later they slept the sleep of the dead.

5

The night wore on. Hunkered down as they were, they only had a couple encounters with interloper zombies. Liam's spears were put to good, silent use. As the sun started coming up, the group came together to discuss the day.

Liam could tell they'd all been thinking about what came next.

Phil made the case they should try to get further out into the countryside. Find an abandoned farm or piece of land where they could regroup and ride out the worst. Melissa wanted to scout out from Liam's ruined neighborhood to find like-minded souls to join their group. She argued the bigger the group, the better chance they had to survive. Liam's parents had agreed they wanted to find Marty, but they had no suggestions on where to even begin. It left Liam and Victoria to answer that question.

"Victoria and I feel responsible for Grandma getting captured and taken away. I know what you'll say—that it wasn't our fault—but nothing can change our minds short of having her back with us. We've been trying to put our heads together to think of where she might have been taken but we're very short on clues. What I do know is this: I gave Grandma my phone just before she left on that helicopter. My hope is that somehow we can get a text through to her and—God willing—she'll figure out how to use my phone to send a message back telling us where she is."

Everyone seemed to perk up at Liam's revelation.

"There are a lot of assumptions, but if we can find out where she is we still have to figure out what we can do to get her out. We aren't exactly a crack commando squad." He looked around, thinking of the calamity they had just survived, and knew he could have been tossed in with worse survivors. In fact he'd spent some time with a group of twenty or so eighty-somethings. They were probably all dead by now.

"So Victoria came up with a short-term plan, a type of triage she called it, whereby we'll go back to the Boy Scout camp I left the other day, and use that as our base camp for future efforts. At least we know we'll have friends there, and we'll have a secure base from which to operate. Once there, maybe we'll be inspired to pick up clues to find Grandma."

He looked at Melissa. "They're going to need help with security, that much I can promise you. Also, I told them if I ever returned I would bring back weapons to help them fight off zombies and other threats. That might be the price of our admission."

He turned to Phil. "The other thing they're lacking over there is food. There are thousands of people and lots of water, but no food. If we can provide them some opportunities to get food—say from abandoned farms—it might further reinforce our value to them."

One thread was consistent through almost all the books he'd read on zombies. If you couldn't contribute to whatever survival group you happened to end up with, you were no good to anyone. Doctors would be near the top in terms of value. Soldiers would be important. Insurance salesmen or data entry clerks with no other skills would soon find themselves hungry. The wild card was pretty women. Many books placed high value on pretty women no matter what other skills they had. He knew deep down what that meant. As he looked at Victoria, Mel, and even his mother he felt an involuntary shiver at what awaited them if he and the other men failed. It was why he was adamant they go right to the camp.

He intended to present his group as being a valuable addition to the Boy Scout leaders. He knew Mr. Lee would have no problems accepting him. It was selfish to say, but he needed a good solid base so he could dedicate his time to solving the mystery of where Grandma had been taken. He couldn't do that if he was running around hiding from zombies, trading bullets with criminals, or zigging and zagging to avoid falling Air Force bombs.

There really wasn't much argument from the core family and friends. Old man Paul was adamant he wasn't leaving his home, even if it was lying flat. He insisted he still owned the land and was going to protect it until his dying breath. To Liam it seemed foolhardy, but his older companions seemed to admire his dedication. A few other neighbors came and went, none of them eager to move on to parts unknown based on the word of a kid.

Liam was used to it. He often thought he could be Jesus himself, citing his own scripture and working miracles, and someone in the crowd would criticize his age. But his reasoning was sound in this instance. There was nowhere else to anyone's knowledge that had been picking up the pieces and providing some hope. Most people were content to salvage from the dying world, or take from those left alive. Neither of those activities had any long-term prospects. Maybe it was too early to talk about rebuilding, but certainly now was the time to organize the people who would eventually do the heavy lifting of repairing the world.

Liam's dad summed up their mission plan. "So all we have to do is get our guns and ammo, walk through the back roads of the county, and then knock on the door of the Boy Scout camp to see if they'll let us in? That sound about right?"

Liam nodded.

His dad finished with words he'd almost forgotten. It was something he said often when he was letting Liam practice driving this past spring.

"Liam, you're driving!"

Let the exodus begin.

APOCALYPSE PYRAMID

As much as they wanted to rush out and get to the Scout camp, they had to find suitable transportation for everything they had to carry. Finding a working car on Liam's street was impossible. There were no salvageable vehicles of any kind left in the wreckage. It was unlikely they could find a car by going to other neighborhoods either. Scavengers looking for gas had taken care of most cars abandoned on the roads—their open gas caps hung out like dry tea bags—and anyone still holding on to a working car would protect it with their lives. No one felt like assaulting neighbors to steal their ride.

They decided to use Liam's remaining bike and trailer as a type of pack mule to carry a good portion of the guns, ammo, and other goodies. Liam was disappointed to see his dad had only saved one big bag of rice. He knew he had many more in the basement.

"Yeah, sucks about the rice, but I only had the time and energy to bury one of them. If I had access to a tractor I might have been able to get them all. It certainly would have helped our situation to have a nearly limitless supply of food."

Melissa seemed impressed. "What were you saving all that food for? If you don't mind me asking."

"Not at all. Well, it all started with Mormons. You wouldn't know it by looking at them, but one of their church's guidelines is to always be prepared for the end of the world—true story! Their church instructs them to have at least one year of food per person per household, and even has recommendations on what you need in terms of the food itself. I think they call it an Apocalypse Pyramid. The foundation for the whole thing was dried rice. For the three of us, I probably had 1,200 pounds of rice stored in my basement and garage. Most of it was in 30 or so airtight five gallon buckets, but this last bag was a recent purchase and I didn't have time to put it in the proper bins yet. Since I knew it was fresh, I grabbed this one."

"So you figured the end of the world would come and you and your family would ride out the storm on top of your Apocalypse Pyramid and everything would turn out fine?"

Liam knew his dad was serious about preparing for any emergency, but he had never come out and said specifically what his plans were. Looking around the wreckage of his neighborhood, and comparing it with the rest of the world he'd seen in his travels, he judged it was unlikely anyone could survive sitting alone in their basement.

"Well, I admit I seriously underestimated the swath of destruction generated by a worldwide collapse due to a plague. I thought maybe we'd have an EMP or terrorist attack in America. It would be bad, but eventually things would get back to normal because the rest of the world would be there to help. But this," he waved his arm at his street, "this plague is everywhere. Every street in the whole world probably has zombies pounding down doors. I've seen fires. Looting. Vandalism. It's everywhere. My preparations were never going to be enough for something like this. Maybe if I'd built a castle in the middle of nowhere and invited a small city's worth of people to help me defend it..."

He seemed to stare off into space for a few moments.

"...but I made a mistake. And I made it worse by breaking up my family at the worst possible time."

Phil, being a policeman, had made preparations too. Liam watched him grab big duffel bags of supplies before they fled his house. Was he also a closet survivalist?

"Phil, you seemed pretty prepared when we were at your house. Was your basement loaded with rice too?"

He started with a laugh. "No, I wasn't as prepared as your dad. My concern was keeping the peace in my neighborhood in the face of urban unrest. Have a shotgun and an AR-15 over my shoulder and man a roadblock to check who came up my street, that sort of thing. In my wildest imagination, I never envisioned a worldwide collapse, an EMP, or a devastating plague. We didn't even deal with those in our training scenarios. Mostly we trained for toxic spills on the highway, riots of shoppers on Black Fridays, and laying down spike strips to stop a high-speed car chase. My bags of goodies won't do anything to keep us fed."

And that was going to be the problem of the world. Getting fed. One half of the population was trying to eat the other, and the other half was dodging those biters to find food of their own. And no one was being charitable when finding a can of Spaghetti-O's was an extra few days of life.

It would only get worse. Liam's wide reading of end-of-world books said all roads lead to cannibalism. Not the dead eating the living...he wasn't sure if that was really cannibalism. Instead, the living eating the dead would proliferate as other food sources dried up. There was no way around that dark destination if society couldn't hold itself together.

Rather than continue down that line of thinking, he brought himself to the present to help the final loading of their "vehicles" for their trip.

They found a serviceable wheelbarrow and tossed the bag of rice in that. Between the bike and the wheelbarrow and everyone's backs, they were able to get all the important stuff. Not nearly enough once it was consolidated into the small caravan.

"It felt like we had more than what we have here."

"Don't look so beat down, Liam. The most important resource you will ever have is the one on your shoulders. We can scavenge food, eventually we can grow it. The weapons are important so we don't get robbed, or overrun by the undead, but even guns aren't the end-all of survival. Your work with the spears illustrates that perfectly."

Dad always knows just what to say.

2

They departed as the sun went down on the ninth day since the sirens. At the bottom of their street, close to where his friend Drew was last seen alive, Liam stopped to say a few words.

"Goodbye, Drew. Thank you for getting my Grandma safely to my street. You kept your promise to do that for me. Your parents would be very proud of you. I'm sure you're with them now—they can tell you themselves." He gave a weak chuckle, but couldn't say anything else.

His mom stepped up. She'd been unusually quiet of late. Liam noticed right away, but attributed it to all the excitement she'd seen the last few days.

"Dear Drew. I can't thank you enough for helping my Liam get home, along with his grandma. You were the answer to my prayers of the past week. I've never wanted to see anyone so much in my whole life, and you brought him to me. I'm so sorry you couldn't join us in this celebration. We will never forget your name and what you did for us. Rest in peace now."

"Amen," they all said in unison.

The group left the neighborhood for the sparsely populated county road. Liam and Victoria were on each side of the bicycle as it pulled the heavy bike trailer. Each held one side of the handlebar to propel it forward. The bike itself was loaded down with guns hanging off each side. There was no way to ride it anymore, but it was perfect for this task. They were able to wrap the guns in some old carpeting so it wasn't obvious what they were. No use making it easy for potential brigands to select them. They were playing the part of dirty carpet salesmen.

Liam's mother pushed the wheelbarrow. She wasn't a physically strong woman, but she was in good shape—she, like her husband and son, was a runner—and she preferred to push it rather than be part of the security detail. She said she wanted to leave that to the professionals.

Liam's dad and Melissa walked about fifty yards in front of the cargo haulers. She was in the lead, and Jerry was about ten yards behind her. Their function was to keep watch for possible problems ahead and prevent the rest of the team from getting ambushed. Melissa had a curious knack for whistling like a bird, which they agreed would be the sign to halt. Once it got dark, it would practically be their only safe method of communication.

Phil was the final piece of the parade. He had a black duffel slung over his shoulder. He was about twenty-five yards behind the cargo, and kept watch for surprises from behind.

They followed the same route Liam had traveled the previous morning. He ran into so few problems they all agreed that was the right path for the return trip.

Liam wanted to chat with Victoria to see if she was doing OK, but he didn't want to risk the operation with distracting gabbing.

I'm learning patience. Grandma would be so proud!

They were on the road for less than an hour when the first curveball appeared. Someone had spray painted white words on the dark street surface. They weren't there on his previous passage. The letters were huge and the words consumed the entire two-lane road from one side to the other.

"WARNING. LOOTERS SHOT. SNIPERS AHEAD. HIGH RISK. REPENT! CHURCH OF OWENS."

Liam remembered the name Owens. Those were the guys he'd met on his last trip who went to his high school. He knew their house was coming up, but in the dark he had a hard time judging distances. A mile ahead? He recalled it was on a long straightaway. Perfect for a sniper. And those good ol' boys looked like avid hunters.

The group had pulled back together to discuss the development.

"I know these guys," Liam began. "I ran into them on my way out here. They were big into camouflage clothing and looked like they'd been hunting since they were in diapers, but they were nice enough to me. We even went to the same school. They said I was welcome to return, but none of this," he pointed to the words, "was here."

Melissa replied, "Do we have any options to take a different route? Maybe another way would be safer? I don't like the idea of snipers picking us off in the night. Especially friendly snipers."

The group searched for an answer acceptable to everyone. Liam had a small light over his county map, but nothing jumped out at them as a slam dunk. A detour was attractive to avoid this particular threat, but Liam had no knowledge of other routes. There could be worse problems on those roads. He argued that he at least knew these people and could talk to them.

Victoria backed him up. "I trust he knows these people."

The fear of the unknown proved stronger than the fear of the known. No one could make a strong case for backtracking and finding an alternate route.

Melissa remained practical. "OK, so how do we get down this road without getting shot?"

"We sing." Victoria had their attention. "I grew up in a religious household. We sang all the time. My mom loved to sing when she did her chores. At the time it drove me crazy, but now I'd give anything to hear her silly songs."

"It seems like a risky proposition, but Liam knows these guys and also the sign mentions religion. In that light, this seems like a good gamble." Liam was pleasantly surprised his dad was backing him up.

They lined up in a tighter formation and began walking forward, into the moonlit night. They couldn't agree on any religious song they all knew, so they chose one verse that was very simple.

"Michael rowed his boat ashore, hallelujah!"

Melissa refused to sing, but she offered to whistle in harmony. Together they made quite the rolling church choir.

Liam was able to put the words together with volume, but he was enamored by the sweet vocals of his partner. Victoria's voice was stunning to him, even with something so simple. At one point, he nearly tripped on the bike's pedal because he was looking over at her. When she saw him, she knew what he was thinking and softly spoke to him over their mule. "Twelve years of choir practice!"

Wow!

They walked for about ten minutes, constantly repeating the one line of that song. Twice a zombie stumbled up the road embankment to try to ruin the fun, but both times Melissa used a stake to forcefully dispatch the intruders. Liam felt unnaturally buoyant at the energy they were throwing off. Nothing like a happy church song to push back the evil of the world. Even if it was just his imagination, it felt good.

They approached the home where Liam had previously been stopped by the group of young men. From out of the dark came, "Halt! Who goes there!" as if they were knights of old.

Liam took a chance. "Hail ahead Northwest High School! Boy Scout and choir group incoming!"

They were right up on the mailbox when he heard clapping.

"Well met, Boy Scout!"

The boys were practically right in front of them, hidden in a blind inside a nearby hedge. Exactly where you'd expect to find a group of hunters.

If these were his enemies, he'd already be dead.

3

"Don't you guys know any other lines to that song?"

Liam suspected Victoria did, but they all stood there shaking their heads.

"Well, neither do we. Guess we didn't pay attention during Sunday School."

Some chuckles from inside the bush.

Liam tried to convey their mission succinctly.

"Hey again, guys. I came through here two days ago. I'm hoping you remember me?"

"Oh, sure we do. You're practically the only person who has come through here that hasn't done something stupid like pull a gun on us. I can't understand if we look like idiots or what, but it has happened a few different times. That's why we designed this blind, so we could cover ourselves anytime someone comes through and gets crazy on us."

"Is that why you guys wrote that stuff on the road back there?"

"That was my momma's idea. She said it would keep the worst people away and only honest people would try to enter with such threatening warnings."

Liam didn't think that was exactly true. "Not to doubt your mom, but wouldn't the worst threats see your warning as a challenge, and then try to sneak in from a different direction?"

"Yeah, but we're pretty good operating in the woods. My cousins are out in the night right now. A couple neighbors are also out there. We look out for each other. Got to do what you can. Momma's idea has turned some people away. We've watched them during the day."

"Do any vehicles come through here anymore?"

"A couple of ATVs have been through. Those were neighbors from a few properties down the road. They have family up that way. Oh, a military convoy came through the other day, not long after you did. They didn't even slow down and we didn't make ourselves obvious to them. Don't want them to Third-Amendment us."

"Third Amendment?"

Liam's dad knew it. "They didn't want the government to quarter troops inside their house. It's difficult to say if we are at peace or at war, and that can determine the rights of the homeowner. I'm inclined to believe this is a state of war, which means the government can pretty much do whatever it wants."

Liam actually laughed. "You mean like firebomb homes, kidnap teenagers and 100-year-old ladies, and kill anyone who happens to get in the way?"

His dad gave a knowing smile in the glow of various flashlights.

"Anyway, we're going back to the Boy Scout camp so we can find a way to rescue my grandma from the CDC. They want to experiment on her. Kill her, I think."

That seemed to strike a chord with the young men. A man with a full beard about eight inches below his chin came out of the blind. "My grandpa, God rest his soul, was a spry 90-something before all this happened. He lived with us in our house. We kept him on the main floor because he couldn't do steps very well, but he was on all kinds of medications and oxygen. When the power failed us, we had a small genny, but that didn't last very long. When that gave out, he didn't last very long. I think he just let himself die. I'm sorry they're doing that to your grandma. It ain't right."

Liam thought of all the old folks he'd seen at the government camp. Each of them likely had family missing them terribly. He remembered how ornery some of them were, and revised it to "some of them had family missing them." No sense sugar coating it. Old people could be jerks too.

"I'm sorry for your grandpa."

They all stood there for a few moments, no one really sure how to proceed. Melissa broke the stalemate.

"Do you guys have any intel on what's ahead on this road? Anything we should watch out for?"

It turned out they had spent a lot of time getting to know their road.

"Zombies are everywhere, of course. We haven't seen any evidence of organized resistance or criminals. Everything is clear to the intersection of the highway a couple miles that way."

Liam remembered *that* intersection. He was held at gunpoint by a drug abuser while he was riding his bike on his previous trip through there. It was a massive traffic jam of dead vehicles and dead drivers, centered around a cement truck which had plowed into them all, and surrounded by a ring of stripped and useless cars. It would have been very difficult to get a large vehicle through the mess. Bikes would be a snap, relatively speaking.

Liam found himself liking these country folk. He wanted to continue a relationship with them, even if they never came back through here. It would be good to know someone doing good work out here, in case they ever needed a place of last resort. He was saddened by his morbid realization he was already planning ahead for when the Boy Scout camp got wiped out.

Grandma would give me a pep talk right about now.

"Excuse me for a moment. I need to talk to my dad."

Liam pulled his dad aside, and quietly asked, "Dad, I've read a lot of books about zombies and it struck me these people would be good allies. If we make it to the camp, it would be nice to know we have friends down here. If we don't make it to the camp, we'll have some place to retreat."

"Excellent thinking, Son. Nice to see all those video games and silly books didn't take away your brain." He smiled at Liam.

Despite the friendly tone, he tried to ignore the insinuation. That was the old Liam.

Jerry offered a proposal. "Our plans are to join up with the Boy Scouts up to the north of here. If we survive this trip and make it there, it would be great to tell them we have allies down here on their south side. In exchange, it would give you somewhere to go if you find yourselves in trouble. You're the only group we've found—besides ourselves—in this part of the county."

The young man with the beard said he needed to run inside and talk to his mom. To Liam, it was funny the kids acted as liaisons between the parents. Between groups. Maybe this was the first step in an alliance that would last for a thousand years.

Feet on the ground, Liam.

It wasn't long and the bearded guy came trotting back.

"My mom agrees to your terms. She wants me to go with you to scope out the place and establish boundaries. No time to waste, she says."

Liam looked to the house, wondering about the woman inside. She seemed really adept at this new reality. Some people did better than others "rolling with it."

The bearded guy was "Bo" though he didn't say what it was short for, if anything. He carried an expensive semi-automatic shotgun and had two pistols in a holster on each side of his waist. He was dressed completely in camouflage—hat, long pants and long shirt—despite the summer heat. It looked like he would disappear in any wooded environment.

He said goodbye to his relatives, though he didn't seem particularly put out. Like he expected to be back in no time. Liam hoped that was true.

He also ran behind his house and came back with a sleek-looking bicycle with skinny tires.

"This is my brother's bike, but he won't mind if I use it."

"Hell I won't!" retorted the bush.

They were saying their goodbyes when Liam remembered he had one more question.

"What is the 'Church of Owens' that you wrote on the road?"

One of the other boys spoke up. "That was my aunt's idea—Bo's mom—she's a preacher. She said people will have more respect for religious figures in the End Times."

Liam didn't say it out loud, but he was pretty certain she was exactly wrong on that point. He'd read books on the Tribulation, formally known as End Times in scripture, and religious people were in for a rough ride in that scenario.

But Liam didn't believe this was Biblical End Times. He was certain Grandma would have been taken if the Rapture was real.

No, this was much worse.

4

Bo pushed his bike next to Liam and Victoria, in the middle of the caravan. Liam wondered if the slim bicycle would be able to hold the large man. He had to be every bit of six-foot-four inches and 250 pounds. But he looked very fit.

They shared some small talk while they were still near Bo's house, but things quieted down as they got back out into the wilderness of the road. Almost immediately, they heard Melissa grunting as she dispatched a zombie. A few moments later they had to swerve around the body.

Bo whispered, "Wow, she can really take care of herself."

"You're telling us. She's a bundle of energy."

Not long after, they crossed over the outgoing set of spray painted warning signs on their way out of Owens' territory. They approached the intersection Liam had feared. The group tightened up, and they laid the bikes in the nearby tall grass while they tried to observe what was ahead. In the moonlight, the intersection looked positively haunted.

Phil reached into his duffel, pulled out an apparatus, put it on his head, and flipped down what looked like binoculars over his eyes. He whispered, "Night vision, courtesy of a Homeland Security grant to the department." Then he spent about five minutes scanning the intersection in front of them.

"I see a few patches of smoke, but no movement of people or zombies. As best I can tell, we can cross to the other side. Wait!" He was now looking to their right, which was on the uphill side of the intersection. "I can see a loose group of people walking away, up the road. I can't tell if they're zombies, but it would be my guess." He then looked in the other direction, slightly downhill. The highway was four lanes wide, but it had a median in the middle to separate the two directions. "It's hard to tell from so far away. There may be more people that way walking in this direction."

Stay or go. The gamer's dilemma once again.

Like so many decisions of late, the fear of the unknown beat out the fear of the known. They *knew* one group had just passed. The second group *might* be heading this way. If it was daytime, both groups would be on them. They decided to chance it.

They walked toward the intersection. Because he had been through here before, Liam explained how the only clear path through the debris and car jam was on their left side. He tried to detail how it wound along the near lane of the highway before crossing the median. On the far side, the path came back to the intersection. The route was basically a large letter U. He'd had the advantage of much more light to pick his way across. Now they had to do it at night, with strangers lurking in the shadows.

The path was confusing to explain, but the only dangerous section was right at the beginning. The intersection itself was along a small ridge line, so the main roadway going north and south was elevated above the surrounding wooded landscape. Liam noted how vehicles trying to get through this choke point were forced to drive on the steep incline next to the highway for a hundred yards or so to the south, before there was enough free space up on the road itself. Even the shoulder was blocked. In the light of day, it looked precarious. Now...

"We have to go to our left along that embankment. Then we'll see the opening up on the roadway where you can get back to level ground. It should be no problem on foot."

He crossed his fingers.

Mel and Jerry went ahead into the darkness along the incline. Bo followed with his bike. Liam and Victoria with their loaded contraption dropped in line next. Lana and Phil were behind; they worked together with the unwieldy wheelbarrow.

He had to push the bike upright from the lower side as he walked along the hillside. There were deep ruts in the grass from four-wheel drive trucks plowing through here recently. He imagined Hayes and his Humvees had probably been on this same hill the day before. Victoria did her best to steady the bike it fitfully rolled along the uneven ground.

Liam thought of something Grandma had told him about the rhythm of life. She'd said life has a rhythm, and once you get used to it you can see things that don't belong or that aren't right. He got that feeling as they walked. A sort of deja vu mixed with a premonition, signaling a disruption.

He felt his heart beating in his chest as they stepped through the difficult terrain.

Beat.

He stumbles in some loose dirt.

Beat.

He tries to compensate as he grips the bike.

Beat.

Victoria is surprised and the handlebar starts to slip from her.

Beat.

The bike leans heavily in his direction.

Beat.

"I'm losing it!" she shouts.

He didn't want Victoria to tumble with the bike and trailer. It was going to happen no matter what she did. His only option was to spring out of the way so he wasn't hit by it. That's exactly what happened.

The overloaded bike tipped to the left. At first he thought the trailer might keep the bike from going all the way over, but it didn't. Instead, metal bent and broke. Liam jumped out of the way, Victoria lost her grip completely, and the whole contraption slid and bounced loudly down the hill. It was fifty or so feet to the bottom; enough space for all the cargo to explosively depart the rigging they'd made to hold it all together.

Everyone else watched helplessly as the bulk of their weapons disappeared into the darkness.

He should have been taking things seriously, especially knowing what was up on the roadway heading his way, but his thought at that moment was of something he'd wondered about on day one of the disaster. "*Am I* that guy *who does the stupid stuff and brings ruin to the group?*"

He ran scenarios in his head. *That guy* who gets bit by his girlfriend because he was too stupid to know she was infected. *That guy* who stops the car to take a leak, only to be attacked at a delicate moment. *That guy* who can't even manage a simple bicycle and dooms them all to battle zombies in the dark.

He hated the thought, but there was no denying he'd screwed up.

There was no time to decide who he was. He had to run.

"Get to the bottom!" Melissa tried to be quiet about it, but had to be loud enough for everyone to hear at once.

They all started down. There was no way to secure the wheelbarrow on the side of the hill, so Mom and Phil held it tightly as they moved down the incline, but it also got away from them. They had gone about half way so it wasn't such a disaster, but it still tipped the bag of rice and other gear onto the grass and then bounced loudly on a concrete drainage channel at the bottom.

All my fault.

Liam was the first one down to the edge of forest along the highway throughway. Liam found it hard to see what had become of his bike and the cargo. Melissa was down shortly thereafter.

"We can try being quiet down here, but it's probably too late for that. Have your weapons ready. There could be lots of them." She saw Liam trying to gather random pieces of their gear. "Don't bother picking up yet. There's no time and we can't risk lights."

Liam readied his weapon instead. Victoria did the same.

"I'm sorry, Liam, I couldn't hold on."

"Totally my bad. I tripped and couldn't find my balance." He was more concerned about her rifle. "You said you know how to work an AR-15. Do you have any extra rounds with you?"

"No, I just have what's in the clip. Thirty rounds, I think."

He didn't think the cusp of battle was the right time to correct her terminology. "Me too. I didn't anticipate the need to carry more mags since we had a wheelbarrow full of ammo with us."

Never take anything for granted. Never.

"There are 1,000's of rounds of ammo within fifty feet of us, spread out after they tumbled down the hill," she said with a wisp of regret.

All of them took positions at the bottom of the steep hill. Mel and Phil were on the left. Lana and Jerry were on the right. The three young adults were in the middle.

In a couple minutes the first head popped over the edge of the highway above them. Looking for the sounds and tastes of fresh human meat.

She brought friends.

5

Liam carried four weapons. The least useful was his pocket knife. It would barely be classified as a weapon under most circumstances, but certainly not for this one. The next least useful weapon was probably his small .22 caliber Ruger Mark I. It had a nine-round mag, and Liam actually had a few extra rounds in his pockets, but it was difficult to aim in the dark, and there was no margin of error when shooting zombies in the face. Reloading in the dark while in close combat would be impossible. Next was the spear he kept lashed together with his rifle. The stout stick was useful for piercing the brains of zombies and could be reused many times. The primary downsides were you had to be strong to use to more than a few times, and it was ineffective against multiple close enemies. His most useful weapon was his AK-47 from his dad's stockpile. Practically a collector's item, the distinctive rifle found its way into Liam's house because it was so cheap to buy. His dad had ten of them. It could put a deadly round into the brain of a zombie from a reasonable distance, though in the dark, its usefulness was reduced greatly. Still, of them all, the AK was his go-to first line of defense. With careful husbanding of ammo, he and Victoria alone could take down sixty zombies. The thought of needing more was enough to make his knees wobble.

The others had similar rifles or shotguns at the ready. Liam stuck his spear into the hard-packed soil of the weedy grass so he could grab it if he ran out of ammo. Victoria did the same next to Bo. They agreed whoever ran out of ammo first would use those backup weapons. Victoria also had one of Liam's Mark I's in her holster, but she only had nine rounds for it.

The filthy robed woman up top screamed and began her descent. Almost immediately, she tripped on the same ruts responsible for Liam's accident moments earlier. It was almost comical as she fell forward and tumbled down the hill in a raggedy ball of arms and legs. She came to rest directly in front of Bo—right in the middle. Liam hadn't seen a zombie get disoriented, but this one had trouble getting back up. Rather than take the easy shot with his shotgun, Bo slung the gun over his shoulder, grabbed the spear at his side, and slammed it home. The woman was hard to see in the low light, but the gruesome sounds of the spear plus the pangs of death were horrible. Liam braced for things to get worse.

More came over the top. Almost all of them arrived from their left. A few were walking along the embankment from that direction, though most were coming straight over the top as if they were in the jumble of cars to begin with.

About half the zombies met the rut and tumbled down the hill. Most were out of control as they seemed to lack any sense of balance once they went from flat to hillside. In moments, there were a dozen falling down the hill.

Then it got loud. Liam had been around firearms his whole life, but always with the approved safety goggles and ear protection. These days, people did away with such frivolities. It was just explosion after explosion from the barrels of their guns. He almost longed for OSHA to come write them a ticket for having an unsafe work environment.

Most dropped to a knee to steady their aim. Hitting things in the dark was already difficult. Hitting tumbling things in the dark, while aiming for their heads, was a whole new level of crazy.

Those who rolled down were comparatively easy to dispatch. Once they reached the bottom, they were exposed on the ground while they tried to recover. The moonlight was enough to find their heads. The real problem were the random zombies who stayed on their feet as they sped down the hill—not quite a run, more of an ungainly bounding. They closed the distance with the shooters dangerously fast.

The first person to go down was Jerry. He was hit at full speed by a lanky man and together they fell over into the wooded fringe behind them all. Lana was experienced pulling zombies off her husband, but her action took them both off the firing line while they contested the outcome. It left a lot of territory for Liam to cover.

He was already on his knee and lined up his shots as carefully as he could, but he still missed a lot. Even when a zombie was hit in the head, its momentum kept it going down the hill—adding to the chaos.

In less than a minute, Liam's rifle was out of ammo.

How did I go through thirty rounds that fast?

He threw it down and pulled out his Mark I. It gave him nine more shots before things would get personal with the spear.

Meanwhile, Phil and Mel dealt with the same problems. They had to take a few steps backward so they had some level ground in front of them where the descending ghouls could come to rest and be dispatched. They were much more disciplined than Liam and Victoria, so the hammers of their guns kept things even on that side.

In the middle, Bo, Liam, and Victoria took a step or two back from the hill to make room for the stack of undead developing there. Bo was still using the spear. Despite his heft, he darted among the injured or disoriented zombies lying at their feet and put them out of their misery. He dodged and ducked between Victoria and Liam with athletic grace as they all sought targets.

"I'm out!" Victoria threw down her rifle, just as Liam had done. She went right for her spear, rather than her pistol. She tried to help Bo.

Liam couldn't get a read on the chaos around him. To his left, he heard his parents yelling and screaming as they rolled around in weeds. To his right, he only heard the regimented banging sounds of the expert shooters. The middle?

We're screwed.

More zombies came over the top.

"We need a new plan!" Liam yelled it, but didn't know to whom it was directed.

His mom answered.

"We have to pull back. Jerry's injured."

Jerry was howling in pain, but managed to shout over all the noise, "No! We can't leave the supplies!"

"Dad, just leave it. We can come back for it. Let's move!"

He didn't know if anyone would listen to him, but he grabbed Victoria and she readily followed. Soon they were all following Liam into the dark woods.

Ahead he had trouble seeing anything. The bright flashes of the guns had ruined his night vision, and the moon was unable to penetrate the thick canopy of leaves above them. He had forced a decision for them all—and it could be a decision that killed them all. What if they ran into another group of infected in this direction? He'd remembered how zombies seemed to end up in pockets in the woods around the Boy Scout camp, like they'd gotten lost and were waiting for something to guide them out. Something alive.

He didn't know how badly his father was injured. Maybe he couldn't keep up?

He stopped in a small dry rocky creek bed; the others came up behind him. Several small flashlights bobbed his way. Phil and Mel were last, constantly picking off the fastest pursuit.

"Where's my dad?" Looking around, he added, "and where's my mom?"

"Dad! Mom!"

"We're coming!"

They weren't far behind; his dad leaned heavily on his mom. In the darkness it was impossible to see his condition, but his heavy grunting painted a dire picture. He had no time for a checkup. Other grunts and moans weren't far behind his parents.

"Keep moving."

It was as intelligent a plan as he could come up with at that moment. Everyone followed.

In a few moments, Liam found a small rocky outcrop blocking his path. He could tell they were facing the start of an incline up the next hill, and this formation provided the perfect defensive position. If he could get them all up onto the top of the rocks.

"Everyone up on these rocks. We're going to fight them from here."

He kept it simple. Everyone in the group grasped his plan as soon as they saw the rocks. Find a way up, wait until the zombies show up, then fight them from a raised position.

"Just don't let them grab your feet. That will be the end."

He didn't need to spell it out. He'd seen men and women pulled from the flat railcar he'd rode out of St. Louis. It had also provided an elevated fighting position. But there were untold zombies pursuing them a week ago. Enough that they stacked up and made unholy ramps for others to climb.

Surely there couldn't be that many? Unlike the rail car, they could move along the rocks if there were too many. They could start running up the next hill if things deteriorated. That is, if his dad could move. He tried to get a read on his father.

Jerry made it up, but was lying on a rock, behind Lana. Liam could just see him in the darkness. Condition unknown, but not looking good.

They'd had just enough time to arrange themselves in a loose line, facing the direction from which the zombies hurtled out of the darkness. The risk of shooting each other was minimal.

Liam wondered if he would be *that guy* that gets shot by friendly fire.

Or worse, shoots my own friends?

So much to worry about in the seconds before contact.

The zombies weren't fooled by the retreating humans or by the darkness. They weren't as fast, but they stayed on track as they approached the rocky area.

They had also thinned out. The trees and uneven terrain of the woods ensured the mass of zombies was staggered. They attacked the group in ones and twos, rather than all at once.

The height of the rocks made using the spears kind of awkward. To be effective, Liam had to drop to one knee to get the leverage he needed to thrust downward into the heads of the zombies. He also found himself constantly worried about tipping or being dragged over the side of his perch. A few times, he had to jump the rocky terrain to find new perches.

After some initial gun fire, the entire group reverted to their spears. Even Bo had borrowed Jerry's, and joined the horrible melee. Soon all he heard was the sickening slurps of spears finding their homes in the skulls of the plague victims, followed by a dull crunch as the bodies fell onto the forest floor. The huffing and puffing of the men and women thrusting the spears played counterpoint to the death they handed out.

Liam found the rhythm both horrible and beautiful. In one of the increasingly longer lulls between zombies, he debated if Grandma would call this the rhythm of life? Personally, Liam felt the sounds of life's harmonies were gone forever. The laughter of children. The patter of rain. The rustle of leaves. Those songs were for the living with a bright future. Hearing them now only reminded the listener of what was lost.

All that remained was the cacophony of a dead and dying world.

The horrible music played for a long time, but went silent with the dawn.

They survived to see the tenth sunrise since the sirens.

TROJAN HORSE

The dawn brought a new perspective on the destruction they'd wrought overnight. Liam looked around the rocky outcropping where they'd found sanctuary; bloody, discarded bodies were strewn everywhere. They were stacked two or three deep, but nothing like he'd seen on the railroad journey. They were too spread out here.

His dad was fortunate. He wasn't bitten.

"Your mother says I broke my fibula. It was that very first zombie that ran me down. It pushed me back and I fell over a tree root and he landed hard on top of my leg. The force fractured my bone. It hurts like hell." He laughed a little to show he wasn't giving up.

Bo and Phil helped him walk back through the woods toward the road. The others provided security with their spears. There didn't appear to be any additional zombies afoot, at least not in the woods.

When they arrived back at the bottom of the roadside hill, they were amazed at how many infected they'd killed there. The use of firearms knocked down a lot of zombies in a short period of time, probably giving them the edge they needed to retreat and survive the night. Without the spears, they'd probably all be dead.

"We need to give those Boy Scouts a medal or something." Liam was being serious. Boy Scouts loved awards and commendations. It was part of their DNA.

They started to clean up the mess of the fallen bicycle and wheelbarrow. Guns had been flung everywhere, the bag of rice had been partially damaged, and boxes of ammo were spread among the dead bodies in their little combat zone. It was like a sick Easter egg hunt.

Liam focused on the bike. He was positive it would be ruined, but it looked remarkably intact upon closer inspection. The fabric of the trailer had several big rips, but the frame was fine. In the end, the only major structural issue was the arm that hooked up to the rear frame of the bike. It had been bent pretty bad, and didn't seem likely to survive being bent back into proper shape. It was only a hollow aluminum tube.

They decided to collect the guns and put them on the bike again, just as they had before. They put most of the ammo into the wheelbarrow. It was so heavy Phil was put in charge rather than Lana. Since the trailer arm was broken, Bo had an idea to use a stout log to pull it by hand. Liam found the proper piece of wood for the job. It was about a ten-foot straight section of a young sapling. It took some time with his pocketknife and some larger knives carried by the others, but they were able to get it down. The key feature was a notch in the bottom where a second shoot was growing upward. It provided a kind of hook at the end.

By the time he was done, most of the debris was cleaned up and waiting for him up on the highway. They put things together in between several cars so as not to be easily seen by anyone or anything else. Liam used his hook and slid it underneath the two-wheeled trailer, anchoring it to the frame by pulling it forward. Now, they could pull the little trailer by hand. The last thing he needed to do was put his dad back there.

The trailer was built to seat two small children side by side, facing backward. A full-sized man like Jerry was hard pressed to fit in there, but it was up to the task. The makeshift ambulance was completed when they found an empty suitcase in the traffic jam. They put the extendable handle under the frame of the trailer, wrapped up with the wooden hook. This allowed Jerry to put his broken leg into the suitcase as its small wheels rolled behind the trailer. It was ugly, but it worked. Liam and Victoria both pulled the trailer. Lana walked behind Jerry. Bo was in the lead with his shotgun at the low ready. They used his bike for a few guns and some equipment they stuffed into Phil's duffel.

They grabbed another empty suitcase and put the mostly full bag of rice in it. Lana pulled that behind her.

Finally, they cleared the big intersection. On several occasions, Bo used his spear to repulse aggressive straggler zombies. Once he fell to the ground after badly misjudging the speed of an oncoming walker. The two tumbled together. It happened with lightning speed. One second Bo was fighting like a pro. The next minute he was in mortal danger.

Lana had made a living out of saving her husband the past ten days.

"Keep him off you. I'm here!"

She used her spear as a baseball bat first, and got the attention of the blood-slick and sick-looking male zombie dressed in short pants and a tank top as it squirmed on top of Bo. He had the good sense to pull up his knees to keep the thing off balance and off his skin. It allowed Lana's "bat" to hit him solidly in the head; the momentum carried him to Bo's side. It was off to his side, so he could roll away. By the time he was up, Lana stood over a still corpse.

"Thanks. That was close!"

He wiped sweat from his brow in the early morning sun.

"Don't mention it. I'm glad I could get to you in time." Then, as she looked back at the group, she doled out a piece of advice. "If they ever get you down, keep moving. Keep them off balance. Keep something between *its* mouth and *your* skin. As long as we stay in a group, you should only need to keep them at bay for a few seconds and we'll be along to help you. We have to look out for each other. Always."

Liam knew it made all the sense in the world. What he never expected was to hear his mother giving him advice on how to survive in a world filled with zombies.

I assumed it would be the other way around.

2

The second half of their journey was anticlimactic. They struggled along with the bike and trailers, and made terrible time. They discussed resting in the trees but everyone was anxious to get to the safety of the Boy Scout camp. So they pushed on.

They had nearly reached the last intersection before the camp when Lana's phone beeped as if it received a text message. Everyone stopped, shocked at the unfamiliar noise. The beeps and rings of technology had already faded from their memories.

This is Liam. At Lone Elk Park at a gov camp. Just broke free. Beware Hayes. Heading for home. Have grandma. 7d since sirens.

"You sent this three days ago; I already got it. It's how we knew you were coming home and had Hayes to worry about. But now it's showing up again."

"I wonder if this is intentional? Maybe someone is controlling the cell towers. Someone we may have met before?"

"Hayes? He already has Grandma; why would he want you too?"

"Us. Why would he want *us*?" Liam reminded his dad.

"OK, so maybe not Hayes. Then who?"

Melissa was a little less paranoid. "Maybe this is just a coincidence. Sometimes a cigar is just a cigar."

Liam scratched his head at the reference, but had no ideas. Maybe he *was* getting too paranoid.

"OK, the question is, do we try to contact Grandma while we can?"

The group huddled together. They stood in front of Jerry in the trailer, since he couldn't get out. "We may never get another chance to do this. If we can find out where she is, it's worth the risk." Liam was ready to jump on the chance.

Victoria was uncharacteristically hesitant. "Maybe we should think this through, Liam. If someone is tracking your family, they'll be watching for your message. That might lead them right to us. They'll surely realize we're heading for the Scout camp. That could put everyone there in danger."

Melissa agreed. "Whoever is out there, they have sophisticated intelligence assets, not to mention the use of the US Military. For all we know there's a B-2 bomber up in the stratosphere just waiting to plug in coordinates to deliver its payload."

Liam had recently seen a B-2 bomber doing just that. It was part of the bombing done on the zombie horde back at the St. Louis Arch. Day three of the collapse. That seemed like months ago.

The group argued the pros and cons for a couple minutes. All the while, Liam felt the sands of time slipping away. What if the network shut down for all eternity?

His father sat quietly. Listening. "I feel like there is something afoot here. The network came up for a purpose. Whoever did it probably has the resources, like Melissa says, but we need the network to contact Liam's phone so we have a clue where she's being held. I think we all know the risk, but I vote to try. Better now than trying it inside the camp where there are people to worry about."

Liam felt relieved. Mainly for his dad's confidence in his plan, but also—he admitted to himself—he was glad his dad was there to make decisions again.

Everyone else agreed, or at least didn't argue. Victoria was quietly kicking a stick on the ground.

Liam got to making his call on his mom's phone, but was disappointed to find he couldn't make a voice call. He went right to text. "Grandma may not know anything about texting, but she's a smart cookie. She'll figure out how my phone works. If she has the phone on her and can access it, she can even tap to reply directly to this message."

He sent a simple message asking her to tell him where she was. He pushed send and watched it as it left his phone. The network didn't give him any indication his message had been lost, so he took it to mean it actually went through.

Everyone held their breath, waiting for the big reply.

A few minutes went by before the group started to fidget. Liam had time to look at the low battery indicator. They'd need a way to recharge it soon. He'd probably passed a dozen car chargers back at the intersection.

Eventually they all went to doing other things. Even Liam was ready to admit they should get back to their task at hand.

"Hey, I wonder if I can text anyone else? Let me try JT." Just before the world went to hell, JT text messaged him by accident. He alluded to the fact he and his family were evacuating the city because of the exploding crisis, but Liam was too thick-headed to appreciate what was happening until it was too late. Now he wondered where his friend had gone.

The message he tried to send stalled in his phone; it was unable to connect to the network.

"It's down again."

His dad spoke quietly. "Convenient." With a dramatic sigh he made as if he were looking up at the sky. "We should keep moving."

They all returned to their walking formation. Soon they traveled the last little way to the camp. Liam kept his mother's phone in his own pocket, determined to be ready for any replies. He imagined the infrastructure of the world: the cell towers, the network operation centers, and the lines themselves. Everything had to work just right for any signals to go out or get back. And with everyone left alive running from zombies, there would be no one around to fix even the most minimal problems.

Figuring out where Grandma was located was a race against the entropy of civilization itself.

3

"Halt!" The voice came from the woods to their right.

"What's your business on this road? This is Boy Scout territory."

The group looked at each other, then at Liam.

"My name is Liam Peters. I left here the other day with my grandma and another Scout named Drew. I said I would come back with my parents. Mr. Lee knows who we are."

Some voices were evident, closer in the woods than they would have expected. They seemed to be arguing over what to do. Many seconds later, a young boy tumbled out of a bush. He was covered head to toe in mud and leaves, which made him blend perfectly into the landscape.

"Liam!" The boy ran up and gave him a big hug.

Liam knew he should recognize him, but with all the debris on his face it was impossible. Perhaps sensing his confusion, he let him off the hook. "I'm Preston. Remember me?"

"Of course! You don't look the same with all that camouflage. You look awesome."

"Thanks, Liam. I've been on guard duty at this gate since you left. I just knew you'd come back."

Preston had fought zombies with Liam in the woods of the Boy Scout camp days earlier. They lost several friends in a gruesome battle with the undead. Liam had assumed it ruined the boy, but he seemed to have bounced back.

"You guys have a gate out here now?"

"Yep, we have gun guys up in the woods. I'm more of a greeter guy down here."

Liam suddenly felt the weight of eyes on him.

"Preston, these are my parents and my friends. Can you take us to Mr. Lee?"

"Sure thing, Liam." Then to his mates in the woods, "I'm heading to Endor. I'll be back as soon as I can."

Liam could see two other boys in the weeds, near the bush Preston used for cover. They gave him the OK, asked him to bring food, then went back to whatever they were doing.

When they got a few paces further down the road, Liam couldn't resist asking about Endor—the mythical forest moon in one of the *Star Wars* movies he'd grown up watching.

"Oh, Mr. Lee wanted to name everything in our camp after things we kids would know. He selected his main security base and called it Endor. I guess he thought we were all *Star Wars* fans. I would have called it Hogwarts myself."

He wasn't a big Harry Potter fan, but the naming convention made sense. He asked about other names in the camp, wanting to become familiar with them.

"Well, after that he tried to get us to vote on the names, but we couldn't all agree on anything." He gave Liam a knowing laugh, as if kids couldn't agree on the color of the sky. "What else? Oh, there are some groups of tents that have given themselves names unofficially, mostly silly stuff. The only one that stands out is the Umbrella Corporation. They've been going out of the camp to abandoned houses nearby and taking any patio umbrellas they find. I don't get it, but they all think it's hilarious."

Liam got it. The Umbrella Corporation was the name of an evil company that built a plague in a series of zombie movies and games. But he couldn't quite get himself to laugh at the joke. For all he knew, there really was an evil corporation behind all this.

"So, you guys are scavenging nearby houses for food and stuff? How are people holding up?"

Liam realized he was hogging the conversation, but no one else seemed interested in talking right now. The tension and disappointment of the text message seemed to have taken the wind out of their sails.

"Yeah, we have to. There's no more food left in the valley. There have even been a few riots from hungry campers who thought other areas were hording food. Mr. Lee set up the foraging teams to try to keep everyone fed, but they aren't coming back with much. 'Cept maybe zombies."

"Have you had any more attacks?"

"Lots, actually. Remember those two kids who died when we were carrying your grandma off that hill? They ended up in camp that same night you left, and did a lot of damage before they were put down. After that, we had to get serious about security everywhere. No one has really slept well since then."

They arrived at a dirt two-track path off the main road to their right, into the property owned by the Boy Scouts. Preston indicated that was the way they needed to go.

Liam's father was rolled carefully off the smooth road onto the dirt and the jostling seemed to cause him a lot of pain. He insisted they continue. He wanted it to be over with.

"This dirt road cuts north and south across the whole property on this side of the camp. Out here where there's nothing but trees...and zombies." He laughed less excitedly this time. "You can avoid the main valley out here. That's why we moved our roadblock out past this road. We didn't want people sneaking in our back door."

After many minutes of walking, Preston indicated they needed to take a smaller spur heading up a steep rise. He said it would take them directly to Endor, and that it wasn't far.

They had a lot of trouble with Jerry on the hill. It got very steep near the top. They had to walk up the wheelbarrow first, with three people pushing. Then the bicycle with all the guns. That took four people. Finally, Jerry. That took everyone.

When they reached the top, Liam recognized where he was. The three-story wooden tower where he and the other Scouts had fought and protected Grandma against an onslaught of the undead. It was not a pleasant memory then, or now. The boys had dragged scores of the dead into a big pile and burned them. The ash pile was nearby.

"Liam!"

Mr. Lee waved at them from the top. He was a tall middle-aged man with a short black beard, and wore the typical dress uniform of a Scout leader: tan short-sleeved shirt loaded with patches and awards, khaki short-pants, and hiking boots. He descended to meet them. Several nights ago, Liam had left this camp with an agreement he would try to return with his family and friends, and with a little luck, with weapons. Liam stood proudly by the bicycle with more than a dozen long guns hanging off its frame. He had kept his part of the bargain.

Mr. Lee, upon seeing Liam and his caravan of goodies, offered only one statement.

"Well done, Scout."

4

There was no time for pleasantries, and almost no time for proper introductions. After their initial small talk, Mr. Lee got right to business.

"Liam, your family is here in the nick of time. We have several problems happening all at once. Where do I begin?"

He seemed to think it over while he paced back and forth, focusing on the ground the whole time.

"OK, our main problem is food. Most of the boys are going out in foraging parties to bring back food from abandoned houses. We team them up with adults, but it's still very dangerous work for these boys, and the yields have been meager, to say the least. A lot of people are still in those houses."

Liam wasn't surprised. Everything he'd heard about this disaster indicated it had been taking place for weeks before the final collapse. That meant people were consuming food, supplies, and fuel during a time where those items were all getting scarce, but before most people realized those things were never coming back in stock. This was most acute in gasoline, which was how most people's cars ended up stranded on the highways. They left the house with whatever remained in their gas tanks—often it wasn't much.

"Close behind food is security. We aren't sure why, but more and more zombies are penetrating our defensive ring and making it into the camp. Needless to say, we're all on edge here. Your weapons will help us reach out to cover more area out here. In the meantime, we've started on a wooden fence but haven't made much progress."

"Have you had any additional visits from the military?" Liam was responsible for bringing the military to their doorstep three days ago when he was here. He was holding his breath for the response.

"No, thankfully that's one problem we haven't had." He seemed to consider that statement.

"Actually, scratch that. The military hasn't been back at our front gate, but it has been on the property. I was saving the job for a proper fighting team, but as I said, things have been thin here. Do you guys want to help me bring back an MRAP?" He wore a devious smirk.

"Say what?" Melissa's ears perked up.

"Yeah, we found the vehicle stuck in the mud further along on the dirt road you just left. There's a marshy section toward the north boundary, and it looks like they were trying to get a convoy up that path when they ran into some soft ground." He chuckled openly.

"But I need some adults with guns to go with me to help get it out of the mud and provide security from any...un-friendlies."

Melissa jumped at the opportunity. "I'm all for getting it, but if it's stuck in the mud how are we going to get it out? Those things must weigh as much as a small tank."

"That's what's so funny. It's down to the axles, that's for sure. But the thing is 6-wheel-drive. It's almost like they didn't try. They just left it there to rot."

"Maybe they were off taking a leak and got overrun?"

"Or they left it there as a trap."

Victoria hadn't been very talkative since she was out-voted in contacting Grandma.

"Victoria's right. Mr. Lee, you know we were being pursued the last time I was here, and this MRAP is probably the same one Hayes used when he came through here—actually now that I think about it, he did mention he lost an MRAP looking for the tracking beacon we took off Grandma. You put it on a deer, didn't you?"

Mr. Lee smiled like the Cheshire Cat.

Liam smiled too at the thought of that small victory. Not only did it divert his attention while Liam escaped the camp with Grandma, but it helped deprive Hayes of his main offensive asset. If he'd had it when he showed up at Liam's house, things might have ended much differently.

"If Hayes had to leave his prized pony in the woods, I'd bet anything he left some nasty surprises for anyone who happens along. He's sneaky like that. He'd call it tending the details. Victoria's right. It will be trapped."

She gave him a casual smile.

Well, it's something.

Melissa was undeterred. "I think we should check it out. Trap or no, having that vehicle would give us a tactical edge over any intruders. We have to think about our long-term survival. It's worth the risk."

The group talked it through, and in the end, only Victoria and Liam were against the risk of springing the trap.

Liam sensed the mood of the team; he pulled Victoria aside.

"I don't like this any more than you do, but I think we have to go to provide help for these guys. We can't split up now or we're going to die."

"We could wait with your dad. Surely he isn't going?"

He hadn't considered that. Of course he wasn't going.

"No, I'm sure Mom won't go either now that you mention it."

Victoria continued to look apprehensive.

Liam took a chance and grabbed her hands in front of him and looked directly in her eyes.

"I'm sorry we overruled you about calling Grandma."

She seemed to soften. "I'm sorry too. I'm so tired of all this death and destruction. I was hoping we would get to this camp and we'd have some time to rest before we went looking for trouble again. That's why I didn't want to call your Grandma at that exact time. I do want to rescue her. I do. And now we get here, and even before we see the camp itself, we are already pursuing another dangerous goal. I'm scared, Liam. Scared of Hayes."

He didn't blame her. She'd been shot by the man.

"Victoria, I'll back you up on this. I'll always have your back, even if we don't always agree on details of our planning and...stuff." Not his best speech. "But you have to understand, I thought you were dead. Now that you're alive, I feel I can conquer anything. No challenge scares me. I can face anything with you by my side."

He felt her squeeze his hands. She pulled him in and gave him a hug. With everyone else around, he was kind of glad she didn't want to kiss him.

She spoke quietly, "Liam, I'll follow you anywhere. Just don't leave me alone. I kinda like having you around." She gave him a burgeoning smile.

That was the old Victoria talking.

"Deal."

They broke the hug, but as they stood there, Liam found his own bravery and leaned in for a quick kiss. He was afraid of zombies, government agents, bombers, and breaking a leg—but he refused to fear his own girlfriend.

He ignored anyone who might be watching, and was very pleased to notice she met him halfway.

It was decided. They were going for the MRAP.

5

It felt like a repeat of his last foray into these woods. He joined up with a team, this time without Grandma, and was out in the wilderness in no time. He traveled with what he considered the "A" team. Mr. Lee. Phil. Melissa. Bo. Himself and Victoria. Mom and Dad were back at Endor, tending to Dad's leg. He felt OK with that, knowing they were safe. The group also had several older Scouts and a couple of adults Liam learned were the dads of those same kids.

Everyone had spears—there were plenty in the tower—and everyone had some kind of semi-automatic rifle along with extra mags and ammo. By agreement, Liam's dad shared his armory with Mr. Lee and the Scouts. The AK-47s found good homes with several of the men, though Liam kept two for he and Victoria.

The group also grabbed several of the dozen different backpacks in the tower. "We collected the things we thought we might need up here from the folks down in the valley. Nothing fancy, mind you, but we always need packs when we head out for patrols so that was one thing people were willing to provide. Calls for food never resulted in donations."

Liam knew the problem with this whole valley was food. They had plenty of fresh water thanks to an artesian well on the property, but the forest had little in the way of foodstuffs for so many people. Even the handful of deer culled from the nearby woods fed a few people out of thousands.

The Scouts were carrying two long wooden structures that looked like ladders. Mr. Lee explained they were going to drop them in the mud under the tires and use them as grips for the tires so they could back out. He said it was the best they could fashion given their supplies.

They were also pushing the wheelbarrow with some tools and equipment Mr. Lee had assembled from the cars in the valley.

"Anyway, enough about me. Who's your new girlfriend here? Didn't you lose...uhh." He hesitated as if he'd just driven into the wrong neighborhood.

"Yeah, it's OK. I told you the military killed my girlfriend. This is her." He let the paradox sink in for a few moments before he continued. "Well, actually I *thought* she was dead, but thankfully I was way wrong on that score. After I left here with Grandma and Drew, we rode our bikes across the county until we reached my house. Hayes was holding Victoria as a hostage, then he blew away my house, and finally he took Grandma away in a helicopter." He knew he was leaving a ton out of that story, but he didn't want to relive all the bad parts in the middle. One thing he did need to share: "Drew is dead."

"Oh man. I'm so sorry. Did he have family here?"

"No, he was alone. That's why he went with me."

Mr. Lee looked at Victoria, perhaps to change the subject. "Well, I'm glad *you* made it alive. Liam was distraught at your loss."

She smiled and nodded. Evidently she didn't want to share any more of her story.

Mr. Lee took the hint and continued speaking to Liam as they walked. "In the few days you've been gone, the place has grown quite a bit, but fewer and fewer of the new people are Boy Scouts. It's caused problems with those who have been here from the beginning. I'm afraid we're in for rough times as food gets harder to find. Part of my desire to secure that MRAP is to have some security inside the wire, if you get my meaning."

They talked about trivial things for the remaining few minutes until they reached the stranded truck. It wasn't all that far from the watchtower, which was itself about a mile or so into the woods outside the main valley. Mr. Lee pulled them into a circle before they got too close.

"From where we are now the dirt road goes to the left and right of us. If we go straight down this hill the MRAP will be visible. Half of us are going to sweep around to the other side so we have eyes over there. We'll all stay behind the truck as it sits now, so if we need to shoot anything near it, we aren't firing across the road directly into each other. Always keep that in mind."

Lee looked at Melissa and suggested she lead the team going across the road. She and Phil took off with Bo, and three or four of the Scouts. They took one of the ladders too. That left Mr. Lee, Victoria, and himself on this side, along with a contingent of two Scouts, plus their fathers.

They agreed to start moving toward the truck in twenty minutes, which went by quickly. Soon enough, they descended the last small hill and could see the MRAP as promised.

It was a beast of a vehicle, designed to protect its occupants from being blown up by large explosions set beneath it. Liam recognized it from one of his books. This one had six big tires and was painted in the light and dark colors of the local woodlands, instead of the sandblasted tan common in the desert. The primary weapon was a high-powered Gatling gun on the roof. Liam saw what it could do to his own house. It would be an awesome weapon to control.

The rear doors hung open, as if they were flung wide in a hasty retreat. If this was a trap, it seemed a dumb thing to do. All six wheels were up to the axles in mud, but much of the mud pit had dried since it became trapped. Someone could easily walk up to the rear doors at least.

They studied the area for other people, or zombies, but the only movement was their own group in the woods across the road. They moved closer to the truck from their respective sides. Their weapons were hot, but were pointed down at the ground as they walked. In a few minutes, they peeked into the back of the truck; there was no one inside.

Mr. Lee held them up about twenty yards from the open doors. He told everyone to hold where they were and fan out to keep an eye away from the truck. The real threat now was zombies sneaking up behind them as they focused on the extraction.

"Liam, I want you and Victoria to come with me."

The three of them moved closer. At the same time, Phil and Mel were doing the same on the other side of the road. They met at the truck. Liam and Victoria climbed inside the open back door.

Once inside, Liam couldn't help think it. "Wouldn't it be funny if this was an elaborate trap to capture the two of us?"

What if?

Victoria chuckled uneasily.

Liam recognized this as *his* MRAP. The very same one he had survived riding in for nearly a day. It had been abandoned in haste on his last ride when it was disabled at a roadblock by an unknown group of attackers. Hayes said they were looters, but he lied about everything.

Liam hunched his way into the front compartment. The security netting which had kept he and his elderly friends packed in the back was now pulled to one side. He could freely access the driver's position. He plopped in the seat, while Victoria did the same on the passenger side.

"Where should we go?"

"Denver?"

"I hope your credit card still works. We're going to need a ton of gas!"

They both laughed at the thought. Liam kicked open his door slightly so he could talk to Mr. Lee now walking up the driver's side exterior, on the other side of the muddy section of the trail.

"How's it look down there?"

"The mud doesn't look that bad. I think they just didn't want to put in the effort to get it out. We should have no problem with the tools we brought. The ladders should help."

Liam felt relieved. The whole operation was going surprisingly well.

He looked around the dashboard, wondering how to start the big vehicle. Surely Mel or Mr. Lee knew. He noticed the key was still in the ignition down and to his right. It also had a piece of paper attached to it. Someone had taken a sheet, folded it over several times, then skewered it with the key so it hung in place. The message was obvious: "Read this note!"

He motioned to Victoria, and invited her to open the note.

"Things are going so well. I just know that note is bad news."

She looked at him like he was crazy, then grabbed the paper and began unfolding. Quickly she skimmed it.

"Dang it. Liam, you win the award for smelling bad news."

6

"To whom it may concern. If you find this MRAP and can get it out of the mud feel free to take it for a spin. Just be aware we're coming to take it back. Thank you for your attention.—DH."

"Douglas Hayes. It has to be."

"PS. Please return with a full tank of diesel. That's all it says."

Liam was crestfallen. "I wonder if anything has changed now that we killed most of his team and sent him running? You think he'll still have the resources to come get this thing?"

"I don't know. I think we have to assume he'll be back. We can't underestimate him," she replied.

Mr. Lee stood outside the open back door.

"What's going on in there? You two getting comfy?"

They showed him the note, removing all the humor from his face.

Liam expected Mr. Lee to make a decision immediately, but he surprised him by asking for his opinion.

"You've dealt with this guy before. What do you think we should do?"

Liam looked over at Victoria before answering. She gave him a slight nod, reinforcing his own notions.

"I...uh, we think we have to take it. If Hayes is coming back, he probably won't just leave us alone in Camp Hope. It would be better to have this on our side. Maybe it will be a bargaining chip."

Victoria finished his thought. "Plus, we can use it in the interim. No sense letting it sit out here doing nothing."

And that set in motion the extraction process. The Boy Scouts were professionals at organized tasks, and under Mr. Lee's leadership, they had the MRAP back on solid ground in under an hour. The ladders proved to be too fragile for the huge truck, but they were able to drag some nearby logs and wedge them under the tires. Mr. Lee and one of the dads had also brought a winch in the wheelbarrow—he pulled it off a Jeep—and bolted it on the front bumper. They needed every advantage to get it out of the deep, muddy ruts.

The whole group packed in the vehicle and returned south on the dirt path. Melissa intimated she had driven one before, so she was the designated driver.

"This will come out on the blacktop road, and then we can re-enter the camp at the main gate." Mr. Lee's tone hinted at saying something more.

Liam gave him a look in response.

"Well, it's just—"

He sat on the rear bench seat with everyone else. He looked down when he resumed talking. "I hate to complicate things. We really need this thing. But I should tell you the council instructed me *not* to try to salvage it."

That shut everyone up.

"Is that why you had us go get this *before* letting us go to the camp? Liam's father really needs medical attention," Victoria wondered.

Mr. Lee ran his hand through his hair. "Look, I'm sorry. You'll see when we get there why I needed to do this. The council never leaves their fortress. They don't know what's happening out here. The whole place is going to collapse if we don't defend ourselves."

A few minutes later, Mr. Lee spoke as if he forgot something important. "Don't worry about your parents, I had them sent to the infirmary as we were leaving."

It made Liam feel a little better.

The ride was short. The only excitement was running over a couple zombies wandering the wooded path at exactly the time the truck was passing through. They finished the short ride on the paved road before they were at the front gate area. Mr. Lee invited Liam to stand up with him so they could both look forward and watch as they arrived at the camp.

Liam saw how much the atmosphere had changed.

The field near the front gate had a few cars parked in it when he left. Now the field was completely full and dotted with tents, campers, and canopies of every shape and size. It was hard to tell how many people were there. Hundreds at least. They were technically outside the formal property of the Scout camp, but adjacent to it.

They pulled up to the front gate. The last time he'd been through here, the entrance was called a gate, but it was really just a road intersection. Now there was a line of cars parked lengthwise to keep any vehicles from turning in and driving up the valley into Camp Hope.

Mr. Lee moved to the front so he could wave at the boys manning the front gate, and then he opened the door slightly to yell down at the them. The car blocking their path was promptly moved.

As they wound through the campers on the mile-long drive up the valley, Liam saw a whole new camp. Every possible open space had either a tent, a tarp, a camper, or a vehicle of some kind. There were even some plywood lean-to's. Whereas previously the campers concentrated on the narrow but flat bottom of the valley, now he could see tents and tarps well up into the woods on each hill flanking the valley. He thought there were a lot of people on his last visit. Now it seemed to be double that. A huge jump in just a few days.

His mind turned to one of the many traumatic events of the last ten days—the bombing of the zombies at the Gateway Arch. It was early in the crisis and the refugee camp at the Arch was at least as big as this one, minus the tents. Few people in the city thought they needed to bring living accommodations with them at that early juncture. Still, as the zombies overran the camp, the Air Force unleashed hell by bombing anything alive or dead in the vicinity. This valley would present a similar target, especially if someone in the military got wind zombies had infiltrated the place.

Is that what we're doing here?

He ran the scenario in his head. Liam's friends find a mysterious MRAP in the woods, conveniently left close to camp by Hayes—a man who has made Liam's life an increasingly depressing version of Hell. Somewhere between the third and sixth circles. So they bring it into the camp where it sits like a giant bull's eye. Maybe it has a tracking device? Maybe it gives them legal authority to come retrieve it?

Bottom line—Liam and friends become responsible for the fall of the camp.

He didn't share any of this with Mr. Lee or bounce it off any of his partners. He felt there had to be a time when paranoia was just paranoia. Hayes couldn't have known he was going to almost get killed trying to trade Victoria for Grandma. He couldn't have known his force of Humvees would be annihilated by Liam's parents and their neighbors. He couldn't have known it would be Liam who would be in the MRAP, even if it was found and recovered. There were too many variables.

But something nagged him like a lone flea in the small of his back.

"My job is all about the details." Hayes had said something to that effect several times.

Was the MRAP just another of those details? Insurance if his plan to capture Grandma failed back at Liam's house? It nearly did. He admitted it did make sense, if one believed Hayes always stayed a step or two in front of his opposition.

As they moved slowly up the camp's main road, Victoria's voice echoed in his head. "Liam, you win the award for bad news."

He glanced back at her, seated with the others. She had been watching him because he caught her attention right away. They shared a big smile, and he gave her a wink.

He turned again to the outside world and had an epiphany of sorts. He was with loved ones. He had powerful allies in camp. He had access to a devastating military vehicle and a cache of high-powered weapons. The folks in the tents he was driving by had far less.

I'm one lucky kid.

He rode that smile until the MRAP came to a stop.

KEY INSIGHTS

As they rolled up the road, more and more people became interested and kids began to follow along. Mr. Lee decided he needed to stand on the outside step and wave, so it was clear the truck was not a threat. Thus by the time they came to a stop, a considerable crowd surged around it.

"So, what do we do now? Go hand it over to the council?"

Mel was joking, but as soon as she said it, they all looked at each other with serious faces.

It seemed obvious to Liam once it was said. Of course the leaders would want control of the biggest, baddest piece of military hardware in the area.

She continued, "Okay, it appears we all believe the council will take this off our hands. Do we want that to happen?"

Just then Mr. Lee stepped back in the front door. He seemed to sense the tension. "What?"

"Mel here thinks the council is going to take the MRAP for themselves." Liam wanted Mr. Lee's unfiltered feedback before they were inside the building.

"Hmm, I hadn't thought of that. I assumed I'd be in charge of it since I'm the head of security. I can't imagine what they'd do with it otherwise. Drive it themselves?" He laughed, but with hesitation.

They shot around ideas for a couple minutes, but in the end they knew they had to at least report the vehicle was on the premises. They decided Mel and Phil should stay inside the MRAP, ostensibly to move it to its next location.

Liam and Victoria got out with Mr. Lee and Bo and together they walked through the energized crowd toward the administration building front door. He heard more than a few people exclaim they were being saved. It left him unsettled as he walked into the headquarters for the valley.

He was hit by the contrast from his last visit. Instead of the organization inherent in the Boy Scout community, everything was in disarray. The new batch of arrivals changed the nature of the camp, and not for the better. At least not where hierarchical order was concerned. People sat everywhere inside the main open space on the ground floor of the building. Gone were the tables representing various branches of the Boy Scout order—food, shelter, and the camp leadership. Now it was just one big jumble of people.

Mr. Lee conducted them directly to the stairs. Liam remembered how the leaders retreated up the stairs to have a quiet place to discuss real business. They were interdicted at the foot of the stairs by two men with serious-looking black rifles. Liam couldn't identify the makes. Not AR-15s or AK-47s. His knowledge of rifles was not very robust. The men were not professional-looking military men, but they didn't seem like inept guards either.

One of them knew Mr. Lee. "Hey, Lee. You bring back that tank? The council is shaking in their boots up there."

Mr. Lee took it in stride. "What? Do they think I'm Julius Caesar coming to Rome?"

The guard shook his head and smiled. "I don't know about Caesar, but they *are* scared. The front gate radioed ahead you were coming. Sent this place into a tizzy."

"Well, it's not like we shot up the place coming in. We okay to go upstairs, Brian?"

"Yep."

Liam was nervous as he followed Mr. Lee up, though he couldn't explain it. The council had given him no reason for concern the last time he'd been through here, and he appreciated their situation with so many people in the valley looking to them for answers. He'd felt the same back on the bridge with the Arnold councilman. That man withered away under the burden of leadership, and gave Agent Duchesne his opening. Liam *really* hoped he wasn't on the verge of creating more enemies.

When they were halfway up the stairwell, Mr. Lee stopped. He turned to them and spoke quietly. "I don't know what to expect, but let me do the talking."

No one argued.

The last time he was up on this level, Liam met with the council in an empty conference room. Now, the entire level was swimming with tables manned by Boy Scout leaders. Apparently all the organization that had once been downstairs had been moved upstairs. But the order and efficiency was much reduced.

They walked over to an area of the big room where the council was sitting in folding chairs, talking quietly with some of the other leaders. Mr. Lee took them right into the discussion.

"Mr. Lee! Great to see you." It was an old, frazzled-looking man on council.

Liam wondered if he really was glad to see him. Not all the leaders were there. Only four of the original six were present.

"Jason. Thanks for seeing us on such short notice."

"Well, we couldn't exactly ignore the fact you brought that military truck into the camp, could we? And after we *all* agreed we would *not* bring it into our valley."

"I know. I know. But everything has changed. I ran into my friends here, and the man who owns this truck held this girl hostage, then shot up his house, then kidnapped his grandma, and then blew up his entire neighborhood—"

"This is why we mustn't get involved!"

"*They're coming back.*" Mr. Lee said it matter-of-factly, and with quiet certainty. It had the intended effect; it got their attention.

Liam shifted in place, uncomfortable in the extended silence. He bumped into Victoria, and they traded terse smiles.

Everyone in the council's corner spoke quietly now.

"How do you know?"

"They left a note, it said 'we're coming back.' It's the same guy hunting Liam. If we don't have the MRAP, they're going to come in here and we will have no way to defend ourselves."

"Lee. We don't want a war. We just want to survive. We want the government to come back and help us, not kill us."

"Then shouldn't we have the baddest war machine in the neighborhood on our side? To keep the peace? What if it's not the government, but instead a rogue motorcycle gang? What if a horde of infected walked up your child-lined street out there? There are a million reasons we should have this truck. Only one why we shouldn't. I don't know about you all, but I like to *be prepared.*"

He'd thrown the Boy Scout motto in their faces. Liam wanted to say more, but held his tongue out of respect for Mr. Lee. He'd seen nothing but open warfare with zombies and bad guys since he'd left the library so many days ago. Surely the council had to see the logic?

2

The council's decision was bureaucratically inspired. They wanted the MRAP placed outside the valley so they couldn't be blamed for taking it. They didn't care where, or how, and they put Mr. Lee in charge of getting it done.

The tone of the previous conversation made Liam's segue clumsy. "Before we go, I want to introduce a friend of mine from not far up the road. This is Bo, and he and his friends provided aid in getting me home and back. They would make good allies to have on your southern border."

The council seemed put out, and briefly claimed they had bigger problems dealing with all the new arrivals, but relented and invited Bo to converse with them. They let Liam know he was no longer needed.

When he caught up with Victoria and Mr. Lee on the stairs, he was fuming. "Don't these guys have a clue what's happening around here? They don't care about defense, and they hardly seem to care about anything I say."

"Liam, not everyone thinks like you do. Hell, most people don't. These guys are used to rules and regulations dictating society as well as their little place here in this valley. You've been out of the valley and know it ain't pretty. I've been out on the border of this place and I've seen enough of it."

Liam had a spark of inspiration. Something that would put Mr. Lee firmly in the realm in which he was now operating: high paranoia. He started to grin at the thought, which Victoria noticed right away.

"You have a plan?" she asked.

"Let's get back to the MRAP. We have to go park the thing, don't we?"

Mr. Lee nodded. He was smart enough not to press for details while standing in the same room as the people trying to chase them out.

As Liam climbed the steps up the back of the truck, he watched Bo cut through the diminishing crowd. He walked with a tight grin and a feint head shake as he pulled on his deep brown beard. He climbed up and joined Liam as they sat in their seats.

Mel and Phil were in the front seats, watching. "How'd it go? You all seem to be in a hurry."

Mr. Lee instructed them to slowly return to the front gate.

"The council wants this vehicle out of their sight. They can't imagine a scenario where it would be good to have a badass weapon parked on their front lawn as a deterrent to any would-be attackers. We have to think of a place to park it. We want it to be close in case we need it, but it has to be out of sight. Out of mind for these wimps."

Bo added, "And they weren't interested in any kind of partnership with my family either. They invited us to come here and stay to help with security, but they saw no use in working out any kind of cooperation. They're more worried about finding tents for the new people, including me." His tone was doused with sarcasm. He picked up his shotgun and began breaking it down to clean it.

"Wow, it's the definition of a no-brainer to shore up your defenses by allying with groups nearby." Liam didn't know if it was true in real life as much as he knew it was true in the online games he used to play with his friends.

Victoria saw the emerging picture. "So, they want the truck out of the camp, but we know we have to stay close because we're going to need this thing at some point. Where should we go?"

Mr. Lee was about to say something, but Liam jumped ahead. "We should take the MRAP and go check out the Elk Meadow facility. It's just over the hill and across the highway. If the place isn't ash, it may

75

have some supplies we can use. If we have to keep the truck outside the valley, we might as well use it for something that can actually help the campers. We may not have much time."

He paused with an epiphany, "And it's not just Hayes. This place is falling apart. The council is losing their grip. Returning after the few days I've been on the road has put the whole place in contrast from the last time I was through here."

Mr. Lee, sitting on the bench opposite him seemed to chew on that. "Hmm. As head of security, I suppose I should be defending the camp from such accusations, but my job has mainly been to help defend against the infected moving through these woods. I don't do water cooler gossip *or* politics. But now that Liam said it, it would explain the heavy security inside the administration building. I was surprised they let you guys in with your weapons. Maybe my authority got you in, or maybe they were just sloppy. I wonder if they're asking themselves the same question right now? Maybe Liam is right. While we have it, we should put it to good use. As far as I know, none of our scouting parties have gone up that way. Most residences we've been searching are to the east and south because they're closer."

From up front, Mel and Phil shouted agreement.

The MRAP waddled down the valley on the tight crowd-choked road, exited through the front gate, then turned right toward the highway rather than left back to the dirt road to Endor. They began the short drive toward the highway and their destination.

Victoria leaned over to Liam. "Are you worried about going back? Didn't you say that's where they ran experiments on the old folks?"

"Nah, I'm not worried. It's probably bombed to smithereens, but there were some odds and ends on the ground after my subdivision was blown up, so maybe there's something worth salvaging up there." He looked to see if Mr. Lee or Bo were listening. When it appeared they were talking to each other, Liam continued as quietly as possible in the noisy space. "My real fear is finding the group of eighty-something's we left after we all walked out of the destroyed front gate of that place. At the time, I didn't think they would make it a mile by themselves, but later I wondered if Hayes found them, and they told him where Grandma and I had gone. Maybe they're all dead."

"Well, if they're dead, it wasn't because of you. If Hayes collected all those people, and killed them, that's on him." She turned so she could look directly at him. Her pretty green eyes were the usual distractions. "You've had a lot of things go wrong since we met up. Believe me, I know. But you have to stay focused on what you can control. You can't take responsibility for what other people are doing in a world gone insane...I need you...to stay strong, so I can be strong with you. That's how we're going to survive this thing. And besides, you've had a lot of things go right, too..."

She gave him a wide smile, missing tooth and all.

They held hands throughout the rest of the fifteen-minute ride. The big truck easily punched through the wrecks and debris littering the highway, had no issues avoiding any of the pedestrians—some living, some dead. A short distance from the front gate of the elk preserve the MRAP pulled over and stopped.

From up front, Mel said, "You guys might want to see this. I think we found some of your friends, Liam."

He moved to the front of the cab. Just off the side of the road, a dozen or so elderly people were piled in a ditch. Even from this vantage point it was clear many had been shot, several had clothes stripped from them as if they'd been the victims of looters. As best he could tell, none of them had become zombies.

Everyone in the cab observed the scene in silence for a minute or so. Liam made sure Mr. Lee got a good look.

Victoria took a peek too. "Do you think Hayes did this?"

"I thought he was capable of anything, but this?" He felt his emotions welling up. "There could be no legitimate reason to kill innocent men and women like *this*. They may not have had much of a chance given their age and supplies, but they hardly made it a hundred yards from where I'd last seen them. I don't know. Maybe."

"Could someone have been waiting for them to walk away from you?" Phil asked.

Ahead, the gate to St. Louis County Lone Elk Park beckoned them to search for answers.

3

The front gate to the elk preserve was exactly as Liam remembered it. When the military evacuated after the containment failure siren went off, they rammed through the closed metal gate. They couldn't be bothered to open it so it could be re-used later if needed. Liam figured if he was in the military and had every available resource, a simple elk pen would seem pretty expendable. To civilians like him though, having a strong fence around your survival camp would be a godsend. Maybe it would be worth fixing at some point.

The MRAP proceeded in. The pavement was narrow for the big truck, but with no traffic, people, or zombies, it wound through the park for only a few minutes. On a low hill overlooking a small lake they observed the remains of the huge olive green tents of the government research facility.

Everyone gathered near the front while Mel narrated, "The planes did a number on the place to be sure, but they weren't very thorough. Most of the tents are down, but not all of them. Even those on the ground look like they were blown down by the compression of the bombs, rather than direct hits. We might actually find something here."

They did a better job bombing my house. How nice of them.

"OK everyone. Be careful out there. Might be un-exploded bombs laying around." Mel said it, saw everyone looking at her, and continued, "Really, I have no idea. Bombs aren't my area of expertise. Just seems like prudent advice."

She and Phil shared a knowing laugh.

They all exited through the front of the truck, and spread out in their search. Victoria and Liam went in the direction of the remaining big tent. He told her it was the tent where he'd seen the experiment, and where the colonel became infected. Essentially it was ground zero for the destruction of the whole place.

"What do you expect to find here? Are you looking for something in particular?"

"I'm not sure myself. All the medical testing that went on here had to have generated some paperwork. Some clues as to what this virus is all about. What caused it. Why it spawns zombies. But the troubling thing to me—besides the government bombing my neighborhood and stealing my grandma—

"—and shooting your girlfriend!" she interjected with a smile.

"—and shooting my girlfriend, is the fact there didn't appear to be any answers here. The colonel may have known more than he let on, but I was there when he died. His last words weren't about the virus, they were about how much he loved his family. He gave me the photograph so I'd know them if I ever met them. If he had *any* clue how to stop this thing, wouldn't he have given it to me?"

"That makes sense." She was a little bit ahead when she stopped and turned around. She looked like she was about to say something when she swayed like the world was tipping. Liam would have rushed to help her but he felt the same effect. Liam's mind raced through a series of images, settling on a view over a city as if he were high up, looking out a window. Then, nothing.

They were both were on the ground when they came to. None of the others were in sight, meaning no one likely saw what had happened. Victoria sat up as Liam pushed himself off the ground and dusted his creek-stained jeans and his dark "Vote Roland" t-shirt.

"What the hell just happened? Did we both fall down at the same time?"

"It looks that way. And I had the strangest visions as I stood there —"

"A city?"

"How'd you know that? Was that some kind of shared vision?"

Liam looked around; imaginary sensors scanning for solutions. Nothing was obviously out of place. No projectors. No mind-control orbs. His mind searched for science fiction explanations, but there was nothing there but the semi-perforated tent and lots of debris.

He helped her up, noticing once again how her pretty eyes offset the bruises, black eyes, broken nose, and missing tooth. He was momentarily happy to be with her, no matter how much destruction was around him.

"What?"

"I'm smiling because you make me happy. But also, I don't know, that vision made me feel happy, too. Reassured in some way. I can't explain it."

"Hmm. I see what you mean." She smiled as she held his hand. "Like we can do anything when we're together. Like we *have* to do something together."

I wonder if she is talking about...

Liam stood there with a dumb look on his face. Not sure what to say next.

"No, dummy. Get the dirty thoughts out of your head." She smiled broadly as she continued, "I'm talking about something *really* important. Like saving Grandma. Saving the world."

That brought him back down to reality.

"Of course! Yes, that's why we're here. I was *totally* thinking the same thing." They laughed, and Liam admitted it gave him the strength he needed to lead her into the tent. She stayed close.

He acknowledged again how much better he felt to have her by his side.

The zombie apocalypse would be so much worse if I was on my own.

He knew how it felt; he went a long time thinking she was shot dead. Now it was like she was reborn.

4

The tent was dark, but not a consuming darkness. The bright of the day seeped in at various points, including the many holes from the shrapnel; they provided enough light to see most of the interior. Liam tied off the flap so the door would provide light even as they went deeper inside.

He knew the front room was the reception area, devoid of anything interesting. He jumped when he saw what looked like a hand reaching under the tent in the corner, but it was his overactive imagination. He pushed the flap into the middle chamber—where he expected to find the table where the old man was strapped down. But when he entered the space, he could tell the man was no longer in the operating theater. Even in the reduced light he could see there were no bodies nearby. He'd just vanished.

Impossible. He was shot in the head.

He searched his memories. The last time he'd been here, the colonel took him into the woods to show him the secret of this camp. The special flavor of zombie they'd found. Was there something special about the man he knew was 106 years old? A man who had died in front of his eyes several days ago?

He spoke to lessen his anxiety. "Did I ever tell you what they kept hidden out in the woods of this camp?"

"You said the Air Force bombed the camp itself and a pit where they dumped all the bodies."

"Ah, that's true. There was a big pit. They dumped a bunch of old folks after they pumped them full of zombie blood to see what happened to them. But the other thing in the woods was a corral with two zombies the colonel said were from Chicago. They had a special skill, I guess you'd call it. They could climb."

"Wow. That's huge. It means even a fenced in place like this wouldn't be safe."

Crap! I hadn't thought of that.

"Um, true. But also it implies there are even more kinds of zombies out there. The man they had in this operating suite was 106, but he acted strange when he was infected. He spoke in a strange language. The last thing he said was that he was sorry and—" Liam tried to remember the sequence of events, "And then he purposely and calmly bit the colonel. The colonel then calmly shot the old man and walked out the door."

"It sounds like it was scripted, Liam, now that you say it like that."

"The only thing the medical team could say about that was they could have saved the camp if they had immediately killed the colonel. Like it happened every day with them. Looking back, it seemed an odd thing to say."

"But if the colonel wanted to destroy the camp, why the complexity? He could have just let any old zombie loose, run the siren, and then he'd still be alive."

"I don't know. All I know is he set things in motion when he left the tent, then the camp cleared out surprisingly fast—minus the test subjects. They left them for dead. It was just me, the colonel until he shot himself, and the elderly test subjects in the end..."

Liam stood there for a few moments, lost in thought. Victoria paced around, thinking out loud. "So the camp cleared out, including the people who wanted the colonel dead. Didn't you say he gave you a picture of his family? Did it have any clues on it? Can I see it?"

Liam kept it in his front pocket, though he didn't readily know how long he expected to carry it around. It was a five-by-seven inch photograph showing the man's wife and son. The boy was about Liam's age, at least at the time the photo was taken. On the back, written on a white mailing label, was an address. He said it was the address of his wife. He handed it to Victoria.

"I don't see any clues on this, other than the address of his family. Maybe they know something, but it will be a while before we go to Colorado to ask them."

Victoria held the photo in her hand. She moved closer to a notch in the canvas so she'd have more light. She ran her fingers over the paper. She looked at it from multiple directions. Then, she held it up to the daylight, as if looking at an x-ray.

"Hey! There's something under this label. It's a tiny square of some kind."

She handed it back, and sure enough he saw it too. He had completely overlooked the label, as it was white and appeared to be a convenient way to write on the back of the glossy photo paper. The square wasn't any bigger than his pinky fingernail, and it was hard to see with the writing on the paper and the fact the whole thing had been folded several times.

"Now that I see it, I know what it is. This is a micro memory card. With the proper adapter it fits into a computer port so it appears like a small hard drive. I use these a lot to transport files to and from school. If we were at Grandma's, I'd even be able to put this in my computer. Currently, I have no way to read it."

"OK, this is *something*. He knew it was important but he didn't tell you about it. Was he hoping you were just a nice guy and you'd travel across three states to deliver an old photo to his family? Are they expecting this to show up one day?"

"At this point, I don't even know what I know. He did mention he couldn't trust me." After a brief pause, he continued his line of thought. "This changes my whole interaction with him. I need some time to figure it out. Let's keep this between us for now. He entrusted this to me, and I entrust it to you, but I don't want anyone else to feel obligated to keep this secret. At least not until we know more. He said there were other groups out there...one of which caused the whole thing. I wish I could ask him."

5

"Liam! Victoria!" They looked at each other, then moved for the door out of the tent. Mel, Phil, and Bo jogged their way.

"We found something you should see."

Mel and Phil each carried a messy stack of papers, as if they'd been laying on the ground. Bo was carrying just one. "Here you go, Liam. You should read this."

Liam took the paper, scanned it, then said, "I knew it. This is it." He began reading, "To Colonel McMurphy. From CDC Mobile Headquarters, Black Mountain, NC. In response to your request for information on the mission of our Forward Operating Group in St. Louis, I can only express my utmost confusion at your insinuation our team is lying to test subjects about the survivability of their experiments. Kidnapping subjects would never be a procedure we could condone. Furthermore, we currently have no teams within 250 miles of St. Louis. Our nearest teams are in Minneapolis and Denver. We have no record of anyone named Douglas Hayes on staff, though I admit HR has been hit or miss since this outbreak began six weeks ago. I'm sure you understand. Good luck out there. —Felicia Iminez, Deputy Director, CDC Operations."

Mel added, "This was actually sitting in the tray of a fax machine lying on the ground. It must have arrived very near the end of this place. We picked up as many documents as we could find, though we have no way of knowing if any of them are of any use."

"We also pocketed some bottled waters and a handful of fruit that survived the bombing. It was a cruel joke, but the tent closest to the bombs was the camp's kitchen and food storage. Almost nothing of value survived."

Liam looked up at Mel. "Thank you. Thank you guys for coming with me to find this. At least we know something more about Hayes."

She replied, "He may not be with any agency, or maybe he is. Hard to say. There are literally hundreds of agencies involved in health these days. Maybe he figured it was easier to just say he was with the CDC, since everyone recognizes that."

Phil carried on, "But what agency *could* it have been? We know he had access to air power, helicopters, soldiers or men pretending to be soldiers, and he fit into this camp as if he owned it. That sound about right, Liam?"

"I guess—"

Bo racked a round into his shotgun. He looked into the nearby woods. Liam's eyes followed. Things were moving there.

"Time to go folks!" Phil took off for the MRAP. Mel kept pace.

Liam surveyed the camp, wondering what they were leaving behind. He noticed a zombie as it clawed out from under a part of the tent they'd just vacated. It was badly burned, with tattered medical clothing, and it was bathed in dirt and mud as if it had been buried. Not hard to imagine with all the craters near the tents. He ran with Victoria as other infected emerged from around the edges of the forest.

Bo trailed, but stopped a few times to check the pursuit.

Liam jogged past the small tent where he and Grandma spent a little time on their last visit. It was blown over, but not destroyed. He knew the place where the colonel had shot himself was nearby, but his body was nowhere to be seen. It was gone, just like the older man's body on the operating table. The force of the blasts must have been powerful.

Everyone made it safely to the truck. Once inside, they could see the zombies wandering into the camp. Liam took a hard look at them, concluding they could only have come from the big pit in the woods where bodies were dumped after the experiments. He struggled to remember if the bodies had all been shot in the head before they were placed in their grave, but at the time he wasn't curious about the pathology of their deaths.

The MRAP growled to life and weaved through wreckage on the way out of the destroyed camp.

Colonel. If you're out there, I'll try to find your wife and son. I renew my promise to you.

6

The trip back to camp was mostly uneventful. They retraced their route, and knew what to expect. They did see a single motorcycle pass them, going the other direction on the highway. Mel called them up from the back compartment when she saw it coming their way. It was the first motorized vehicle they'd seen—aside from their own—in a long time. The rider made no effort to stop or slow down or otherwise acknowledge them. Liam didn't blame anyone for not stopping for the military.

Liam, Victoria, and Bo returned to the back and tried to look through the remaining stack of papers. They hoped to find something useful before they arrived back at the Boy Scout Camp.

After several minutes, Victoria found a short note directed to the camp from a Homeland Security department. It was an authorization for Douglas Hayes to continue his research at the camp, including his methods for subject acquisition. Furthermore, it listed him as *Doctor* Hayes.

"Well, don't that beat all. He said he was just a truck driver for the CDC."

"Liam, he still might not be a doctor. Nothing about the man should be taken as fact. Maybe he sent this himself?"

One of Liam's earlier self-revelations was that once the zombie apocalypse befell mankind, a person looking to reinvent himself would have no problems doing so. You could erase your past and become practically anything, as long as you had the practical skill to fake it. You couldn't say you were a doctor and expect to get away with it. The first time you had to make a diagnosis it would become obvious. But a doctor would have no problem pretending to be a truck driver, especially in a world where trucks were scarce. The only question was why.

It made more sense if Hayes *was* a doctor. It would explain his keen interest in Grandma. His command of resources, including Army personnel. An Army doctor?

"Mel, could an Army doctor command troops in the field?"

"Yes, though it would be unusual. Maybe less so now, but they do have rank and could command troops."

"But aren't doctors supposed to help people? Doesn't shooting my girlfriend disqualify him from the academy or something?" Still, "doctor" felt right. He hated to use the term, but he thought it anyway. An *evil* doctor. Maybe a step down; a *sinister* doctor. Just the kind of person who would thrive in an environment of plague, death, and zombies. It was a bit cartoonish, but he couldn't think of a more reasonable explanation.

His question turned out to be rhetorical. No one volunteered an answer.

The remainder of the documents provided a few additional snippets of data, but little in the way of information. Protocols for destruction of camps. Composition of security details. Numbers of infected tested at the camp—224. Very little in the way of clues.

One tantalizing piece of data was in the header of an email sent to the colonel. The hardcopy didn't give an address, but listed "Riverside Operations Center, St. Louis, Missouri." The message referenced medicines and other supplies they had on hand for shipment to various research facilities, including Elk Meadow. Someone had used a highlighter throughout.

He leaned over to show Victoria. "Check this out. It seems to imply this place is some kind of supply hub. Colonel McMurphy mentioned a base of operations in downtown St. Louis. Maybe this is where they'd take Grandma? But why doesn't it list an address?"

"Maybe they didn't want anyone to know where the stuff was coming from?" she volunteered.

"Or maybe they all knew where it was, so putting an address was silly. No one on Earth probably knows the postal address of the St. Louis Arch. You don't need it to find it."

"So, all we have to do is find someone from this camp and ask them for the address of their secret headquarters in the middle of the collapsed city we just spent days escaping?"

Liam laughed at the thought. "Yeah, and while we're at it, we'll ask them for a ride to get there. Save us all the effort!" He thought about it for a second. "OK, it's a working theory for where she is."

RIVERSIDE

Marty knew she wasn't awake as soon as she saw the birdbath. Almost two weeks ago, her very first encounter with a man purporting to be her late husband, Aloysius, had been at this very spot—her backyard. The man wasn't really her husband, and she wasn't really in her backyard, but she couldn't say for sure who he was or where she was. It was more real than a dream, but she wasn't really awake either.

"Hello, Marty."

"You aren't really Al. You don't have to pretend."

"I'm sorry. I have to say it helps me relate to you better. May I continue the charade, if you will?"

She hated to admit he was right. She feared what other form he might take.

"Oh, alright. I guess it helps me, too."

The avatar of her husband walked over the bright green grass of her backyard, and stopped at her favorite birdbath. It was a gift from her family for one of her big birthdays; the eightieth, she guessed. Before the infected came, she loved to sit on her back porch and watch the birds playing there. It brought her peace. As close to Heaven as she could get in this world.

"Heaven. An interesting concept. In a universe defined by the cold of absolute zero across the infinite depths of space and time, your warm rock called Earth would be Heaven by almost any definition you could conjure."

"Even with infected walking all over it?"

"Hmm. I guess that depends on if you're still alive or one of the living dead. But do you recall what I told you in an earlier meeting? The infected are still human, and they'll be walking the planet when it's finally engulfed by the Sun if they aren't stopped here and now. That's why I chose you to fulfill your mission with your two young friends."

"Liam and Victoria. Yeah, you said we were a trio of heroes. I fear they're trying to get themselves killed by rescuing me from these people. I encouraged them to be heroes, but they don't appreciate the danger they're in."

"On the contrary, my dear Martinette, you don't understand the danger *you* are in. They understand it better than you do, I think. They don't know it as intimately as you do because they aren't here with us now. You know you *must* survive or all of humanity could be lost."

"What if I don't?"

"Then the cure dies with you. Eventually everyone will succumb to the plague, or die resisting it. Even those who survive the next few years will die off soon enough. The thought of having kids in a world ruled by the undead will eventually decline the pool of survivors to a point the human race can no longer endure as a species. If you had a supercomputer you could run the numbers. I've seen it in other...worlds/simulations/archives." He chuckled to himself. "Actually, I *do* have a supercomputer. As part of my research, I've found the pool of surviving humans is dwindling far faster than expected. Though most humans survived the initial crisis, time is indeed growing short for them as the number of zombies rise."

They stood near each other in the simulated backyard of her house and watched the bird bath. It had water in it, but there were no birds to be seen.

"It doesn't make sense. Why am I responsible for saving humanity from this plague? You said before it was because I was close to Hayes. Now that we know Hayes is deeply involved, why not send in the Army? Give the President a visit with this information. Why put three —nobodies—at the center of this fight for all of mankind?"

Al took a full minute to consider. He walked slowly and deliberately around the birdbath several times.

"Do you have any doubt that what you see here is actually how you see it with your own eyes? The complexity of translating the reality of this—place—into something you can process is beyond reckoning. Yet it gets done. Would it surprise you to learn there may be other Marty's talking to other Al's in backyards very similar to this one? I once called myself a close approximation to an angel. You may believe I am infallible—truly an angel in the 'wings, harps, and white clothes' tradition. Those may yet exist. I've not seen a fraction of existence, though it would not be braggadocio to say I've seen a near-infinity's worth of it more than you. Suffice it to say, I am not infallible. I'm not even the best at what I do. But I do serve the Light. I do serve the one true God."

He stopped at the birdbath and looked directly at Marty. "But I do make mistakes." The being pretending to be Al actually managed to look sheepish.

"So, I was your mistake? That explains a lot, though it doesn't make me feel any better."

Al laughed out loud. "No, my dear. Let me finish. You are the *exact* person I wanted for this crisis. It was your age—along with a few complimentary parameters—which enabled you to hear/decipher/recognize our call."

"There! Why did you say it like that? This/this/that? Who are you, really? I think I need to know."

"I told you who I represent. Isn't that enough?"

"You said this universe was at a tipping point between good and evil. Why don't you just cut with the mystery, tell me what I need to do, and we can get it done together?"

"A delightfully human response. I've admired you from the beginning. But as I imagine you already know, if a creator interferes with his creation to the point he dictates what happens, it really isn't a creation at all. A creator could just snap his fingers and arrive on the final day of the simulation, everything neatly wrapped up. But what purpose would that serve? Why start it at all?"

Al continued to pace around the birdbath while he moved his hands over the reflective water in a kind of pattern. "Instead, imagine a creation of wonderful chaos. If there *was* an omnipotent being behind it all, wouldn't absolute chaos and uncertainty ensure He wasn't dictating everything that happened? And perhaps that being would ensure general chaos by allowing his agents to continually introduce new stimuli, even to the point one might think it was 'evil.' That would be the last thing you'd expect from an omnipotent being, would it not? Agents of the Light. Agents of the Dark. Agents of order. Agents of chaos. All designed to complicate the universe to the point of infinite unpredictability. *That* would achieve a near-impossible result for an omnipotent being, wouldn't you think?"

"It has a certain logic to it, but to what end? Why put humans through the ringer like this? Does that mean God has no involvement whatsoever in His creation?"

"Ah, my dear Marty, I love your spirit. All I can tell you is that if God didn't care at all, He wouldn't allow me to be here, either. But there are more pressing and important questions you should be asking. Like how to work that phone you've been hiding in your pocket." Al pointed to her fuchsia-colored pants pocket where Liam's phone rested.

"You must summon Liam and Victoria. They will come to you. Together, unified by your shared experiences and emotional interconnections, you have the best chance of anyone to access the 8088 room." In a prior visit, he showed her a locked room behind a window containing an old 8088 model computer sitting on a wooden table. It was part of an elaborate construct which included a seemingly magic waterfall nearby. "I assure you what you will find in there is much more powerful than your nominal recreation of a personal computer. Inside lies salvation for you and for your planet."

She reached for her pocket, but instead found herself back in her bed. It was dark once again. She didn't think she screamed when she woke up. Another small victory.

2

The MRAP idled outside the front gate of the camp. Liam and his friends were trying to agree on where to secure it. They couldn't park it inside the camp because the council was dead set against it, but leaving it outside the camp left it open to theft from anyone who stumbled upon it.

Mr. Lee came up with the only viable solution. "We'll hide it in the woods near the watchtower south of here. Technically it'll still be on Boy Scout land, but as per the council, it will be outside the camp itself.

It will allow us to access it when we need it, prevent it from being easily stolen, and keep it close enough to the main camp to be useful in case we're attacked."

Phil and Mel nodded vigorously. Victoria and Bo also seemed to agree. Liam couldn't think of a better idea, so he too lent his support.

"Wow, we all agreed on something," Mr. Lee laughed. "If only dealing with the council was this easy!"

As the truck rolled down the pavement and headed for the dirt track leading to the watchtower, Liam moved closer to Victoria so he could talk to her in private near the back of the truck. She was looking in his direction with a smile on her face.

He returned a smile and asked, "What do you think happened to us back at Elk Meadow? Why did we both pass out at exactly the same time?"

He expected Victoria to have an answer prepared. She was planning for a career in medicine, so certainly had to have been thinking about the incident since it happened. But she surprised him. "I can't explain it. I don't even have a guess. Shared vision isn't something I've ever studied or even read about. Maybe it was some kind of suggestion put in our head by the stress of the bombed out camp? Something there, but beyond our comprehension."

"Something that made us both think about a city when we were in a bombed camp in the woods? That's your answer?" Liam smiled, but he was also serious.

"I know it makes no sense whatsoever. Neither do zombies. Strange things happen at the end of the world."

Liam couldn't argue with that. In fact, many of the books he'd read on zombies resorted to magic or the supernatural to explain the goings-on of zombies. It seemed too far-fetched, even as he was immersed in the same zombie world he'd read about so many times. But his were just people infected with a disease. They weren't animated by the supernatural. It could not have been magic.

While thinking, he looked at her surreptitiously as the truck plodded down the bumpy road, and was amazed once more how attractive she was and—

"Your arm!"

She looked down, not surprised. "Yeah, when we passed out, I fell to this side and my arm must have landed on something in a weird way." A large and ugly purple bruise the size of a small apple was present on her upper arm just above the elbow.

"Well, it complements your face." He gave a taut laugh, not sure if she found it a laughing matter.

"Ha! Very funny, pretty boy. How is it you have no bruises at all? You don't have a scratch on you. Are we on the same adventure?"

Liam shrugged his shoulders with great exaggeration, but let it drop. He continued their conversation at a slightly lower volume. "I've been thinking about that vision and trying to recall my feeling while looking at the city I was seeing. I felt something—not an emotion exactly—but something close. I felt *old.*"

A knowing look swam across Victoria's face. "Yes! And I think I know who the old person was, too."

They didn't bother saying the name out loud. They both arrived at the only logical conclusion given all the evidence.

It was Grandma.

3

After parking the MRAP, everyone walked the short distance to the watchtower. They passed through a woodland construction zone as men and boys worked on a makeshift fence using downed trees. They hadn't built very far from the watchtower yet, but Liam was glad to see progress.

He and Victoria decided to continue down into the valley to find his parents. The boys at the Endor tower felt confident they would have been taken to the makeshift infirmary in the same building where he met the council earlier.

Phil and Mel offered to stay close to the MRAP, which Mr. Lee agreed was a great idea given the circumstances. He asked them to join their security rotations.

Mr. Lee said he was going to stick around the watchtower and catch up on the fence progress. "Thanks for the tour, Liam. You've shown me how far we have to go on making this place safe." He went off to his troop.

Bo also stayed to help out the Scouts on the hilltop. "I have lots of experience helping my daddy build fences around our pastures. At the time it wasn't much fun, but it looks like these guys need the help. Not doing much anyway. Not like I'm going to walk back home on my own." He smiled as he shouldered his gun and headed off to the tower.

After they all broke up, Liam felt guilty for acknowledging he was glad to *finally* be alone with Victoria. They walked down the long singletrack trail toward camp, Victoria in the lead, when she stopped, turned around, and moved purposely back up the trail to meet him.

His heart smashed the gas pedal as she approached.

Yes!

She talked in a conspiratorial tone, "Do you think Mel and Phil like each other?"

No! Not at all what I was thinking.

He humored her as he pretended to think about it, then found himself drawn into the question.

"Well, I do know they hated each other that first night they met on my street. I think she used the word 'rapists' to describe me and Phil." He was uncomfortable even saying that word. "Phil seemed to genuinely dislike her when they first met, too. But they fought together that night and have been fighting together in close quarters all the time you and I have been off doing our thing with Hayes and friends. Maybe they've reached an understanding?"

"But didn't he just lose his wife last winter? Didn't his wife even say something through Grandma on that bridge when we escaped on that train?"

It was true. Phil's deceased wife spoke through Grandma that day, though no one—herself included—could understand how it happened. His wife had been gone for six months. He had no frame of reference to know if that was enough time to move on.

"I dunno. I'm uhh—" He wanted to say he was inexperienced talking about women, but he didn't want to paint himself too heavily into that corner. "—not sure what adults might think after losing a spouse." Then he thought of himself and his realization earlier in the day. "I wouldn't blame him if he needed to share this with Mel. I think this whole disaster would be ten times worse if I didn't have someone to care for and worry about."

"Yeah, I wish my Grandma were still alive. Heck, I wish my parents were with me so I could take care of and worry about them too."

"I, uh, actually meant you."

Victoria gave him a big, gap-tooth smile. "I know, you big dummy. I'm just being silly. But I really appreciate it, and I'm also glad I have someone to care for and who cares about me. I'd probably still be sitting back at the Arch waiting for help to arrive if you hadn't come along."

Left unsaid was that she'd more likely be dead, since the Arch had been overrun with gangs, then zombies, then was bombed extensively by the United States Air Force.

They stood there in close proximity for many seconds before Liam was brave enough to wrap his arms around her and pull her in for a hug.

"Would it hurt your mouth if I kissed you?"

He was halfway serious, since she had banged her mouth and lost a tooth during their explosive reunion, but he was also looking for an excuse to suggest he wanted to smooch. His instincts still weren't honed in interacting with her on a romantic level. Hell, the whole world of zombies was the exact opposite of romance, so being romantic was even more cumbersome. At least, that's how he justified his ineptness.

By way of an answer, she stood on her toes so she could reach his face from lower on the trail, and for the first time since they'd met, they engaged in a long passionate kiss. By the time it was over, Liam's head spun in delight and his initial nervousness seemed a remote distraction.

It ended much sooner than Liam would have liked, but Victoria apparently couldn't stay on her toes any longer. She dropped down to her normal height, then quickly spun and resumed walking down the trail.

With her back to him, she spoke to no one in particular. "So, there's this boy I met at the end of the world. A handsome young lad. He's very shy for some reason. But I think that makes him very sexy. I'll have to tell you about him someday."

Liam was somewhat embarrassed to be described as shy, but she looked back with that same big broken smile and it dawned on him she was playing with him. He followed her down the trail, unconcerned with any of his perceived shortcomings. He knew he wasn't perfect, but with his charming feminine friend by his side, he felt invincible.

Despite the hormones flushing through his system, he was able to hold on to an important piece of his brain during their walk down.

This is where you were attacked the last time you went down this trail. Danger!

Rather than catch up to Victoria and swoop her up and profess his love—

Do I love her?

—he pulled out his pistol and was at the ready. They carried their rifles over their shoulders, along with several magazines each, but somehow the little pistol gave him more confidence.

He wasn't going to let anything happen to his girl again.

A vow he knew was impossible to keep.

4

Nothing happened on the way down. He holstered his gun as they approached the outer ring of tents and people. He didn't think it would be out of place to be carrying a gun there, but he didn't want to cause any commotion. Guns often scared people, even after everything they'd seen.

"Let's head for the admin building and find my dad."

In a few minutes they had wound their way through the tent city and stood at the front doors.

"Liam, I'm going to hang out here and wait for you. I need some time to clear my head from the past few days of chaos and going in that crowd is just too much for me right now. I'll be right over there by the creek. Come get me when you're done?"

A strange emotion zipped across his mind as he wondered if she wanted to be away from him, but he tried to remain pragmatic and understand her needs, too. He pushed the doubt aside. "Sure thing! I'll find you when I'm done."

They traded smiles and she walked off; he pushed through the doors of the stuffy building.

It was still a chaotic mess, but it was late in the day and it wasn't nearly as crowded as it was earlier. He had no problem finding the infirmary, as a pathway of sick and injured pointed the way down a small hallway to a set of double doors. His dad was among those in the hallway, sitting with his bound leg out in front of him.

"Hey, Dad. How you doing?"

He expected a warm greeting after being separated for so many hours, but he only got a weary nod. "Tired as hell. They set my leg and got me squared away, but they don't have much in the way of painkillers."

His leg was wrapped in a decidedly makeshift-looking cast. More like a couple sticks bound together with some belts. Better than most people had it "out there." Jerry had the look of a man in a lot of pain, including the beads of sweat and the taut facial features.

He sat down next to him. "I'm sorry you're in so much pain. If it makes you feel any better, I'm also sorry for causing so many problems the past few months. Getting myself kicked out and all that. If I'd known this was coming, I think I would have done a few things differently in how I handled myself with you and Mom."

Jerry strained a laugh. "Thanks, Son. I think if any of us really knew what was coming, the last few months would have been entirely different for us all. Weapons training. Stockpiling food. Defensive plans. Bugout locations. Backups of backups. I can think of a hundred things I planned on doing but never got around to because they never seemed urgent. Now we're well into it and here I am doing nothing at all to help you or your mom."

Liam was hoping for some sort of reciprocal apology, but took it in stride. It was better than any discussion they'd had this year. Instead, he moved back to a subject he had asked his dad days earlier. A subject he pointedly avoided answering straight.

"Dad, how did you know to stockpile all those guns? You knew something was coming, didn't you?"

Jerry leaned his head back against the wall behind him as he sat on the floor, apparently thinking. Liam waited patiently. Several moments later, he popped his head back up, looked both ways in the hallway at the other injured folks, and then returned, "I've always done all I could to protect you and your mother. The less you knew about my sources the safer I thought you'd be. But now that everything has gone to hell, I really don't think government agents are lurking about listening in on conversations like this one."

Liam looked around, suddenly self-conscious that he could be the subject of surveillance by one of Hayes' men. But no one nearby played the part. Most looked positively sick or dying.

His dad noticed him looking intently at those nearby. "What?"

"It's just you said something about government agents. I've been dealing with them a lot lately. They took Grandma. They shot Victoria. They destroyed your house. They took my picture on a bridge. I'd say the odds are pretty good we *are* being spied upon right now."

His dad managed a real laugh. "Congratulations, Jerry. You've raised a son even more paranoid than you are."

Both smiled at the joke. "No offense, but if you'd seen that medical camp over in Lone Elk Park when it was in operation, you'd have no doubt what the government was capable of doing. Paranoia is a survival trait nowadays."

"Well, suffice it to say that yes, I did know something was coming. Someone in our family called me—don't ask because I swore to not tell anyone, save your mother—and gave me information that something big was coming and that I needed to be prepared to leave home on a moment's notice."

He looked around before continuing in a quieter voice, "So when the sirens went off, your mom and I were totally prepared to hop in a car, go to Marty's where we knew you were safe and sound without access to a car, and we'd all be on our way to somewhere out in the country to safely watch it all blow over. What I didn't count on was that the world would fall apart everywhere at exactly the same moment. I counted on being the first guy out the door. Instead, I was the one millionth person out the door. Your mom and I barely made it onto the highway before things broke down. Crashes. Gunshots. Running people. We knew where you were, but it was days before we could get there...and by then it was too late."

Liam had so many questions, but for some reason he was most troubled by one of the most mundane. "So can you tell me if you sent me to live with Grandma because of TEOTWAWKI?"

"Tea ought what key? What are you saying?"

"Sorry, I figured you'd know that one. It means the end of the world as we know it. Did you know the world was ending? Is that why you sent me to Grandma's?"

A more strained laugh.

"No, Liam. I really did send you to Grandma's so your mother and I wouldn't kill you."

He paused to reflect on the past six months leading up to his exile at Grandma's. The arguments over responsibility. About time management. About doing what you said you were going to do. All the little details he so often got wrong in the eyes of his parents. All the things that seemed to drive his parents crazy. All the things *he* always felt were unimportant. He had to admit he often made things worse by yelling, slamming doors, and generally being an unreasonable punk.

Why was I acting young and stupid?

"Young and stupid" and "just being a kid" were allowable two weeks ago, just before the sirens took down the world. He'd been forced to mature or die. Maybe he'd have done it no matter what, but he was thankful once again Victoria had come along and helped him man up during those early difficulties. Sure, he thought, he did cry in front of her a couple times, but to be fair all of society had come unraveled. Everyone was crying at some point; she cried and talked in her sleep and he thought no less of her.

Somewhat satisfied at his answer, and wanting to give his dad some time to rest, he excused himself.

"Where's mom?"

Jerry had leaned his head back against the wall again. This time he answered without opening his eyes.

"She took that bag of rice to the council as payment for my medical services. I tried to stop her, but she's as stubborn as you are sometimes. Or you're as stubborn as her. I get them confused."

In the Old World, this might have been a jumping off point for some sort of argument. In the New World, it was just taken as the joke it was meant to be.

5

He left his dad to rest. He thought about trying to find his mother, but didn't want to tangle with the leaders again. He wasn't even sure he could get up there by himself with all that security. Instead, he hovered near a window facing the creek where Victoria had gone to rest.

Should I give her more time?

He easily spied her a hundred feet away. She sat on the bank of the creek, and was talking to someone—a young man—a bit further away. He seemed filthy, even from this distance. His first instinct was to run out there, but he knew that was stupid. They were just talking. So, he waited.

He quickly bored of watching them. He surveyed the huge camp and saw only tents as far as he could see from his window. The narrow valley was filled to capacity.

One area where the Boy Scouts were able to keep control was the judicious use of the water from the creek. With so many people living so close to the waterway, boys patrolled up and down the bank to make sure no one poured chemicals into the water or tried to use it as a latrine. Liam saw the boys actively walking up and down both sides of the creek even now. Water was a precious resource, though he knew the real key to this valley was the large artesian well further up the creek. They didn't have much food to spread around, but with clean water, it gave them an edge most people probably didn't have in the wider world.

A few minutes later, he returned his gaze to his girlfriend—he loved saying that—and saw her arguing with the guy.

What the!

She tried to grab him by the arm, and he shook free immediately, took a few seconds to observe the vicinity, and then pushed Victoria hard enough she fell down the steep creek bank out of Liam's view. He ran from the building in a flash.

The young man ran away from him along the creek, but his first concern was Victoria. He dashed to her in time to see her struggling to climb back out of the creek bed. She appeared dry and in one piece, though her clothes were still soiled from the previous creek she'd been in.

"That new guy needed to check in to camp but refused. I tried to pull him over there as a joke, and he pushed me down here. I guess he ran away?"

She peered up from the rocky slope, trying to see left and right. "I didn't see which way he went."

105

"I did." Liam took off, knowing she would be fine.

He was sure someone else had to have seen the incident, but no one joined the pursuit. He felt a surge of anger that no one helped and it doubled with his burning desire to have words with the fleeing suspect. Liam, a natural runner and the slightly-above-mediocre star of his below-mediocre track team, kicked into overdrive running in pursuit.

It didn't take long and he could see the man ahead. He wore a filthy white t-shirt and brown cargo pants with white sneakers. He wasn't a very large man, so his stride was about equal to Liam's.

The man realized he was being followed, which both sped him up and changed his trajectory. Instead of moving down the creek corridor, he made his way into the thick of the tents on the valley floor. The advantage of speed was lost immediately. Instead, with ducking and weaving in random directions through the myriad of tents and tarps, Liam steadily fell behind.

He considered calling for help, but didn't want to cause a commotion over a situation he still didn't understand.

The runner made his way toward the front gate. That became apparent after a few minutes of zigging and zagging through the crowd. The question smoldering in Liam's brain was, why?

The man left the tents and was up on the comparatively clear access road. It led from the front gate, up the valley, and past the admin building. Everything ran next to the creek, making it really hard to get lost. This guy was following the most basic directions.

Soon they were both on the paved road. Not far from the entrance. The man had a fifty-foot lead. He appeared to be giving it all he had to get to the front gate.

Maybe he's from outside?

A touch of panic now. An outsider? Liam actually backed off a little. He chose a nice even pace so he could pursue but not exhaust himself like the other man. He figured he was being pretty smart about it.

The man reached the front gate. None of the guards made any motion to stop him. Liam's anger peaked at the realization. They were trained to stop people going the other direction. Again Liam considered yelling ahead for help, but he had already halved the distance. His adrenaline pumped and he had tunnel vision to close the last twenty feet and catch him. He felt his holster, knowing his gun was there. He was ready to use it if needed.

The man crossed the road and ran into the overflow tents in the field. Liam had confidence he could follow him, no matter what he used as a diversion.

The camp exit was in a heavily wooded area, with poor visibility on the access road going left and right of the gate itself. As Liam ran out the gate and crossed the road, he chanced a look left and right. Even though there was no longer any traffic, the old habits died hard.

Clear left.

Clear—

He came to a dead stop in the middle of the road; the running man opened an insurmountable lead. Anyone looking at Liam would laugh at the sight of his mouth hanging wide open. But no one looked at him. Everyone who could see it was doing the same thing as Liam: gawking.

A convoy of military trucks had parked on the shoulder; they were visible as far as he could see on the windy road. Some around him probably knew what they were, but not why they were there.

Liam knew.

Hayes was back to collect his precious MRAP.

He brought a lot of friends.

DON'T MAKE PLANS

Someone bumped into Liam's dangling right arm as he stood in awe. Liam turned slightly to confirm it was Victoria.

"What are you doing? We have to keep after him."

She had her back to the military convoy. She watched the escaping man as he headed into the field of tents, but he didn't care.

"We can catch him! He's slowing down."

He remained frozen. Finally, she turned around and joined Liam in the wide-eyed spectacle. Men and women soldiers stood outside their vehicles. Some had fanned out to the sides, but they didn't act particularly hurried. A small group walked toward the front gate; toward Liam and Victoria.

"This can't be happening," Liam said quietly.

He grabbed Victoria by the arm. Running was not an option. The troopers were much too close. If they wanted him, they had him.

"Greetings!" said a jovial-looking officer as he walked up. He was flanked by several tough-looking Marines in woodland camouflage uniforms, helmets, and with weapons drawn.

"I'm Lt. Colonel Joseph Brandyweis with the 2nd Battalion 2nd Marines. I've been tasked with investigating this camp for civilians known to have stolen U.S. Government property."

Here it comes. We're caught!

"Wel-welcome to Camp Hope." Liam didn't know what else to say.

"Will you two fine folks take me and my friends here to the administrator of this facility?"

It was an order, not a request.

"Sure. We'll take you." Liam held Victoria's hand—tightly.

The colonel waved to the lead Humvee in his column, then said something into a small radio. In response, the front vehicle and two more behind rolled toward the front gate. As the first one pulled up, he instructed them to get in.

"This will be faster than walking." He gave them a once-over. Liam figured he looked guilty—he had sweat pouring off his forehead from his pursuit. "Don't worry, my friends. We aren't here to hurt anyone. We're the good guys!"

Liam had heard that before. He was pretty sure the good guys were gone for good.

When they climbed in, Liam was overcome by the smell of cooked meat. He was practically drooling. How long since the last decent meal? Days.

"You guys want some deer meat? I don't have much, but you're welcome to what I have."

Victoria didn't hesitate. "Oh my, that would be incredible."

"We've been traveling a lot these last couple weeks. Sometimes we stop and get food from pre-positioned government stockpiles, but more often we dismount and hunt deer. Always in season now, huh?" He gave a hearty laugh.

Liam took the venison, though he hesitated before eating it. He looked at Victoria and saw her enjoying her small serving. He decided if he was going to be captured this easily, he'd at least get a good meal out of it.

He was well into the small serving when the colonel asked about the condition of the camp. Who was in charge? How many people? How big was the valley? Liam and Victoria answered honestly, until he directed his questioning at them.

"So, how did you kids end up here?"

Liam looked at Victoria, her face giving no clues to her thoughts on how to answer.

"My family lived near the interstate. When the zombies chased out all the people from the city, both groups used my street as a battlefield. Our house was destroyed. Our neighbors killed. We decided the one place we'd might find some help was at this Boy Scout camp." Liam told himself he didn't really lie. He learned his lesson about mentioning his wayward grandmother to anyone in government.

"And what about you?"

Victoria was quick to respond. "I was part of a summer medical internship at Barnes Memorial Hospital downtown. When the plague began spreading, I made a run for it. I escaped, along with many others from downtown, by walking out. I found this place by accident." After a moment's pause, she added, "My parents are still in Denver, so I'm hoping to make it out there again someday."

"Denver, eh? Well, I'm sorry to say no urban area is intact these days. I've not seen Denver, but I've seen downtown St. Louis. They can't be that different. I wish you luck in finding your parents."

Liam felt brave enough to ask a question he knew was borderline self-incriminating. "You said you're looking for thieves here? What did they steal?"

He got a cold stare in return, but nothing further was said.

He knows.

2

Liam guided the Marines to the main building, introduced the newcomers to the guards, and then was told to stay put on the main floor. He and Victoria mingled in the bustle of the crowded room, but he felt very much alone.

"It seems odd they wouldn't take us upstairs. Maybe they aren't here for you. Uh, sorry. They aren't here for *us*."

Victoria talked to him, but he had trouble focusing. The volume of chatter in the room had exploded once the Marines came and went. His belly was temporarily sated, but the venison didn't sit very well. Taken together, he felt oddly out of sorts.

He tried to calm himself as he leaned against the rear wall of the large room. Slipping out was an option, though other Marines now patrolled around the building. He could see them through the big ground floor windows.

"I uhh, don't know. Should we try to get away? Where would we go? Won't that look like we're guilty?" After a moment, he said, "I need a minute."

Victoria pulled up a piece of wall next to him. "Thanks for chasing that guy down. He seemed like an OK guy up until that point."

Liam reoriented. He'd been absorbed with his own problems, and ignored hers. "You said he pushed you down when you tried to take him to check in. I saw that part. What was he talking about before he pushed you?"

"He mainly asked about the camp. How long it had been here. How many people we had. Was it safe to bring his kids. Stuff like that."

"Did he ask about supplies or security?" Liam's ill-feeling was not improving.

"No, but he did ask where the creek water came from. I told him I didn't know. I've never been up the creek."

"It sounds like he was probing for information. I've read about this many times in my zombie books. Survivor groups will scout each other to find strengths and weaknesses. Many times it's a prelude to an attack if they think they can take the weaker group." He paused to think for a moment before continuing, "But how big would their group have to be to consider taking on an entire valley of people like this?" He fanned his hand out over the tents sprawled outside the windows of the building.

Neither of them answered for a long time. Liam's stomach still danced, but started to improve. He no longer felt like he was going to embarrass himself by getting sick.

"I guess it's a good thing the Marines showed up when they did. Maybe they chased off the group which sent the scout?" She always searched for the positive.

Liam's nerves were rattled by the appearance of the Marines, he was tired from his brisk run, and he'd generally been in a bad mood since Grandma was taken. As a result, he sought the negative in everything. "I guess that depends. What if the group is strong enough to take the Marines too? Maybe the Marines are the bad guys..."

Victoria pulled herself off the wall, turned, and appeared ready to chastise him. But just then someone called for him from up the stairs.

"Liam Peters! Front and center in the council chambers!"

Victoria's demeanor softened. Instead of the admonishment he thought was coming, she instead just gave a long sigh. She reached in to give him a hug.

"Good luck."

She held him for a moment before she pulled back. He was relieved that instead of leaving, she took his hand and led him to the stairs.

We're in this together. Thank God.

His stomach, and his will, hardened for what was coming.

3

When they reached the top the stairs, the Lt. Colonel was huddled with a couple of the council members. They motioned him over. Camp security guards and Marines formed two separate cliques on opposing sides of the room, as if wary of each other.

The colonel spoke first. "I don't recall asking for the young lady."

Liam was ready for that. "Where I go, she goes."

Liam felt eyes drilling into him. They could, of course, toss her out and there wouldn't be anything he could do about it. His mind spun down a network of possibilities from there. Would he refuse to cooperate? Was he putting her in danger? Could he fight? The small pistol on his hip was rubbing him as if in reminder...

I must be going crazy to even think I have a chance against Marines.

"Then let's get right to it. I'm told you know where to find Douglas Hayes."

Liam felt his face flush. He may also have felt a dumb look on his face as he stood facing the military man.

"Liam? Do you know where he is, son? It's vital we find him."

"You want to find him? Why?"

He glanced at Victoria, but she shared the same look.

"As I was telling your camp leaders here, we want to find Mr. Hayes because he's a vital link in solving the mystery of fighting this outbreak of..." The colonel didn't want to use the Z-word, Liam knew authorities believed it trivialized their condition. "...plague victims. Hayes and his team have been conducting their own research the last several weeks and have gone off on their own. They've taken a lot of equipment and personnel from legitimate government researchers. Some would say he *stole* those resources. We also know he's been rounding up test subjects outside the purview of his bosses. An Army

Colonel at a camp near here was asking questions about Hayes' methods."

Liam felt sick again, but not because of what he ate. This was confirmation of what he already suspected about Hayes and his intentions with Grandma. He didn't know which was worse though; an out-of-control government bent on researching the outbreak no matter how many people they had to kill during trials, or an independent and secretive group of researchers doing the same, beyond the control of the aforementioned all-powerful government. Either way, there was no excuse for the piles of bodies he'd seen at Elk Meadow, or what they did there.

Maybe he could finally get some answers.

"I want to help you, Colonel. I really do. I will if I can. But Marines blew up my parents' house. Didn't Hayes order that?"

The LtCol studied him for a moment and seemed to reach a conclusion.

"The world is chaos now. My area of operations is the entire state of Missouri, but I can only control what's directly in my line-of-sight these days, and even that's getting hard to do. My bosses sent me out with minimal intel and frankly it's a miracle we found you here. What I do know about your house is yes, it was Hayes who ordered the strike. But what we can't figure out is what kind of clearance he had to authorize said strike."

He closed the distance to Liam and spoke a little quieter.

"We sent another unit to investigate what could have rated a full-blown strike. We should have sent a team to gather information on a target *prior* to wiping it off the map. Now..." He shrugged. "The official report, brief as it was, stated there were no obvious signs of contagion beyond the uniform standard of infection everywhere else.

That's a fancy way of saying there were plague victims, but no research facility or high value target."

He drilled into Liam's eyes.

"Son, do you know why he'd select your house?"

Where do I begin?

Aware that he'd already told a white lie when they first met, he had to explain why he lied initially, then he laid out their first meeting with Hayes under the Arch, his strange interest in Grandma, and the subsequent kidnappings, escapes, and firefights which summed up their give and take relationship. He also mentioned Victoria's capture and shooting by Hayes. He finished with the bombing of his boyhood home.

"So, the reason Hayes blew up your neighborhood was payback? Can it really be that simple?"

"I don't know, sir. He warned me the planes were coming—said he owed me one because I spared his life earlier—so on the face of it the whole thing seemed like a waste of resources. But he did kill a lot of my neighbors."

"I'm sorry, son, I really am. You're a better man than me. Someone shoots my girlfriend or wife," he tossed Liam a wry smile, "they get a dirt nap. Is there anything you can tell me about his whereabouts now that he has taken your grandma? I think we both want to find her."

Her?

Liam had been pretty forthcoming in his storytelling, but he did leave out one significant detail. He made no mention of the age factor and how Elk Meadow had revealed the link between the virus and very old test subjects. He wondered if the LtCol already knew about that. The answer would reveal whether he was looking for Hayes, or for Grandma.

"He picked her up in an unmarked private helicopter. It could have been from a TV station, a hospital, or maybe some government agency. I can't tell you which." Liam ran the scene over and over in his head, and those were his best guesses about the origin of the helicopter. In other words, he didn't have a clue.

While waiting to see how he reacted, Liam realized something else. The LtCol was here, looking for *him*. Somehow his name had been associated with Hayes. Which means Hayes must have put him in his reports. Reports accessible by this Marine. But how did they know he would be here, in this camp? It seemed too convenient. Too lucky.

Liam's natural fear of the government, inherited from his father, was red-lining.

The LtCol wasn't telling him everything.

I really wanted to trust you, too.

4

Liam was relieved he wasn't under arrest, which was where he figured he'd be by this point in their conversation. The LtCol continued to ask questions, but none of Liam's answers led to any new revelations about where Hayes and Grandma might have gone. He even told him about the paperwork they'd found referencing "Riverside" downtown, but it was deemed not credible. "I can't go all the way downtown on a hunch."

Liam willingly shared almost all of what he knew, minus what he witnessed at Elk Meadow. Liam couldn't be sure, even now, whether this man knew about the significance of his grandmother. He intended to keep it that way.

"Don't you have any way to track people?"

Like you tracked me.

The LtCol was hard to read, but he thought the man's eyes might have widened at the suggestion. His response was less helpful.

"If we had a way to track him, we would already have found him. He has to be accessing our network, but we don't know how. I'm in the dark here, and I don't like it. The only clue I have in this whole mess was an early report from Hayes' team from underneath the Arch where he mentioned your name. We followed that lead and found your street blown to hell. We realized Hayes had authorized the strike order and we wanted to know why. We dug into more of his movements and discovered through our signals intelligence Hayes had been at this camp. It was a long shot to find you here, but we ran right into you. Amazing good luck. The trail can't go cold from here. You have to help if you can."

Liam wondered if there were any leads he overlooked. He'd been thinking about Grandma since she took off in the helicopter, but to no avail. Should he tell him Grandma had his phone? If they could trace his phone to her location, would they immediately go collect her? Would they let him go too? Would they bring her back? Probably none of those things. His mind drifted as he tried to solve the puzzle.

Victoria pulled him toward the big glass windows overlooking the camp. The LtCol made no effort to follow.

"Liam, are you there?"

He snapped awake. "Hi! Yes, I'm just trying to think of what to do next. My mind isn't cooperating though. Do we have any hope of finding her on our own? More importantly, do we trust him?"

For a brief moment, he thought of asking his parents. He'd been on his own long enough in this carnage he'd almost forgotten they were still around to help. Did he think of himself as a son or as a boyfriend these days?

No. I'm a survivor first.

The word sounded harsh, like metal on a grindstone. But better to be harsh than dead. So many others had given up, succumbed to the plague, or were caught by the zombies. Others were captured by their own government and used as guinea pigs. The man in the room with them was part of that government, no matter how well-meaning he might be.

He didn't need to ask his dad. He already knew what he'd say.

Trust no one from the Federal Family.

Easy enough. But where do you go from there?

Victoria looked at him, patiently waiting for him to make up his mind. In turn, he focused on her emerald greens. He hardly noticed the bruises and blemishes around them. Did she know what he was thinking now? Liam knew she did. He saw an almost imperceptible head shake.

Things were only going to get more complicated. It was no longer possible to offload the problems of being a kid onto the adults in the room. The new world had no respect for age, and it mercilessly penalized stupid people of all ages. Liam resolved not to be stupid.

He looked to make sure no one could overhear them. "We can't stay here with these people. If these Marines know we're here, it won't be long before Hayes knows. He may decide to decimate the valley simply because he can. We can't be responsible for that..." His thought trailed off as he looked out at the camp he'd begun to consider his new home. His parents were here somewhere, too. He suddenly had a deep resentment for Hayes, the government, the military—and whoever started this zombie plague. It was an inconvenience of the highest order.

He inwardly chuckled at the lunacy.

Victoria picked up where he left off. "OK, so we need a plan. We need to walk out of this camp where no one will find us. Do you and I run off? I was joking before, but this seems like the time to try it. We need to regroup and figure out how to find Grandma."

Can we do it without the Marines?

Liam honestly couldn't answer that. He couldn't trust them. But could he use them just as readily as they would use him? He looked over at the LtCol, now engaged in quiet conversation with members of the Boy Scout council.

Liam knew what had to be done, though he didn't have a clue how to make it happen. "How can we get out of this room, get out of this camp without being seen, and have enough gear to survive?"

It was somewhat rhetorical, but Victoria answered him. "Getting out of this room is easy. We just tell them we need to collect our gear. Then we head back to our tent, grab some supplies, and disappear."

"Just like that?" Liam knew there was nothing "just like that," anymore.

"We'll, I admit there are bound to be some kinks. Let's hear your plan, Mr. Smarty."

They both shared a conspiratorial giggle, a little louder than intended. It caught the attention of the LtCol.

"Have you two thought of anything that may help my search? I really need to be moving on."

The council members became visibly agitated. "Moving on? We thought you were here to protect us."

Soon the LtCol was overwhelmed with questions.

He tolerated none of it. "Listen! I'll only say this once. We are U.S. Marines. Not your personal security guards. We're here on a mission to save humanity. We need to be Charlie Mike *as soon as possible*. We're leaving."

Their mission is my mission: saving people.

And then the way forward presented itself.

He was going to help the Marine Corps after all.

5

The chaos in the room grew as more people came from downstairs. The guards on the stairs either heard the LtCol say he wasn't staying, or other Marines on the lower floor had spread the message they weren't sticking around. However it happened, the result was madness.

Liam briefly considered trying to sneak out right then and there, but knew that was stupid. Better to play it safe.

They returned to the main discussion.

"Colonel, I think I have a way to help you find Hayes and my Grandma but you have to take us along. Victoria and I are going to grab our gear and go with you in your vehicle, if that's all right?"

The LtCol appeared distracted by the raised voices in the room, but he had the sense to detach one of his Marines—a burly-looking man with several stripes on his arm.

"Jax, keep an eye on our young friends and make sure they aren't harmed as they gather their gear."

With that, he redirected his attention to the council. The message was clear. Get lost. But not *too* lost.

Victoria gave him a troubled look as they walked out of the room. The trio moved down the stairs and out into the tent city. Word was spreading almost before their eyes.

Cries of "The Marines are leaving!," "They aren't here to help us!," and "Make them stay!" permeated the desperate campers.

He walked hand-in-hand with Victoria, hands clasped very tightly as the energy built around them. Jax, who wore the name Jackson on his uniform, seemed unconcerned with all the fuss, but he had deftly moved his weapon from his back to a place under his left arm. Not openly hostile, but easily accessible.

Why'd we get the bad-ass professional?

Closer to their own tent, Liam checked the distance between them and their overseer and decided to share his plan in a quiet voice. "I'm going to get in our tent first. Then you tell him," he nudged his head backward to Jax, "that you want to join me in the tent before we leave." I'll take it from there.

Victoria nodded.

Several people watched Liam and his two friends walk into their section of the camp. Some nodded. Some were openly hostile to the Marine. Apparently word had spread well ahead of them that the Marines were abandoning them. Many probably didn't know the Marines had even arrived.

Liam didn't wait for an invitation from Jax to go into his tent. He just whipped open the zipper and plunged in.

He got right to work with his pocketknife on the back nylon wall; he ripped it partially open so he and Victoria could sneak out the back and get a head start on a run. He knew they would be seen eventually, but the woods were thick not far from their tent—so they'd have a chance to lose any pursuit. No way Jax would shoot them.

Liam reflexively gulped.

No time for doubts. Victoria said her part and climbed in. She zipped the front zipper, then saw what he'd done to the back panel. The course of action became obvious at that point.

Liam whispered, "Follow me out the back and run like hell. We're going for the MRAP over the hill."

Victoria nodded.

Liam cut the last little bit of fabric off the back of the tent and it fell to the ground, giving him a perfect view of the woods.

Unfortunately, the view was blocked by the imposing presence of Jax. "Do you kids think I was born yesterday? I know five-year-olds with better plans than you."

He had his weapon out, but pointed at the ground. "Get your stuff and let's go."

Liam smiled innocently as he retreated back into the tent. "Well, that didn't go as planned."

"You tried, Liam. Now it's my turn."

She partially unzipped the front zipper, turned around at him with a big grin and a wink. She did something that quite literally shocked him. She screamed at the top of her lungs, finished opening the zipper, and spilled out the front.

Liam was left in stunned silence. He turned around and looked through the rough cut of the rear of the tent and saw Jax as he moved toward the front again. He looked all business.

"That soldier tried to pull off my shirt!" Victoria screamed while forcing herself to sob.

Oh, shit.

Liam came out of the tent to see a dozen armed men and women running up from the scores of tents in earshot. None looked too happy to have to deal with a Marine, though the screams of the girl could not be ignored.

Jax came around the tent with his weapon drawn.

"STAND DOWN" he yelled in his most commanding voice.

The arriving civilians stopped in their place, but not for long. More followed.

"I SAID STAND DOWN!"

Fewer people were affected.

The plan worked too well. Liam worried someone might get hurt. He stood up next to Victoria as if to comfort her. He made an exaggerated effort to speak so everyone could hear him. "Victoria, would you like me to talk to this Marine to get *his* side of the story?"

The crowd of men and women were twenty feet away, but spreading around him. He had to know his chances of surviving the flash mob was dwindling.

"Yes, please speak to him!"

Victoria was acting scared, but Liam thought he could detect real fear in her eyes.

"Everyone, give me a minute to talk to him. Please."

No one seemed overly anxious to escalate beyond coming to a rescue.

Liam moved over to Jax, and directed him to the rear of the tent. He spoke quietly. "Do you have a pencil?"

"What the hell are you talking about?"

"A pencil? You know, to write with? I want to get you out of this alive. Victoria and I only want to be left alone, but if you give me a pencil, I'll write down how to find my grandma. That should soften your return to your unit."

He didn't look happy, but he pulled out a stub of a pencil and a scrap of paper. Liam noticed it had some words printed on the side, in tiny gold script. It said, "Trust in God."

He looked at it for a long moment, then wrote something. "You were right. My plan was as sophisticated as a five-year-old's. Hers..." He made a swooshing sound with his mouth.

He handed the paper and pencil back.

"That's the phone number to my cell phone. Currently my grandma has it wherever she is. Maybe you guys can do some fancy tracking on it or something. You have a better chance of finding her with it than I do and I have to believe you are less hostile to her than Hayes."

Jax seemed to consider this new information. "Then why are you running away?"

He had a point. Maybe going with the Marines would be the fastest way.

Trust no one.

His dad's maxim on life.

He looked into Jax's eyes and felt himself wanting to believe this man, this U.S. Marine, was honorable.

"The government took my grandma. The government shot my girlfriend. The government bombed my house into scrap. I wish I could trust you and the colonel. I really do. But I have to go my own way, away from any agent of that government."

With that, Liam spun around before he could be talked out of anything. The desire to trust the Marines was overwhelming.

He spoke to the crowd.

"I think there's been a slight misunderstanding. Victoria and I were merely wanting to go our own way, and this Marine accidentally tried to stop us. Would you good people make sure he gets back to his unit at the council's HQ? It's very important he not be harmed. Scout's Honor."

Liam thought about whether he could really make this request of these people, but he was surprised to see several step up as if to provide escort.

For his part, Jax played along. He made no effort to talk the crowd down or reason with them. He simply fell in with them and led them back through the tents. No final words to Liam. No threats. Just business-like in his demeanor. He'd come to appreciate that in the real world there were seldom big speeches.

Once they were sure he was gone, they ran into the woods like cross country stars.

TRAJECTORIES

"We have to find Mr. Lee. I just hope he's up in his watchtower where we left him."

Victoria struggled to keep up with Liam as they ascended the steep wooded path. As she arrived, he asked, "You OK?"

"Yeah, just worn out. First running after you, then the excitement of the Marines, now more running. I think I'm exhausted because lying down in those bushes and calling it a day seems like a really good idea right now."

She nodded and he followed her gaze.

"Well, you don't want to lay in *those* bushes. That's a tangle of poison ivy. My Boy Scout plant identification badge is still paying dividends."

Victoria scrunched her face in a "thanks Mr. Know-it-all" gesture, but they both laughed.

They resumed the trek the rest of the way up the hill and arrived at the watchtower they had left earlier in the day. It was a bustle of young Scouts running to and fro. Some worked on the fence. Others ran off into the woods. It was part of the communication system Mr. Lee had rigged up to talk to other checkpoints and keep the perimeter free of zombies and other intruders.

Liam saw Mr. Lee on the lowest level. He waved at them, though he looked very busy.

She grabbed his arm. "Wait, Liam. We have to discuss what we're going to do next. We need a plan so we don't look like a couple of kids just running away from our problems."

"That sounds like an after-school special." He was smiling, but she wasn't.

"OK, I guess now isn't the time for humor. I think we should all get in the MRAP and go follow the Marines and see where they go. I gave them Grandma's phone number and I bet they have access to the cellular network and can get a message to her so they can find out where she's being held."

"What if she doesn't have the phone anymore? What if it was taken from her?"

Liam felt his face turn serious. "She still has it. I have to believe she does."

"What about your parents? Are we going to leave them in the camp?"

Liam could feel his stomach turn over. "I should have tried to get them out. I didn't even think of it."

"Do you want to go back?"

Liam took a long minute to think. "We can't. We'd never make it back under the nose of the Marines, and even if we did somehow manage to get dad out, his leg is busted. He would have to stay in the truck the whole time. My mom has to stay with him too. They'll be fine in camp, for now."

Victoria nodded.

"So the next question is, who do we get to go with us? You and I can't drive that thing on our own. We really need Melissa."

Liam looked around, but didn't see Mel. "Yeah, and having Mr. Lee, Phil and Bo along wouldn't hurt either. We could assemble our A-team again."

Privately, Liam worried he had asked too much of his new friends already. Going out on another excursion for "the young kid"—with a low probability of success to boot—was asking a lot. Especially when they were somewhere relatively safe already. Victoria was right. They had to come to this with a coherent plan.

My plan sounds childish; save my grandma.

Liam turned the pages of his mind, searching through the books he'd read about zombies to try to arrive at his own solution, but he had to admit most scenarios like this started with noble intentions and ended in death for at least some of the noble warriors. Asking people to risk their lives for him was not the trivial request he thought it was just a few short minutes ago. It made going off on their own seem more palatable, even if it meant it would be much more difficult. Still, he wanted to give it an honest shot to enlist the others.

With suitable embarrassment, he managed to ask her how she would present his plan so it didn't sound juvenile.

"I think the answer is Hayes," Victoria was deliberate in her response, "and his seeming inability to just leave you alone. We already know he has Grandma, so getting help to rescue her can't be ignored. But the bigger picture is the protection of this camp. We have a reasonable expectation that if Hayes knows we're here, he could attack the camp just like he did for your house and street. By leaving to rescue Grandma and stop Hayes, we are protecting the camp from further harm."

Victoria snapped her fingers as if surprised. "That's it! We aren't going to rescue Grandma 'just because.' We're going to stop this once and for all so both the camp and Grandma can be safe. That sounds reasonable, doesn't it?"

"Actually, that sounds very reasonable."

Except for the part where two kids take on a secretive military-biological Army unit.

They approached the Endor watchtower hand in hand.

2

"Guys, I wish I could go with you, but this camp needs me here. The Marines have really stirred things up in our happy valley. I think people saw their arrival as the end of their time out in the wilderness— the sheepdogs were back to protect them. But as word got out the Marines were just visiting, they...well they didn't take the news too good."

"We saw that coming up." Liam left out the part where they escaped from their Marine overseer.

"We also saw firsthand what the Marines are looking for. Rather, who they're looking for. You won't be surprised to know they're looking for Hayes, same as me—us."

"That figures. How did they end up looking for him here?"

Liam looked at Victoria. She shrugged her shoulders in the universal "I have no idea" answer.

"He didn't say precisely, other than to tell us he got really lucky. Hayes put my name in a database, and he followed the bombs. That's how he put it."

"Hmm, sounds like we could be in real danger now that the Marines know you're here. Hayes knows, too. You can take that to the bank."

Victoria gave Liam a knowing look.

After a thoughtful pause, Mr. Lee continued, "I still can't come with you. As head of security, this is when the camp needs me the most. As you can see, my runners are working hard to keep our ring of security positions in contact. Liam, people are trying to leave already. What's that saying? Rumors have traveled to the next county before truth has laced up its shoes."

He must have understood the dejected looks on their faces, so he continued. "I do think Melissa and Phil will be back soon. They're doing some running for me, too. I wouldn't be surprised if they wanted to go out and explore again. I don't think they like what I've got them doing." He laughed, but had a distant look in his eyes. "If only we had some more radios."

Mr. Lee excused himself so he could get back to managing his runners.

Victoria pulled Liam away and they sat up against a nearby tree while they waited.

Several hours later, he woke up to find Victoria sleeping next to him, still with her back up against the tree.

The sun was low and the shadows of the forest were long.

He stood up, unsteady as he rose.

Victoria was jostled awake. "How long was I out?"

"No idea. I'm just waking up, too. I guess we really needed a nap."

Mr. Lee was still in the tower, as were Phil, Melissa, and Bo. They were sitting and standing on the first floor.

He pulled Victoria off the ground and together they made their way back to the structure.

"Ah, you're awake! I have good news for you. Melissa has agreed to drive for you, and Phil and Bo are joining you too." He paused and looked at Melissa before continuing, "We discussed how useful the truck could be in defense of the camp, but I understand why you want to find your grandma and stop Hayes from doing whatever he's going to do to her, and to us. I think that mission is more important than killing any random zombie. Just promise me you'll bring the truck back?"

Liam didn't know what to say.

"We promise." Victoria responded for him.

"I do have one request. Can you tell my parents I went out looking for my grandma? I don't want them to think I fell off the planet."

Mr. Lee assured him he would send a runner immediately.

They descended the back side of the hill to the wooded hollow where they hid the MRAP. They clambered in, sealed the doors, and Mel fired up the diesel.

"We got word from our runners the Marines spent a little time looking for you, but bugged out about an hour ago. There was some ugliness as they left, but nobody got hurt, thank the Lord. They haven't gone far however; the convoy is parked not far from the entrance to the valley, though we don't know why they haven't moved from there." She turned in her seat to face everyone in the back of the vehicle. "So we have to decide how we're going to track these guys."

No one was quick to offer suggestions. Liam literally had no ideas.

She continued after a suitable pause for feedback, "OK, I vote we head north out of the woods and find a position overlooking the highway so we can observe the convoy as it passes. There's an old water slide on a bluff I know. We can probably follow them using the path they have to cut through all the detritus on the highway. We can't get close, but we should have no problem tracking them wherever they go. Right to your grandma, Liam."

It was a plan. Better than anything he would have thought up.

Nice to have friends.

3

The little dirt track through the woods was not much wider than the military truck. The dwindling light of the day made it seem narrower than it was as he looked out the front window. He heard the branches drag across the side plates as they passed clumps of trees. Sometimes branches would make a loud snap as they got caught on the apparatus of the chain gun up on top. They'd been through here before, so had confidence they'd come out where they needed.

It was only a fifteen minute trek to the edge of the property, even at such slow speeds. They emerged from the woods on the back side of a dusty open space adjoining a small neighborhood. Melissa stopped the MRAP as they were in the last of the trees.

"You guys want to look at this."

They gathered as best they could near the cramped space of the driver's compartment. Liam looked out on a whole subdivision of smoldering homes. It was hard to tell how many houses were once there. Maybe thirty or forty. He shuddered as it reminded him of his own ruined neighborhood.

Victoria asked, "Did Hayes do this?"

"No, this is something different. Not a bombing anyway. Each house was torched. There are no craters and—" Melissa hesitated as she looked out, "there's one house still standing smack in the middle."

Liam noticed it, too.

Phil, in the navigator's seat, asked the question they were all thinking. "Do we proceed?"

Liam sensed they were asking him. "The gamer's dilemma?" He smiled, trying to make light of the situation, but he felt they had no idea what he was talking about. "I guess we have to go on," he finished more seriously.

Melissa cautiously rolled the MRAP across the field and toward the remaining house. It looked lonely among the dozens of ruined frame houses on the empty streets. Liam didn't know why she would head for it. After all, they could just as easily skirt the whole subdivision by driving through the backyards of a few houses to reach the access road.

"Wait," he shouted.

The truck slammed to a stop. Liam almost fell over.

"Uh, sorry. How do we know that house isn't some kind of trap?" After he said it, he felt guilty for thinking himself important enough to warrant a trap, but in his defense he did have his home bombed.

Melissa and Phil studied the house carefully.

"They really made sure you'd see this, Liam."

Liam looked at Bo. "Well I see it. I vote we just get out of here."

Melissa offered her suggestion. "Let's at least drive around to the front of the house and evaluate from there. The road looks intact and unless they have a rocket propelled grenade there's nothing that can harm us." She looked back at them with a wry smile.

They all agreed to at least get close and check it out.

Melissa sped up as they approached. She turned the last corner so they could all see the front facade of the last house still standing.

Liam heard a few gasps. He merely put his hand on his forehead.

I told them we should have just left.

A word had been spray-painted in big block letters on the white double garage door.

"LIAM."

4

For the second time in the last several minutes, Victoria asked if this was Hayes' handiwork. This time no one offered an answer. He felt the eyes of his friends on him.

"I don't know anymore. Before I met those Marines I thought only Hayes knew my relationship to Grandma. Certainly he was the only one who could possibly know Grandma had my cell phone. But I told Jax about it before we left camp, so I guess the Marines could have written this, too, if they were fast about it. Maybe they announced it on an open frequency so all levels of government know who I am. I just can't say."

"We can't just sit in here talking about it. This ain't just Liam's problem. We can see for a mile around us. No people. No Z's. Let's check it out." Bo shuffled to the back doors. When no one made an effort to stop him, he opened them.

"I'll go with you." Liam really wanted to stay in the truck, but he couldn't let Bo take all the risk while he was safe and snug.

When Liam jumped out, Victoria came out after him. He gave her a look.

"What? I'm not just going to sit back there by myself."

They all had a little laugh and marched up the level driveway of the house. Liam's name loomed large, adding to his displeasure that things seemed to always be about *him*.

Bo kept things light by saying, "You're famous, dude," as he walked up the few stairs to the front door. He jiggled the handle; it was locked.

"Maybe the back door is open."

He walked away from the front door as Liam tried to open the garage door. At first he thought it was locked, but it rose a few inches. He called for help. With great effort, the three of them were able to get it nearly all the way up. With no electricity for a garage door opener, it took sweat power.

They froze in place. They held the garage door above them, hovering between getting it all the way up and letting it crash back down. In the almost-empty garage was a large 55-gallon drum with the unmistakable outline of a bomb on top, complete with blinking lights.

Thirty seconds passed. They were frozen.

The door of the MRAP opened and Phil yelled from the street, "What do you guys see in there?"

Liam blocked a straight view of the device from Phil's vantage point. He scooted over—still holding the door—so it became clear.

The only response Liam could hear was muffled cussing.

"Do we drop the door?" Bo asked. "Run for it?"

Liam had read enough and watched enough movies to know there were a million ways to make a bomb explode. Trip wires, lasers, sound waves, chemical mixtures, proximity sensors, or even the good old fashioned button. Maybe the door opens and knocks a bowling ball onto the bomb.

Or maybe the door closes and explodes.

Once again, Liam faced a life or death choice.

Melissa came running up the driveway at full speed. "Let me see it!"

"What, you're a bomb expert too?" Liam asked, while straining to hold the door.

"No, but I played one on TV. Just let me look in there."

She approached the open door and took her time scanning the garage, including the door itself. With great care, she made her way over to the big drum, staying as low as possible. With exaggerated slowness, she stood up next to it.

"OK, I don't see any wires connected to it or the garage door. Someone put some heavy weights on the door, but they seem useless. I think you can push the door open and then back away."

"No way," Bo said. "We don't really know what's going to happen with this door. If we open it, maybe it explodes. If we close it, maybe it also explodes. Y'all should clear out and I'll close the door. At least we know it has already been closed and didn't explode. We don't know what happens if it goes all the way up."

Liam couldn't argue with his logic, though he didn't like the idea of leaving him behind even with such a remote chance of the thing exploding.

Victoria was already on her tippy toes holding the door up. She probably couldn't hold that position for much longer.

Melissa accepted Bo's suggestion, telling the rest of them to clear out. She left the garage slowly, but then ran for the MRAP once she was out.

"I'll be ready to move once you two are in!"

It left the three of them holding the door. Victoria was visibly straining.

"You can let it go, Victoria. I got this. You too, Liam."

They both let go and Bo took the burden. He didn't seem the least bit strained.

"Um, I'm sure this isn't goodbye, but thanks." Victoria said it almost reverently.

"Yeah, thanks, man. See you in a few."

Bo turned his head and smiled through his beard. "This is gravy. Beats the heck out of laying fence. Trust me on that."

In moments, Liam and Victoria were back in the MRAP and it was backing up the block.

Melissa parked it so they were facing the house, about fifty yards away.

They all watched as Bo let down the door as far as he could, but he had to let it go to avoid hurting his fingers and it slammed noisily to the pavement. He appeared to pause after it was done, as if he expected an explosion and braced for it.

"Why didn't he run?" Liam asked.

"Whatever's in that drum would have blown up an area bigger than he could escape."

"Then why are we so close? Shouldn't we be in the next county?" Liam mused.

"Relax. Nothing can hurt us in here."

Bo finally stood, gave a thumbs up, and started walking toward the street to meet them. Mel had released the brake and applied the gas.

Seconds later, Bo dropped flat on the driveway. He looked back into the woods from which they'd originally emerged.

"What the—" was all Liam managed to say.

Bo's head lifted up and then ducked quickly back down.

Phil had his weapon in his hand in a flash, "Someone's shooting at him! We have to—" But before he could finish his sentence, and before Melissa could get to him, the world in front of them turned black.

5

The violence of the explosion hit them in a split second, and it rocked the huge truck. It was strong enough to toss debris into the front windshield, and cracked it in several places. Something heavy crushed the passenger-side windshield pillar and spidered the glass in front of Phil. A dark cloud of smoke and dust enveloped them while debris rained down for several minutes.

As the smoke cleared, the evening had almost moved from dusk to night. When it was just a gentle trickle of falling matter, Victoria asked, "What just happened? Where's Bo?" Liam could see nothing was left of the house. Even less than the charred hulks of the burned homes. There wasn't even much of a fire. Nothing was left to burn.

Melissa and Phil both had identical looks of shock as they stared out the front.

Liam wondered why he wasn't in shock.

How would I know?

He answered the question. "Someone was shooting at him from the woods. Maybe they hit the drum behind him and set it off? Or..." Liam's mind was in conspiratorial overdrive these days, so his next statement came quite naturally. "Someone was aiming for the drum to get it to explode on purpose. That...should have been me."

"Liam, no," Victoria said softly.

Mel snapped out of her reverie. "Yes, he's right, someone set it off deliberately. That's why there were no wires or timers. They were waiting until we were all there before setting it off from a distance. Not quite as sophisticated as the improvised bombs we saw over in Iraq, but still effective. They had us all pretty much dead to rights when we were inside the garage, but maybe they thought we were *all* going to get out of the MRAP."

She seemed to regain her composure the more she spoke. She stepped on the gas and drove with purpose toward the subdivision entrance. "I don't know what this is about, but if it was a trap, there may be other ambushers waiting for us."

Sure enough, as they exited the subdivision they saw a disorganized gaggle of civilian vehicles to their left, parked off the county road. Several men and women ran around as if the explosion had set them in motion. Many of them were armed with big black battle rifles.

"Kill them," Liam yelled. "They murdered him."

Mel turned the rig to the right, but she stopped in a few moments. She left it idling in the middle of the road.

Liam had no idea how to fire the chain gun. "Someone shoot the Gatling." He pointed up at the roof.

"I will, Liam."

They were in full view of the men behind them, but no one was firing. He didn't know if they had begun chasing them, or if they were innocent bystanders. He didn't really care. Mel was operating the controls for the chaingun. Liam heard it rotate on top, and then rip out shells for a second or two. He was about to cheer when it stopped.

A few moments later, Mel returned to her driving position and continued up the road at an almost leisurely pace.

"Did you get them?"

"Those folks won't be bothering us anytime soon."

"Did you kill them all?"

Mel turned to look at him with a very serious face. "Liam, things are very fluid here. We have no idea who those people are. We can barely see them. We can't just go around shooting men, women, and maybe children—even if I think they were guilty. I put some rounds across their bow."

At that second, Liam felt it would have been a justified killing. But he knew he could never know for sure if those men were with the ones who shot at Bo, or if the ones who shot at Bo were actually trying to blow up the house and kill his friend. There were too many variables to have black and white anger.

"You're such a nice kid, Liam. You have to view everyone out there as a potential bad guy now, but you don't have to kill *everyone*."

Liam and Victoria returned to the back seats while Mel and Phil drove and rode silently in the front. Bo's hat still sat on the bench. He'd taken if off because it was so hot in the back. It made Liam feel his absence immediately.

The truck rolled on. He was sure something didn't sound right with the engine, but his ears were still buzzing and ringing from the explosion. He was content to sit close to Victoria and simultaneously fume and grieve. It was several minutes before anyone spoke.

"Guys, we have problems up front. Again."

Liam saw what appeared to be several families with small children walking in the same direction they were driving. It would be possible to drive through their loose formation, but he judged it would be very risky with so many children present.

"In Iraq, I heard of women and children being used as decoys and human shields for hardcore insurgents, but this looks innocent. Still, keep your eyes and ears open."

An older, thin, gray-haired woman dropped back from the main detachment so as to speak with them. The main group wasn't waiting for her.

Phil cracked open his door so they could communicate. It groaned loudly as it fought the bent support of the windshield. Liam could only hear her from his vantage point, but she spoke loud and clear.

"Hello ma'am. Why are you all out on the road like this?"

"We come from a subdivision back yonder. Some a-holes dressed like deer hunters come through and killed everyone they could find, then started burning our homes. The menfolk did what they could to stop them while we got away. We're supposed to meet them at a school not far up the road."

"How many men were attacking you? Were they professional soldiers?"

"Naw, they drove regular trucks and wore camo like they was hunters, not soldiers. Don't rightly know the difference, but soldiers don't kill civilians for no reason. My children are old and grown, but my husband stayed and fought with the other men."

"Do you know why they might have left one house intact? Right in the middle?"

"Nope. I saw them torch my house. After that, I didn't care. That's when the men gathered us all up and sent us quick on our way. What was that big boom we heard?"

"Oh, that was a bomb in the last house."

"I guess the men gave them a good fight and let us escape. Nothing worth dying for in those houses. I should keep moving."

Phil tried to yell some more questions out the door, but the woman wasn't interested. "Well, that's that. An unknown group of bad guys took down a whole subdivision for no apparent reason. Then they set up a trap specifically designed to draw us in and kill Liam. Sounds like a lot of people died in that effort, too."

Liam replied in a mechanical tone, "Do we get involved with these people? Isn't it my fault they're on this road? Lost their homes. Lost their..." He bit his tongue to prevent the tears waiting just behind his eyes.

He looked up and saw three faces looking at him with concern.

"How can we help? Won't we put them into even more danger? We have no food or water for such a large group. We can't even protect them for any length of time. And every minute we delay is one less minute to reach and follow the Marines."

Melissa focused on the tactical situation. "The highway is behind us. It probably isn't safe to go back that way and engage whatever group was back there. If we go forward we can loop around and eventually get back to the highway, but we could just as easily loop around to the south and deposit these folks at the Boy Scout camp. We have plenty of gas, and other than a cracked windshield, she seems good to go." She rubbed the dashboard as if the truck were alive.

Victoria added, "We can't just drive past these poor people and leave them in our dust. Like Liam said, we have to take some responsibility for this. If they knew it was his name on that garage, they'd probably want to string us up. We should at least help them to their rendezvous with their men."

Phil turned dark. "Bo paid in blood for this subdivision. What happened here with the burning and the killing—it's happening *everywhere.* You guys saw it in my own neighborhood all those days ago. Society is burning up like newspaper in the fireplace. Soon it will just be ashes. Then things are going to go downhill from there. I came on this mission because I made your grandma a promise. I feel sorry for these people, I really do, but my allegiance is to my tribe here in this vehicle, and Liam's grandma, wherever she might be. We have to take care of our own before we can hope to save anyone else."

Liam sat down in the back once again, in thought.

He tried to process all the facts in front of him. Like any number of zombie books he'd read, he was faced with a no-win scenario. He was thankful for the small miracle that this dilemma didn't directly involve fighting off zombies, though fighting with other humans was just as disturbing. He was used to making decisions in his online game. Save the princess or save the village. In the game, there were always ways to do both if you navigated the decision tree in just the right way. Was there a similar string of decisions that would allow him to save these people *and* save Grandma? There had to be.

Or I could lose Grandma and *watch these people die.*

"We help these people to safety, then go get Grandma. At worst, she would probably jokingly scold me for trying to rescue her, but I think she would use an honest-to-goodness curse word on me if she knew I abandoned these kids when I had a chance to lend them a hand. If we can't count on anyone to do the right thing anymore, then Phil will be right. The world will be burnt to a crisp."

After a minute of introspection as the truck rambled along behind the women and children, Phil spoke up. "Liam, the threat of Grandma cursing at me is enough to agree with you. And your idea makes perfect sense. We save these people, *then* we save her."

Mel got them busy. "Liam, would you be kind enough to man the rear window and make sure no one is following us. We'll watch on the remotes too. I'll keep us just behind the group and we'll see where the night takes us."

Liam looked West; the last glint of sunlight dipped below the treeline behind them. Someone out there had just tried to kill him in the most destructive way he could imagine. The Marines were moving toward Grandma, leaving him behind. Hayes had her somewhere out there. Civilization itself was enjoying its last hurrah. Zombies roamed through it all. It seemed there were nothing but insurmountable tasks ahead of him.

Victoria's hand touched his shoulder.

He looked at her in the dim cabin. She smiled a faint smile.

"We'll get through this, Liam. We all want to find Grandma."

Her eyes were islands of calm on a stormy sea.

He resumed his watch, thinking about the one friend who wouldn't be helping him anymore.

Goodbye Bo.

THUNDERSTRUCK

Only a handful of the subdivision's men made it out. Three men showed up to the rendezvous at the school, and they were in a hurry to keep moving once they found the women and children. The survivalists, as they called them, were behind them the whole way. Phil suggested they return to the Boy Scout camp rather than stay near the school. After some deliberation, everyone agreed it made the most sense to join up with a stronger outfit. One man even claimed to be a Boy Scout, saying, "Once a Scout always a Scout."

Liam and Victoria got out of the MRAP to walk so they could fill it with the smallest children and the weakest older ladies. Older kids, and a few women to watch them, climbed on the roof. It helped the entire procession move with haste.

Liam learned from the survivors they had been assaulted in a swift strike on their neighborhood by an unknown, but large number of "gun-wielding duck-hunter type characters." Initially they went from house to house killing any men they found, and capturing women and children. But then they started using rudimentary catapults to toss bottles of gasoline onto nearby houses, setting them on fire and chasing out the occupants. There was no defense against it once the houses started to burn. The remaining families rallied on the far side of the subdivision, and that's where they enacted the plan to help the women and youngsters escape while the men made an effort to buy them time.

Still, no one could explain why there was only one house left standing, and they had no idea anyone had written anything on the garage door. Liam was content to leave it at that, rather than explain it was his name.

Several times throughout their walk they thought they could see dim lights far behind, but no one could say for sure. Liam was ecstatic to be challenged by someone at the edge of the Scout camp. They'd finally have some friends to help them.

"Halt there! What's your business? This is Boy Scout territory," cried a small voice in the night.

Liam chatted with the boys manning the forward checkpoint, and word was supposed to be sent to Mr. Lee's team about what had happened. A boy took off up the trail.

Phil and Mel discussed whether the survivalists were trailing them. They suggested the checkpoint be pulled back so none of the boys got hurt, but the boys wouldn't go. They did agree to move deeper into the woods and assured everyone they would observe and report, rather than confront anyone coming up the road during the night.

The MRAP continued up the paved road as fast as the people outside could walk. They headed for the front gate. Liam had a strange desire to see his parents. He assumed it was because he was surrounded by kids who had just lost their fathers.

They were almost at the gate when shots rang out far up the valley. First, just a few. Liam and Victoria stopped in their tracks, looking at each other in a frozen pose of surprise.

A few more shots rang out. Then nothing.

He felt himself leaning forward as if to continue walking, and another shot rang out.

"We better hurry to the council."

They left the newcomers and the MRAP at the front gate. They jogged up the small road. Just yesterday they had both run the opposite direction as they chased the young man who pushed Victoria into the creek.

Liam spoke as they jogged. "It can't be a coincidence that guy who pushed you was probing our camp at the same time the survivalists were attacking the subdivision on our northern boundary."

"I was beginning to think the same thing. The only thing worse would be if he worked for a different group that was going to hit us from a different direction."

They both got a nervous laugh out of that as they reached the administration building. Liam figured it would be shut down and everyone would be asleep, so he was surprised to see it was a hub of activity even in the pre-dawn hours.

And there, just inside the doors, were his parents.

2

Liam's father still nursed his broken leg; he sat on an ancient metal folding chair. When Liam walked in, they were all over him.

"Liam! Thank God you're OK." His mom ran and hugged him as she said it.

"Yeah, good to see you, son. Forgive me for not standing." He tried to laugh, but Liam saw he was still in a lot of pain.

"We can't get out of here. The doctor wanted to make sure it wasn't going to get infected since we have so few medical supplies available. He said it was cleaner in here than in those dirty tents."

"Yeah, we saw you and Victoria run out with that Marine, and we saw him come back *without* you. We knew it was crazy, but we couldn't help but imagine he offed you in the woods. We didn't know what to think until we heard the MRAP was back at the front gate.

They said you'd spoken with the guards along the road so we lined up here to give you a welcome home."

His mom still didn't let him go. Instead, she grabbed Victoria and pulled her into the embrace as well.

"Just so happy to see you both."

Liam would have been embarrassed in the Old World to have his mother show such affection in front of his girlfriend, but in this new one, he was perfectly fine. He knew she might be gone tomorrow, or he himself might be a fine mist after a massive fireball explodes out of some nondescript garage.

"I'm glad to see you guys too." He wasn't necessarily going to tell them every scary thing out there, but he had to tell them something. "Things are getting worse out there."

"We heard there was a doomsday cult making trouble north of here?"

"A cult? No, they were survivalists—or so we've been told. We didn't actually see them up close. They burned a whole subdivision to the ground. We found a big group of women and children on the open road and we brought them back here before they could be rounded up by the bad guys. Most of the men didn't make it."

Liam looked at his dad as he said it, knowing his father would understand what he was saying.

They were still in the doorway, so it was easy to hear renewed shots in the distance. His mom finally released the two kids. It gave Liam a chance to see how much activity was going on inside the building. Scores of flashlights bounced back and forth between the lantern-glow of the various rooms. He saw head-lamps and hand-held flashlights heading out into the distance and coming toward them in streams from the tents. Liam thought it was kind of magical. The moment was broken when several men and women charged through the doorway. One of them was Mr. Lee.

"We need to talk to the council! We're under attack!"

Mr. Lee shouted, but noticed Liam and his family and diverted to them.

"Liam! Thank you for the warning. The runner from the checkpoint got to us in time to warn us, which I can tell you probably saved a lot of lives. At this hour, it's easy to be lax, but with the prompt of possible trouble our boys were on high alert. I really don't have time to explain everything going on. I need help out there."

"We're in." It fell out of his mouth before he even thought about it. Night fighting in the woods wasn't really something he was proficient at doing.

Are any of these Boy Scouts any more prepared?

His conscience reminded him of the reality of where they were. They were all in this together no matter how much experience they had on paper. Fifteen-years-old or fifty, it made no difference now. He'd seen some of those same Boy Scouts fight like lions in hand-to-hand combat against the zombies.

As Mr. Lee moved away, Liam faced his parents again.

"I know you two have to go back out there. I wouldn't expect you to cower here like children. Even though I can't help but think of you as my little baby boy." She began to tear up. She still clutched his filthy shirt, as if unwilling to separate.

Liam couldn't remember his mother ever being this emotional. It was affecting him as well. He didn't want to start sobbing like that little boy she envisioned. To compensate, he looked at his dad. "See ya, dad. You guys have weapons in here?"

He nodded in the affirmative. He then held out his hand for a handshake. After all their difficulties the past several months, he'd forgotten the last time they'd shaken hands or hugged. Maybe New Years.

Liam took it with a firm grip. The unusual displays of affection from both his parents were making him dangerously close to losing it.

"OK, we have to go. We'll be back as soon as we can." He turned around and was hasty walking out the door. Victoria followed.

When they were into the tents, he stepped off the main path. He felt the tears forming in his eyes. "I'm sorry, I didn't want to get emotional in there. I've never seen my parents like that." He wiped his eyes, only making a cursory effort to keep her from seeing him.

"Well, they did think you were dead. Gunshots are ringing out in the night, getting closer. They don't want to lose you for real. Frankly, I feel the same way. We're heading into a dangerous situation *again*. We can't be kids anymore, just sitting on the sidelines while the adults take care of things for us. They've known that for a long time, as have we."

Is this what it feels like to be 25? 55? 105?

Liam briefly considered telling Victoria to stay with his parents, to keep her safe. But he knew how that conversation would end.

3

Liam and Victoria stood outside the building waiting for Mr. Lee to organize things on the inside with the council. He took the time to check their rifles, organize their magazines, and lighten their loads. His backpack had nothing but the brick-sized 1000-round box of .22 caliber ammo, still mostly full. He had nothing else extra to toss out. They each had one of his dad's surplus AK-47 rifles with one thirty round mag in the body of each weapon, and three spares. No water. No food. No medical supplies. Liam also had one pocket knife and one mysterious photograph.

They looked each other over to ensure they had no loose clothing or other obstructions that could get them killed. Shoelaces were tied.

"Your clothes stink."

"Oh really? And what do your mud-soaked clothes smell like?"

"I'm a lady. They smell like roses."

They had no opportunity to change since they survived the bombing of his street and jumped in the muddy creek. They both reeked, but so did the rest of his friends and family.

She had tried to buoy his spirits, but all he had in him was a polite chuckle.

He pushed out the thoughts of the dead, and tried to regain his focus on the moment. They each had their little Ruger .22 pistols, though his felt insignificant next to the larger semi-automatic rifle slung over his shoulder. As he found back at the dead intersection, it would only be useful as a last resort.

The faintest light of the morning appeared as Mel and Phil jogged up. They both looked like death warmed over. None of them got any sleep on the journey in, but driving and navigating while watching for bad guys all night clearly took a toll.

"Hey, guys. What's the plan here?"

"We're waiting for Mr. Lee. He's talking with the council and getting a plan together for how to defend the valley. Once he comes out, we're going to link up with him and see what he needs from us."

"Does he know we have the MRAP here? Surely he does."

"He didn't tell me anything. He was in a hurry." Liam looked at Mel. "How would you defend this place, Mel?" She'd surprised him several times the past weeks with her quick understanding of tactical situations. In all that time, he still didn't think to ask her about her military background, or how she ended up selling shoes.

She had already formulated a plan.

"This valley is impossible to defend from all directions. We aren't professionals, and this isn't a movie where stupid heroism wins the day.

We have thousands of innocents, most without weapons or any means of protecting themselves from flying bullets. The survival guys will already control all the hills, or at least the hills they need to assault this valley. Our only good options now that we've lost the initiative are to either get everyone out and use our shooters to facilitate that escape, or try to draw in the enemy to the place and time of our choosing and strike them hard. I doubt we could evacuate anyone before the place was overrun. That leaves only one realistic option."

Liam tried to think of what he'd do with the MRAP. "Maybe we could wait until we see them down here in the valley and then shoot them with the chaingun on the MRAP?"

"How would we avoid slicing and dicing unarmed civilians? That gun isn't exactly a precision instrument. Even less so in the low light."

"What about the Marines? Are they still close by?"

"No!" Mr. Lee had just emerged from the building as Victoria spoke. "We've kept our eye on the Marines, but they cleared out just before dark last night. We have no idea where they went, other than north up the interstate. We can only depend on ourselves in this fight."

Several armed adult men ran out of the administration building. They were the core of Mr. Lee's defense force for the valley. He explained they were a mix of ex-military, law enforcement, and competent listeners who could also shoot. There were only a precious couple dozen of them gathered now.

Melissa pulled Mr. Lee aside toward Liam. "Where are your men heading? What's your plan?"

They discussed the plan cooked up between Mr. Lee and the military guys. They were going to launch an immediate counterattack by taking a long route down the valley and then work their way around the back of the attacking force to catch them off guard.

"We don't have time for a counterattack. Your boys don't have the discipline to pull it off. It would be tough for regular army under these conditions and with such bad intelligence. You need to put your men where you know the enemy is going to be—here in the valley bottom. Put a token force in the administration building and along the creek bed, draw in the enemy, and then give them the building. They will then stack their troops in there because it's the only hard cover around. Then we hit them hard with the MRAP when they're grouped up. Kill the stragglers."

Mr. Lee seemed to waver.

"Lee, you can't leave the valley in the hope you run into them. By the time you've made contact, they will already be here killing your people." Melissa spoke to him softly, almost pleading with him.

"You're right. God, I just need five quiet minutes to think." He ran his hand through his thinning hair. "We talked about that very thing inside, but some of these military guys want things their way or the highway."

"You trust 'em? Sounds like a blue falcon trying to take himself off the field of battle..."

They discussed the plan for about five minutes. It wasn't enough time to cover every eventuality, but it was enough time to address the fundamentals. Melissa was very keen to convey that the plan must be as simple as possible. Mr. Lee rounded up some of his lieutenants and together they established a new plan. Liam listened in, but offered no opinions. He knew he was out of his league, and for once he was glad. He would be worried if he knew more about tactical matters than the people supposedly in charge of security.

The only divergence from Melissa's plan was that a few of the ex-military men insisted on going around the hills to hit them from behind as originally planned. No one argued with those guys, and Liam had to admit it would be sweet to have someone taking the fight to the enemy. *If* they got there in time. A team of four took off at a run down the road.

Liam risked injecting a question into the planning session. "Mr. Lee, who's defending us up on the hills right now?"

Mr. Lee smiled. "Liam, I asked the kids in my pack to call me 'Mr. Lee' to teach them respect. I guess it kind of caught on for everyone. But I want you to know, I'd prefer it if you just used my first name. Call me Lee."

Liam was honored.

Lee continued with a sadness in his voice. "I sent several two-man teams of older Boy Scouts and their fathers to harass the invaders from random positions. I instructed them to shoot from afar and run—stay alive—but I fear many of them are dying too. But we desperately needed the time to organize a defense down here. My assumption was that any attacker would need to secure their flanks before advancing. Needless to say, I don't want to blow their sacrifice."

Liam had no idea if it was a good or bad plan. The crack of gunfire intensified in the hills; Scouts were in peril out there.

Mel was right. This is nothing like the movies.

His hands were shaking.

4

Everyone was put to work to execute the plan. Mel and Phil ran back to the MRAP, while Liam and Victoria split up so they could each get people moving out of their tents and toward the far hillside—away from the attackers. He felt something unsettling as she ran from him. He watched until she was consumed by the stirring campers and he could no longer see her...

Liam had to yell at people and get them moving. Most needed little encouragement since the shooting was loud and clear on the hill above them. But there were holdouts. Some men and women refused to abandon what little they had in their tents, and were willing to fight and die for it, no matter how long the odds. Nothing Liam could say would change their minds, and he didn't waste time arguing.

Maybe they'll delay the enemy, giving the rest of us a chance.

Thousands of people running across the valley in the dim twilight was a sight to behold. The area closest to the administration building where Liam operated was also the area with the highest percentage of Boy Scouts. They coordinated and executed the evacuation in a remarkably short period of time, given the pressure of the situation. But even the best of the best weren't fast enough for the worst of the worst.

"Come on! Run!"

He ran toward the administration building with a lagging group of men and women when he heard some gunshots close by. In the low light, he couldn't tell if the shots were coming his way or going the other. His fears were confirmed when a large man in a white t-shirt crumpled in front of him. The red splotch grew on his backside.

Shots from behind.

Rather than push his luck to keep pace with the stragglers, he ducked down between a couple of large tents and found his way inside the smaller of the two. He took off his backpack because the box of ammunition rattled obnoxiously as he ran, and stashed it under a blanket to hide it. His hands shook almost to the point of uselessness. He couldn't help himself. He unslung his rifle so both hands had something to do while he readied himself for any encounter. A round was in the chamber, so all he had to do was drop the safety to get it ready for action.

Footfalls outside ran by, but he was pretty certain they weren't from campers. They were quiet and disciplined. His suspicions were confirmed when they conversed in hushed, winded, voices.

"We've got them all on the run, sir."

"Understood. Push through these people and continue until you find the primary target. We have—"

Liam took a step back in the tent, and stepped on something which made a large pop. He didn't have time to curse himself. He pulled out his pocket knife and got to work on the orange rear wall of the tent. In ten seconds, he was out and running; he stayed low while putting distance between himself and the infiltrators.

He expected yelling and orders to pursue him, but the men were either too disciplined or—worse—pursued him silently. The thought got him running.

He went perpendicular to the survivalists coming off the hill, but in the darkness and confusing tent city they couldn't see him before they were on top of him—if at all. Several times he crossed paths with a survivalist just as he ran by. They skipped civilians and kept pushing in. He thought it was pretty risky to leave anyone behind your main attack, but now that he was there...

I can make a difference.

He tried to be as quiet as he could and snuck his way into another of the abandoned tents. He grabbed what turned out to be a shoe and briefly stuck his arm out the tent flap and tossed the shoe as hard as he could on the path where he was heading. It was the oldest trick in the book, but people kept trying it because it seemed to work.

He heard several people run by, but there was no way to check which direction they were going. He no longer heard voices or foot traffic nearby. If he had pursuers, he felt he'd lost them. Still, it was several minutes before he considered leaving the relative safety of his tent.

As he huddled there, his heart rate kept going up. He could hear his blood beating through his eardrums. His mind fed him suggestions of delusions of grandeur. He knew if he was in a movie, this would be the time he could sneak behind the lines and kill the enemy general, and single-handedly win the battle for the good guys.

"Listen, this is *not* a movie. The golden rule is to not do something dumb."

He was deliberately talking to himself inside his head. He felt it had to be done to keep himself straight under such pressures. A big part of him really was drawn to being a hero at that moment, but he was tempered by a vision of Victoria chastising him for even thinking it.

While he deliberated, the volume of gunfire increased from the area near the administration building. The plan was to draw the enemy fighters in that direction—

Something tore through his tent; it whirred as it went by. Suddenly his position *behind* the enemy became a liability.

This is why I don't devise military strategy.

5

The night should have given way to the light of dawn, but when a few drops hit the tent, he understood the delay. A flash of lightning lit up the inside of his hideout. The immediate burst of thunder made the gunshots sound quiet by comparison. The sound rumbled up the valley.

He had to give them credit, they couldn't have picked a better time to attack.

Almost like they knew.

He was on his stomach to minimize the risk of any stray bullets heading his way. He thought of his next move as the pitter patter of rain slowly increased. How long had he been out here? The battle seemed to reach a crescendo near the administration building.

Lightning. Thunder. Gunfire. Death.

The cycle repeated many times over the next few minutes as the rain increased to a torrent. He loathed going out in the dark rain, but knew staying in the tent wouldn't serve anyone. Thinking of Grandma, he said a short prayer for protection, and slowly made his way to the front flap. He could see nothing beyond the next tent. Even flashes of lightning seemed to be subdued by the darkness of the heavy rain and dense cloud cover.

The gunfire, and the screaming, finally got him moving.

His plan was to swing wide of the battle and move down the valley. That would ensure he wasn't in the main line of fire behind the survivalists, and give him the best chance of linking up with someone on his own side.

He ran like hell. Instantly soaked, he held his rifle down, hoping to avoid getting water in the barrel, though he wasn't sure if that really mattered. He passed no one, though at times he thought he heard crying in tents as he ran by.

Music and lyrics from a childhood movie popped in his head.

Just keep running!

In ten minutes, he had looped around the entire epicenter of the battle, and went back up the creek bed running down the middle of the valley. He stopped when he guessed he was about 100 yards south of the administration building. He could see the flashes of gunfire everywhere up there.

As scheduled, the MRAP rolled up the tiny road toward the building. Liam braced for what it was about to do—end the battle. He cautiously made his way a few yards up the creek to see if he could find a better vantage point. He noted, but ignored, several campers hiding their families around him. He had to see how this ended.

Lightning. Thunder. Buzzzzzz. Buzzzzzzz. It looked like dragon's breath, and it was pointed at the administration building.

The MRAP sank its teeth into the building for several short bursts; the enemy was getting a taste of their own medicine.

"That's for Bo, you duck mounting bastards!"

No one could hear him over the rain, thunder, and constant gunfire.

The intensity of gunfire flared as the MRAP poured thousands of rounds into the infrastructure of the building.

Then it died down considerably.

Within moments, it stopped completely.

The MRAP advanced into the grassy field next to the road. It paid no heed to the tents it crushed.

He slung his rifle and climbed up the soggy incline of the creek—he gripped small tree trunks to steady himself in the mud—and ran across the ten or fifteen yards of ruined tents to get behind the MRAP. It would be the epicenter of the surrender.

When it stopped, Liam ran up and banged hard on the back with the butt of his pistol. He took a few steps back so Phil could see him on the remote camera or out a rear window if he was up.

One of the rear doors began to open. He still held his pistol, but it was pointed down; an afterthought. His rifle was on his back, forgotten. The door opened fully.

Intense gunfire flared at point blank range, both in front of him and behind him. The person who opened the door was thrown back into the compartment. Liam threw himself to the ground and tried to claw his way under the truck for cover. Gunfire continued, though the

MRAP moved ahead and began to turn to the right—directly for the nearby creek.

More gunfire from behind him on the hill. Directed at the MRAP.

How did the enemy get up on the hill?

While low in the wet grass, and among the tents smashed down by the truck tires, he watched in horror as the MRAP drove over the lip of the creek bank, and disappeared.

He was too terrified to move.

Gunfire ceased once again.

He lay in the grass for another fifteen minutes.

The storm ebbed. It became a light drizzle.

It was lighter now. Liam spied the area. The administration building was chewed up. All the windows were broken out. Smoke poured out from points inside.

He feared the increasing light would give him away, but he was petrified. He admitted he couldn't force his muscles to move due to fright. If the MRAP was destroyed and his friends were in it, then who was shooting from up on the hill behind him? Would they shoot him in the back if he ran to the creek?

Finally, after an eternity, he heard a voice from far away.

"Give Liam Peters to us and we'll let everyone else walk out of there."

He heard the director of the movie yell "That's a wrap!"

6

Minutes went by. He still couldn't move himself from his position in the tall grass. As the daylight increased he could tell he was exposed, but not by as much as he feared. No one was mowing grass these days and it was particularly tall where he had fallen. There were also the many downed tents in the area.

He sensed a couple people walking nearby. He chanced a slight turn of his head to see what they were doing, and was rewarded with a good clear look at two people from the camp waving a white sheet of some kind. One of them was Lee. The other he didn't recognize. They walked toward the administration building.

He was unable to turn his head to see where they went, but he heard them perfectly.

"That's far enough," said one of the survival guys. "We're sending someone over."

In moments, a pair of voices were close to Lee and his partner.

"Hello. I'm...Red. Y'all fought bravely, but it's over. You've lost. We can either kill everyone right here, right now, or you can turn over Liam and a few others, and walk out of here alive. It makes no difference to me, although it would be nice to save the ammo if you'd just hand him over."

"Liam is a member of this camp. What has he done that would warrant this type of assault on innocent women and children?"

He heard soggy footsteps move closer. He could imagine the two parties closing together to discuss terms. When they resumed speaking, it was in a much quieter tone.

"Listen, friend, I don't have to tell you jack. We have enough men to sack this entire valley, but we only get paid if we take Liam off your hands. That's what we intend to do. Having the rest of you dead or alive is a non-factor here."

"We'll give him to you."

"Charles, what the hell?" Lee asked. Hushed voices continued.

"We can't risk the whole valley for one kid. If they want him, they can have him."

"Smart man, maybe we'll deal with you, huh?"

"No, we can't give him up just like that. For all we know, they're going to kill the boy for no reason if we give him up."

"We just need to capture him. Bring him back alive. We'll be super gentle with him."

Lee knew some of his travails with Hayes, but not all of them. Still, Liam was pleased to hear him defend him.

"Why Liam? He seems like a pretty solid kid. Not someone who would warrant such an attack. He do something bad?"

There was a long delay. "What the hell, it doesn't matter to me. The kid blew up a research facility that was close to unraveling the mystery of this plague, and then killed a bunch of old folks for sport. If we bring him in, we get two MRAPs in the deal, though I would have really liked to have the third one you guys shot up and sent over the edge of the creek."

"That was *our* MRAP."

The man laughed out loud at that. "Ha! You let our specialists walk right into your camp and steal it from under you. You don't deserve it."

"I guess you don't either, seeing as you drove it off the ledge."

There was no talking for a long period of time. Liam could imagine them staring each other down. The survivalist finally broke the silence.

"You have thirty minutes. Give us Liam or we burn your people alive inside that building. We'll be watching from the creek. We'll shoot anyone who leaves the building, so you might want to let 'em know."

It wasn't the survivalists inside the administration building. It was *his* people. The campers from the valley. Were his parents still in there?

It almost made him raise his head to look. But something told him to keep still. Play dead.

He was so confused, and staring at the grass didn't help.

He was prone for several moments before he heard a low voice.

"Liam, don't you dare move."

Lee.

A long silence followed.

MIGRATIONS

Liam couldn't tell what was going on around him as he lay in the tall grass near the site of the recent battle. He didn't know who was in charge, who had been killed, or whether he was going to be turned over to the enemy. The drizzle had become a mist and the night had given way to morning.

He nearly fell asleep in the wet grass as the adrenaline of the battle was subsumed by the exhaustion which never seemed to go away. But he jolted awake when he heard a commotion from up on the hill behind him. It started with gun shots.

More survivalists? He wondered if they surrounded the whole camp now.

Someone screamed, "Infected!"

He heard the familiar sounds of loading weapons, checking ammo, and racking slides. Those around him were redoubling their efforts at preparing for war.

A deep voice shouted from up the hill, "Marines inbound!" In moments, footfalls through the wet leaves approached.

The survivalist negotiator was still somewhere close by. "This better not be a trick." Then, louder, "My guys, hold your ground."

Liam heard men, women, and children running. Muffled chatter was all around. Impossible to tell who were friends and who were enemies without looking up. He *really* wanted to look.

A Marine spoke between great gulps of air.

"Unbelievable. Look at all these children," he sounded frustrated as he said children. "I don't know what you all have got going on here, but trust me when I tell you your only hope is to stop the horde of zombies behind us. They wiped out our unit and are coming over the hill behind us. They're relentless in their pursuit."

"They wiped out your MRAPs? How's that possible?"

The Marine seemed to hesitate before responding. "Well, I don't know about the main column but our detached team was keeping an eye on the highway over this hill. The zombies massed up along the roadway like they were returning to the city. They stumbled on our position and we've been running ever since."

They were spying on us too, no doubt.

Liam didn't blame them. It made perfect military sense.

Men, women, and children started running back across the valley— sloshing like so much bathwater in the basin—now going in the opposite direction they'd fled this morning.

Liam heard his signal.

"Liam. Start crawling back toward us. Stay low." It was Lee.

He used his arms to push himself backward in the wet grass. He had no way of knowing how far he had to go, but it couldn't be further than fifty or sixty feet until he reached the small road. He knew there was a shallow ditch for drainage on each side. He could use that to make better time away from the admin building.

All the people who cleared out for the survivalists were running off the hill behind him, across the field, and into the creek and beyond. A couple kids tripped over him while on the run. Parents picked them up and dragged them away without a second look at him.

Gunfire increased on the hillside.

Do I keep going backward?

"Liam. We're out of time. You need to run for it!"

He stood up. Lee ran toward him. Zombies were messily draining out of the woods, even as shouts and shots continued to ring out from up on the hillside. Many people were almost certainly surrounded by the thousands of zombies in his field of view.

His feet refused to run. It was a flashback to his first zombie on the first day—yoga girl—and his inability to do more than watch his death approaching. Only Lee's firm grasp of his arm brought him back into the moment and got him on the move.

A handful of Marines were nearby. They had knocked over a couple picnic tables, tipped them on their sides to form a V-shaped wedge— the pointy part faced the arriving zombies. The open part was just enough room for the three survivors to protect two additional wounded Marines lying high up in the V, both with combat shotguns on their legs. Liam thought it was both brave and impossible. He immediately felt compelled to go help them, but Mr. Lee's grip was insistent—as if he knew Liam's thoughts.

In seconds, they stumbled down into the creek bed, and turned south to run away from the administration building and the survivalists still holed up somewhere nearby.

"We have to make a run for it until we meet some more shooters. We can't hold them off with so few of us left, but maybe the duck guys can take it in the face." He laughed sarcastically as they splashed down the shallow creek.

Liam looked back at the building. A few campers with rifles were at the ready in the shattered and broken second floor windows, anticipating the wave of death heading for them. He saw a few survivalists, mostly in the creek bed. Some were backing away. Some were sticking it out.

Everyone wore a mask of fear.

With one last peek at the zombies, he understood.

They're endless.

2

Marty went for another test. The windows on the penthouse level of the hotel faced the main part of St. Louis, not toward the Arch. In the daytime, she recognized lots of landmarks, especially the stadium where the St. Louis Cardinals played baseball. If she could ever figure out Liam's phone, she could lead him right to her. She felt it in her right hip pocket as she walked down the hall, reassuring herself she still had it.

The "nurse" wore a bio-hazard suit. Because she was so short, Marty couldn't even look into the face of her captor. The person moved like a woman, but she admitted she was guessing. Most of the nurses she'd ever met were women, so it seemed reasonable.

As expected, they guided her to a plush seat, and helped her sit down. The cushion sank so far down she didn't know if she could get out on her own. She laughed at the notion it was intentional to keep her from running away.

Soon they wheeled in a gurney with another elderly person up top.

No one had talked to her since she arrived. At first she was thankful for the privacy, since she spent time trying to manipulate Liam's phone, but eventually she tired of that and just wanted someone to talk to. She tried to engage with the nurse helping her, but they were adamant about not saying anything.

It left her with nothing but the screams of other patients.

Each time she was brought here, the elderly victim was carted in, and many minutes later, the screams would start. First it was intermittent, but eventually the screams would become so intense she would watch the door for fear something horrible would spill out. Angie had made those same horrible sounds back at the beginning.

Liam mentioned they deliberately infected test subjects back at Elk Meadow, though part of her wondered if it was really possible. It sounded like something a conspiracy nut would say. She didn't think Liam was a conspiracy nut. But *intentional* infections? She'd seen dozens of people go in, sometimes two or three at a time. They couldn't all be dead.

As expected, the screams began on today's subject.

It was dangerous, but she decided to pull out Liam's phone. They never came for her until the screaming was long over with. This would be a prime time to see if she could finally get a connection to Liam.

The screen of the phone showed her a picture of Liam's face giving her a "shush" symbol over his mouth. She knew that was the last picture he took of himself before he slipped his phone into her pocket when they parted last. She knew how to "open" the phone because it said "slide open" right on the cover. What she didn't know was how to contact Liam. When he gave the phone to her, he probably didn't realize she could no longer call him because she had *his* phone! He didn't leave a number, and she hadn't had to memorize a phone number in decades.

Through trial and error, she poked and thumbed her way into the address book for the phone. Who would be the most logical person to call now, she wondered? Probably her grand-daughter-in-law; Liam's mom. Her number was in the system, but when she tapped the digits it always said the phone was unable to connect to the network. No real surprise given the state of things. She tried it a few more times as she ignored the screams.

To her surprise, it rang.

3

Liam kept running.

Plagued with exhaustion, he stumbled and landed face down on the smooth rocks lining the creek bed, even before he knew it was happening.

Lee picked him up and practically tossed him further down the creek—away from the zombie hordes spilling over the bank behind them.

"Run, Liam!"

He almost missed the scream from Lee over all the other campers yelling and cursing at their own stragglers, as well as the constant chatter of gunfire. Without ear protection, the sound of guns was painful. But it was the only sound keeping him alive.

"Come on, we aren't going to die in this creek!"

Lee pulled him through the shallow water. Here and there, a zombie crashed over the edge of the creek to their right. Sometimes Lee would put it down with his rifle. Other times another camper would do the necessary task. Liam still had a hard time making his feet move.

The smell of gunpowder fought with the stench of the walking corpses approaching them.

They reached a point in the creek where the bank seemed low and flat to their left, allowing them an easy egress into the main part of the valley. Something seemed to satisfy Mr. Lee when he saw it because he pushed Liam hard to get out of the creek.

As they gained the top of the bank, he could see the zombies flooding out of the same woods he and Grandma traversed that first day they arrived.

Many of his fellow campers were unable to escape and were overwhelmed by the sheer numbers pouring forth. Those in the creek were faring a little better because the barrier slowed the onslaught enough to fight or escape. But too many armed campers vacated the creek and made a run for it. Fewer guns meant fewer zombies put down.

Lee paused.

"What are we waiting for?" Liam's breathing, and his feet, were getting back to normal. The initial shock and frenzy inside the creek was wearing off.

"We need to figure out what's happening here. Running around without a plan is going to get us killed."

The creek was a mass of confusion. Upstream, scores of zombies lurched for people in every direction. Nearest to him, and downstream, hundreds of campers also ran in every direction. Some fought with guns. Some fought with spears. Some carried small children to safety. Others appeared to be panicked to the point of helplessness. A few tried to hide...

After all the planning. It ends like this?

"I want to save this place, Lee."

"I do too. Trust me. OK, I see our goal. You see that clump of trees up on the hillside?" Lee pointed it out as they crouched in their position. "We're going to run like hell over there and then see if we can find anyone with a gun. We have to pull things together or everyone is going to die in this valley."

Liam couldn't argue with the logic. "Do you see Victoria anywhere?"

Liam received no answer. Instead, he was pulled forward again and they began to run across the relatively flat, tent-covered field between the creek and the beginning of the hill forming the south side of the valley.

Several times he saw other runners fall down after being shot.

"Who's shooting at us?" He yelled to the crouch-running leader, but it was more for his own sanity.

"Everyone!"

Liam saw handfuls of campers holed up in small clumps, as if they paused from running to defend their patch of ground. He'd seen the same thing when the survivalists attacked. Some were firing wildly into the crowds, uncaring if they were zombies or not. Others were picking their targets with more care.

He looked over his shoulder to see the zombies coming out of the creek behind him.

He then heard the unearthly Buzzzzzzzzzzzzzzzz sound from the MRAP. Then another, longer buzz. Someone was still alive in there, and taking it to the zombies. The sound of the chain gun sounded louder somehow in the confines of the creek. The rattling went on for several more long bursts, but ended with a short one. He waited for more, but none were forthcoming. It wasn't because all the zombies were dead...

They arrived at the treeline moments later. He was surprised to see Lee had collected two of his guys as they ran. Now they were a team of four, though none of the men looked particularly soldierly in the face of what was behind them.

"All right, guys. We have to do two things fast. One, we have to get more shooters. Two, we need to shoot the zombies in the face as they come through these tents. Once they're in the woods, it's going to be too late. Many people can't even stay ahead of the zombies on open ground. Climbing hills will be the death of them. I want the three of you to organize firing lines up and down the valley along this treeline, do you understand? I'll be right here in the middle."

Liam felt the butterflies in his stomach in response. Lee was putting him in charge of something major. Something that would save lives. He wanted to put on a brave face, being the youngster.

"Understood." He gave Lee a quick Boy Scout salute, then took off at a fast jog.

He didn't really know what to do or say, but he began shouting to the throngs of people ahead of him. "All shooters to me! Form a line! Protect the kids!"

He ran up the valley. He could have easily run the other way. The way with fewer zombies! The way with fewer survivalists! He remembered Mel's words about those soldiers running off when they were needed the most. He was proud he was doing right by her. He also thought of his grandma and how she would be praying for him as he headed into the maelstrom.

As he ran he imagined he heard his mom's ring tone.

But that's impossible.

He shouted louder.

4

His first obstacle was the huge wave of frightened campers as they ran for the literal hills. The area nearest the administration building had the biggest crowd. After the initial battle between the survivalists and camp defenders, most people had huddled in the creek bed since they had nowhere else to go. Now, they ran for their lives right past the survivalists.

Liam jumped into the crowd, shouting the whole time.

"I need shooters! Follow me! Protect the kids!"

Another sixty seconds and he was through the central stream of people. He managed to pull six or seven men and women with guns out of the crowd. One was from the survivalist group, but appeared anxious to help quell the zombies.

Do I say something to him?

"OK, we're setting up a line of guns along the treeline up and down the valley. We need to hold the zombies in this valley or they're going to tear up the women and children as they go up the hill to safety." He paused for many seconds while he tried to catch his breath.

He must have drifted because one of the men coughed to get his attention.

"Yeah, so try to grab other people with guns and stand your ground here. I'm going to continue up the valley to do the same."

A woman he recognized, but didn't know, said, "No problem, Liam."

As he walked off, the survivalist sidled next to him. He looked like he'd been flopping in a mud pit. He wore full camouflage gear and had attached some branches to himself for additional visual deception. But his mud had streaked in the downpour earlier. He came across as the kind of guy not happy to have his stuff ruined.

"Mind if I go with you and help?"

He wanted to say no, but he didn't have time for an argument. Killing zombies had to take priority over everything else.

"Sure, we have to hurry."

As they ran, Liam shouted his message. From time to time, he'd stop to arrange small groups of gun owners. The whole time the survivalist shadowed him, offering no commentary or assistance.

Get lost, buddy!

If only he could order the guy away using his mind.

After another ten minutes of running Liam knew he was out of time. The sound of gunfire behind him intensified. The zombies had finished consuming survivors on the other side of the creek and were all coming across to his side.

He turned around to head back. He found a last little group of men and told them to gather more support from further up the valley, where there were no zombies. Mel's words echoed again. He could leave the battle and just go gather men in safety up that way. If he was *that* type of guy.

He took a deep breath. "You know what to do. Someone has to keep going up the valley to warn them and organize resistance. I'm going back to join the fight. My family is back there."

The men nodded and were off.

I wish survival guy would volunteer to go up the valley by himself.

He began jogging back to the main fight. After running only a few moments, the man grabbed his arm and asked him to stop. Liam's rifle was slung over his shoulder while he ran; it was useless in an emergency of this sort. He knew he'd have a better chance with his pistol on his hip. He tried to be casual.

"Hold up—Liam. I want to ask you a question."

The man was slightly taller and bulkier than him, but had a sallow and wet look about him—like he'd been suffering in a malarial jungle for a long time. He looked unnatural.

"Umm, OK."

He tried to separate himself from him, but he wouldn't allow Liam to leave his personal space. It was intentional, but made to look innocent.

"Hey, bud. I don't mean no trouble here, but you're the Liam we're here to find, right?"

A million things swirled through his head at that moment. But the most prominent thought was how stupid he'd been the past few minutes. The survivalist stood right next to him with his rifle drawn and pointed in his direction. Not an overt threat, but the threat of a threat. It took away his own options.

"We have to keep moving," was all he could think to say. He turned around and took a step down the valley when he heard the unmistakable sound of a reload and a bolt release on an AR15. A round was in the chamber of the gun behind him, no doubt facing right at his back.

"I don't think so."

Liam put his arms up. He thought someone might see him and come to help, but was distraught to realize they were mostly hidden from view by dense foliage in their vicinity. The man chose this spot for a reason.

"Are you going to kill me?" He still faced away from the man.

"That depends. I was given very specific orders to kill you if I could. I'm also cleared to kill your parents if I find them. But my associate also said I could take you alive if you were with your grandma—he was going to give me a little something extra for you both. Don't see no grandma, though. Don't matter to me anymore. This whole valley will be dead by the end of the day. I could kill you, take that sweet antique gun you have, along with your ammo, and be a relatively rich man in the wild. Who's to say you didn't die in this zombie attack?"

Liam didn't think there was anything special about his rifle, but he considered all the men and women now running for dear life who would give anything to be able to defend themselves.

Anything.

Liam was back in the movie. His next line was scripted.

"So, who is it that wants me captured alive?"

Who is the mastermind behind all this?

"Mmm-hmm. I bet you'd like to know that. Why don't you drop that gun slowly and take a few steps away huh?"

He did as he was told, but kept talking.

"Was it Hayes? Did he send you out here?"

His gun rattled to the muddy ground. Next he dropped his magazines. Here and there he could see campers scurrying, but none were coming directly for him. No help out there.

He was violently grabbed by the man, then forced backward. He fell. Rather than slam down to the rocky soil, he got wedged between two tree trunks. He was turned so he looked up at the man. A man with his weapon pointing directly at his eyes.

"He said you were dangerous, but not very photogenic. That means *ugly*, kid." He laughed. "And smart. Said you were a real weasel." The man spat at the ground, as if in emphasis of his disdain having to say those words. "Frankly, you remind me of the little punk kids that used to make fun of my boy." He pushed the barrel closer, "A BOY KILLED BY THIS PLAGUE! You think it's funny to destroy our only hope of a cure?"

"But I didn't do any of those things they told you."

"SHUT UP!"

The anger was evident on the man's face. The malicious tone to his voice was no better.

"The world has gone to hell, my family's dead, and my orders are to kill some jerk kid in Missouri. Do you know what it's like to kill women and children? It changes you. It changed me—that much I know. We had to kill them and burn that whole subdivision to the ground because of *you*."

He moved his rifle so it was up against Liam's sternum. Liam tried to move his body so he could grab his pistol in his hip holster, but he had sunk further between the two trunks and his arms were wedged at his side. It would be comical if it wasn't going to be the cause of his death.

Liam struggled hard, almost getting one of his arms free. He reached for his holstered gun, which was in clear view of the man. Liam didn't care. He wasn't going to die without trying to defend himself.

"Nice try, kid. I guess I'll just take the gun."

The man pulled his rifle backward off his chest and took careful aim at Liam's face again.

An inane thought sputtered out of Liam's head.

Did he back up so he wouldn't get blood on the muzzle?

Liam's closed his eyes.

Crack! A gunshot from very close by.

On reflex, his eyes opened. The man had not fired.

A second shot.

His chest opened up. A loud gunshot clap immediately followed.

The man looked up to someone behind Liam, surprised.

"You? Nawww."

Then eight or ten continuous cracks of gunfire.

The survivalist sprouted several more holes in his chest. All Liam could see was the big hole of the barrel of his gun wobbling over his chest. Was something deadly going to reach out and zap his own life? Finally, with no fanfare, the man tipped over backward.

Liam was well and truly stuck. Even with one arm free, he was wedged so completely in the uneven space he couldn't get leverage to move himself. He was so tired. All he could do was wait.

He was shocked when a woman came into view.

"Liam, thank God!"

Victoria! Thank God indeed.

His exhaustion conspired with the release of adrenaline and he teared up involuntarily. He couldn't help himself. His mythical hero status was very much in doubt.

5

Victoria pushed and pulled Liam so he could shimmy out of his prison, and held him close.

"I saw you back down the valley when you came across with Mr. Lee—I mean Lee. I tried to catch up to you. I almost caught you when you met up with this loser," she gave the man on the ground a little kick "and something told me to hold back. So, instead of running up to you, I ran up a little higher on the hillside here so I could watch. I saw you for a while but lost you in this clump of trees. When you didn't come out, I knew something was wrong. I made my way closer just as he threw you down. I wanted to run in screaming and shooting, but he was pointing his gun right at your chest. I don't know how I held my fire now that I think about it. But he pulled back for some reason and I took that as my cue. I remembered what you taught me, and I aimed for the biggest part of his body. I missed him the first shot, but I hit him with the second. When he didn't fall down, I opened up. I think I missed half of the shots, but I got him with the other half." She laughed nervously.

"I was so scared, Liam." She was in tears too.

"I wish we could curl up together in one of these empty tents...but we have to get into the fight. Can you believe this is really happening?"

"I know; this doesn't seem real. These duck hunters. The zombies. That freak storm. Everything seems fake."

Liam picked up his rifle and the ammo he dropped, and he also grabbed the gun from the survivalist and slung that one over his shoulder. He searched the man for extra ammo or other supplies, but he had none. Just what was in the magazine he was carrying.

Has a human's worth really been reduced to the number of bullets he can carry?

As an afterthought, Liam searched the man's pockets.

"This guy talked like he was important. He might have something on him which would help us figure out who he worked for."

But other than minimalist survivalist gear—a fork/spoon combo, waterproof matches, and so on—he had nothing of importance in terms of intel on his upper body. Liam did find a sheet of paper tucked into a cargo pocket on one of his pant legs. His pants were covered in mud and filth, but the pocket itself was clean.

He pulled it out and unfurled it. "Well, that makes perfect sense." He read the names on the sheet. "Liam Peters. Lana Peters. Jerry Peters. This must be the list my parents mentioned. They said their names were on it, but they didn't mention mine."

They were the only remaining names on a list consisting of three neat computer-printed columns. The other names had deep black lines through them, as if they'd been redacted. They were unable to read any of them. Next to Liam's name someone wrote in "kill or capture," while it only said "kill" next to his parents' names. At the end of the list, one name was hand-written in the margin. It was Victoria's. Rather than kill or capture, it simply said "known accomplice."

They both crouched in silence. He wasn't sure what to say, though after having a gun pointed at his face, he felt better than he imagined he should. He folded the sheet and put it in his pocket.

"We have to keep moving. We'll look at this later."

They were off and running once again. As exhausted as he was, Liam felt that extra "something" he always felt when Victoria was around. It pushed him to keep going.

"Thanks for saving me, by the way. It's almost old hat now, huh?" They both laughed at the dark humor as they reached the first group of fighters on their journey back down the valley.

This was a group of about ten men and women, all with rifles. Most of the civilian campers had been cleared of this part of the valley, so they were free to shoot at will at any of the zombies coming out of the creek. The creek was a bit steeper here though, so not many zombies made it out. They were going elsewhere...

Liam made a command decision.

"Hey guys, can a couple of you come with me further down the valley? I'm sure there are more zombies down that way."

Several of them looked at each other with the "stay here where it's quiet or go to where it's dangerous" expression, but in the end, three volunteers stepped forth.

More running.

They reached the next strong point. This time there were about twenty shooters in a rough line fifty yards long. Liam spotted the survivalist immediately; he was hiding behind a large tree and shooting at the approaching wall of zombies.

He turned to Victoria, and spoke quietly. "What do we do with that survivalist? I can't just go over there and kill him, though that seems to be what they want to do to me. I don't know how to deal with this."

Victoria seemed to ponder the situation, but Liam was disappointed she didn't provide a solution.

He settled on, "We should keep going down the valley."

The sound of gunfire was overpowering now. Liam yelled but Victoria signaled she couldn't hear him, so he grabbed her and pulled her along, much as Lee had done for him.

He kept an eye on the survivalist character as he ran behind him in the cover of the woods, but the man made no effort to follow him or even look at him.

I guess it would be too much to expect him to leer at me like a hungry wolf as I ran by.

In his mind's eye, he saw that very image. He ran a little bit faster until they were clear of the whole group. Victoria stuck close behind.

They stopped about a hundred yards down the valley to rest and evaluate. He saw a couple zombies amongst the mélange of tents and tarps out in the valley. Surely there were more lurking out there, but it was hard to see all the way across the littered field.

He dropped to one knee, lined up his shot, and missed the closest zombie. Even with the small red-dot scope he was unable to make a second or third shot. He was shaking too badly.

Soon the two zombies moved in their direction.

"How is it I'm scared to death of these two zombies after seeing hundreds pour out of the woods earlier?"

Victoria responded by shooting the two zombies at twenty-five yards. It took her several shots for each one, but she got the job done.

"Liam, you were just in a traumatic situation back there. It's OK to be scared. Let's go find our friends."

They slung their rifles, she took his hand, and they jogged together toward the main fight taking place further down the valley. In a few minutes, they found it.

Liam's shaking wasn't getting much better so they decided to use tree branches on the edge of the woods to steady his aim.

Zombies were much thicker here, but so were the shooters. Liam and Victoria were able to contribute as part of a group of about two dozen men and women lined up along the edge of the woods. Behind the line, women, children, and unarmed men made their way up the steep hillside out of the valley. The recent rain showers made the leaf-covered slope a slippery mess. Lots of people sat on the ground at various points, apparently unable to go further. Others helped as best they could. Several elderly people waited right at the bottom.

Liam had a vision of Grandma sitting there. It helped him refocus his energy on protecting them by shooting zombies in the valley.

Zombies scared Liam to death, there was no doubt about that. But under concerted fire by dozens of semi-skilled shooters in fixed positions, the zombies couldn't make much progress. It was no more than 100 yards from the creek to the woods, which was nothing for a scoped rifle and a skilled marksman.

Liam needed them to get in a lot closer before he was able to half-reliably shoot a zombie in the head to put him down for good. After several shots, he noticed his scope had come loose and clanged loudly on the AK's top cover with each shot. That was part of his aiming problem.

Minutes went by. Liam squeezed off his first magazine of thirty rounds. He'd already used a few rounds earlier. The second mag went quickly because a small clump of zombies had found its way directly in front of Victoria and himself. The third magazine was depleted a couple minutes later. He soon had only one magazine left.

And our pistols. Ha!

He studied the number of zombies; they weren't going to have enough ammo. Even with his pistol and whatever was in the extra rifle on his back, he wouldn't have enough. A few other shooters had stopped too. Things would snowball quickly if fewer and fewer guns were fired.

In the space of a minute, he un-slung the survivalist's rifle he salvaged, fired off twenty or so rounds, and it was empty. He had no more ammo for it so he set it down next to him.

"We aren't going to make it. Look up the hill at all those people. We're running out of ammo down here. We need a movie rescue to happen. Marines. An air strike. Something!"

Close by, one of the shooters shouldered his rifle and lifted a piece of wood off the ground.

The spears!

The spears were a Boy Scout specialty.

"We have to find some spears!"

There were lots of spears not far from their position. Up the hill behind them, all along the ridgeline, Lee had put checkpoints for the outer perimeter of the camp. One of those points had to be close by. Lee mentioned they stored lots of spears in each checkpoint as part of their overall defense against the infected.

"We have to get to the top of this hill and get spears from the nearest checkpoint."

His throat ached as he yelled into the pandemonium of the gunfire, but he had to tell the men and women fighting down here they had to get up the hill to swap their gunpowder for spear power in order to survive this onslaught. Even knives would require getting in biting range of the monsters.

They seemed to understand the word "spears" while he was pointing up the hill and pointing at the man nearby holding his wooden weapon. In return, he got various thumbs-up signs and they began to peel off the firing line to go up.

Liam and Victoria retreated toward the muddy hill.

6

They were met by a dour gaggle of elderly loitering at the base of the incline. There were ten or twelve people, mostly women, who had apparently decided not to climb to the summit. Many of the fleeing shooters saw them, hesitated, then ran on when the women shook their heads vigorously in the negative. As Liam arrived, he had to stop.

"You have to try to get to the top." He shouted it as loud as he could. The moans and yells of the zombie horde was all-encompassing.

The closest old woman calmly shook her head no. She made no effort to move, or speak. He realized they were all praying. Several had

Rosaries in their hands. A couple grasped the crosses on their necklaces. One ancient man wore a yarmulke.

It was too much for Liam. His emotions churned like the battle around him. He was distraught to see these people were destined to die in this dirty forest.

"Liam. We—" Victoria choked on her own words, "we have to go. We can't save them."

A firm hand pulled him away to follow the other young people. He hated himself for thinking the deaths of the elderly would give him a head-start on his own escape.

The muddy leaves were much worse than they appeared from the bottom. He imagined himself in a movie scene where the monsters pursue an ever-slowing hero in a bladder-loosening chase. Without any path up the hill, they had to lunge from sapling to sapling to keep from slipping back down.

"Victoria, don't look back. Just climb."

The gunfire fizzled out behind and around them.

The screams at the bottom began.

I'm so sorry. I really am.

"Don't look back. I'm serious!"

He made sure she was ahead of him. Any other time, he would be happy to have such a nice view, but not today. He wanted to catch her if she fell. If he missed, she might end up dead. That meant they both would die...

Liam didn't take his own advice. When he had the chance, he looked back. Some of the last gunslingers struggled up the hill, the same as him. There were only a few. Thirty or forty dirty zombies at the vanguard of the horde started their way up, too. They were clumsy, but indefatigable.

The race was on.

"Victoria—"

"Let me guess! Don't look back?" She laughed, but Liam recognized it as her nervous and slightly fatalistic laugh. Perfectly appropriate for this situation. But she was also stubborn. She grabbed a stout tree and turned herself around.

Did her knees just buckle? I thought that was just a cliché?

She said nothing, but climbed again. Liam followed. Several times they helped struggling campers stuck on the slope, but there were fewer and fewer living humans around them.

The slope grew less steep up top, and they were able to run. To their dismay, they passed more and more campers who reached the top ahead of them, but stood around doing nothing. They looked exhausted. It would take no time at all for the zombies to chase down these people.

They reached the small Scout checkpoint and finally had a piece of good luck. Scouts were already there, working on getting spears into hands of those who could fight. Many boys were on the ground, frantically whittling more spears.

"Can we make a stand?"

"We have to try," Victoria answered.

Liam yelled, "We need spears. There are still people stuck on the hill, and the zombies are right behind them."

A boy nodded, then tossed him two spears from his dwindling stockpile.

"Make them count."

He returned the nod.

"Gather your spears and come with us!" Liam yelled it to no one in particular, but was pleased to see a dozen or so men and Boy Scouts joined up.

"We're going back down this hillside to try to engage the zombies before they can get a footing on solid ground. If we can get them while they're still climbing, we might have a chance." He wasn't sure if he learned that in one of his books, or through real world experience. Things were starting to blend together.

No one argued, though a couple of the men instead ran with their spears down the *backside* of the hill, away from the zombies, to points unknown.

Liam couldn't bring himself to curse them. Part of him envied them.

Instead, he and his compatriots ran toward the battle, hurtling themselves into the transition zone between the muddy hillside and the more stable hilltop. They didn't have to wait long.

A few of the last survivors from the shooting line made it up mere feet ahead of the pursuing zombies. They looked wrecked as they crawled by. No one was going to make them stay and fight.

They spread out as best they could, found comfortable fighting positions, and waited for a few moments before the first climber arrived. It came up under one of the grown men. With one skilled poke, he skewered the face of the assailant.

Then a few more reached the line. Liam still didn't have one in his area, but Victoria did. She tried to reach out to the zombie, but she unceremoniously lost hold of her spear and it fell down the hill.

Liam thought he caught her cussing, but he wasn't sure.

She began climbing out again, but the zombie she missed lunged and grabbed her leg, causing her to fall and start backsliding.

Liam didn't hesitate. He was doing it almost before he thought it.

Un-sling rifle.

Bring to bear.

Aim.

Shoot.

Miss.

Shoot.

Miss.

Aim center of mass on the zombie.

Hit.

It didn't kill the zombie, but if a zombie could be surprised—this one acted surprised. He let go of Victoria and she climbed once again. Another woman piked the zombie.

He re-slung his rifle, glad he didn't expend all his ammo down at the bottom.

He then got to business on the zombies closing in on his fighting position.

The next hour was a mental fog.

He remembered seeing Victoria come back into the fray with a fresh spear.

He remembered seeing several of his allies get grabbed as Victoria did. Each time he would un-sling his rifle and try to help the victims. A few times he got lucky, but he had to admit hitting moving targets was not as easy as they made it seem in the movies. Several people were bitten and pulled down the hill. Eventually he did run out of ammo. He wanted to save some in case Victoria needed help again, but he knew he couldn't sit doing nothing if someone else was in similar trouble. His last bullet saved the life of one of the other women fighting on the line with them.

And seemingly all at once, they ran out of zombies. No more were coming up their hill. A hundred or more lay sprawled on the hillside below. Some he recognized as campers.

7

Victoria and Liam studied the Boy Scout spear builders as they continued to work after the fight was all but over. The boys cranked out as many as they could, and showed no sign of slowing down.

"We can't ever be unarmed, even for a second, can we?"

Liam knew she was right, but it seemed an impossible proposition.

"Do we carry spears into the shower with us now? In bed? How can we be armed all the time?"

"I'll guard you when you take your shower." Victoria flashed a wry smile as she said it, taking the edge off a dour morning.

As a topper it was drizzling again, making everything extra slippery and messy.

"I guess we should go help clean up the straggler zombies and see if we can locate my parents. We need to find some ammo, too." Liam patted his shoulder strap, indicating he was talking about the rifle on his back.

They could hear very sporadic gunfire from down in the valley and throughout the woods around them. Liam wondered if it meant everyone was fighting hand-to-hand with the zombies, or they were truly gone. People around him started to relax. There were no zombies anywhere in their field of view on the wooded hilltop.

They found a group of young men who wanted to go down into the valley. No one said it, but Liam guessed they were a lot like him— they wanted to find their families. As they all walked away from the checkpoint along the ridge, Liam was surprised by two teenage girls who dropped in behind them all. They were covered head-to-toe in blood, like they'd been crawling in dead bodies. Liam thought they might be blondes, but couldn't really say for sure. They each had a spear, similarly slathered in blood.

Liam shared a look of concern with Victoria but otherwise kept walking. They followed the ridge for a while, then turned right and descended on a main trail, rather than going down the slippery slope on the side of the hill. Even so, they had to move slow. Several times on the way down, they had to stop while someone in the group dispatched a wandering zombie. More often than not, it was the two girls who would rush in with gusto to kill the prey.

I'm not sure if I'm impressed or horrified.

He didn't want to risk antagonizing them by saying anything to Victoria they might overhear, but he thought she had the same wary look on her face as he did.

As they came to the valley floor, they saw the killing floor where most of the survivors had made their final firing line at the edge of the woods. The valley looked like a tornado came through and knocked all the tents and tarps over; a second tornado came through and dumped blood over everything. It was only missing the Four Horsemen, though many dogs rooted through the abandoned tents searching for lost masters, or food.

Liam recognized several of Lee's men standing off to one side, near a group of trees on the edge of the valley. He pulled Victoria away from the others. As they approached, he saw the military men who had left on the long, circuitous route around the entire battle. They appeared clean and fresh, though winded. He had no energy to state the obvious to them: they were useless.

None of the crowd disbursed as he walked up so he pushed his way through. What he saw broke him.

Lee was dead. He'd been brought down by a zombie, then changed into a zombie, and was put down by a Boy Scout spear. His uniform was a bloody mess as he lay on the unnaturally green grass in this spot. They'd arrived just in time to hear a witness.

"...so Lee and the other guy made it most of the way back to the trees when they got surrounded by them things. They were able to fight with their guns for a little while, but it was too much. They were overwhelmed. Killed."

Liam looked at his friend one last time, and noticed something odd. "Why does he have those belts on him?"

It was obvious once he saw the whole picture. Lee had removed his belt and wrapped it around his arm; it was lashed to the leg of his partner. The other man had a belt wrapped around his own arm, attached to Lee's leg. Lee knew he was a dead man after getting infected. They both did. They tied themselves to each other so they couldn't get up and walk away and hurt anyone. It was the best they could do in the time they had left.

"My God. He prevented his zombie self from harming anyone in the camp."

Victoria leaned against his back, as if unwilling to view Lee's body in all its horror. "He was a hero." She started to cry into his shoulder blade.

He stared at the bodies as people came in and out of the circle to see the fate of one of the camp leaders. He tried to summon the sadness, but his own ups and downs had drained him. He just wanted to move on...

He melted back into the crowd, and Victoria was next to him. They crossed the field, avoiding several badly wounded zombies who somehow still managed to grab, claw, and bite with whatever appendages still functioned. He thought of the two girls. They were fifty yards away going to town on the doomed zombies up that way.

They're going to need counseling.

The mangled bodies were thickest near the administration building. Lots of living people were hovering around outside the confines of the shredded structure, many with the thousand-yard stare common in survivors of a desperate battle.

He was intent on finding his parents to ensure they were OK, but he couldn't help but notice the area around the small contingent of Marines was hopping with activity. A dozen men were pulling zombie bodies from a huge pile around the wedge of picnic tables. He and Victoria investigated.

Incredibly, the scrum of zombies revealed survivors. The two wounded Marines who were furthest inside the wedge had managed to survive. Somehow, under the massive pile of bodies, they managed to hold them off. A small cheer went up as the two men were pulled from the makeshift fortress. They also found two tiny children inside the wedge. The Marines weren't content to just save themselves.

As they watched it unfold, a woman walked up next to them.

"Mom!" Liam gave her a quick look for injuries, then gave her a fierce hug.

He pulled back and looked for his already-injured dad.

"Where's dad?" He felt his stomach turn over at the depth of that question.

"He's fine. Still in the administration building. We were told we would be evacuated before the battle started, but I guess the memo got lost. It's really a miracle we weren't all killed by the big machine gun. I pulled your dad into that hallway, and into the basement as soon as shots started punching through all the glass windows on the outside. He wanted to fight of course, but he could barely hop the few feet down the steps."

Liam looked around at the horror. "Mr. Lee's dead. Zombies." He said it, but it was really the fault of the survivalists for starting the whole thing. Or his fault for getting the survivalists involved. Or... He saw there was no end to that thought.

"I'm so sorry. I know you two had a connection. Are you going to be OK?"

That's the million dollar question.

"Yeah, I'm good. Just going to take some time. You know?"

Nothing further was said as they all looked over the ruined campground. The administration building might be salvageable, but it was littered with holes and broken windows. The MRAP pumped thousands of rounds into the structure. He was afraid to ask how many people died inside. He knew it must be a lot. There were dead bodies on this side of the valley, just like on the far side. The zombies rampaged through here, but got chewed up by the mass of gunfire and the concentration of good shooters. The Marines took more than their fair share of the horde.

"OK, Liam. I have to get back to your dad. Be safe out here."

Ha! As if that's possible.

"I will, mom." He almost let her go, but he shouted, "I love you, Mom," before she had gone too far. She turned around and expressed her love for him and for Victoria.

"See you guys in a bit," she said as she continued her departure.

After she was gone, he looked at Victoria. He pulled her into a private space on the edge of the woods, checking for lingering zombies the whole time.

"We have to go find Grandma now, or we may never get the chance. I really don't want to know who else is dead. You and me have to go out on our own. No fanfare. No nothing. Just walk out unnoticed and get it done. If we wait and try to gather more help, we may never get out of here. Zombies could swarm again. The survivalists could shoot me on sight. Anything could happen. It's you and me on this list." He patted his pocket where the list of names was hiding. "We can't stop until we find out who put our names there. I think we both know his name. Find him, and we find Grandma."

Victoria wore a serious face. Liam had learned to read her facial expressions and knew she was in. Before she could answer verbally, he gave her the key piece of information he knew would guarantee her assent.

He held up his mom's phone. There on the screen was a text message from Grandma. It said exactly where she was.

Victoria nodded. While looking at the phone, she solemnly pledged, "Grandma, we're coming."

GREEN WATER

Getting away was easier than Liam had thought possible. They walked out with hundreds of others. On their way, they grabbed whatever ammo they could scrounge from the dead, as well as a few tidbits of food and bottled waters. Liam found the orange tent where he'd stashed his backpack so they had something to carry the supplies. Several of the zombies had energy bars in their pockets, like they'd all come from the same place.

"Why is everyone leaving camp? Didn't we win this morning?"

He wondered the same thing. "You and I have been outside this valley several times. We know how much worse it is out there. I bet lots of these people have no idea how far everything has sunk. They won't get far probably. If we ever make it back here with Grandma, I bet most of these people will be back. Unless..."

Liam paused, not really knowing if what he was about to say could possibly be true.

"...there's somewhere safe out there now. Maybe set up by the government? Someone's handing out energy bars. Or was. If there's nowhere around safer than this valley, we're all in for a letdown."

The Marines still functioned, so the government had to be operating. But even the Marines were chewed up—literally, he was sad to admit—so the thought of any government agency being able to save them was remote.

"In the books, the government always tries to shore up humanity, but it always involves setting up camps behind fences of some kind. But the problems, at least in the books, are that the population of the camps always get out of hand, the plague always gets in, and the government is always too rigid and unable to adapt to rapid changes as the disaster unfolds. They can deliver pallets of water and energy bars, but if they run out of ammo, the whole thing falls apart. Maybe we just live in a backwater and aren't seeing some serious firepower being applied to the zombies, but it looks to me like this war is lost."

He looked at Victoria, expecting a reply, but he could see the stooped shoulders and hangdog head.

"Look, I'm sorry. Yeah, things are bad. But we've survived this long. Look at what we just did! We survived those duckers and a whole field full of zombies—at the same time. I'd say we're pretty well able to take care of ourselves, better than most of these—"

He realized he was talking a bit loud around the other people walking out the front gate.

"—most of those people who didn't survive out there."

He stopped and grabbed her arm, pulling her close.

"We're going to get through this. When I was looking at the map back in the MRAP I saw we aren't far from the Meramec River. If we can find a boat, we can float the river downstream until it hits the Mississippi. From there, we can make our way up that river until we end up downtown. We'll be right next to the hotel where they're keeping Grandma."

He tried to keep his face bright and smiley as he said this next part. "It'll be a piece of cake."

She smiled at him through misty eyes. "We're not warriors. This isn't natural human behavior." She paused. "I know we'll save her. I'm just tired of always fighting. Being on the run. Being hurt. Being hungry. You don't have to lie to me. I know it won't be easy—nothing has been easy since..."

Her eyes were unfocused and distant, looking beyond him. It worried him on a level he couldn't vocalize. In the two weeks he'd known her, she always had direction. Always had the look of someone with a plan, even in those early dark days. But not now.

Time drifted on and she showed no sign of returning. Liam tried to finish her sentence. "Nothing has been easy since we met, that's for sure."

Come back to me.

She blinked.

"Ha! You got that right. Nothing has been easy since you rolled Grandma's wheelchair over my hand. How many weeks ago was that? How many weeks since the sirens?"

The big tornado sirens may have signaled the end of civilization, and he recalled how scared he felt as they were going off, but now he craved their sound, if only as a reminder of the more civilized time just prior to them.

"Not even two weeks. Can you believe it?"

Liam worried she was going to drift off again, but instead she focused hard on his own eyes. He thought she was going to say something, but after a few moments, she merely pulled him in for a long, firm, embrace. He could sense people shuffling by on both sides, though he felt he was frozen inside an impenetrable bubble. He held on tighter.

2

Later, as they walked down the highway toward the river, he tried to steer the conversation toward something that didn't involve death, zombies, or the collapse of everything around them. It was no small task.

"Did I ever tell you about my childhood trips to the lake with my grandparents?"

"I don't think you've ever told me anything about your childhood."

She laughed, which he took as a good sign. The dark cloud hanging over her trailed behind them instead of directly above.

"Ah well, that's why we're heading to the river right now. I spent a good portion of my childhood on small fishing boats and canoes. In fact, the very first thing I can remember as a child was being in a boat. Actually, under it. My grandparents liked to take me to one of their favorite lakes down in Kentucky. We'd load up their canoe with camping gear and then they'd take me out onto the lake, to a remote cove where we could have some peace and quiet. We'd find a nice sandy beach and make it our home for a week. My favorite activity was playing in the water, of course. And my favorite water activity was to flip over the canoe with Grandpa and play underneath. It felt spooky to see the dark water below us."

He paused to prepare for the punchline.

"Well, Kentucky Lake is massive. Barges use the lake to transport stuff up and down the riverway. They make *huge* waves because they are so powerful. One day, while playing under the canoe, I heard loud screams from Grandma just as some unusually large waves slammed into us. I banged my head on the floor of the canoe and took in some huge gulps of water. I panicked. I kicked and flailed, all the while my grandpa tried to steady the canoe above us. Fortunately, the waves were big but few. As they passed, Grandpa pushed it off. Grandma was there in a flash, dragging me out of the water with a strength that sticks with me to this day. I remember being thrown to the ground and the water escaped my lungs. She saved my life."

"Wow. Grandma Marty has always been a hero."

"What? No! I'm talking about my grandparents...on my mom's side." He laughed heartily. "Can you imagine my 94-year-old great-grandma rescuing me from the water?" He immediately stopped laughing. "Oh wait. I guess she did save me a few times recently."

More seriously, he continued. "Yeah, the funny thing is, at the time it didn't bother me. It didn't prevent me from swimming again as a child. I probably swam under the boat that same day again, if they let me. Today however..."

He hesitated again, unsure how he felt about this part of the story.

"The thing I remember most is how green that water was. When those waves rolled through, and I was in over my head in water, I just saw a deep, almost bottomless...green. You imagine water is black, but not there. Not that day. I regained my mind smelling that faint hint of dead fish on the shoreline. I can't go near water without recalling that incident. Even walking near water makes me a bit nervous."

Victoria held his hand as she gave him a sideways glance.

"So, you want us to take a boat ride, yet you're deathly afraid of the water?" Her tone was sarcastic, but she asked a serious question.

In his head, he saw that green water. He tried to push it aside.

"I know. I probably shouldn't have even brought it up. But, well, I guess I feel like I can tell you anything now. And besides, once you've had zombies trying rip you apart, a boat ride seems positively quaint—even if it does scare me to death."

He laughed to wallpaper over his fear, but was relieved when Victoria squeezed his hand.

"Don't worry. I've never been on open water. Not many places to sail in Colorado. We'll make a great boating team!"

She made like she was pulling him, trying to get him to the water faster, but then settled back down with a snicker.

"What's so funny?"

"I was just thinking that this plague has blown away even the thing that scared me the most prior to its arrival. My nightmares back then seem trivial now."

She seemed to drift off a while. Liam let her go this time. It only lasted ten or fifteen seconds.

"I guess the plague did me that one favor. Now, my scariest memory is that first night on the run when the zombies came. It's like a dark window that blocks everything that happened to me in my life before it. Both good and bad. Every bad thing that's happened since then— going up in the pitch black Arch, riding that train, getting shot, the mess back in the valley—is each its own black box of emotions, but nothing has exceeded the level of fear and despair of that first night. Maybe I'm broken?"

"No!"

No more than me, at least.

"No." He repeated in a calmer tone. "We've all seen lots of things that should scare us to death, but I think we're getting used to the fear. Once you've seen the dead walking, is there really anything else that's gonna make you poop your pants in fright?"

"You're disgusting!" He could see she wanted to laugh.

"Well, I won't tell if you don't." He gave her a wink, to which she gave him a withering look with a scrunched-up face. She was finally healing from all her bruises. Even the fake disdain on her face was a welcome sight.

"I'll tell you one thing though: my biggest fear right now is that we haven't seen the worst yet. I feel like we're heading right for it..."

The words hung in the air as they detached from the scattered group of refugees on the highway. A small river was just ahead. They made their way down a short hill next to the roadway, and arrived at the waterfront of the Meramec River.

His palms began to sweat.

3

There were no boats in view. They were along a part of the river far from any boat ramps or other places where a boat might be tied up. Up and down the river they saw nothing but the highway overpass and foliage-draped shorelines.

"It's beautiful down here."

Many birds chirped happily, adding to the illusion of peace. Liam just wished he could have presented her with a boat, to make himself feel better about bringing her along on this journey. She volunteered, but he felt he had to keep her safe and show some intelligence. In the old days, it might be described as hot-dogging to impress a girlfriend. Today it was survival. He had to improvise.

"I guess we should start walking." A small muddy path along the high-water mark of the river snaked away. It was empty of any foot traffic, alive or dead. That made it promising as a next step.

"Onward. Let's see if there are any boats downstream."

Be confident!

They followed the path for an hour before it began to change into something more substantial. The dirt changed to gravel, though today it was all still muddy and wet after the hard morning rain. Several sections were eroded by wide gulleys, as if maintenance had been neglected for a long time.

The gravel path merged again with a blacktop trail of about the same size. The walked together onto a large golf course nestled along the river. Today it was wild and untended.

"Wow. A golf course sure goes to pot quickly if the maintenance crew becomes zombies." He wasn't a golfer, but he knew what a golf course should look like.

They kept moving along the river while they enjoyed the better quality path of the country club.

"I wonder if we could steal a golf cart?"

While pondering what he thought was a really good idea, Victoria spoke again. "Or what about *that* boat? Bingo!"

She pointed to a small white rowboat that was next to a small pond on the golf course. Its purpose was likely decorative, but it seemed functional.

"No, you're supposed to say 'fore' here."

They laughed as they walked to get a better look. With little effort, they slid it into the water, jumped in, and paddled around the surface of the tiny pond. It was painted white, and it did show off a lot of wear and tear, but they made it work for them.

"Let's get this to the river," she said as they hopped out.

They strained to pull the rowboat up the shore of the pond and get it going through the hundred yards of rough toward the river.

"You know this is the part of the movie where the zombies come at us just as we're close to putting this in the water?"

"Liam! Why would you even say that? I'd come over there and slap you if I weren't exhausted."

"Yeah, sorry. My filter turns off when I'm scared. Oh. I didn't mean that. I'm not scared at all."

But he looked over his shoulder, fully expecting that by thinking it, the zombie horde would spring the trap. She picked up on his nervous behavior.

"Hey! Zombie boy! Stop thinking that. Focus on what's ahead. Getting Grandma."

She's probably dead.

After he thought it, he thanked his lucky stars he didn't let that one out.

But seriously, she is.

Stop it!

"OK, Miss Smarty Pants. What would you like to talk about?"

"Tell me more about Grandma. Why did you go to live with her? I mean, you've told me the general stuff. I want to know the details."

She said the word "details" as if it were a tawdry tabloid story. Liam knew she was just teasing him, but he momentarily took offense that his past life could be in any way considered a tawdry tale.

"Well, I told you that my parents and I fought a lot this year, though I can't tell you the one thing that started all our problems. My dad and I used to be really close, but this year has just been a challenge. It's like he became a different person. And—"

Do I tell her all the details?

"—I guess there was that one time I punched him."

"Ooh. Do tell." She sounded like the town gossip.

"We were in our living room. He and I had been yelling at each other for ten minutes about my behavior. He said I was out of control because I went out with my friends the night before without telling him exactly where I was going and when I'd be home. He wanted to ground me for a month. A whole month! I guess I was losing it already, but then the phone rang. Of all the times to take a call, my dad actually shushed me while he answered it. I stood there seething, my anger growing at his attitude toward me."

He chuckled.

"Anyway, when he was done I went nutso. Lots of things were said. He got up in my face. I got up in his. I...threw a dumb punch that landed on the side of his head. It was embarrassing how weak I was—I'm not much of a fighter—but after that, everything changed. My dad's anger turned to raw shock. I knew I had crossed a line. I felt so bad, my anger drained away. But it was too late."

A long sigh.

"Instead of punching me, he walked away. He can be an ass, but he's not violent. My mom was in another room, and he went to retrieve her. It took a few minutes, but they both came into the room and informed me I would have to go live with Grandma because it just wasn't safe for me to be there. I was gone the next day."

Liam's blood thumped in his ears with the tension of reliving the event. They were nearing the river. His relief loosened his tongue some more.

"Dad drove me to Grandma Marty's the next day, saying nothing the whole way. He could really pour on the silent treatment like nobody's business. Grandma let me in and said I could stay in the basement. I was embarrassed by the whole thing beyond words—kicked out of my own home—so I said nothing as I trudged on by with my suitcase and backpack. I spent the next couple of weeks getting over my anger for the most part, wondering why I was so mad in the first place."

They took a short break to catch their breath.

"I recently asked my dad if he knew this plague was coming. Was that why he sent me to Grandma's. He said no, it was just a lucky coincidence. But once you've seen men and women dying in droves with a horrific plague, you get a new perspective. On what you've done in the past to people you love. On the very concept of coincidence. Something happened between my dad and I at the start of this year, and I don't think any of what followed was coincidence. On the other hand, I can't figure out why, if he knew this was coming, he didn't stockpile food at Grandma's? Why not arm me with a real rifle for survival, rather than counting on the small guns you and I had to use? Why not send me and Grandma to Montana or some huge bunker where we'd be safer than this mess?"

He nodded his head, as if pointing to everything around them.

"And if I'm honest with myself, it makes me mad to think that if my dad *did* know all this would happen, he deliberately sent me to Grandma's knowing I'd be unprepared. I know deep down he would never put me in harm's way, but I can't stop thinking that thought. Crazy, huh?"

"Not at all. I'm with you—your dad would never intentionally hurt you. To me, that means he didn't really know all this would happen. Maybe he's telling the truth about coincidence. We'll just have to ask him when we get back. Deal?"

"Yeah, sure. If—when we get back, we'll get to the bottom of this little conspiracy theory. Keep an eye out for some tinfoil for me. I'm going to make a tinfoil hat when the time comes. He likes that sort of stuff."

Liam couldn't decide if he would be happier knowing his dad was just lucky in sending him to live with Grandma or that he sent him into the hot zone knowing he was going to be in danger. He was long past the age of believing his dad was an all-knowing hero, but he wasn't too old to believe his dad wouldn't do everything between Heaven and Hell to protect his son.

The splash of water brought him back to the moment.

They didn't waste a second. Victoria jumped into the boat and Liam pushed off as he jumped in. They both turned around and were relieved to see an empty fairway all along the river. They weren't being chased.

Not by the dead anyway.

Shut up!

4

It was nearly lunch time as they settled into their boat ride. They had lifted a couple candy bars off a dead survivalist as they left the valley—a theft for which they had no regret. They shared part of one after the exhaustion of launching the boat.

"Mmm, this is so good."

Liam answered with a similar non-verbal vocalization.

Victoria was in the rear of the little boat, laying up against the back while looking toward him. He faced her while sitting on the single plank in the middle which doubled as a seat for pulling the oars. They could continue talking to each other while they slowly, so slowly, deconstructed the chocolate bars into tiny pieces.

They drifted down the small river without the need to paddle. This gave them the opportunity to rest, as well as observe the world passing them by. The tree-lined banks on each side were well shrouded by foliage, though they saw nothing but more trees through the gaps.

Liam pulled out his pocket knife and began to etch into the wooden stock of his AK-47.

"That's vandalism."

"Not if I own it." He looked up. "You remember when Phil said the guns were our Moses? At the time I thought it was just a clever saying, but he was spot on. Without guns, we'd be helpless victims back in that camp, waiting for some imaginary government to come rescue us." He went back to carving. "Not this boy. I'm giving this thing a name. I shall call him *Moses.*"

He finished his carving and showed it to her. She rolled her eyes, but humored him.

"Very nice."

"Yeah, well. It is." He couldn't think of anything more intelligent to say about the gun, so he continued with navigation. "I think we have a long way to go on this river before we reach the Mississippi. On the map, it seemed to wind all over the place. This may take a while."

They agreed that while things were quiet one of them would nap while the other paddled. Victoria glanced up and joked that since he was already in the seat, she would let him paddle first.

Liam was so tired he wanted to lay down next to her, no matter how cramped the space, and just let the boat go where it may. But he was disavowed of that bad idea after the first small set of rapids they approached. Not rapids exactly, but faster water as the river narrowed next to a gravel bar. He had to paddle a few times to avoid running into a large rock in the water. An easy maneuver if you're sitting at the oars, but it would be a rude awakening if they were just drifting along while sleeping.

She was out in moments. Not surprising, given the circumstances. It gave him a chance to admire her without his usual awkwardness. Her brown hair was a nasty mess, pasted with dried brown blobs of mud from their struggle up the hillside. He figured they'd all have shaved heads soon enough.

Victoria's face was angelic, despite the fading bruises and cuts he saw there. While she slept, the taut seriousness of her face drained away too, restoring her teenage beauty.

Is this what she would look like dead?

His mind just wouldn't keep quiet, but he figured it was an honest question. With so much death in the air, thinking about it nearly all the time was the new reality. She did indeed look different as she slept.

This is what she looks like in another universe, where zombies don't exist.

She wore a simple black t-shirt with blue jeans. She picked jeans, she said, from his mom's wardrobe because she had a knack for being tasty to mosquitoes. So, even though it was deathly hot—there's that word again—she opted for the long pants simply to avoid bugs. She was very down-to-earth in that way. He could only imagine what some girls he'd known from school were going through. No makeup. No hairdryers. No nothing. Of course the boys were no doubt complaining about the lack of video games or sporting events on the tube.

Continuing his overview, he smiled at the sight of her holster with his little .22 pistol on her right hip. She had laid down the AK-47 on her left side. It rode in the boat next to her like her best friend.

He turned around to check his course and held the oars up while he studied a new set of problems. Bridges were ahead.

He continued rowing, but remained alert.

The first bridge was for a four-lane highway. It was all concrete with two large piers pushing down into the dirty green water. While it would have been busy with four lanes of vehicle traffic in the old days, there was little chance of anyone being on the deck just now. Unless they were up to no good...

He propped up *Moses* next him. There was a round in the chamber, though he kept the safety on so he wouldn't accidentally shoot himself or anyone else. The air naturally cooled as he went under the large structure, temporarily escaping the glare of the sun. He had an urge to yell something as he went under, knowing it would be amplified in the semi-confined space, but he checked that irrational childish impulse as soon as he thought it. Having fun was the anti-survival skill these days.

He was more concerned about the next span. It was a lower railroad bridge and even though it was a hundred yards or more downriver, he could see nets and wires had been strung below—as if to ensnare boats traveling this very path.

He thought of rowing back upriver to avoid it altogether, but he ran things over in his head. If this was a trap, going backward would only get him killed. He knew he couldn't paddle against the current fast enough to escape anyone running along the shore. He'd have to try to push through using the momentum of the current.

As he approached, he noticed the nets had significant amounts of debris down where they touched the water. It gave the appearance a neglect on the part of the would-be trappers.

Closer now, he saw gaps in the nets on the far right, between the shoreline and the concrete pier holding up the rusty metal framework of the bridge twenty feet out.

He paddled furiously to that side. As he approached the nets, he had to nearly paddle backwards so he could avoid the big pier, but the current caught him and tossed him cleanly to the inside and through the gap. A small lean-to made of tarps was under the bridge, with a large opening facing the river. As he floated by, he looked directly into the hole, and saw the bottoms of a pair of boots. But he also thought he saw—

Eyes in the darkness.

He waited to see if anyone would run after him or start shooting. Or start moaning. All the while, he paddled downriver like his life depended on it.

After about a minute of hard paddling he saw—nothing. Just like the golf course, his mind constructed pursuers, but the world would not provide them.

Did I really see eyes?

He knew there were still people left alive. The river would be a natural focal point for those looking for food. And that would bring in the zombies, searching for the same.

As the boat rounded a sweeping turn and the bridges fell from view, it struck a large piece of driftwood. Victoria woke up with a jolt.

"Holy moly, Liam. You're soaked with sweat! You look like you've been paddling in a competition."

"Nah, just a hot day."

"Oh, well do you want to switch? I don't mind paddling for a while."

He thought about telling her to go back to sleep, but the nets spooked him. The eyes terrified him. His fear of water was a minor quibble now.

"Maybe we should both keep our eyes open, you know, for security."

She glared at him for a few seconds, clearly seeing through him—he knew her facial expressions—but she didn't complain.

Since there was only one sitting plank, she sat next to him and worked the left oar. It was less efficient but they still made decent forward progress.

Together they continued down the river.

Come zombies or high water.

5

Working in tandem, they paddled down the river for most of the afternoon without incident. Liam felt the stress of each moment, as he expected trouble at each bridge, each sandbar, and each revealing curve in the meandering stream. Many times, he saw men and women wandering aimlessly on and near the river banks, but by staying low in the boat they managed to avoid being seen by the infected.

They also saw scores of dead bodies in the water. They were heaviest near the bridges linking Arnold with St. Louis, where the effort to contain the plague in those early days was fierce. People had fought, and died, for those bridges. Clouds of flies greeted them as they went under each span.

"We're only seeing the undead. I figured there would be a lot of people down here fishing and stuff. Is it possible no one's left alive out here but us?" He chanced a look over the side, not sure what made him think to do so.

Maybe zombies are walking on the bottom, below us?

He knew he was being irrational, but he ensured he was sitting as close to Victoria as possible in the middle of the boat just the same.

Ahead, he saw a landmark he recognized. "There's the bridge we crossed all those days ago with Grandma." He laughed a dark laugh. "The bridge we helped destroy."

The trussed railway bridge was partially collapsed on the south side, thanks to the big wrecking ball the police had used to prevent the zombies from getting to their side of the river. The large crane and ball were the only sentinels left to guard this wreckage, though the bodies of a few zombies wrapped in the bent girders still writhed and grabbed for them.

There was a ghostly howl coming from the current rushing through the hollow metal dipped in the water. As they slid underneath the good side of the remaining structure, Liam reflected on everything they'd seen and done since passing across this bridge on the third day after the sirens. He looked at Victoria and guessed she was lost in similar thoughts.

"We've come a long way since that day. Lost a lot of good people."

This time it was Victoria who wouldn't let him get himself down. "Yes, but look at us. We're still alive and happily boating underneath this very bridge where we thought we were going to die. As far as I'm concerned, given the alternatives, I'd say our prayers were answered that day."

"True. We got across the bridge. The bridge was blown. We were saved. But when will it end?"

"God doesn't give us any more than we can handle."

"That sounds like a motivational poster." Liam gave her a friendly chuckle.

"Well," she said while echoing his laugh, "maybe it is. But that doesn't make it any less true. God is watching out for us."

In his former life, Liam would have argued about the presence or absence of an all-powerful God. He wanted to argue it. But what came out was tempered by all that had happened since the bridge.

"I hope someone is watching over us. Watching over Grandma. But we still have to do this ourselves."

They shared a moment of silence as they watched the bridge behind them. Then it was back to business as they approached the end of the river.

"I can see the Mississippi ahead. We'll have to stay close to the left bank so we can turn upriver when we get there. Why don't you sit in the back again so I can paddle us around the corner?"

As they glided for the turbulent waters of the confluence, Liam saw a familiar, if unwelcome, sight. Far across the big river, he saw two of the Marine Corps V-22 Ospreys flying fast and low near the water— heading upriver toward downtown St. Louis. Momentarily frozen by the sight, the boat drifted further out into the watery chaos of the junction than he intended.

"Hang on" was all he could say. The boat was very small and there was no way for Victoria to hang on to much of anything. Her only job was to sit in the rear and keep watch in front of Liam to see where he was rowing.

"I think the current is weaker along the shore. Let's aim that way."

Liam wasn't about to argue as he heaved the oars with all his strength. A few tense minutes was all it took to ensure they'd not be drawn further down the river, instead of going the direction they intended. He brought it as close to shore as he dared. He settled in and they made slow but steady progress upriver.

"Let me know when you want to switch."

Um. Now?

The small boat served them well on the small river, but it became a challenge in the faster water of the large river. It helped a great deal to stay close to the shore where the current was weakest, but Liam felt himself losing steam.

"I'd be happy to switch, but paddling in this stuff is going to exhaust us both in no time flat."

He pulled the oars for a while longer then handed them off to Victoria so he could rest. He suspected her slighter frame and weaker upper body wouldn't be able to dig the paddles as fast and hard as the river required. Still, she wouldn't take no for an answer and managed to find a rhythm that worked for her. She pulled her weight. The boat moved upstream.

At dusk, after many shifts at the oars for each of them, they were done. They happened upon an empty container barge anchored near shore. In the old days, this river was a superhighway of barge traffic. Today, nothing else moved on the water but debris—including lots of bodies.

"Let's tie up to that thing and climb aboard if we can. As long as there are no zombies inside the hull we should have a truly safe place to rest tonight. Help guide me in."

Liam pulled the oars with soft grunts as they approached the long, flat barge moored thirty feet offshore. It looked like it was sitting low in the water; it was loaded with something.

Please let it be food!

In short order, they'd tied up and found a ladder up the side. No zombies jumped on top of them, and no human defenders waved them off, either. Liam was so tired he didn't really care what was inside the hold. Even the thought of a zombie didn't scare him. He was willing to shoot just about anything to lay his head down.

He struggled up the ladder with his sore arms and raw hands and was relieved to see neither humans nor zombies. He turned down to Victoria as she climbed the final rungs of the ladder behind him.

"You're never gonna guess what we get to sleep in tonight."

She got to the top, and paused. "You know, I don't even care."

6

When they escaped St. Louis, he and Victoria spent a lot of time riding a train. They were forced to hop rail cars so they could reach the engineer in the front. Unfortunately, many of the gondola cars were empty, requiring them to slide down into them so they could run up the other side. The bane of their existence during those jaunts were the empty coal haulers, which were filthy with black dust on their insides. In the end, they were covered head-to-toe in black soot, and they carried it with them long afterward. The undersides of his fingernails were *still* black.

Neither of them protested as they settled down on the coal pile. After weeks of cat naps and fitful nights tossing and turning, deep sleep came fast. The soft rhythm of the river, the crickets and other bugs squawking in the nearby trees, and the facade of safety helped Liam achieve his best sleep since the disaster started. The dreary cloudy morning came fast on the heels of the night.

When he woke, Victoria was already up and moving. She sat nearby, patiently trying to clean off some of the smudges and grime caked on her arms and face. She had nowhere to wipe but on her shirt. She had somehow gotten his pocket knife and had cut a swath of her shirt so it was about four inches shorter all around, exposing her midriff. With the long strip of cloth, she managed to do a decent job of cleaning up.

She noticed him. "Oh, hello. Good morning." Her words were accompanied by a big smile, though her eyes were still travel-worn.

He responded, or so he thought, but his eyes were glued to her exposed belly. He knew he shouldn't stare, but...

"Hello Liam? You in there?"

He snapped to. "Oh sorry. I'll take two." He smiled a guilty smile.

"Two what? Are you even in there?"

She tossed the filthy piece of her shirt; it landed right on his face.

"I left you a little clean area, so you can wipe that silly expression off your face." But she was laughing. "Sometimes you act like you've never seen a girl before."

"Well, I, uhh..."

Don't say something stupid.

"Never saw a girl as pretty as you."

Smooth.

"No, I mean—"

"Liam, it's OK. Really."

He took a deep breath. "No, I should tell you that you are literally my first girlfriend. I don't know how to act around you. I don't know what's polite and what's not. I know there aren't a lot of options for either of us right now, but if I'm going to lose you, I don't want it to be over something stupid like ogling you too much. I guess what I'm trying to say is, being around you when you're not in zombie-fighting mode—when you're just a girl—makes me more nervous than being in the middle of a horde of the undead." He tried to end it with a little laugh.

"Well, first of all, you aren't going to lose—"

They both heard it. The familiar drone of zombies. It came from the nearby shore. Liam knew they were safe on the boat. He told himself it was a foolproof hideout.

And how many books have "foolproof" hideouts?

They popped their heads over the edge of the barge's hold.

All right. A "nearly foolproof" hideout.

Hundreds of zombies walked on the shore, all of them walking up the river. Gaggles of them were far down the bank, and more were far up the other way. It was like an undead funeral procession, marching slowly to some unknown beat.

They dropped back into the hold. In a whisper, Victoria asked, "Are we safe here? Can they get over to us from the shore?"

The barge was anchored away from shore, but it had a large cable running from the front to an anchor point somewhere on shore. A skilled person might be able to cross the wire by going hand-over-hand as they hung down from it. Liam had seen it done by some of his friends back when they used to spend time along the river.

"There's no way they can get over here using the cable, but I don't know if zombies can swim."

"Well, we have to get on our boat and keep moving. There's no end in sight to that line." The shoreline was straight for a few miles. She was right.

"I know."

He knew some zombies could climb. He saw two such climbers at Elk Meadow. Colonel McMurphy said there were many different flavors of zombie out there, though they were tied more or less to the city where they were spawned. The climbing zombies seemed to be a specialty of Chicago. Perhaps swimming zombies had come down from a city up the Mississippi river, and these zombies were walking back upstream now?

They briefly wondered if they could unhook the barge so it would float away from shore, but the size of the tie-down cable made it clear they would need tools to detach it. They cursed themselves for tying up the rowboat on the shore-side of the barge. If it was on the other side, they'd be free and clear before they were noticed.

"It will probably take us sixty seconds to get on the ladder and step down to the boat and get clear. We'll just have to take our chances."

Victoria didn't argue with him as she grabbed her gun and other belongings from their campsite.

"Let's do this nice and safe. Don't panic when you climb down and we should both be fine."

"Don't panic in the face of a horde of zombies. Got it."

Victoria went first. She climbed onto the rim of the barge and casually began her descent down the ladder. Liam followed and stood on the rim above her for a few moments. In that time, he could see her business-like approach was working. She went over nice and easy and made no noise and didn't appear nervous. In no time, she was below him in the boat, ready to go.

But she was noticed. A cry went up. One of the zombies sprinted toward the barge at a high rate of speed.

Zombies can't run that fast!

It plowed into the water, as if unaware it would sink. It pushed into deeper water with purpose. Worse, other zombies moved his way too, though most walked like "normal" plague victims. Liam began his descent.

The fast zombie managed to get surprisingly far into the water before it was too deep for him. He continued under the surface; Liam lost sight of him. In the strong current, he guessed the zombie was going to be swept behind the barge. A few other runners had their sights on the boat.

He set foot on the wooden plank. Victoria tried to untie the knot which kept them in place, but the old rope of the rowboat was well-frayed and looked confusing to untangle.

Something made a thud sound on the bottom of the boat.

Impossible!

Liam resolved not to look over the side. The rattle on the floor was the knock of panic.

"Victoria, hurry!"

She made a humpf sound, as if she couldn't be bothered to respond.

Another vibration on the bottom of the boat. Zombies poured into the water, screaming, clawing and flailing at the sight of two living people in a land of the dead. He knew they could stack up and get themselves to high places.

"Victoria?"

"I'm trying. This knot is really stuck."

"The knife! Use the knife!"

Don't panic.

Liam couldn't tell if Victoria cursed. She seldom did, but he allowed this was one time when it was appropriate.

She fumbled with his pocketknife as he looked to the shore and the waters between it and their boat. It boiled with arms and legs of the many zombies who managed to walk and run here from earshot of the boat. More streamed out from the trees along the shore. It wasn't hard to see what would happen.

Tons of zombies. One arm comes over the edge. We tip and die.

The boat jerked, and they were floating free. Victoria made the cut.

Liam grabbed the oars and paddled for their lives. His shore-side oar hit the head of one of the zombies wading in the water. The swimmer made a clumsy grab for it. His far-side oar sank in the water for a weak stroke. He couldn't swing them properly.

"No, push us away from shore!"

He saw the problem. If he could only use his far oar, it would push them *into* shore. Zombies desperately tried to grab the other oar, as if they knew it was attached to the food they wanted inside the craft.

Don't panic.

Victoria turned around. "Let the current take us backwards."

Liam sat with a blank look on his face, until it dawned on him. He gave one firm reverse tug on the far side oar, hoping it would push them both backwards and up against the barge as they drifted. He then secured both oars so they were out of the water.

Victoria readied her rifle, and even aimed at a few zombies that almost reached them, but none managed the full distance. The boat drifted downriver for more than a hundred feet until it cleared the back of the barge. He dropped both oars and paddled with gusto to go around the barge and continue up the river. He guessed the zombies in the water just kept going until they were caught by the undertow and pulled downstream. Not many zombies came back out of the water.

Will they walk the bottom to get us?

Shaken, Liam paddled like a fiend in the deeper water for an hour as they put the incident behind them. They could see zombies on the shoreline walking north with them. Sometimes one would notice them and turn to walk into the water, but mostly they faced forward and kept to themselves. A rare few of the "different" zombies loped by the others with fleet feet.

Many hours later, exhausted, they reached downtown St. Louis. The closer they came, the fewer zombies they saw near the shore. They grounded the boat on the cobblestones of the famous riverfront landing of the city of St. Louis. They couldn't have gone any further upriver if they wished. Someone had blown the interstate highway bridge; the deck had fallen straight down into the water and the wreckage blocked the entire river from Missouri to Illinois. A colossal jumble of barges, towboats, and huge pieces of driftwood hugged the upriver side of the mess. The tangle presented a formidable barrier to river traffic, had there been any.

They pulled the rowboat high up out of the water. It slid easily over the stonework. They wanted to park it under the edge of the downed bridge as it provided some cover on the otherwise open landing. They froze when they got close. Under big neutral-colored tarps were two fancy rubber boats with small but powerful-looking outboard motors. They too had been dragged up the cobblestone and left there. A nearly-dry trail of water went all the way back down to the river behind them.

The rubber boats were still dripping wet.

GOING IN CIRCLES

"Well, we're back in St. Louis. So glad we escaped, aren't you?"

Victoria responded with a small growl.

With rifles slung, they started up a long piece of collapsed highway. It had fallen along with the main bridge, but it formed a ramp so they were able to walk up onto the raised highway into downtown St. Louis. A car coming the other way would drive from the highway, down the ramp, and into the river.

When they reached the top of the ramp and crossed the tangle of broken concrete and rebar at the joint, they were relieved to see the elevated highway passed next to the Riverside Hotel and Casino—Grandma's prison. They walked the mostly empty interstate—the Army had blocked the approaches to this bridge early in the disaster—they talked about the boats.

"It can't be coincidence the zombies on the shoreline were heading this way, as well as two strange boats, Ospreys of Marines, and of course, us. Is Grandma *that* important, do you think?"

Before he could answer, he became distracted by the spectacle of destruction below them. The once-beautiful St. Louis Arch parkland had devolved into a hellish landscape of stripped and burned trees, huge craters, and an untold amount of trash and debris, including lots of bodies and body parts. There were countless buzzards picking at the remains. The smell...

"I didn't think the birds would touch a zombie."

Liam wondered. "I don't think they're *all* infected down there."

"It looks like the Army and Air Force really did a number on them."

"Yeah, we were there, remember?"

"In my wildest imagination," she spoke wistfully, "I wouldn't have thought the bombs could wreck the place so thoroughly. It almost looks like the moon down there."

There were black scorch marks on the lower portions of both legs of the Arch, but otherwise it looked intact. Liam took some measure of comfort from that. He knew the Arch would one day succumb to the forces of nature, but it didn't happen in the recent conflagration. Something survived. Something beautiful in a world of ugliness.

"In answer to your question, yes. I think Grandma is more important than we think. This can't all be coincidence."

Victoria looked over the ruin of the Arch grounds. "It's like a siren song. We were beckoned to this horrible place, where we'll be smashed on the rocks." She continued on a different track. "I really hate Hayes. I think I could kill him for all the grief he's caused us. I owe him one for shooting me, at the very least. I mean, here we are at the end of the world, zombies and plague swirling around us, and this jackass has to spend his time kidnapping and shooting people. How messed up is that? He told us he was looking for a cure. I call bull shnikes on that. Doctors trying to find cures are not running around town shooting little girls and kidnapping old women and bombing innocent people in their neighborhoods. And now look at him in his fancy tower! We have to waste our time going to save Grandma because of him. I have a hundred things I'd rather be doing right now—including finding my parents thankyouverymuch—but this turd requires more of my time than a three-year-old. I'm sick of it!"

"Wow, your cursing is really coming along," he said with mirth.

She glared at him in a way he recognized as something near pouting.

Liam didn't know how to respond, so he grabbed her hand and started them toward the hotel. No use delaying. But it turned out to be a mistake, at least at that moment. They saw the base of the building.

"Oh God, no," she said.

Liam fell to one knee as he used the railing on the side of the bridge to steady himself.

"See? This is what I'm talking about! Why in the name of all that's holy did Hayes need to lock himself up in the one tower that has a million gazillion zombies swarming around it? Oh, Liam, how are we going to get into that mess?"

She sat down hard next to the guard rail of the bridge, so the hotel was out of her field of view. Liam sat down next to her. The smell was horrific, but he was disturbed to realize it didn't affect him as much as it did a week ago.

"I know this is hard, but we can do hard things. Together. Grandma is at the top of that tower, and I can see now this has all been pre-planned by Hayes: Grandma, the massive swarm of zombies, and now us. It all ties together. We just have to figure out how. I need you, Victoria. I really need you."

Deep down he felt something he couldn't describe; it was both new, and familiar. Maybe it was love. Maybe it was just affection. He felt a powerful, almost subliminal, emotion toward Victoria. He would kill every zombie down there with his bare hands if he had to. He would kill anyone to protect this girl. It was partially a protective instinct, in the same vein of protecting his family, but it was so much more...

"Victoria, I—I know this sounds absolutely crazy. You're my first girlfriend, I know that. But everything we've been through. Everything I know about you. I want to always be by your side. I want to fight by your side. Die by your side if I have to. I can't explain the emotion I'm feeling. I—"

"I feel it too, Liam. It's like a wave that just came over me."

She looked at him, and he realized they were both crying in happiness as the emotion wrapped around them. The both embraced as they sat on the pavement, enjoying the feeling of loving and longing for each other.

Liam, unsure of himself in matters like this, blurted out, "Is this what love feels like?"

She seemed to remember something unpleasant, and pulled away. "Um. Yes. I mean I guess so. I uh—" she looked down at the roadway. "Oh, Liam. All I know is that I can't walk into that swarm without you by my side. Really, truly, by my side. If that is what love is, then yes, I love you."

Liam, prone to gaffes when he was nervous, let slip a doozie. "Well, we should get married if we survive the Apocalypse." Knowing he was likely making a huge mistake, he ended it with his telltale laugh.

To his surprise, she simply said, "Deal."

His smarmy mind, usually quick with a retort, was dumbfounded into silence.

2

They both recovered from the emotional outburst as the sensation receded, like a broken wave dragging itself back out to sea. But the core of the emotion still remained. He felt it was like a strong trunk of a tree had been planted in his mind. One that would forever tie him to the girl sitting next to him.

"Shall we try to find our way into the hotel? I'm kind of anxious to get this thing over with now." He wiped away his tears and gave her a starry-eyed wink. He was relieved to see she smiled back with a big natural smile.

They followed the highway overpass for a couple hundred yards, always staying away from the edge so as not to attract attention from the zombies below them. The hotel had a large flat platform on the roof, with a "Riverside Hotel and Casino" sign hanging off the side near the top. The hotel was mostly made of glass but was accented by beige stonework at the top and bottom.

"I think we just found the Riverside Operations Center." She referenced the paperwork they'd found back at the Elk Meadow camp. "This has to be the place."

They heard muffled gunshots coming from inside the building.

"Sounds like a real battle is going on in there. You think it's the people from the boats?"

"Your guess is as good as mine on this. But it makes me uncomfortable with all that shooting going on while your grandma is over there." They both looked up and saw small drones in the sky above, and a larger one looping high above. Whatever was happening inside had lots of onlookers.

A few more minutes and they were almost parallel with the hotel. The rounded building was about thirty feet north of the elevated highway. Someone parked a huge green garbage truck nearby, among a handful of smaller abandoned cars. A stout metal wire was attached to a handle on the side of the truck, then it went over the side of the bridge and through a window of the hotel on a floor just below.

"I think this is how they got over there," he said, proud of the patently obvious use for the wire.

"Yeah, it looks really dangerous, too."

"We have our way in, though. Dangerous or not, it has to be safer than what's below." Liam risked a look over the side and saw the crowd of zombies. There were thousands of them, probably tens of thousands. Liam didn't know and didn't really care.

"So how do we get from here, to over there?"

"In the movies they make it look easy. You just swing something over the wire, hang on, and slide in through the window."

"And what if you aren't in the movies? How do *those* people do this?"

He knew he had to answer her question sufficiently for this to work. Just a cursory search of the area proved to him there would probably be no easier way of getting in than this crazy scary over-the-zombie-crowd rope ride. His probe led him to the truck, and his answer.

"We can use pieces of this truck to make handles for sliding. Piece of cake!"

"You sure like cake." She smiled, but warmed to his suggestion.

In short order, Liam was able to put his pocketknife to work cutting carpet and pieces of plastic to make something to throw over the wire which would allow them to slide down and into the hotel without burning their hands. He wasn't prepared to say it would be as easy as in the movies, but he felt more confident than he did walking up to the garbage truck in the first place. Victoria didn't look worried, though he thought she looked about as wary as anyone would be who was about to ride a thin wire over a deadly horde of zombies into a hotel which had the welcoming aura of a hive of hornets.

He discovered her worry was placed somewhere else entirely.

"Liam, what we said back there, I don't know if it was real or some weird side effect of the plague or the end of the world or what. But—"

"No, I get it. It did seem too good to be true. I understand—"

"Let me finish!" She stomped her foot. "I was going to say that even if what happened to us was fake, my feelings for you are real. I know we are young and all, and that we are in the fight for our lives every day now, but I truly do love you. I've seen your love this whole time we've been together. The way you treat your grandma, the way you treat your parents, and the way you treat me. I've watched you searching for answers about God, which is also very important to me. With a sniffle, she continued. I've realized that things are never going to be the same. Big weddings, the white picket fences and the apple pies—those are things of a past era. We've embarked on a new journey, in a new world, with new rules. I believe in my heart you are the person with whom I want to share this journey. My consideration was complete before we had that—whatever it was—back there. It just amplified that feeling, is all. But I want you to know my true heart was already made up. That this is real."

Liam had never felt happier in his entire life.

"I love you, too!"

He then grabbed his makeshift handle, slung it over the wire, gave her a big smile, pushed himself over the bridge, and whooped it up as he slid over the horde and into the dark broken window of the hotel like he owned the place.

Only after he was inside did he comprehend how dangerous it was and that he'd left his wonderful girlfriend out on the overpass without so much as a lick of instruction.

"And the winner of boyfriend of the year is..."

3

Liam ran back to the third floor window and was relieved to see Victoria toss her handle over the wire. Like him, she sat on the bridge railing, held onto the crude handle made from the truck's gutted interior, then pushed off. In moments, she was heading for him at a slow but steady pace.

He looked down.

What the—

He didn't appreciate the size of the zombie horde while they were walking on the raised highway. From his new vantage point he could see the zombies took up every bit of space around the base of the circular hotel, and they packed every street leading up to the hotel. They were unnaturally quiet for such a large crowd of zombies.

Victoria gave an exclamatory yell as she arrived. He wasn't able to tear himself away from the zombies to help her.

"You could have at least helped catch me, though I'm glad someone put that mattress there," she said as she came up behind him. She too saw the endless sea of the dead.

"I'm glad I didn't look down."

"Why do you think they're so quiet? Are they all looking at us?"

"They probably heard you whooping like a teenager at the amusement park," she giggled.

"Yeah, maybe."

"Let's keep moving." She tried to pull him away from the window. He resisted at first, but then relented.

After he vacated the window, the distinct moans and yelling of the zombies went back up to level 11. He had an inspiration to pop back to the window to see if they fell silent again, but when he did so, they just continued moaning. Some did look up at him and appeared to reach for him, but it seemed random. He thought he was seeing "normal" zombie behavior now, though he still couldn't identify what that might be.

He followed Victoria out the hotel room door, and finally noticed the ripe stench in the confined space. It made the background nausea of the horde outside—and the Arch bird feast—seem almost pleasant.

"Wow!" His quiet exclamation mimicked the look of shock on Victoria's face.

They ran back into the room with the open window and went to work ripping up the bed sheets, trying to fashion makeshift masks they could use to fight the deathly fumes.

Victoria came out of the bathroom with a little bottle of hotel shampoo. "We can rub this on the sheets we put on our face. Maybe it will hide the smell. Even a tiny bit can make a difference."

In a few minutes, they were back out the door with their olfactory defenses bolstered. It did help, but didn't come close to completely hiding the smell. Liam's eyes wanted to water.

All the rooms of the tower were on an outer ring on each floor. The interior of the hotel was hollow, with about fifty yards from one side to the other, giving the appearance of the inside of a smokestack. They were on a circular walkway ringing the entire floor. From the railing, they could peer down to the ground floor. Normally it would have been an enchanting garden. Many plants, shrubs, and small trees tastefully decorated the atrium. They were being trampled by hundreds of zombies milling about down there. Yet, the truly disturbing feature of the lobby was the large pile of bodies.

"May God forgive us." Victoria's voice was muffled by her scarf, but Liam concurred. Only humans could have created the huge pile of bodies.

"Those are all elderly people—" Liam's voice cracked as he tried to voice the obvious. "Do you think?"

"No. I'm absolutely sure Grandma isn't down there."

Liam searched his feelings. He, too, felt she was still alive, though he wasn't sure why he had such faith. Looking at the pile of people just like Grandma, he realized he felt anger more than anything else.

"Let's keep moving." He swung *Moses* off his back and showed Victoria that he was clicking the safety off. She did the same.

Time to get serious.

A few steps later, they found the first zombie. The bath-robed woman had been shot in the head and lay sprawled on the otherwise cheery carpet. Looking ahead, they saw many more zombies had been killed on the walkway.

"Someone has been through here. Well-armed. But why don't we hear shooting anymore?"

The shooting had been constant as they walked up to the hotel, but somewhere along the way it stopped. Liam laughed inwardly that gunshots were so common now he thought nothing of them.

He observed the design of the hotel. Each level of suites was ringed on the inside by the large walkway with a metal railing. He put himself on the six o'clock position of the hotel. At three o'clock and nine o'clock, he could see dim EXIT signs above doors, suggesting stairwells. At the twelve o'clock position, almost directly across the void, he could see a pair of clear shafts; they were for elevators. The elevator cars were nowhere to be seen. Looking up, he guessed they were at the top. Studying the other levels, he was dismayed to see dark figures lurking on several floors.

"This doesn't make any sense. How could zombies get inside the hotel and up onto these levels? One closed door at the bottom and it would prevent them from reaching all these levels. Surely some of the stairwell doors would have been barricaded? Was the place abandoned and left totally open?"

Victoria drank in the view as she responded, "I think someone had to have let them in. I can see doors down in the lobby, and all the glass looks broken. Even if that were an accident, I can see at least one of the stairwell doors down there, and it has a bar or something propping it open. It's that one over there."

She was pointing to three o'clock.

"We should go over there, to the *other* stairwell. See if we can go up." He was pointing to the nine o'clock stairwell.

Victoria didn't argue. They quietly and deliberately moved that direction, staying as close to the inner wall as possible. Liam didn't want to chance being spotted by any of those dark shadows on other floors.

A couple minutes was all it took to reach the large metal fire door at the stairwell. It hung wide open. In the low light it was hard to tell why. He gripped his rifle tightly. His finger wasn't on the trigger, but it smashed the side of it just above the trigger guard.

When they reached the door, they found the blockage: a body.

It said "hello."

4

"You kids shouldn't be here."

The bald man wore a nondescript black uniform. He had a rifle, though it was lying haphazardly next to him. He had gore covering his leg below his knee. A nearby female zombie clad in rhinestone-lined jeans and a bloody tank top—with a detached head—was possibly the culprit.

The man followed Liam's gaze. "Yeah, that's the bitch that got me. They can chew faster than you can believe. She was searching for an artery so she could drain me. I was so mad I removed her head and threw it over the railing before I took my seat here to wait for the end..."

Then, to himself, he said, "I was planning to take at least one more."

Victoria said, "We heard shooting in here. Did you shoot all these zombies?" She motioned back over her shoulder the way they'd come.

He didn't answer directly. "Is there a door open? How'd you get in? I thought we sealed all the doors on this level."

Liam searched for an answer that didn't involve the truth, but he couldn't think of anything. He was just about to respond with his best effort when Victoria spoke up.

"Not sure about the doors. We came in through the window. Me and my boyfriend were driving on the highway until we found the bridge was out. We got out of our car and got chased. We were lucky to find a wire to this hotel and we had just enough time to slide down before we were eaten by the infected."

"And the guns?"

Victoria was nonplussed. "Who doesn't have guns anymore?"

It was true enough, but given where they were, he felt he had to add some veracity to her story.

"Cost us twelve chickens for the pair of them. We coulda used the chickens, but we're trying to get across to Illinois so we needed the artillery more."

"Well, you can look around at this place. I think you'd have had a better chance out in the open. This hotel is crawling with these bloodsuckers. I'm gonna be one soon, too. Not for long, I hope."

As if in emphasis, he coughed up a large wad of—something—and spit it on the floor next to him. Liam knew he was close to turning. He'd seen it before, notably when he saw the colonel from Elk Meadow change. McMurphy had the courage to kill himself when the time came. Would this man?

Seeing the bloody mess he'd coughed up, the man began cursing. Not at Liam or Victoria, but just in general.

Liam felt it was worth risking an innocent question. "How did you get here? Did you come across that dangerous wire, too?"

The man stared at the floor as he spoke. His words were slow and deliberate.

"I started my day in a warm bed with a warm woman if you can believe that. Phone rings and it's mission time. Jump in a truck. Drive. Jump in a boat to cross a river. Then we have a brilliant plan to get into this place..." He faded out for a half a minute before returning "...shoot a wire across the gap. Then seal the doors. Always running from infected. Ha! I wasn't fast enough as you can see."

"Where were you going? Is there safety in this building?" Liam tried to paint a look of innocent hopefulness on his face, though the dim light may not have helped.

The man seemed to be fading fast. "Only the Army's fortresses are safe. Never leave a fortress if you're lucky enough to get in one. They're the only thing that went right in this bag of dicks called Doomsday."

Liam had to risk a more direct question before the man left and the zombie arrived. He'd seen the transition happen many times, and was seldom the same from person to person. The bald man's head was now resting on his chest.

"Sir, were you sent by Douglas Hayes?"

At the mention of the name, the man sprang to a semblance of awareness. He grabbed his rifle and pointed it—somewhat randomly—at Liam.

"Tell me right now who you work for."

Liam froze. In moments, the gun swayed dangerously. The man was on the edge and having trouble holding the weapon in the air with his waning strength.

"Hayes has my grandma. We think he's going to kill her."

The gun dropped completely to the floor. Whether it was because of what he said, or just fatigue, Liam couldn't tell.

"Son, look over the rails. They've been killing grandmas and grandpas up there by the pound. Your meemaw's dead. Get out of here."

Victoria spoke directly to Liam, as quietly as she could. "Liam, I'm sure she's fine."

The man coughed several times, loudly. Then, with his head on his chest, "Liam? Can't be many Liams out there. Liam Peters, by chance? Grandma is Martinnette Peters?" He ended with a wet cough.

Liam hadn't recovered from having the man's rifle pointed at him, but now pointed his own gun. "What do you want with Martinnette Peters?"

The man was trembling. He looked into the distance. "Sorry, sir. I almost killed them both. Yes, sir. It's been an honor, sir. I'm—" He heaved himself sideways into the doorway.

Victoria pushed Liam into the doorway as well. They both fell to the hard cement floor on the far side of the man as an explosion erupted. Liam was stunned by the noise and concussion, but was otherwise unharmed. He got to his feet with ringing ears and his normal headache. He pulled Victoria off the ground and they moved out of the smoky stairwell while they recovered.

"Are you OK?" Victoria shouted.

Liam nodded in the affirmative.

They both sat down on the floor nearby. It took a couple minutes before they could resume normal conversation.

"You saved our lives. Thanks. How did you know he would explode?"

Victoria talked at a higher volume than normal. "I saw it in a movie. I didn't want him to raise his gun at you again, so I watched him like a hawk. When he rolled over, I heard a click, and saw the grenade clear as day fall behind him. I guessed that his body would shield most of the explosion, so that's where I pushed you."

"I'm lucky I brought you along. I just stood there like an idiot."

"Well, you didn't bring me along for my girlishly good looks, did you?" Even behind her shampoo-laced scarf, he could tell she was smiling.

"Well, actually..."

The humor belied the stark raving fear he felt at that moment. *We almost died. Again.*

5

"So, what do we do next? Go into the super-scary pitch-black stairwell?" He tried to be funny, which was the only antidote to the dread clawing at his insides.

"The elevators haven't come down for us yet, so I guess we have to."

Liam inwardly smiled that she had a sense of humor. He didn't think he could have survived with someone who was a constant dark cloud.

They got up and searched the man for any clues about who he was or what his mission might have been, but he had no ID and very little else on what was left of his body. He had a small flashlight latched to a black utility belt. Also attached was a holster with a handgun in it. Liam recognized it as a Glock. He tossed it in his backpack. The man wore a piece of steel on his chest—a bulletproof chest plate. Liam imagined wearing the chest plate, getting shot by the bad guys, but then jumping back up to kill them all after they thought he was dead. However, after pulling it off the man's ruined body, he felt the weight.

"I wish I could have carried this bulletproof armor." He held it up to his chest, struggling to keep it there. He never thought of himself as a weakling, but the dead man was larger than he appeared. The armor was oversized for a man of his girth.

"Just do what I do," said Victoria, "don't get shot."

"Now, wait just a minute," Liam retorted. Of the two of them, she was the only one who had actually had a bullet land on her.

"You're so funny. I'd kiss you if I wasn't wearing protection from the stink around us, and we didn't have a headless zombie full of bullet holes and a dead man missing a large chunk of his body right by us. Kinda takes the mood away."

Liam turned to the dark doorway, flicked on his own battle-worn flashlight, and said a quasi prayer. "I will fear no evil."

"Amen." Victoria gripped the dead man's small light and together they headed up the steps.

Almost immediately, Liam said, "Are we there yet?"

"Don't make me turn this stairwell around. I will, so help me!"

"No seriously, are we there? How much longer?"

"For the one-millionth time, I'll tell you when we get there!"

They both giggled in the confined space, trying to push back against the darkness.

At the next landing, they checked the door. It was closed, which was a relief since no zombies could stumble in, but it was also welded shut with the word "Phoenix" stenciled on it with white paint.

The next level was also welded shut. Its door said "Chicago." A few twice-deceased zombies were lying in the stairwell—all shot in the head. They were dressed in hospital scrubs, though it was unclear if they were the doctors or the patients.

"Why do you think someone would seal these doors?"

Liam could think of a few reasons. The most obvious was to keep out the zombies, but zombies were already in the building, on every floor, if his earlier surveillance was correct.

"I don't know," was all he felt like committing to at that moment.

At the fifteen floor, they found the bodies of two U.S. Marines. The area around them was scorched and blackened, as if an explosion ripped through there. The bodies were badly mangled, though Liam avoided studying them in any detail.

"So now we have Marines, a guy dressed in black wearing body armor, and a hotel full of zombies. Was this a popular nightclub or something?"

Liam responded, "This hotel is so new I don't know if it was even open before the sirens went off. Dad drove me by here a couple times and I saw it going up, but I don't have a clue why it's so popular now."

After many tiring minutes, they reached the final door in the stairwell. It had the number thirty on a placard next to it. Unlike the floors below, each with a different city or region stenciled on it, this door was unmarked.

Liam ascended the last few steps and put his ear to the door. He heard nothing obvious from the other side but did notice there was one small hole in the metal next to his head. He noticed more holes in various locations on the door.

He shut off his light and Victoria did the same.

As their eyes adjusted to the darkness, the door revealed many more punctures.

With a whisper, Victoria stated the obvious.

"Bullet holes."

OLD FRIENDS

"OK, I'm outta here."

Liam made like he was going to walk back down the steps, trying to pass it off as humor. He looked longingly into the darkness below him, knowing it was safer than whatever was on the other side of the door.

Still whispering, Victoria retorted, "Har har, Mr. Funny Guy."

"Yeah, I know. I'm just trying to enjoy the day before I get shot up."

He tried to look through some of the bullet holes to see what was on the other side, but they revealed nothing.

He prepared himself to open the door, but paused as he touched it. He turned to Victoria and embraced her. Nothing was said, but it made him feel better. After a few wonderful moments, he broke free, and pulled the large fire door.

A big machine gun was on the floor. It had been sitting on a tripod at one time, but was now lying on its side in an alcove to his left. A massive hole was in the wall of the hotel room directly in front of him. A spacious circular room with a glass ceiling was to his right. The top level of the hotel was a posh lounge with many small tables and chairs and lots of planters. Rows of slot machines were parked in a central area, though they were still wrapped in shipping plastic. Most of the furniture was overturned, and bodies were everywhere on the floor.

The circular central lounge was flanked by the penthouse suites on one side, and by some kind of Japanese restaurant on the other. The Kanji letters were listed below the English name Kyushu View. On the far side—in the 3 o'clock stairwell alcove—he saw another machine gun on a tripod, still upright. It had a flashing red light on top, and if his eyes were true, the machine gun was swiveling in his direction.

"Run!"

He plunged ahead into the breach in the wall, tripping on the debris as he did so. Victoria tumbled in after him. Together they hugged the floor awaiting the sounds of the big gun. Its silence almost disappointed him.

"Sorry, I thought that other machine gun was going to start shooting us."

Victoria took it in stride as she sized up the new room.

The construction plaster of the wall had blanketed the floor and was extremely slippery. They both crawled away from the downed wall and regained their footing on a shaggy carpet. The penthouse was huge.

"So this is where the rich people stay." Victoria whistled in amazement.

Everything you'd imagine in a million-dollar suite of an expensive hotel was in front of them: large kitchen, a massive en suite hot tub, stainless steel decor, several bedrooms, and big comfy sofas overlooking a million-dollar view of downtown St. Louis and the entire cityscape beyond.

It would have been perfect if it didn't also contain a handful of dead Marines.

Liam dragged himself to the closest man and was dismayed to see he was shot, not bitten.

"The day has come where I actually prefer dead bodies to be killed by zombies, rather than other men. What does that say about me?"

Victoria put her hand on his back as she spoke. "I think it's normal. I'm scared to death of anyone who's willing get into a fight and kill Marines. It looks like they succeeded, at least in killing these men. It can't be for any good purpose. Unless—"

"Unless what?"

"Unless the Marines are the bad guys." Liam considered himself to be the conspiracy theorist, with his conspiracy theorist father to thank for that, but Victoria now gave him a run for his money.

"Think about it, Liam. Someone blows your neighborhood to hell, and the Marines are there. Marines show up at Camp Hope, and out of the blue survivalists attack the camp. Maybe they were working together? Now, in a creepy tower filled with zombies, where we know your grandma is being held, we find more Marines. That seems like a lot of odd coincidences if they aren't really the enemy here."

"Yeah, I guess I see your point." He didn't want to believe it. "But let's keep moving. Grandma's probably in worse danger than we thought. As long as she's up here and not..."

"Just keep going. She's here."

He stood up and she led him to the far wall. It was also breached wide enough for soldiers to pass through.

The next room was similar to the first. They managed to avoid slipping and falling as they came through. More Marines were dead in this room, but there were also dead soldiers with different uniforms too. It was apparently a swirl of fighting—the room was a disaster area of broken furniture and scorched walls. All the glass of the outer windows was shattered or blown out. It made him feel as if he were going to be sucked out the opening, though he knew it was just his mind being overprotective.

He reached the first of the non-Marine soldiers to check him out. He didn't need to be an expert to identify the stitched tag on his shirt.

U.S. Army.

2

They were surrounded by both dead Marines and dead U.S. Army soldiers.

"Were they together?"

Victoria checked out the bodies, too. "Why do they all have bullet holes in their heads?"

Nothing? No shock at that statement?

He looked straight at the dead men, all shot in the head, some with their brains spilled out, and he felt no revulsion at the spectacle.

He tried to block out the question by focusing on solving the mystery.

"Hard to tell. We know there are at least three factions involved now. Marines. Army. And the black uniform guy and his friends."

"Hayes could be his own faction, don't you think?"

"Dunno. This is getting out of hand though. Is there any hope of finding Grandma if all these men fought and died around her? There's no way she could have survived fighting this bad…"

She grabbed his shirt and pulled him along. "Don't give up. Just keep moving. Remember, *we* are her faction." She tapped her rifle with her free hand.

She brought them both to the door to go out. There was no breach in the next wall, meaning whoever left the room had to have gone out into the main lounge area.

Maybe they're watching us now?

There was no way to hide their approach in the well-lit lounge area, so Liam poked his head out the door to see if it drew any response.

Nothing happened. He could see the alcove on the far side of the room where the machine gun sat, but from this vantage point he couldn't see the gun. He supposed the Marines were trying to flank the heavy gun. Now he was taking advantage of their tactics.

"At least the Marines did us the favor of getting us around that machine gun. No matter if they're the good guys or bad."

Victoria said nothing, but squeezed his back to let him know she heard him.

"Wait here and cover me. I'm going to run past the elevators to the next room. The door is open, so that might be where the fight continued."

They both double-checked their weapons before he stole a quick kiss and ran across the open space. He eyed all the tables and planters where he could take cover in the lounge if a bad guy saw him, but he made it all the way to the planned doorway without seeing anything. Except—

About twenty feet from the doorway, he saw someone had cut a large hole the translucent floor. The whole lounge was floored with a thick glass-like material designed to let light filter down into the main atrium of the lower hotel. The floor was intact except the five-foot wide hole nearby. Someone had surrounded it with chairs from the lounge. Victoria ran up after him, patting him on the back again to acknowledge her presence.

He judged the distance between the open door and the hole in the floor, as well as whether anyone inside the room could see him if he walked to the hole.

"Liam!" Victoria whispered; she wanted him to stop.

He ignored her and walked to the edge of gap.

I have to know.

Victoria chose to stick by him rather than hold up the wall, though he noticed she was turned sideways with her rifle swinging to and fro. She was protecting him from any threats.

Cautiously, he bent over the 300-foot drop so he could look straight down into the hotel and the lobby floor. He knew what he'd see. The pile of bodies they'd seen while on the third floor was straight down. Whatever took place up here was responsible for the nightmare down there. The bodies had been tossed from this hole to fall unceremoniously onto the macabre funeral pyre.

Victoria peeked into the hole, too. It didn't take her long to come to the same conclusion.

"Why would they toss them down there like so much trash?" She looked back toward the open door, then continued while facing Liam. "Look at me. Grandma isn't down there. I know it in my heart. She's *not.*"

"I hope you're right. My heart feels it, too. But my brain can almost see her down there."

"Liam, no—"

A new voice spoke loudly from behind them, "She's not down there. I promise you that."

Liam didn't have to turn around to know who it was. Since the second day of the collapse, this voice had been haunting him. Its owner had followed them out of the city, only to run and hide at the very last moment when he could have been useful. He tracked Liam and Grandma, kidnapped them, and shot Victoria. He tried to experiment on Grandma, then lost her, then kidnapped her one last time, presumably to bring her to this building. He was the person Liam had grown to hate more than anyone else in the entire apocalypse.

"Hayes."

3

Liam and Victoria spun around, weapons drawn.

"Don't worry, kids. You don't need the guns. I'm unarmed."

He held his arms up as he stood in the doorway of one of the uncleared rooms. He wore a hideous yellow Hawaiian shirt, bulky khaki short pants which mostly covered the bandages on his thigh, and penny loafers. He looked like an older man playing at being young while going to the beach, but then he'd always had a questionable dress code.

He looked them over, then dropped his arms and limped back into his room. "Come on in."

Liam wasn't willing to shoulder his weapon, so he left it hanging at his side—ready if he needed it. Victoria kept hers in her hands, pointed at the floor as she walked. He didn't think she was willing to trust the man who shot her. He didn't either.

They entered the room where Hayes had disappeared. It was laid out just like the other two rooms, but in the front living space there were several blood-soaked gurneys with lots of medical equipment nearby. The rest of the room was shot to hell. Liam shut the door and locked it with the chain and deadbolt.

Hayes walked over to one of the remaining chairs—a large leather armchair—and took a seat. He motioned for them to come sit on a nearby couch with fist-sized holes in the sides. Liam was happy to put the bloody gurneys to his back, though he stayed on his feet rather than sit down.

"Where's my Grandma, if not down in that hole?"

He tore off his makeshift bandana; Victoria followed. The smell was still bad, but not overpowering, on this floor.

"Be careful, Liam. She's in the bedroom resting. But she isn't alone. Please put your weapon down before you go in. I don't want anyone else getting shot."

He looked at Hayes for a long second, then turned and walked toward the bedroom, gun in hand. Victoria followed.

"Grandma!" He yelled it, even though she had her eyes closed. There were also several other people in the bedroom suite.

"Hello, Sam. Or should I say Liam Peters? And welcome, Miss Victoria Hennessey."

A man in dark tactical clothing sat on a chair next to the bed. He was the same agent he'd seen days ago on a bridge overpass over the interstate out of St. Louis. A wave of refugees was on the highway underneath, and Special Agent Duchesne wanted to turn them all back. Liam outsmarted him and convinced his police allies to let everyone escape. He'd used the alias "Sam Stevens" to avoid giving his identity, but the agent took their photographs, and figured out the truth.

"You? What are you doing with my Grandma?"

Another man stood next to Duchesne. He was large and well-armed. Liam remembered him, too. He was on the bridge as the agent's bodyguard. He pointed a huge military rifle directly at Liam's chest.

"Why don't you drop the weapons and then we'll talk?" His bodyguard put the emphasis on "drop."

Liam and Victoria both stacked their weapons on the floor at their feet. Liam didn't want anyone shooting with Grandma sprawled out on the bed in the middle of them all.

At the far end of the room, near the exterior window, the red-headed woman sat on the long window sill. She was dressed in camo fatigues, including the same cap he'd seen her wear before. She was also unarmed.

"Just don't hurt my Grandma and we won't have any problems."

Duchesne stood up, kicking the guns closer to his assistant. "And what if I did hurt your Grandma? What kind of problems would you make for me?"

Liam looked at the bed, then at the man. Then back to the bed.

"Just please don't."

Louder, he called out of the room. "Hayes, why don't you come in and stand over there by your secretary."

The woman glared, but remained silent. Hayes did as instructed, and Liam noted she put her hand on his back when he joined her.

Duchesne slowly wound his way around the room, speaking softly. "Liam, do you have any idea the lengths I've gone..." He came to a stop right behind Liam, then spoke to Hayes instead. "Actually, I think Douglas would be a much better person to explain the length's *we've* gone through to get you. Don't you?"

For the first time since he'd known him, Hayes appeared tired.

"You serious? You want me to tell him everything?"

"At least tell him your role. I think he'd love to know why you've been following this old lady," he thumbed in Grandma's direction, "like a little lost puppy dog." He laughed, though Hayes did not. "Tell him about your delightful experiments here. Go on!"

Grandma was still asleep. Or passed out.

Or dead.

He studied her chest and was relieved to see it rising and falling in slow, even turns.

Hayes didn't respond. Liam didn't know who was in charge here, but he wanted answers.

"Hayes lies about everything. Why would you trust him?"

That got a response.

"I've always told you the truth. Your grandma is very important to our research into the origins of plague—"

"Because of her age, right?"

"Yes, we know that men and women of extreme age seem to react to the infection in a way that is very different than the younger people who get it. You saw that back at Elk Meadow. That was where I put it together for the first time. Unfortunately, that buffoon in charge of the camp let the virus escape and he set us back in our research. Who knows how many people died because of that, eh?"

His glib attitude constantly grated at Liam.

"OK, so the old people have something to do with the plague. Why is there a pile of them on the ground floor of this place?"

He knew the answer, but had to ask it anyway. He saw a similar killing field back at Elk Meadow, though McMurphy assured him everyone was there as a volunteer. In a quieter voice, he preempted his own question.

"Were they volunteers?"

"You can't be that naïve, can you? The elderly are this planet's most important resource. Do you know how fast they're dying now that electricity is gone? Medicine is gone? Medical services are gone? So many of our age-challenged friends were literally living on borrowed time back in the Old World. They never had a chance of living in this new one. Volunteers? No. But they gave their lives doing something that could save everyone they love, so I tend to think they gave their lives happily once I explained what they were doing for us."

"You think all these people were already going to die, so you killed them?"

"No! I'm not a monster. Killing them is such an unfair depiction of what we're doing to them. When we inject the virus, there is a very real chance each and every time they will live. Some of them live for a long time. I admit some of them convert right away. Those are unfortunate, but necessary. You see, the key to this whole thing is that some of them are almost able to resist the virus completely. If we can find out why, it may give us the clue we need to cure the whole population. We draw blood, do tests, send it to—"

"But why just toss them down the hole? Don't they deserve more?"

"I share your concern. I really do. In the camps out in the country, we could bury people with a little dignity, but that takes resources. Fuel for tractors. Manpower. Things that are in diminishing supply. We chose this place because it allowed us to operate up here and easily dispose of the unfortunate volunteers by putting them in the hotel lobby below. We felt it was more humane than tossing them out the window into the crowd of zombies below us."

Liam couldn't argue the point, but it didn't make it right.

"So Grandma is important to you because she's so old. I get it. I hate that this question has popped in my head, but what's so special about her that has made you chase her so many times and keep her alive while so many other old folks are tossed aside like trash?"

Duchesne was back by his chair. He seemed to be enjoying things. His bodyguard hadn't moved. He hadn't even lowered his weapon.

Hayes paced in front of the window.

"Before I tell you that, let me ask you a question. Let me ask you both a question: what kinds of medications are you on?"

Liam looked at Hayes like he'd just stepped in a cow pie.

"This is a serious question, kids. Let me ask you this another way. To protect medical privacy and all that. Have you ever been on medications, for any reason, longer than a week or two?"

Liam searched his memory. For a long time, as a child, he took medication for his attention deficit disorder. He took it for years before he grew out of that particular need.

Victoria looked down, but said nothing.

"I'll take that to mean you both have taken some kind of medication. Now, think about your parents. Do you see them popping pills every day? I'd wager they probably do, or have in the past, or will in the future—well maybe not in our current future, but they would have. Everyone takes medications these days like it is perfectly normal and expected. Even Duchesne over there is on something, I'm sure."

If he was, the agent gave no indication. Liam was less hostile now that he understood the direction this was going.

"The thing that makes your Grandma special is that she has never taken medication a day in her life. No high blood pressure pills. No cholesterol meds. Not even vitamins as best we can tell."

"What about pain pills? She broke her arms a few years ago. Surely she had pain pills?"

"Undoubtedly she did, but the effects fade quickly. She only took them very short term. The main thing is that she has no cellular damage or mutation which is indicative of longer term medications so common in the world today. And, even more peculiar is that at her advanced age she has taken no medications that are so common with her peers. She's almost unique in that regard. I should know, I've examined her blood several times."

"So, you aren't a truck driver, are you?"

Eons ago it seemed, Liam and Hayes discussed his job function at the CDC. He said he was in logistics, and Liam believed this to mean he was a truck driver.

"What? No. I'm sorry I had to bend the truth on that, but my cover is more important than just tricking a couple of kids like you. I'm an immunologist in a world swarming with viruses. I'm too valuable to die in some futile battle against the undead."

"We get it. You're so important you didn't want to fight with us to get out of the city *and* you study the virus that destroyed the world."

"Yes, but I've come to understand something that my—uh, colleagues—have missed. This business with viruses started at the end of flu season in the United States. This spring, we noticed the flu wasn't petering out like it normally would as the weather warmed up and people started getting out of confined spaces with each other. The CDC, along with the World Health Organization, began doing extensive research on the phenomenon. I won't bore you with the details, but the bottom line is that we realized there were two versions of a nearly-identical strain of flu. They were identical on the surface and in behavior but the resistance of the clone was enhanced—making preventative health measures ineffective. We thought this deadly pairing could be solved before a real emergency evolved. Many nations quietly fought the flu internally, though most publicly wrote it off as a last hurrah of flu season. No one wanted to cause a panic."

Liam couldn't remember anything about a flu epidemic, but was a self-proclaimed news-avoider.

"But that isn't what ended the world," Hayes continued.

"You aren't making any sense. What could be worse than two flu viruses working together?" Victoria inquired.

"Because approximately a month ago, just as the flu problem was at its height, we became aware of a mystery virus already present in every man, woman and child on the planet. That virus was custom-made and it worked together with the already deadly pair to form a mutating triad. Actually, we don't know how many versions are out there now."

Liam finally understood. "I'm going to take a wild guess. You had something to do with the mystery virus, didn't you?"

"I understand why you hate me, Liam. And Victoria; I shot you, after all. But you see now the stakes I was dealing with. Why nothing can get in the way of understanding this unholy trinity of viruses ravaging the planet. I assure you I had nothing to do with the mystery virus."

He hesitated as he finished his sentence.

Victoria spoke up, "But?"

Hayes looked at her as he spoke. "But, I know who created the cloned flu virus."

Finally. We're getting somewhere.

"So who ended the world?" she asked.

"The people who released the mystery virus."

"You mean flu virus."

"No, the virus we can't identify."

"I'm not following you, Hayes," Victoria lamented.

"The thing my colleagues don't realize is that the second version of the flu was actually a human-created clone. It was designed very cleverly to be more effective at delivering its payload. Very nearly 100% effective, I'm afraid. Almost impossible to detect the human signature. If nature had been left to take its course, the clone flu would have compounded flu season and become a deadly, but manageable, plague upon mankind. It wouldn't have led to...what we have now."

"Are you saying there are two man-made viruses working together out there?" Liam started to understand the problem. Humans always seemed to be scarier in their actions than Mother Nature. Even the zombies eventually paled next to the potential for trouble from other men and women.

"No, I'm not."

"But you just said—"

"No! I said there's a man-made clone flu virus and a mystery virus. We can't figure out how the mystery virus was made."

Oh. Crap.

4

"A great story, Hayes. But as usual, you leave out the highlights."

Hayes glared at him, but refused to be baited.

"OK, I'll fill in the blanks if you're going to be shy." He stood up again, but stayed close to his tall friend. "We'll start with all the dead bodies in this building. Hayes' little petting zoo." He pointed to the floor. "Riverside? You want to tell them why I had to fight to get into Riverside?"

Duchesne gave a withering look at Hayes, and that seemed to do it.

Hayes laughed tightly.

"Riverside. That's this place. I was assigned to an Army unit when things began to fall apart. I guess the thinking was the military would protect me while I did my work. In the beginning, they were annoyingly strict on following protocol—even refusing to let me cross that bridge when you two saw me talking with them over the Mississippi River. But in a world of fewer and fewer resources, the Army pulled more and more of my protectors away until I was left with only a fraction of what was necessary to guard an operation of the scale I needed. Rules got lax. Orders were lost. I guarded those remaining resources jealously. As communications became sporadic, I explained what I was doing to cure the plague and the remaining men and women agreed to follow my orders until the end. Today, they met that end."

"Killed by the Marines?" Liam asked.

"Nope. The Marines were collateral damage. Most of them died down below, fighting to get in. They came up here and didn't know friend from foe—killed everyone they could—but there weren't enough of them. Most of the killing was by the NIS guys. National Internal Security. One of the labyrinthine layers of government contractors and security. Sort of the Secret Service for the Secret

Service. Even talking about them can get me killed, but seeing as one of them is sitting right in this room, I'm not going to worry about it." He nodded at Duchesne. " *These* boys came in to stop my research. They're the ones who killed both the Marines and the Army remnant protecting me—my research."

Duchesne made a clicking noise with his tongue. "No, that's not it at all. Tell them who *you* really are." The two men stared at each other for a long few seconds before Hayes looked away.

"I'm NIS, too. At least I started out with them." He turned to Liam, "I told you back at your house I was able to pause the hit put out on your family. I could do that because I was originally part of the team that put the list together. But the virus was the priority. Killing one family on the whims of some politician held no interest for me. So I stopped it."

"You tried to stop it. You should know better than anyone, a top-level directive can't be stopped," Duchesne mused.

Liam was naturally suspicious of government functionaries, and he couldn't tell who was telling the truth here. He had several questions he wanted to ask, but had to stay focused on what was happening in the room. "So you're saying that government contractors came in and killed government soldiers and Marines, just so they could take my grandma?"

"No, you fool. I'm saying they were here to kill the 'rogue unit' and usurp my research. Bring it back on the reservation. The only reason they're still here is your Grandma. They couldn't have known she'd be here."

"Yes, she's a peculiar piece of research. A real coup. After all the killing and dying getting in here, I'm trying to make this trip worthwhile to my bosses. My colleagues and I were discussing her fate when you two wandered in."

Victoria addressed Hayes, "But would it kill you to go back to doing research with the government? Surely you'd have more resources than you do out here by yourself?"

He seemed reluctant to answer.

"Hayes?"

Liam was about to ask him, too, but Duchesne beat him. "Why don't you tell these fine kids what this is *really* all about?"

The red-headed woman hopped off the sill, and stood next to Hayes. She wrapped her arm around his waist, bolstering him. Then she said, "*Those* men are trying to destroy all of humanity. *We* are trying to save what's left of it."

"This is Jane. She's absolutely right." He let out a pained sigh. "There are three viruses out there. By a mad piece of luck, the flu this year was a particularly nasty strain. It was similar, in many respects, to the Spanish Flu of 1918. That killed millions, though today, with better medicine and heath care, it wasn't on track to even be noticed—a few extra sick here or there. But someone cloned that virus; made it an even more efficient killer. If things had gone as planned, it would have killed or sickened hundreds of millions worldwide. A terrible plague, yes, but one we could have survived."

After too long a delay, Duchesne prodded him, "But?"

"*But* we realized, too late I'm afraid, there was a third virus floating around. It was several orders of magnitude smaller than any living organism we knew about. We weren't looking for it. We really only know of it second-hand, even now. We can see its effects, but it's beyond our ability to see it with our equipment."

His brow furrowed. "And...unfortunately for you and me and billions of others...the clone virus was adversely affected by the theoretical one—we dubbed it the Quantum Virus because of its size. Our research teams watched as the flu virus was modified in various ways, depending on geography. We've studied dozens of zombies from around the world, each with their own adaptations based on where they originated."

Hayes let out another long sigh.

Liam was horrified, even though he'd seen the Chicago climbing zombies.

"In the end, instead of a manageable disease sickening hundreds of millions, it became a global extinction threat. It could kill every single person on the planet. Only dumb luck saved us. It was released so late in flu season it didn't have time to spread around to everyone through the typical coughing and sneezing."

Victoria's interest was medicine, so she pressed for answers. "But the virus *is* everywhere. Look around. Look out your window. There's nowhere the virus hasn't spread. So how can we have been saved?"

"What you see now is the vector of transmission for the Quantum Virus—the one they dubbed Extra-Ebola. It's spread primarily through saliva—biting. Anyone infected with it dies, but becomes desperate to continue ingesting more of the virus in the bloodstream. It *wants* to be spread into every living human and it uses the human host as the most efficient means of that transmission. It wants to spread into other animals, too, but fortunately there aren't many animals the stupid things can catch."

He looked directly at Victoria. "Our best guess is that just as the clone flu was affected by the Quantum Virus, the clone flu also affected the Quantum. They work together." With a fake laugh he said, "When flu season comes around again, we're going to have a doozie."

Victoria shook her head in disbelief.

Liam listened in rapt silence. He was finally getting his answers. He was dismayed to realize they weren't what he expected. No secret cures were out there. These are the men who would know. And Hayes had been fighting the virus all along. He had difficulty squaring that with the sight of him trying to kill Victoria. Was he himself responsible for hindering Hayes in the discovery of a cure? Something more was going on. One phrase was festooned with neon lights in his head from Hayes' explanation.

"*Our* virus." He spoke it out loud, quietly. "You said, it was 'our virus', didn't you? You made the clone." He pointed at him.

Hayes was good at pretending to be sheepish. Liam had seen it before. This time, his embarrassed look was completely authentic.

"I'm afraid that's true. I helped make it."

PATRIOT SNOWBALL

"Now we're getting somewhere." Duchesne seemed to enjoy Hayes' forced admissions. Liam's questions stacked up in his head.

Before he could ask, another NIS contractor walked in the room.

"The charges are set, sir."

Liam turned, thinking the voice was familiar, but he didn't recognize her.

"Excellent. Grab these guns," he pointed to Liam and Victoria's guns on the floor, "put them somewhere safe. Then just wait outside. We're almost ready." He turned to Hayes. "I'm in a hurry. Tell these kids about their Snowballer Grandma and we'll move on to the next order of business."

Liam involuntarily gulped. He knew this wasn't going to end well. But, he was also terminally curious.

"Liam, surely you've heard of the Patriot Snowball, right?"

"No, why?"

Both men looked at him like he was telling a lie.

"Seriously? That's impossible. Don't you read the news? Watch the news? Anything?"

He was reminded of a similar conversation on the day of the sirens. The librarian seemed incredulous he didn't follow the news in any form or fashion.

"Look guys, I don't read the news, I don't watch the news, I don't do squat with news. Just tell me already!"

Hayes laughed despite himself. "Well, you continue to amaze. I thought you of all people might have guessed what this was all about. Your Grandma Rose never told you?"

"Intel said she never contacted any of the family. She went completely off the grid," Duchesne stated matter-of-factly.

"Well there you have it. Your Grandma started the whole snowball rolling toward Washington D.C. and she was never heard from again. *Still* not ringing any bells?"

Liam searched his memory. Surely he'd remember his own Grandma Rose—she was Great-Grandma Marty's daughter-in-law— doing something to bring down the government. But he drew blanks. His only interactions with her in the past six months were getting a Christmas card with a crisp hundred-dollar bill as per usual, and then hearing his dad and Grandma Marty talking on the phone and mentioning Rose's name. That was *once*.

"I have *no* idea what you're talking about." He looked at Victoria, but she also had no sign of recognition on her face.

"Neither of you kids know what's happening in your own world? Wow."

Hayes sounded condescending, and Liam felt his hackles rising.

"Are you going to tell us or not?"

Duchesne laughed.

Hayes was a little more measured. "OK, after the President was sworn in back in January a movement of malcontents popped up out in Colorado—surely you know your Grandma was a congressperson from Colorado?" He waited to see Liam nod in the affirmative. "The movement started as a highway blockage, holding signs and complaining about crooked politics. They wrecked traffic in the entire city for a full day. When they broke up, a small cadre of people—they called themselves patriots—began walking toward D.C. with the express intent of overthrowing what they called the illegitimate government. They refused to follow an anti-American President."

Hayes watched for signs of recognition on Liam's face, but Liam had none to give. He shook his head and continued his story.

"The protesters regrouped at Liberty, Missouri, stating their cause was Liberty itself. Many more joined up. They continued walking east through the winter and into the spring. They got into Ohio and Rose herself appeared at the head of the column. She made a plea, or threat depending on your point of view, stating that any of her fellow congresspeople who abandoned the corrupt government and joined her would not be run out on a rail when she arrived. No one joined her, but the people loved her. More and more patriots began to follow her as the spring arrived and the weather got better. The joke in the news was that her cause was growing like a snowball. They named their march the Patriot Snowball. And it was rolling right for the seat of the most powerful government in human history."

"Dutch, you want to take it from your end?"

"Sure, *partner.*" He laughed. "I take my orders directly from...the top. Sometimes things need to be done outside the law, you know? My bosses wanted the problem—gone. I warned Rose privately what was heading her way, but she never took me seriously. One day—poof—she disappeared. She escaped us." He let out a fake sigh. "Still, a warning without consequences is worth nothing, so we expanded the order. We jobbed up a list of Rose's family members—

every...single...one—and got to work eliminating them. A small price to pay for threatening Uncle Sam, don't you think?"

Liam finally found his bad guy. He was too exhausted to summon the anger he knew he deserved.

"The Snowballers marched on to Washington and actually made it into the White House, can you believe it? The damned secret service wouldn't protect him against his own constituents. But he got the last laugh. He unleashed the plague on them—he thought it would be cleaner than nuking them. Hayes was busy in his government lab building his Frankenstein when the call from the President came in, and to his credit, he did his duty and released it upon the world. The President put a bullet in his mouth when the dolt realized it was much more destructive than Doc H and his friends said it would be. I guess the old Socialist won in the end. We're all equal in the eyes of the infected."

Another laugh.

"For my part, I had teams out sweeping for your family when the balloon went up. We never found Rose, bless her heart, but we did manage to get a team on your Marty here. Funny thing, too, my report said the agents released a zombie which attacked her private nurse, Angie I believe, who then went in and killed Martinnette Peters. *The report said she was dead.* That might have been the end of the story, and we'd have never known, but her name showed up as 'alive' when Hayes entered her information into his reports from under the Arch. Can you imagine the good luck? I sent two agents to check her house to find out why the paperwork was falsified, and they reported her body was gone. Somehow she escaped an infected right in her own home. I wish she were awake so I could congratulate her."

He bent over Grandma and shouted at her, "Are you awake?" She didn't stir.

Liam knew she had survived because she ran outside her house to escape the sick nurse.

Seemingly satisfied, the agent continued. "Hayes said he was keeping an eye on her for his research, but we were keeping an eye on her, too. It was only after your name came up when I took your picture on the bridge overpass—Mr. Sam Stevens—we put it all together how she got away and where she was going. From there, we tried bombing her, we asked the Marines to grab her, and we even embedded some Special Forces guys into a small group of troublemakers straight out of *Mad Max* to liquidate her in her Boy Scout tent. In the end, it was Doug who brought her to us."

"*Not* to you."

"Well, it's the same thing."

"If the President's dead, why are you still following his orders?"

Duchesne looked at Victoria. "You really think the President is the only one in charge? There are over 500 representatives in the halls of power, not to mention scores of judges, generals, and powerful executives in the defense industry all willing to do *anything* to protect their way of life. They're probably all sitting in their bunkers somewhere, just waiting for their fresh start. The government is going to go on, plague or no plague. My mission doesn't stop just because a few of them are dead, or because things are bitey out in the world. We each have our parts to play. Mine is to terminate troublemakers with professional efficiency. Hayes' is to ensure the plague wipes out the malcontent citizenry. I think he's done a fine job, don't you?"

Yes, bully for him.

2

Grandma was with Al. She was also asleep in the room with everyone standing around her—she could hear them if she focused on their voices—but she was in a dark space, standing outside the door she'd seen before in this place.

"Hello, Marty. Are you ready to open this door?"

She looked inside. The huge ugly computer was still sitting on the wooden table, just as it was on a prior visit. Al called it an 8088.

"What's changed? Why will I be able to open it now?"

"Ah, an excellent question. And one for which you deserve an answer. Walk with me a minute."

Al turned from the door and strolled away. The darkness fell back as if it were smoke, and she could see a whole universe of stars above her, just as she had before. He took her out into the open space near the foot of the waterfall.

"Yes, prior visits I showed you what I needed to show you. This time, you will see it all. Or as much as human eyes can see."

As she came out of the darkness she was overcome with emotion at the scale and beauty of this "Heaven" as she understood it. Where once there was one bright waterfall pouring into a pool ensconced in a picturesque patch of grass and flowers, now there were separate and distinct waterfalls of all sizes and shapes stretching off to the horizon in on either side of her. They glowed like beacons in the night. It was hard to see the darkened land behind the waterfalls, but each had a middle landing like the one on which she was standing. From there, a second shorter waterfall spilled from the landing down to a choppy sea—which also stretched in both directions as well as directly away from them to the horizons. Above it all were stars. An impossible number of stars. So many that the whole scene was well lit by them.

It took Marty's breath away. She stumbled and felt the desire to sit. A rocky bench was off to one side, and she sat heavily and faced the waterfalls along the coast to her left, away from her own. Away from Al.

"Is this really Heaven?"

"This isn't your Heaven, I'm sorry to say. This is the multiverse. Mind you, this is still an internalized representation your mind can accept. But it's a grand reflection of reality I must admit. Your brain truly is a wonderful place."

"This—is real? Not just in my head?"

"Yes my dear. Each waterfall is a completely separate universe. Each waterfall has its own rules. Is run by its own caretaker. Some are young and fresh. Others are more mature. We meet at homeowners' meetings and have tea."

She turned around and gave him her best stink eye.

With a curt laugh, he said, "I'm sorry, Marty. I don't want you to get too taken with what you see here. Some people can't handle it."

"Others come here?"

He smiled. "Let's talk about *you* coming here."

"All right," she said as she looked back to the coastline, "do all the waterfalls drain into this ocean?"

"Yes, all roads lead to the ocean, if you will allow me to mix metaphors. And this ocean gives back to all the waterfalls in ways that are hard to describe with simple words. The ocean is the engine which drives the universes. Perhaps if you observe for a while, you will see."

Marty sat there for a time. As her eyes adjusted to the darkness, she became aware of flashes of light under the water of the ocean. At times, bright and moving, as if lightning was striking under the surface. Sometimes a dim explosion of brightness seemed to encompass the entire ocean at once. It was impossible to see any patterns, but she was content to say she saw the lights. The energy flashes made the water appear as a deep translucent green color.

"It's the most beautiful thing I've ever seen, Al. Or whoever you are. Thank you for showing this to me." Tears streamed down her cheeks, as it became too much to take in. Between the infinity of stars above, and depth of the sea below, it defied description.

"Please Marty, don't be upset by what I'm showing you. Take solace that you are only seeing a tiny fraction of this shoreline. It goes on in each direction, pretty much forever. Your mind couldn't handle seeing more of it at one time."

He sat next to her and changed tact. "You've succeeded, Marty. You, Liam, and Victoria were able to work together to get you here. To talk to me. The final piece is to get inside that door back there."

"It isn't really a door, is it?"

"You're catching on. The door represents something blocking you from doing what you need to do. The computer is the answer to your problem. A problem that should be fixed as soon as possible."

"What problem? And why the delay? Why not tell me this two weeks ago?"

"The balance is delicate, my dear. Zombies roam your world with impunity. Bad men are hastening your collective destruction. Each minute lost is irreplaceable. But as I've said before, the answer must come from you, not me."

Marty sighed. Every visit to this place was more frustrating than the last. She'd seen Liam's memory from one of his books—"

"The book was *Earth Abides*. It's one of Liam's favorites. You'll have to ask him why it's so important to him."

"And why show me Victoria's death?"

"I think you already know that. Your memory of your own daughter's death those many years ago is a big reason why you and Victoria bonded. That, and Liam liked her." He laughed. "All right, that was probably a big part of why you all bonded."

Marty searched her feelings. The dream she'd seen had indeed shown her a memory from her own deep past—one she'd like to forget.

When she was a young girl, freshly married, she got into a car accident in which her young daughter died. It was something she had tried to forget for over eighty years, though every day she thought about her. Of course meeting a young girl named Victoria would affect her judgment.

"Did you put her there, Al? Victoria, I mean. Put her under that tree that day?"

He smiled, but said nothing.

"And when I saw her in the backseat of that SUV. I saw—"

"Yes, you carry your painful memory and she carries hers. She was assaulted by her fiancé—a real dirtbag as she discovered—just after they were engaged to be married. That's what drove her to leave Colorado and go to St. Louis. But the pain was fresh when you first met her. I think you and Liam saved her in more ways than one."

So many questions.

"What about when I saw her in that dark alley? She left a friend behind. She was about to be bitten."

Al took a long time to reply. "Not every vision is an exact representation of reality. She may not have been bitten when she ran that night, but she wishes she was. That's what she sees when she dreams of her escape."

"Oh my. Poor girl."

Victoria had told her and Liam she ran all night to escape the zombies in downtown St. Louis. It made sense if she imagined herself getting caught, it would be while leaving a friend behind.

"Al, please tell me. How will this help any of us in curing the plague?"

Al smiled. "That, my dear Martinette, is the right question, at the right time, for the right person. Come with me and I'll show you."

They stood up, striding for the window.

3

"That's not true. Liam, I admit I released the original virus, but you have to believe me when I say I never intended for it to be *this* effective. I'm really trying to reverse it."

"You're doing a piss poor job of it. That's why I'm here to clean up your mess. Get this research," Duchesne nodded to the bed, "to the fortress over in Illinois where some real scientists can look at the data."

Hayes seemed beaten. It was a look Liam had never seen, for real anyway. He feigned it several times.

"Is there rescue over in Illinois? Can we *all* go to the fortress?"

"Well, little lady, what do you think? Do you think the government is just sitting out there somewhere in a bunker just waiting for its citizens to show up so it can feed and clothe them in this time of need? Is that really your view of what the Federal government is for?"

"I always just thought...you know, they'd want to help out."

"There's a fortress all right. And the US of A Army is parked there right now with its tanks and Humvees and every weapon you can think of pointed *outside* their walls at all the fine citizens that stumble their direction. Living or dead, it don't matter in the least. The whole city of Chicago must have gotten a memo because the dead are stacked ten-deep in the fields north of the fort. They built it too close to population if you ask me."

He turned to face her. "And no, you can't go there. They don't let in just anyone."

Duchesne leaned over Grandma, checking to see if she was awake.

Or alive.

The thought prompted him to ask. "Is she doing OK? Why isn't she waking up?" He felt his heartbeat downshift and start to spin wildly.

"Liam, that's an excellent question. But before I tell you, I need to give you something."

It happened so fast Liam could only reconstruct it after the fact. In one fluid motion, Duchesne sidestepped along the bed and swung his fist. He connected with his stomach, sending him to the floor. When he was down, the agent kicked him hard in the face. He missed connecting with his nose by a couple inches, but the sole of his foot scraped painfully across his cheek. He stayed down, hoping that was all.

Victoria and Hayes both moved in his direction, but the bodyguard yelled something and everyone froze. He couldn't remember because he'd hit the floor pretty hard and his ears rang like mad.

His mind came back into focus as Victoria lifted him. Duchesne had gone back to his chair, but was hunched over with his elbows on his knees, rubbing his hands together. He spoke in a low voice.

"That's for making me look like an ass back on the bridge. I've been wanting to do that since the minute you left my sight. I never dreamed I'd have this chance. I have to say, that felt pretty good."

He sat back up, talking to the room.

"This is what's going to happen. My team and I are going to take Ms. Peters here down to our boat. We're going to get into said boat, motor to the far shore where our chopper is waiting, and live happily ever after in the cornfields of Illinois." He paused with a little drama before continuing. "Well, *most* of us will live happily."

"Will you try to take care of her? Keep her alive?" Liam had asked the same question of Hayes not long ago.

"Are you kidding me? I don't care what happens to your dear old grammy. They can rip her apart as far as I'm concerned. As long as someone who knows what the hell they're doing is analyzing the results —and not *this* goof—she'll have proven her worth. If she has to suffer so the rest of us can live, so be it."

The pain in his stomach was intense. He wondered if he ruptured his stomach or other internal organs. It felt that bad. While hunched over and being supported by Victoria, he continued to press Duchesne. "Take us with you. We'll help you take care of Grandma and go to your fortress, or whatever, and not cause any problems."

"Ha! Not cause problems, you say? Like you didn't cause any problems when two of my agents died in your Grandma's house? Like not cause any problems when you sent a whole army of refugees into the quiet hinterlands of southern Missouri? Like not cause any problems when you skillfully avoided the U.S. Marines and the bombing of your neighborhood? Is that what you mean by not cause problems, because if that's *not* causing problems, I think I'm genuinely afraid of you if you *are* trying to cause problems. You're a lone boy, and you've cost this country millions of dollars, maybe billions of dollars, in terms of lives lost, damage to property, and long-term financial ruin of a significant portion of the population of St. Louis. That's all you and your 'not causing problems'."

"Liam also helped destroy a perfectly good railroad bridge over a river when we came out of St. Louis. You might want to charge him for that." Victoria seemed to revel in goading Duchesne. She did the same back on the bridge.

"Very funny, young lady. I'd punch you, too, if you didn't already have two black eyes."

On his feet, Duchesne said something to the bodyguard and the big man left the room. He then turned to Hayes. "I'm outta time. Do you want to tell them, or shall I?"

Hayes had a downtrodden look. He was either still sulking from his earlier embarrassment or this was something new. When he looked up, he wasn't looking at Liam. He was looking at Grandma. He moved in her direction, reached behind her pillow, and pulled something into view.

"Liam, I'm *real sorry* to have to tell you this..."

Liam didn't hear the rest of the statement. He knew. Grandma had already been infected with the deadly virus. The reason she was so quiet was that her body was absorbing it into her blood, just as Bart had done back at Elk Meadow. When Bart woke up, he was sentient for a while, but devolved into a zombie not long after.

Grandma had minutes to live...

4

Marty walked with Al for a few moments, then she entered her own memory.

"Al, no. Not again. I can't bear it."

"You must, my dear. You must face your darkest fear before you can look ahead."

"But..."

She fell into the dream.

"I'm so happy! Al just bought me a new car. Well, he bought it for us. Mr. and Mrs. Aloysius Peters. I just love saying the name." She twirled in the grass of her backyard like a giddy schoolgirl. She wasn't much older than one.

"I can't wait to drive it. Al showed me the controls. I'm *sure* I can. But he said not to."

She ran on tiptoes from the yard and into her garage. It was fresh and new. She was looking at a polished black Model T Ford. Her mind registered it as a 1926 Runabout—they had just bought it used from Al's father.

She eyed the driver's door of the vehicle. "What would it hurt to drive it? I could take a *quick* ride around the block. Al would never know I was gone."

"I shouldn't."

"Should I?"

Her emotions became confusing here. Marty recognized both restraint and abandon in her younger self. The straight-laced young lady had never done anything so *illicit*.

"I'm an adventurer!"

She jumped in and looked at the spartan controls. She walked through the starting process Al showed her, ending with stepping on the starter on the floor. Her happiness was through the roof.

She proceeded to back out of the garage, deftly working the three pedals on the floor while adjusting the spark and throttle on the steering column.

"I can do this."

She rolled the car forward down the narrow alleyway and paused at the edge of the cross street.

Her elation fused with dread as she wondered if anyone would recognize her, and if they did, would they tell Al his wayward wife was on a joyride in their prized new Ford.

The confusion and danger thrilled her. She released the brake and turned right with a little boost to the throttle. Youthful Martinette's long blonde hair began to flow wildly behind her. She was now in second gear and loving life.

"I'm doing it. I'm so proud of myself."

While the car never really got going too fast, it felt like riding a bolting stallion to her young self. She controlled all that power.

She could see into the backyards of houses as she passed. More often than not, a woman was tending laundry on the drying lines, or holding a baby or two. Those women were securely tied down just as surely as those laundry cables.

"I am, too."

"But in *this* moment I'm free."

Marty recognized the struggle of her younger self.

Her mind was aflutter. Unfiltered joy rode with abject fear. The mixture was intoxicating.

She drove for several minutes. A flash of disappointment as she turned the car around.

"I must get back. Things to do. I've had my fun. I wish Al could be proud of me."

Her feelings fluctuated between desire and regret now. Telling her husband she had taken a joyride would be a minor scandal. Better to just park it and ignore it happened at all. She felt sorry for feeling that way, but sometimes a white lie helped keep the peace in marriage. She at least believed what she thought.

Hair blowing, she spun the iron horse back into the alley, slowing slightly, heading for the wooden corral behind her home.

"I can turn into the garage at this speed. I know I can. I'm doing great."

She made the turn quickly and deftly, ecstatic she could do it, and then slammed on the brake. She felt a bump as the car decelerated, but she knew she didn't hit the front wall because she still had a couple feet to spare.

"That would be a disaster."

"Mercy. What a ride that was."

Car off. Door open. Step down.

And she saw it. The shoe.

Confusion.

"Impossible. It *can't* be."

Slowly, Grandma moved to the front of the car. What young Marty saw was so emotionally powerful she still couldn't see it now. Grandma had completely blocked it.

It was her first baby. Barely 18 months. A girl. Martinette had left her sound asleep in her crib in the backyard when she snuck off for her joy ride. When it happened for real, she had run away screaming. She stole one quick glance at her daughter lying on the cold concrete. Al came and took baby Victoria away, leaving her with nothing but an empty hole in her soul.

Her emotions became a storm of pain and depression.

A voice in her head said, "Marty, you *must* look."

"Al, Victoria is dead. I killed her. I killed my little girl."

"I know, my love. I beg you. Please look at her."

The grief of nearly ninety years spilled out, and Marty was racked with sobs.

"I just can't, Al. Please don't make me."

She felt Al's hand on her shoulder. Far away and yet so immediate in this dream. "I trust you to do this. You are my fighter. Always were."

Young Martinette opened her eyes. She used her hand on the side of the car to pull herself toward the front. Toward what she knew was a tiny ruined body.

Her hands were soaked from perspiration. Her heart was overtaxed from anxiety. She pushed on, rounding the front bumper.

She looked.

On the floor, there was no evidence of her baby. Instead, she saw Liam's phone.

She fainted, but did not wake up.

5

"Hayes. Why? Why now?"

"Liam, listen to me. They were going to take her away. This was my last chance to test my theory. I think your Grandma can survive it. I need to see it happen."

Liam didn't know what he should be feeling. He felt like he did when he first escaped from Angie, nearly two weeks ago. When he evaded her and reached his home, he sat down and felt *empty*. He felt nothing. This moment was a mirror of that one. He felt absolutely nothing at all.

Grandma was dead. It was all for nothing. He was—

Victoria chirped. The whole room looked at her.

A second chirp.

She steadied Liam so he could stand on his own, then with a slightly red face, she pulled her phone out of her bra. When he saw it, he recalled she pulled it one other time. It was within the first few minutes they'd been together back when they'd met at the Arch. She hadn't used it or mentioned it since then.

"I usually keep it off. I've been trying to save the power and only check it once a day to see if my parents tried to contact me. I must have left it on."

She looked at the face of the phone first with shock, then sadness.

"This has to be some kind of joke. Look at this." She handed the phone to Liam.

Reading from the text log, Liam said, "Need to kill the power to building. Stop the sirens." He looked up with confusion. "It says it's from *my* phone."

"Well, where's your phone?" Victoria asked. "I thought you gave it to Grandma."

"I did. Someone must have taken it from her."

Duchesne seemed only half-interested. His tall associate pressed his ear bud, then whispered something to his boss.

"OK, we're ready to go. I like your friend's thinking. We were going to blow the stairwell doors for this building so you'd be trapped in here, but we'll go ahead and place a charge on the power generator on our way out. Yeah, that's a great idea actually. That ought to make things interesting for the whole city, eh?"

"No! If you cut the power all the doors will...unlock."

"And how is that my problem?"

Hayes looked at everyone before making the realization. "You're leaving us *all* here, aren't you?"

"Smart man! I don't think we'll be needing your services anymore. I'd just as soon kill you all where you stand, but I think it's fitting you die at the hands of your own menagerie, don't you? Once we blow all the doors, and the power, this place will be zombie headquarters for St. Louis. With a little luck, the old people you tossed to the ground will come back up and have words for you."

Duchesne whistled and the woman came in with her weapon drawn. She stood by the other bodyguard, their message clear: "Stay back."

"I assume we're all adults here. You know enough not to try anything tricky with my two friends pointing rifles at you all and zombie grandma. No one needs to get hurt. Now, back against the window if you don't mind."

Liam was leafing through every book he'd ever read, looking for the answer to this riddle. How to stop a madman from taking his grandma away from him forever. He didn't think he could take the agent in a fight, nor did he consider even for the briefest second he could eliminate the two guards pointing harm in his direction. Unlike his books, there was no opportunity for him to be the hero.

"Nice and easy, everyone."

The big bodyguard slung his rifle, then picked up the frail form of Grandma from the bed. He was surprisingly gentle, and due to his size, she appeared as if she was a small child over his shoulder. He carried her out of the room, making for the stairwell.

Duchesne walked out next, followed by the woman. She slowly walked backward, keeping them in check. Liam wondered how often it happened to her that her prisoners sprung for her with their bare hands. When she was at the threshold of the door, she pulled it shut. Just before it closed completely, she said, "If we see you come out before we're on the stairs..." She didn't finish it but she raised her rifle in Liam's direction.

When the door clicked shut, Liam flung himself at Hayes. He was partially deflected by Jane, but he made contact with the man's jaw. Liam winced as his knuckles felt broken. Hayes reacted in an instant, twisting himself and Liam to the ground. The battle was over in moments.

"Liam, you have to listen to me. We can still save Grandma. I didn't inject her with zombie blood."

He had him in a headlock so Liam couldn't respond except with gasps of air. After many seconds, he stopped struggling and gave a thumbs up sign. At that, Hayes relented enough so he could talk. He didn't know what to say. He was used to hating Hayes. The new Hayes was confusing him.

"This may be the first time you don't have a witty retort for me."

With a groan, Liam could only say, "Yeah, this may be the first time since we met that I sort of like you. It feels weird. Especially since I just punched you."

They both got up and dusted themselves off. The two women also stepped apart, though they hadn't been fighting.

Liam tried to be nonchalant about the whole affair. "So, about that rescue..."

SINCE THE SIRENS

Jane was Hayes' assistant, or friend, or girlfriend. Liam couldn't figure it out, and didn't ask. She was at the big window of the main room in the suite, scanning the wreckage below the Arch. "I've found them. They're leaving the railroad tunnel."

Liam and Victoria jumped off the couch so they could see. Jane was trying to locate Grandma and her three captors.

"You found her?" Liam asked.

Duchesne said they had boats.

"You might be able to see her. South leg, heading south on the tracks."

Jane gave him the binos and pointed to the bomb-cratered landscape that was once the lush grounds under the Arch. The dead bodies, downed trees, ruined walkways, and the massive flocks of scavenger birds had turned the parkland into an ugly slice of hell. The Mississippi River was the same ribbon of muddy and ugly it had always been, but now it deposited the world's litter into the large pile of wreckage entangled in the piers of the Poplar Street Bridge.

It took a few seconds to orient on the position and adjust the binoculars, but he saw her. A tiny figure carried by a giant and followed by two normal sized people. He was at such a height he could see them, but so far away he couldn't make out much detail. He dropped the binoculars and looked closer to the hotel. The zombies below the building were a throbbing froth of death.

"How did they get by all of the zombies?" He no longer cared about using that word. He had to know how to catch up with Grandma.

Hayes knew. "I'm sure they took the pedestrian tunnel. It goes from the parking garage into the Arch museum. It's all underground."

Hayes had returned their weapons and ammo, and even shared a little food.

"Liam, there's something else in this building. Something you should know if you're going to go out there to get her."

Liam wolfed down a grain bar as he listened.

"This building is designed as a crude prison for the zombie samples we've been bringing in for months from around the world. But it also became the focal point for other pieces of research. One of the key discoveries the long-gone research team made was in brainwave manipulation. The brains of the infected retain a very narrow band of electrical activity—usually core functions such as muscle control, motor functions, and the most rudimentary cognitive functions related to...we assume...sating hunger. They don't run on evil spirits, like the movies." He guffawed, trying to be funny, but he had an unreceptive audience.

"Anyway, we were able to modify all 200-something tornado sirens in the St. Louis area with special equipment which could broadcast on that frequency. When the sirens went off, the message went out to the infected: Run!"

"Hayes, I hate you again."

"I deserve that. But don't you see, it was perfect. The sirens go off and the small number of infected in their homes or sitting in backyards run out to spread their cough. Before all this happened, we actually thought we'd have trouble getting our virus to spread. We worried the flu victims would curl up in bed and we'd miss our opportunity."

"And are they working now? We saw tons of zombies walking back toward downtown when we were in our boat. Is that why they're all packed against this building?"

Hayes laughed, but not in a funny way this time.

"We have digital sirens on the roof of this building. Sort of massive dog whistles designed to be subsonic for humans, but the sound is like a dinner bell for the infected. We were field testing a way to bring them all down here so we could dispose of them. Imagine how easy it would be if we could gather them in one place."

"So we have to get down on the ground, run through the crowd of dinner bell zombies, get into the tunnel, and then deal with the mercenaries before they can get her across the river to their impenetrable base. Sound about right?"

"Yes. That's right. But I do have a plan."

After hearing it, Liam really wanted to devise an alternate plan and dazzle everyone. Unfortunately, he couldn't think of any alternative that didn't involve fighting the thousands of zombies at the base of the hotel in close combat. He'd have to work with Hayes' plan.

"I'm a big fan of George S. Patton. Studied his books. He always had his staff prepare three contingencies for every situation, the assumption being he would never be caught with his pants down. At the Battle of the Bulge, he was able to march his soldiers in the dead of winter to help repulse the Germans a hundred miles away. This was because of his excellent foresight. A detail man. I like to think I'm a worthy student of his ways."

He paused to watch Liam smack his lips. Liam smiled nervously after noisily inhaling the food.

"Sorry."

"All right. Escape route number one was the stairwell you came up —and Dutch went down. I had all the doors of the south stairwell welded shut so the staff could descend without fear of zombies stumbling in during those early days. But that's ruined now."

Liam interrupted. "Why did you put city names on all those doors?"

"Isn't it obvious? It's where we got all the zombies on each floor. Try to keep up."

Hayes walked back and forth in the kitchen area while he explained his thought process. "So, escape route number two is the one I'm giving to you, and escape route number three is one I'm saving for Jane and myself."

"Why do we get this one? It seems really dangerous."

"Because I'm afraid of heights."

Liam couldn't tell if he was serious, but he wasn't smiling which was unusual for the terminally jovial man.

Victoria asked about the third route, but Hayes didn't think Patton would reveal his strategy in detail until it was absolutely necessary. He emulated the dead general.

They hashed over some details while they stood in the kitchen and all of them jumped at the loud banging on the hotel stairwell door.

"I think the infected have come up the stairs now that Dutch has gone back down. He probably wedged open all the interior doors if I know him. We couldn't go down the stairs if we wanted to."

He was resigned to Hayes' plan. He and Victoria let Hayes and Jane lead them through a door to an adjacent penthouse suite where the scope of Hayes' study of Patton was on full display. One of the windows had all its glass removed and was covered with heavy plastic sheeting. A large spool of metal cable was bolted to the concrete floor. Several pieces of rigging and safety harnesses were lying nearby.

"How did you guys know to build this thing? This is amazing."

"You must not read as many zombie and global infection books as your boyfriend. *Always* assume things are going to go to hell. Always."

Liam wasn't going to agree, no matter how right he was.

"OK then. So you unwind the spool of wire out the window, then Liam and me latch on and scoot ourselves down to the roof of the garage. Just like that?"

Hayes responded in the affirmative, though he seemed to enjoy her obvious discomfort.

"I should mention there may be zombies at the windows as you scale down the exterior. I don't think they'll give you any problems— the glass is pretty thick—but I wouldn't window shop on your descent if I were you."

Liam was still deeply disturbed. "Is there anything else you aren't telling us?"

He brought back his normal joviality. "Oh, plenty. I don't have a week to tell you all my secrets. You'll just have to trust me on this one."

Trust you? Over my dead body. Wait—

Minutes later, they were ready to go. Jane peeled back the heavy plastic with a flourish so the room was open to the outside. The effect was dizzying. Liam held on to the spool of wire with a death grip. Victoria, he noticed, clenched his arm with both her hands.

Hayes pulled at the cable so it began to unspool. He attached a heavy piece of steel to the end of the wire and placed it just outside the window.

"We'll let this thing go down to the bottom, then you guys can start your journey." He threw a switch and the spool began to unwind automatically. A small motor hummed as the wire drained out the window. They all watched the wire go.

Moments later, from somewhere in the building below, they heard a loud bang. It was chased by a slight vibration, and then the power went out. The spool ceased rotating.

Hayes' only statement was, "Uh oh." He wore real panic in his eyes.

I wonder if we just lost plan number two?

2

"What happened?"

"Well, my dear Liam, the power went out. He put the explosives on a timer. Dutch was true to his word." He fiddled with the spool as he spoke. "This means we have to get this thing spinning manually. I don't think it will affect your journey, or mine, you'll be happy to know. However, if the power is out below us, the doors are all unlocked now. It won't take the infected very long to push them open and get up here in greater numbers."

"Why didn't you secure them inside the rooms?"

"Must you criticize everything I do?" He looked at Liam with no humor.

"Is this a big deal for us? I mean we aren't going back down on the inside." Victoria asked Hayes, but she looked at Liam.

"Until a couple dozen types of zombies run outside and tear apart St. Louis..." He said it to be funny, but Hayes must have seen the looks on their faces. Instead, he said, "No, you'll be just fine. Let me worry about them. Get into those harnesses before something else goes wrong."

Liam had no intention of ignoring them, but at the moment he had no alternatives. He and Victoria suited up in the climbing gear.

The spool spun freely as more wire fired out the window—pulled by gravity and the heavy weight on the end. It wasn't long before the spool locked up once all the wire was depleted.

"There will be extra slack at the bottom. You have to go now. We need to be going our separate ways."

Not one to argue, Liam maneuvered himself so he was attached to the wire, and then worked his way to the edge. Victoria attached herself to the wire as well, then stood behind him.

Liam couldn't shake the feeling he was about to be betrayed.

"Hayes, if this is how you intend to kill us, can you just shoot us instead. I can't stand the suspense." He was being smarmy as part of his bravado, but deep down he was being honest.

Hayes laughed. "Come on, you said you were starting to like me. I prefer you alive. We've had our differences, and you drive me crazy with your persistence, but we want the same thing now. Plus, as I've said so many times, if I wanted you dead, I would have just killed you with my sentry gun or a hundred other ways and been done with you. I'm not going to murder you for sport."

That gives me absolutely no comfort.

Liam had learned to mistrust anything Hayes said. It had served him well the past two weeks, and despite his apparent falling out with Duchesne, he was still part of the team that destroyed the entire world. That alone was enough to engender mistrust. But he was over a barrel, and was about to be outside at 300 feet...

Liam fumbled his way out the window and steadied himself on the exterior glass as he got his bearings in the shifting perspectives and geometry. He released the control clasp and dropped several quick steps so Victoria could join him.

"Come on out, the weather's beautiful."

"Oh Liam, I think I'm going to throw up."

"Then why didn't *you* go first?" He tried to laugh it off, but he worried she might be serious. He wanted to believe he'd be chivalrous about it, but knew he'd probably be so grossed out he'd toss his cookies as well.

"If I throw up, I'm sorry in advance."

Liam went down a few more paces, willing some distance from her. She came out and gently released her grip enough to drop to the floor below the open window.

Hayes stuck his head out the gap above them. "This is where we say goodbye, Liam. You've fallen into my trap!" He gave a maniacal laugh and retreated back into the room, out of sight.

Oh no.

"If this is the end, I love you, Victoria."

"I love you, Liam."

Liam closed his eyes, waiting.

Twenty or thirty seconds went by when Hayes returned to the window. Liam looked up when he heard the voice.

"You guys are so sweet. I'm just messing with you. A small payback for all the trouble you've caused me. Oh, and watch floor twenty. Those are the ones with pheromones that can make you go love crazy. That could be awkward. Ciao!"

He left with a curt wave.

"I hate him again. Let's keep moving."

"I would, but there's a creepy zombie staring at me inside this room. I can't look away. He's the biggest person I've ever seen—a giant. And his face is—horrible. But his eyes..."

Victoria was a floor above him, so he couldn't see what had her attention. "We don't have time to sight-see. We have to move down. Now!"

She loosed the harness grip and slipped down the wire to meet him. "Oh my. This building is horrible. But at least my tummy feels better now that I know we aren't going to die out here." The breeze picked up, as if daring him to agree.

They continued down the wire. After several minutes, they had passed eight or nine floors. He paused to wait for her to catch up.

"Hey, I like the view from down here."

"Seriously, Liam? *That's* what you're thinking about?" She laughed, but it was forced.

He laughed, too, but when he took his eyes from her he saw inside the window next to him. He nearly jumped out of his harness when a zombie dressed in desert camo army fatigues threw himself at the glass. The pane rattled, and small spidery cracks formed, but it didn't break open. The zombie continued banging on the glass with his head and arms, but it made no further progress besides smearing blood where it impacted.

"Victoria, there's a zombie in this window. Don't let him scare you."

"Don't worry about me. Zombies are nothing when I'm hanging desperately to the side of tall buildings."

He continued but she stopped at the window.

"Oh Liam. You didn't tell me he was cute." She giggled.

Cute?

Hayes' warning echoed in his head.

Are we on floor twenty?

He tried to estimate, but from the outside it was impossible. The soldier zombie continued to throw himself at the window, inches from Victoria. She seemed unconcerned, and dangerously so.

"Just keep moving!"

There was no obvious way to use the clasp to go up the wire. Pulling her might be required...

"Oh. Boo." She sounded pouty, but did move after a long pause.

Liam only let out his breath when she was a floor below the strange man in the window.

Victoria seemed to sense the change too. "That was weird. I got all dizzy and...giddy." She laughed it off.

He laughed too, but only said, "I know the feeling." He wasn't going to bring up his own experience with one of the odd zombies. Back near the beginning, he had expressed his love for a zombie girl, *in front of his grandma.*

On the way down, they peeked in all the windows; they saw many odd zombie behaviors. In some rooms, the zombies merely watched them go by, as if they were drugged. Some ignored them entirely, which was strange for a lot of reasons. Some ran in and out the open room doors into the interior of the hotel. Some rooms were full of zombies fighting among themselves. The blood in those rooms covered the walls and much of the windows too. One large suite was stuffed with children zombies. One room had either dogs or wolves. It was hard to tell as they had shredded the beds and used the materials to fashion hidey-holes. Lots of zombies threw themselves at the glass, but always in a random fashion and to no effect. They were three or four floors above the roof of the garage when he looked in a window and screamed.

"Nooo!"

A group of zombie men in green biohazard suits hit the glass at the same time. The glass cracked audibly. He knew he should just keep dropping, but the horror in front of him was unbelievable. His hands wouldn't move him down.

After the first strike, two of the three fell to the floor at the base of the large pane. The third went to the back of the room. He guessed the man had a chance to break through if he hit it where the spidering was the worst.

"Victoria, move it. Now!"

He dropped down the wire, hoping she would follow. However, she was slow to move.

The glass above exploded outward and the running man fell out the window. His trajectory took him too far above Liam, and Victoria was still too high. He glanced off the wire, and pushed it away from the building. Liam bounced out, then banged hard against the glass of the floor below. The zombie's protective hood flew in a different direction as he flailed at the air on his way down.

"You have to come down fast. That window's open!"

He didn't know if he needed to tell her the obvious, but he wasn't taking any chances. Even so, she was still several seconds delayed before she started to move.

"My harness is grabbing on the wire. I'm coming."

Liam looked up to make sure she got by the open window without incident. He was surprised when a hand reached out and pulled her entirely out of his sight. The strength of the zombie was incredible. It managed to pull him up several feet as it pulled Victoria—and the cable —inside the room above.

Oh God, no. This is it.

One of the green plastic-covered feet near the base of the window popped out the window, then went back inside as if in pursuit of prey. Victoria struggled in the room. She grunted in counterpoint to the moaning gurgles of her zombie captors. She screamed loudly, then shot a gun several times. He recognized the small-caliber pistol.

Victoria "sprang" back out of the window above. She was pulled through the window by the tension on the wire. He also dropped several feet as the slack returned. She dangled about, then steadied herself.

"Go! Go!" She descended below the dangerous gaping maw, and kept moving. She caught up to Liam in a few seconds but grabbed herself just before her feet hit the top of his head.

"There are more!"

Liam looked up and saw them. Two more faces hung outside the window. Not the green-covered guys. One of them was a bloodied woman in a business suit. She jumped out the window. Another took her place. He watched in horror as the woman was only a foot or two from him as she sped by.

The next one yelled from above. More faces found the opening too.

He allowed his clasp to drop him many feet at a time, willing it to get him to the bottom. Several more zombies had either jumped or were pushed out as the number of faces in the window continued to grow. One managed to lay a hand on Victoria as she dipped below them, eliciting a scream. She made better time as they neared the bottom.

Thirty seconds later, a zombie wearing a blue football jersey managed to get his arms around the wire as he fell out. His momentum flung him around the wire as he fell. He spun in circles as he came down, causing the wire itself to vibrate and move. Liam watched the man fall toward Victoria at a high rate of speed for twenty or thirty feet, and at the last moment, his bloodied arms released as if to grab her. He slammed into the glass of the tower and then deflected away from them both. His body rattled on the pavement of the garage.

Victoria had been looking down the whole time.

He looked up with a wan smile and shouted, "Only a few more feet. You're doing great."

3

Liam touched down on the top level of the garage, surrounded by the accumulating bodies of the zombies that continued to fall out the window above. He stepped away from Victoria's path as he undid his harness. When she arrived, they made short work of hers.

"Thank you, Lord, for watching over us."

The roof of the garage was more or less empty of zombies, though the rest of the hotel grounds swarmed with them. They jogged a short distance to get out of the path of the jumpers. One fell every couple seconds now, and they made sickly crunches as they impacted.

"And please help these poor souls," Victoria added.

"OK, we go in with our rifles," he said as he unslung his. "Check to make sure the safety is off. Make sure you can grab extra magazines. Try to keep calm..." Deep breath. "...and kill them."

They checked their supplies; each of them had 30-round magazines in their AK's, with two extra mags each. Liam put his in the large front pockets of his jeans, while Victoria—with her women's jeans and their simulated pockets—had to put hers into her waistband.

He knew this part of Hayes' plan would require lots of gun handling. It wasn't his strong suit, but he hoped he would be good enough. Either that, or he'd soon be a zombie.

Stay positive.

On the grounds surrounding the garage, the roar of the crowd of infected was constant and unsettling. They moved toward the stairwell opening they needed off to one side of the parking area. He took a knee and aimed at the two wandering zombies making their way over the pavement in their direction. He dropped the first with his first shot, but it took two for the second.

"I need to be closer to hit them in the head like that." Victoria claimed to be the poorer shot of the two, but Liam wasn't so sure.

"We'll be plenty close soon enough."

They dropped into the stairwell, Liam in the lead. The concrete stairs were held together by an open framework of metal in the open-air parking garage. One or two cars were on the fourth floor, but little else. As they hit the landing, he observed only a few zombies on the entire level. Rather than engage, he continued downward. "Hurry!"

It was dangerous to allow zombies to get behind them as they descended, but if they kept moving fast enough it shouldn't matter. They couldn't kill them all.

On the third floor, they both had to shoot a pair of zombies who were too close to ignore. As if trying to prove herself right, Victoria missed several shots before bringing one of them down.

"Maybe I need them even closer."

Just wait.

On the second floor, he took a knee and started shooting while he yelled at Victoria to keep moving down. He dropped four or five in just a few seconds. Many more were moving in their direction. Instead of shooting at the rising tide, he followed her down to the ground level.

Zombies swarmed the level. Victoria had shot her way through a clump of them hovering on the bottom steps, but she had trouble with the zombies in the stairwell to the basement level. The rest of the crowd took a few seconds to notice them coming into their view.

Liam yelled, "You shoot down into the stairwell, I'll keep them from following you."

Working together, they fought the horde to a tenuous standstill.

Victoria cleared enough zombies to begin going down to the basement level. Liam had his back to her as he fired at will at the dead circling the stairwell entrance on the first floor.

"Go down!"

He ran out of ammo as he began to follow. "I'm out of ammo. Turn around."

She spun around, and he squirted by to a step just below her. He slung his rifle and in one motion pulled out his handgun and pumped a few rounds into a zombie on the steps below. He holstered the pistol, grabbed a full magazine, and rocked it and locked it into *Moses*. He finished by pulling the charging handle to chamber the first round. The whole action took fifteen seconds, but during that time, Victoria continued to bang away at the writhing dead above them. In the small stairwell, it was like shooting fish in a barrel, even for a novice like her. But soon she too ran out of ammo.

"I'm out!" She had panic in her voice.

Liam turned around and ordered her to get behind him.

She stumbled down the bodies accumulating on the stairs, but recovered at the landing between floor one and the basement. On her knees, she reloaded her own magazine. It took her twice as long to reload. She mishandled the empty magazine and it fell through the crack into the open space of the level below.

"Leave it. Run!"

He was nearly deaf from the noise of their guns, so when she didn't move he was forced to yell even louder. "Get to the basement!"

She heard that, and did as ordered. He ran behind her; the zombies above were free to pursue.

Only a few zombies were in the basement level, so it was relatively easy for them to clear those nearby. Hayes had told them where the door was to the underground pedestrian tunnel to the Arch; they ran for it. A few dead zombies littered the route to the tunnel—signs Duchesne had come through. The infected excreted from the stairwell behind them. Daylight found its way through several stairwells of the level, so he could see their destination. After a mad sprint, they reached the doorway and banged against it. It held fast so he tried to pull it open instead.

"Of course it's locked. Hayes didn't mention any locks."

He was dismayed to see a pair of zombies running. He recalled a snippet from some zombie movie.

No, they're sprinting.

They were about three-fourths of the way across the garage while the rest of the zombies were still shambling away from the logjam at the stairs.

Victoria yelled, "Break the glass!" Then she added, "Maybe Duchesne locked it."

Liam took the butt of his gun and tried to slam it against the door, but it had no effect.

"What is this, bulletproof glass or something?"

"Shoot it out. They're almost here." To add to her seriousness, she got down on her knee and tried to shoot at the two zombies running.

The bang bang bang rhythm was nerve wracking for him. He managed to turn his gun around and aim it at the door.

I wonder if it will bounce back at me?

As he thought the thought, he reoriented his gun so any ricochet would deflect away from them both.

Luckily, it was not bulletproof. It blew out just like normal glass.

Victoria continued to shoot. Each shot like a hammer on his ears.

"It's open. Let's go!" Everything was a shout now.

He tapped Victoria on the shoulder, appreciating her shooting skills. She downed the two runners, but the swelling crowd of zombies bore down on them.

She got up and followed him through the gap.

They ran for their lives into the dark tunnel.

4

Guided by their lights, they ran as fast as they dared down the tiled hallway. He resolved to thank the St. Louis tourism department for insisting this pedestrian-friendly tunnel was built to link the parking garage with the National Monument. It kept them from having to walk the impossible walk on ground level.

The moans fell behind, but didn't disappear.

"Hopefully they'll get stuck in the door like the 3 Stooges." Liam had seen plenty of the bumbling trio. It was a favorite of both he and his father. He could only dream the zombies were *that* mindless.

He thought he heard some footfalls from behind, and he slowed just enough to shine his light backward. A blood-covered male soldier zombie hurtled directly at him. He had only a fraction of a second to act, but he guessed the zombie was going for his light, so he tossed it straight up while he sidestepped in the hallway.

The light smacked the concrete ceiling. The zombie jumped for it, and its speed carried it right by. It tumbled on the slippery tiles, and came to a rest about twenty feet ahead. Victoria still held her light; the beam pierced the bloody eyes of the infected man.

Liam brought his rifle to bear and fired off a wild series of shots. The close quarters amplified the noise and concussive force, causing him to jump even though he was the one pulling the trigger. Victoria's light was unsteady in the chaos.

The zombie moved slowly toward them, unconvinced by the missed shots. Liam's light rolled on the floor, throwing light in mad directions. The monster seemed unable to orient on any one light source, or the humans nearby.

More are coming...

Panic rose in Liam's stomach.

He took careful aim, and put one shot into the face.

Certain he hit it, and with no fanfare, he picked up his own light and they continued down the long hallway.

"Don't stop, Victoria. Run for it."

They never looked back. They reached the Arch museum entrance and encountered two sets of glass doors. The first set was unlocked so they could enter the airlock between the two portals. The interior doors were locked, however.

"Just shoot it." She sounded close to panic, too.

He couldn't see any way to avoid shooting the door. He took some comfort that the outer door was closed, and because it opened outward, the zombies would not be able push it open. But having two intact doors would have made him feel twice as safe.

He shot the glass. They carefully made their way through the broken glass frame and were inside the Arch museum. It was the same place where he and Victoria and Grandma had sought shelter on the second night of the disaster.

"Follow me," he yelled.

The whole complex was underground, underneath the Gateway Arch. The pedestrian tunnel dumped into the large museum about westward expansion—a quaint notion now—which in turned linked with the cavernous ticketing areas. Tunnels led north and south to the legs of the Arch where, in better times, visitors could board the trams to the top of the structure. Two other tunnels led to more glass doors and the outside.

As they ran through the museum, several holes in the ceiling suggested the military's bombs had done their work here. Everything inside the museum had been rearranged, or burnt to a cinder. They could easily climb out any of the many holes they passed, but Liam had a specific place he was trying to reach.

"Why don't we go up, Liam? I want to get out of the dark."

"When I was looking at Grandma through the binoculars, I saw lots of zombies, pretty much everywhere up top. We're going to try to get into the railroad tunnel. That will keep us off the surface and drop us pretty close to the boats."

Behind them, they could hear zombies once more.

"They broke through the glass!"

Liam picked up the pace, which was still pretty slow because he had to weave through the wreckage. Girders from the ceiling were on the floor, along with dirt and other matter from up above. The body of the large stuffed buffalo, which had always stood sentinel at the entrance, had been ripped apart. They passed out of the museum and into the ticketing area where the police and gangs had fought. He finally made his way into the side tunnel leading down to the loading area for the south leg of the Arch. That's where they'd find the final duct work into the railroad tunnel.

They arrived at the open door to the maintenance room; the lock had been blown open.

"Through here."

He ran into the room where they had taken refuge weeks ago, and he briefly looked at the stairwell Victoria had climbed with her flashlight while he was locked behind the grate of the small crawlspace with Grandma. It might have been the death of her if his police friends hadn't gone up and saved her later. With no further reminiscing, he went into the crawlspace with Victoria safely behind him this time.

"Almost there," he shouted. His ears still pounded.

He happened to look ahead at the exit and saw the faint glimmer of a wire directly across his path. A wire that shouldn't be there. He stopped his crawl and peered at it with his light for a short time.

"Whoa!"

Victoria bumped into him.

"What is it? We can't stop. We just can't."

"Uh. I think it might be a booby trap. There's a wire across the tunnel just ahead."

He showed her with his light.

"Oh man. What do we do now?"

"Maybe we could trick a zombie into going down there for us?" Liam was laughing as he said it, but he looked at Victoria's face and saw it light up with an idea, just as his did.

"We can push *something* through there."

With great reluctance, they moved back into the maintenance area. Many days ago, they found a rolling creeper, which they used to get Grandma through the tunnel. Something like that would have been perfect, but they had discarded it just outside the tunnel when they were done with it. The next best thing they found was a metal trash can.

"What if the explosion causes the tunnel to collapse?"

As if to mock the question, they heard moans outside the door. There was nothing with enough heft to block the door.

"All we can do now is pray."

Liam used a broom handle to push the trash can ahead of him in the tunnel. He gave himself maximum distance from the wire, then pushed the trash can as hard as he could with the broom handle. It slid down the slight incline into the wire and he was nearly blinded by the light of the explosion. The concussion roared up the tunnel; though it wasn't powerful enough to injure him, it did cause his ears to go numb.

I guess I didn't think that through.

Victoria said something, but he couldn't hear her. She pushed him firmly to go ahead. She held her light to her face, and though his vision was filled with stars and tears, he could see her mouthing the word.

"Zombies!"

5

The railroad tunnel was shorter than he remembered. Instead of being a hundred feet to daylight, there were but a handful. The bombs had wrecked it. In the place of the covered rails, there was a long gully filled with debris. It was pure luck the collapse didn't block their secret exit.

Victoria pulled him along. He was fully aware of what was going on, but the loud ringing in his ears was very disconcerting, though slowly dissipating. He took that as a good sign. His blurred vision started to return to normal too, the longer he ran in the daylight.

He stole a look behind. No zombies came out of the black hole in the wall.

They will.

The more he ran, the better he felt. Soon they were at the end of the tunnel—where the end would have been—and recognized it as the same spot he had seen Grandma and her captors almost a half hour before. He wondered if there was any chance they were even around anymore.

The cracked landscape made it hard to see much beyond the next hill, but they moved in the direction of the collapsed bridge to the south where the boats were stationed.

"Can you hear me?" she shouted.

He gave her the thumbs up sign as affirmation.

She smiled, but kept moving. She held his hand, guiding him. He felt like he was getting back to normal, but he liked holding her hand so he didn't let go.

He was fully distracted by the soft feel of her skin when they came over a crater lip, directly in front of a rubber boat with four people standing near it.

"Oh sh—"

The soldiers in black were professionals. Duchesne and the big bodyguard carrying Grandma were on the other side of the boat, walking slowly. The woman and a new guy dragged the boat over the cobblestones, but they stopped when Liam appeared. The man in the back pointed his black rifle at them before he could even think about raising his own. He was holding hands, making it virtually impossible to lift a rifle even if he wanted to.

Super-soldier Liam, reporting for duty.

He groaned to himself.

"Drop those weapons."

They complied. Liam pointed to his pistol, indicating he had it and didn't want to be shot for having it.

"Slowly drop the pistols. And the backpack."

The Glock was still in the backpack, though he doubted he'd be brave enough to use it against guys like these.

"Come on down, you two. We could hear you yelling for a mile over there."

Liam felt so stupid. Of course they were yelling. They probably heard the booby trap go off too. Mentally he was smacking his own forehead.

The man ran up and collected their rifles while Duchesne invited them to come to him. The woman had her rifle out, daring him to argue.

END TIMES

The NIS team had dragged their boat through the debris so they could launch in the water north of the downed bridge. Duchesne indicated they wanted to get Grandma right to the helicopter, which was across from the Arch on the Illinois side.

They had brought it through the debris on the near end of the downed bridge, but spent a lot of time dealing with zombies. They appeared tired to Liam, but they were close to their goal.

Just before the boat reached the water, the head of the woman next to Liam exploded.

"What—" Liam blurted out.

Two seconds went by. Enough time for him to wonder if any of the blood and gore had gotten on his clothes. He reflexively looked down.

The man who had been carrying the boat with her lost a good chunk of his right shoulder. The force of the gunshot flung him toward the water; he skidded across the wet cobblestones, into the shallow water.

Hayes and the bodyguard with Grandma flung themselves on the ground in front of the boat.

"It's Hayes. Or his floozy. It has to be," Duchesne yelled to his team.

Liam was paralyzed with fear. He could run away if he chose. His captors were pinned down. But without his weapons he appreciated how much danger they'd be in. He saw the same look in Victoria's eyes.

"We have to stick with them or we're dead," he said to her as quietly as he could manage between the ringing ears and the crunching noise coming off the water. The big jumble of debris at the Poplar Street Bridge had a leading chaotic edge which splashed and spun as the water brought in more junk. Several loose barges bounced in the swell as well, providing the only hint of stability out there.

"Don't you two think of leaving us. We'll shoot you before you get ten yards. We'll need your services to get over the river."

Another shot went over their heads, landing in the water just offshore.

Liam looked back to the tower and could just barely make out two small dots on the roof. Hayes and Jane were trying to help him.

"I need you and your gal pal to push the boat in the water for us. We're going to slide along with it. We don't want your Grandma getting hurt now, do we?"

The implicit threat got him moving, but he looked back to Hayes. Would he shoot him for helping Duchesne? Would he know he had no choice?

"OK, let's do this," he said to Victoria. Together they were able to push the rubber boat the short way down the cobblestones and into the water. As promised, the two agents kept themselves hidden the whole time.

Once in the water, the big man carrying Grandma pulled himself up the far side of the boat and attempted to place Grandma on the floor. He had her most of the way in when a hole appeared in his neck. This time they all heard the crack of the gun up on the tower.

"Dammit, Hayes. You're going to pay for these men!"

"Liam, you and Victoria need to do me a solid. Stand in the water just in front of the boat. I need you to hold it for me, then I'm going to climb in behind you. Remember your Grandma is right at the end of my gun barrel, just in case you were thinking of doing anything heroic."

With great effort, they managed to form a wall and get Duchesne into his precious boat. Liam was mentally prepared for him to simply drive away, but he ordered them in as well. Once they were all aboard, he explained his plan.

"You two are going to be my meat shields. Just sit by me and we'll all make it safely to the other shore. And you, Great-great-great old lady, get up here, too."

"But she's..." Liam assumed she was still sleeping, or in a coma, or whatever she was in back in the hotel room. "Alive?"

Liam knew she was alive because Hayes explained he didn't use zombie blood on her, but he couldn't figure out why or how she could sleep through all the excitement back in the room. His incredulity passed as legitimate surprise. Duchesne fed off that while he tried to start the motor.

"Yeah, we're going to have to figure out what superpowers your grandma has. She survived the zombie plague. She's the most important person in the world right now and that idiot Hayes—the man who claims he's trying to stop the disease—is the one attempting to prevent me from getting her to safety. Isn't that ironic?"

So many things flew through his head as he watched Grandma struggle to sit up on the small seat. Both he and Victoria gave her a hand, though Duchesne was careful to ensure they never opened a gap between himself and the big sniper rifle bearing down on him.

"I can't believe you're OK, Grandma. You survived..."

"Oh, my body is just too old and decrepit to get infected, I guess."

He couldn't tell her she hadn't really been infected. It would decrease *his* value. As it was, Duchesne gave no indication he was going to take he and Victoria to his base, though he was beginning to think that might be an opportunity.

Unless we end this now.

2

Marty found her seat in the boat. She'd been out cold for most of her fireman's carry ride through the Arch. She woke up just as they left the railroad tunnel. Now she was safely in the boat with the man who wanted her to die as a zombie.

Duchesne fiddled with the engine for a few minutes as they sat in the shallow water. Long enough for Marty to get concerned about the increasing number of zombies walking their direction. She took it as a good sign none of them were runners.

As he worked on the motor, he seemed to talk to calm his nerves. "Every two-bit berg and city upriver is dumping their garbage into the river. Even the end of the world hasn't put an end to human stupidity. Good riddance, I say."

Finally, the boat engine cranked over.

"Suck it, Hayes." He reversed the boat from shore, then spun it around. Once they were out on the water, Duchesne allowed them to sit in front of him, since he could sit in front of the motor. Victoria sat next to Marty, while Duchesne made Liam sit next to him.

The water was really moving. It had lots of churn and it tossed small bits of debris among the larger hazards such as rogue boats, loose barges, and driftwood fields. Two bridges upriver had been destroyed, though their decking wasn't visible in the water. Downriver, it appeared that every scrap of debris from all points north had found its way here and smashed itself against the mother lode of detritus.

The blockage started when the deck of the eight-lane highway was blown. She could only speculate on how the blockage grew so large. There must have been long lines of barges that came loose and collided with the downed bridge, and they formed the core holding it all together. As more things arrived at the stoppage, they either threw themselves against immovable objects and were crushed, or they bounced haphazardly in the mad surf until they were thrown on the debris pile out of the water for good.

Big blades of water cut all along the leading edge of the logjam as the fast-moving Mississippi made contact with it. She watched as an empty aluminum canoe twirled and spun in circles as it drew upon the deadly stoppage. It found its way between two 200-foot-long flat-deck barges —also bouncing and banging—and crumpled up as the water caught it and mashed it between the two larger boats.

She made the sign of the cross and said a little prayer.

She was terrified of what would happen if their boat sputtered and died, but she tried not to dwell on that. Instead, she tried to focus on an echo in her head.

It said, "Murderer."

Oh great. I'm hearing voices.

Trying to find distraction, she looked at Victoria; she was staring off into the distance—at nothing in particular.

Before she could engage her to find out how she was holding up, the boat arrived at a long concrete pier, which previously housed a large floating casino directly across the river from the Gateway Arch. Only the faded name was left on the mud-stained wall. Their tiny rubber boat was dwarfed by tie-downs and boat bumpers against the wall of the pier, but Marty's concern remained with Victoria. She had a pained look on her face. Marty began to think the voice in her head was...

"Murderer. Murderer. Murderer."

That's impossible.

Somehow she could sense what Victoria was thinking. Not just words, but also a strong new emotion. Grandma had to really focus on the word as it flitted in her mind's eye.

"Revenge."

The boat neared the wall, but the churn of the river made it very dangerous to try to get close to the ladder going up. Another of Duchesne's dark-clad friends appeared next to the ladder fifteen feet above. He was bent over with his arms out like he wanted something thrown up to him. Duchesne brought the boat around so it was facing upriver, the motor set to go just fast enough to cancel the effect of the current. She turned so she could see him trying to grapple with a tangle of rope. Something snapped against the wall.

"Not a chance, Hayes. You can't hit me from this far out. You're going to kill your precious *Grandma* first."

Suddenly Marty had a brilliant flash of insight, through Victoria's eyes. She immediately knew what was going to happen, and what she must do to stop it.

She pulled her legs over the bench so she faced backward.

Victoria, she sensed, was doing the same.

As Duchesne made a large heave with the rope, Marty looked at her great-grandson. He wasn't looking at her. Instead, he was watching Duchesne as the rope he threw came back down on his head.

He wound up to make another toss.

That gave Marty exactly what she needed.

Just a little push.

3

I am Victoria.

She played it over and over in her head as she crossed the ugly river in the floppy rubber boat. The anger she shared when she thought

Hayes and Duchesne had murdered Grandma. That's how she saw it at least. They were willing to murder anyone and everyone to advance their plan. The death of Grandma was bad enough, but they had both willingly tried to kill millions. Such evil could not stand. Evil was the one thing she'd been taught since preschool to fear, and resist.

Now she sat next to Marty wondering where their future would take them. She was glad the blood wasn't infected—she owed Hayes a modicum of respect for that—but there were millions, probably billions, of people's blood on the hands of the man sitting not three feet away. He was part of the organization that set all this evil in motion.

She gave a quick glance toward Grandma and could see she was in her own thoughts while doing her best to hold on as the boat bounced and swerved on the choppy water.

And Liam? He was sitting with *him*.

Victoria actually *hated* Duchesne. He was a man who reveled in killing Liam's entire family—her boyfriend's family. That made it personal. He also was pretty happy to see the whole world engulfed in zombies because it forced the collapse of the United States. Even her Christian upbringing wouldn't allow her to forgive the man. He sealed his fate when he tried to infect Grandma deliberately *just so he could see what happened.* Transporting them across this river as meat shields against the sniper rifle was just piling on. She resolved this all would end before they left the boat.

Payback time.

Her faith prohibited any thought of suicide, which was funny to her because two weeks ago that's exactly what she wanted. The first night on the run back in the city there were many times she thought about stopping and letting the nightmares in the darkness slither out and steal her away.

Back then I had nothing to live for.

But she ran, tangentially aware of the magnitude of the sin of killing oneself, but also deeply afraid of dying in such a horrible and gruesome manner. She'd seen it over and over...

Then she found Liam and Marty. They seemed like such down-to-Earth people—and Liam was attractive to her in that scruffy-dorky kind of way. He had beautiful blue eyes and was always smiling—the perfect remedy to her life's problems.

She felt herself smile inwardly at that highpoint of emotions during those early days.

But soon after meeting them, she was presented with the opportunity to act as a decoy against the gang members, allowing Marty and Liam—and Hayes, unfortunately—time to escape the Arch. Was it a sin to commit suicide if you were doing it to help someone else live? She'd have to ask Pastor Beth if she ever made it back to Colorado. She was willing to lay down her life, not just for the new friends she'd found in the faceless crowds downtown, but also to sate her own guilt at running away from her mates on that first night. Finally, she was shot by Hayes, and in her mind, she was sure she was going to die. Ironically, it was to be in Liam's house where she'd find salvation. She was shot in his front door as he and Grandma were taken away. Her last thought was a begging for forgiveness. She was done running.

But she was saved—literally—by her Bible. The very one given to her by Liam as an act of friendship; of love. It had to be a sign from God. She prayed around the clock in those dark days, waiting and hoping Liam would find his way back to her. When he did, she resolved to never lose him again.

Now she saw her chance to make things right—to give Liam and Grandma a hope at freedom. As the small boat pitched and yawed in the water, Duchesne was trying to throw a rope to his minion up top. And—

Grandma!

Victoria could sense it. It was an incredible rush of awareness. A sudden urge by Grandma to push Duchesne into the water.

I love you, Grandma. Let me take this burden.

She only had a moment to decide, but she was a girl of action.

Just a little push.

4

Liam bounced in the boat during the river crossing. He sat next to Duchesne who kept himself crouched low as he piloted them all using the small outboard motor. He was left to wonder what fate awaited them on the far bank. *If* they made it to the far bank. He tried to ignore the maelstrom of debris thrashing about a hundred yards downriver from their tiny, fragile, air balloon-ish little dingy. Though the motor had already proven temperamental, he resigned his trust to it. He'd go crazy with stress thinking of all the ways they could die down in that wreckage if the boat lost power. There weren't even paddles...

Just ignore it.

They bounced wildly toward some kind of docking facility on the Illinois side. He wondered if he should try to make small talk with Duchesne as they crossed, perhaps to beg for their lives, but the loud motor made that impossible.

He was a few feet from the two most important women in his life right now. He felt a little guilty he didn't feel quite the same about his own mother, but there was something about his great-grandmother and the adventures they shared that drove him to be a man, to be stronger and more resourceful, to be a loving partner. Being around his father caused him to want to offload responsibility, while being around his mother made him feel he had to more carefully manage his emotions. In short, his parents reminded him he was their child. Grandma's needs required the child to be a man. He knew it was unfair, but he was resolute Grandma made him a better person in her own special way.

And Victoria. He had nothing but good things to say about how she'd helped him these many days as well. She was his partner. His equal, if not his better.

He sighed a contented sigh, knowing they would be fine.

As the boat neared the large seawall port, Liam felt a weird emotion swirling through his head. Was it betrayal? Maybe. The word was there, but it had nuance. He focused hard on what he was thinking and feeling. He thought he heard words, but wrote off the impossibility. He couldn't hear thoughts. But still...the emotions formed into words.

Betrayal.

But not exactly.

Betrayal. And Payback.

He worked through it. The word became obvious as the boat bounced near the seawall.

Revenge.

Liam knew he was a bit slower than the women with emotions. Spending days on end with Victoria taught him a lot about the differences. It took him extra time to ruminate on the meaning of emotional words, and try to understand how Victoria saw the same things in entirely different ways. But that's what made things interesting, even in the most mundane settings.

Now he sensed some kind of powerful emotional link with Victoria.

And Grandma?

The boat tossed on the nasty water, sloshing waves back and forth between the boat and seawall. All the while, Duchesne was tossing ropes around. And—

Whoa!

The emotion was overpowering. *Both* women were broadcasting a message—was it body language—that Liam understood. He assembled the message in an amazingly brief time; he knew what was going to happen and what he had to do. He wasn't about to let either of those women do what they were planning, but he couldn't give away their plan to Duchesne.

Victoria. I've got your back.

Grandma. Thank you for teaching me to be a better man.

He stood up, catching Duchesne at the perfect moment of vulnerability. The man was tossing the rope in a ridiculous way, trying to get it high enough so his friend up on the top of the seawall could catch it and tie it off. The opportunity was golden.

Liam figured he was going to give him—

Just a little push.

Yeah, just a little one.

When the moment came, he threw himself at the distracted Duchesne. He was joined in perfect unison by the other two. Liam watched in horror as the rear of the boat pitched downward at the worst possible time.

In one confused mass, all four of them tumbled over the edge.

5

Liam's first thought, after popping out of the water after their big splash, was how bad the water smelled. On a good day, the Mississippi might smell like diesel fumes and dead fish, but today it smelled like diesel fuel, dead fish and, well, just death.

When they hit the water, he was able to grab Grandma's top so when he popped out, she popped out as well.

Victoria was further away, but thrashing hard to push Duchesne away from Grandma. He broke away from her and attempted to make for the seawall. The problem for him, and for them all, was the current. It pushed them all back out into the main channel because of the swirling eddies along the debris-strewn shore. The seawall gave no purchase to someone swimming below, and in no time, they all drifted in the main channel, a quarter mile from the end of the line.

Victoria made it to Liam and Grandma. She immediately took some of the load from him as Grandma was unable to swim on her own.

"I should tell you both," she said as she spat out some nasty water, "I can't swim."

"No, Grandma, you shouldn't have told us that." He laughed, despite it all.

They were into the strong current twenty-five yards offshore. It drove them in the direction of the massive disaster wrapped around the gigantic catastrophe. They tried to paddle and swim toward shore, but with Grandma in tow they just couldn't break free of the main current. They were in the event horizon.

Victoria responded in a weak voice, "My God. Look!"

From their vantage point, the wreck became more imposing as they neared. There were well over fifty barges wedged into the side of the bridge; some of them canted dangerously as they bobbed up onto the debris. The tips of others pointed up out of the water while the bulks of their hulls remained hidden beneath the waves. They watched as an open-topped 200-foot barge ran into the pile ahead of them. It came to rest nearly sideways, and listed toward the surface as it was absorbed by the massive frontal wave. The powerful current reached inside—it was empty—and simultaneously held it in place as it began to fill up.

No, not empty. Oh no.

As the runaway barge tipped further and further in their direction, Liam could see into the hold. It contained a large number of bodies. He scanned other barges on the pile for signs they too were holding similar cargo. He assumed it was illegal to fill barges with dead people and send them downriver.

I'm going to blast those towns upstream when I write my book.

They were going to drift into the blockade. The only variable was where. Even that wasn't much of a question since they had very little ability to alter course.

All along the front edge of the debris field, large pieces of driftwood smashed into heavier objects such as concrete or barges—and they broke apart with sickening cracks. Wooden and fiberglass boats shared a similar fate. The only things that seemed to survive the impacts were the barges themselves. Most went in front-to-back, which made swimming near them suicide. There was no possible way to climb on either end in the tumult. If they could approach from the side, they still didn't have a great chance, but it wasn't exactly impossible either.

"Guys, we have to swim hard for that sinking barge with all the bodies in it," Liam shouted.

They didn't have time debate it. The women made no protests, and paddled with Liam in the direction he wanted to go. It was a tough swim, and it took them further out into the channel, but there were no similar pieces of safety between them and either shore.

He gave one cursory head spin, searching for Duchesne. He hoped he'd drowned, but figured they'd not get that lucky. He did see rope guy running downriver along the shore. He wondered if he would try his luck out on the flotsam and jetsam to save his boss.

He thrashed his legs under the water, and drove the triad into the current heading straight for the sinking barge. He hoped their timing would be right to suck them directly into its hold, and they would have a little time to climb out before it tipped over or sank.

Risky. Very risky.

His mind fought against the illogical notion of heading *for* the grand disaster before them.

Please God, help me get Victoria to safety. Please God, help me to get Grandma to safety. And please God, if it's your will, help me find safe harbor as well.

The noise from the blockade increased as they approached. The cracks of wood. The groan of the metal hulls. The chaotic splashing of water and debris out front.

25 yards.

15 yards.

They were on the glide path he wanted, but he continued to kick as hard as his tired body allowed.

"Swim as hard as you can as far as you can into the barge. We need to get in and find a ladder before it capsizes." Already the barge had a severe list. Liam hoped for a little luck, or a little help from God.

5 yards. They were in the spray of the leading waves.

The barge had filled most of the way with water and had settled down as the heavy load stabilized. It continued to fill, but they were able to get across the upriver lip of the barge's hold without too much trouble. The cargo sent panicked shivers down Liam's spine. Up close, the stiff dead were terrible.

Victoria screamed, "Oh God, no. No!"

If this was a normal sinking boat, Liam would be scared enough. Getting across the thirty feet of the hold as it filled with water would be a major challenge. But this barge was filled with dead bodies, and as it filled with water, it shifted and rearranged them. All of them seemed to have bullet holes in their heads adding to their grotesque appearance. They were once zombies...

"God almighty. Poor souls." Marty wailed as she too succumbed to the horror. She recoiled as she touched them.

"Don't stop. Just get through them," Liam shouted with fear in his voice. He pulled Grandma across.

He had no choice. Without guns, knives, or spears, the only weapon they could wield was speed. There were easily a thousand dead bodies floating in the eight feet of red-tinged water inside the barge hold. The darkness at the bottom, and the movement he imagined there, nearly caused him to "break and run" as they said in his computer game. He wanted more than anything to just swim ahead and leave his friends behind. Wanted more than anything to be out of this deathly sick water forever. It was completely irrational and was the last thing he would do at any other time. But now, he was ashamed he even thought it.

The middle of the barge wall did have a ladder leading out of the hold up to the narrow deck around the hull. But the strong currents flowing into and around the hold made getting there difficult and slow.

He felt his legs and lower body being pushed, pulled, and punched by whatever was below. Taken with the cracking sounds from crushed debris and the noise and spray of the filthy water, he found himself overwhelmed with stimuli. It took everything he had to reach the ladder, and it took every ounce of his being to let Victoria go first so she could help get Grandma up the ladder. Meanwhile, he left himself *exposed* to the lurking evil below the waves.

The barge started to tilt more severely. Victoria was at the top, but Grandma was still on the ladder. She was unable to lift her leg from rung to rung and hang on at the same time. Victoria had to come back down and lift her slowly and deliberately up each rung. It was slow going.

"You have to hurry. Pull her up!" he said with something approaching anger. Lower, he said, "Please." He felt a lump in his throat as he couldn't shake the thought something was going to grab him from below. So many bodies, some of them almost had to be reanimated zombies. It was how it happened in the movies.

He gripped the ladder as the whole barge shifted. He stepped up a rung as Grandma started to move up. The water inside the hold met with a new influx of water from over the side, and the wave action shifted the horrible cargo, bringing corpses to the surface again and exposing him to the stench of the recently deceased. It was a powerful and disgusting miasma of rot and death.

And they are moving down there.

He was paralyzed with fear for several long moments as his imagination reveled in the drama. Finally, he checked on the women. He was shocked to see the ladder was empty. They had made it up and moved out of his sight on the top deck. He had to assume they were safely on firmer ground—well, as safe as anyone could be in the middle of the river on a great shipwreck wrapped around a highway bridge.

The barge continued to tip upward, and the water pulled him down as the boat shifted. The cargo hold was nearly topped off with water. Some was rushing back out. Would it sink by tipping straight up and down as he had seen with other barges? He didn't have time to wonder. It tipped back down to a shallow angle, and was held there by the rush of incoming water. Amidst the sloshing cadavers, he turned around to try the ladder again. It wasn't as steep now though the boat was starting to shift downward once more. He'd have to hold on carefully to each rung so as to not slip off, and he'd have trouble getting over the lip at the top, but it wouldn't be impossible.

He had just found purchase on the rungs with his feet when something grabbed his leg and pulled.

The shock forced him to slip from the rung he'd been holding for support. As he dipped below the waves, he reminded himself to thank God.

You saved two out of three of us. Thank you.

He waited for the bite, too exhausted to fight it.

6

The expected bite never came. As he regained the surface, a living person used Liam's body to pull himself up and over to grab the ladder. In a moment of resignation, he could only watch as Duchesne ascended right over him. He held the ladder and kicked at Liam to get him to float out into the dead bodies. An effort which worked. He went underwater as he slid backward through the frozen arms.

When Liam came back up, he saw Duchesne made it to the top of the ladder. Liam struggled to stay afloat; he pushed off the bodies as they shifted in the current.

Don't look at them.

He ignored the rotting faces and focused on Duchesne as he crested the top. He waited while the boat tried to settle again. The lower it got, the easier it would be to gain footing on the deck. This gave Liam the opportunity to catch up. He pulled himself through the bodies, grabbed the ladder, and hauled himself up. A few rungs were all it took to reach the man's lower pant leg.

Liam wrapped his arm around Duchesne's ankle and flung himself outward. Whatever Duchesne had been doing, he lost his grip and fell roughly into the pool of undead. Liam held on the whole way down. It wasn't a soft landing for either of them. Duchesne was beyond angry.

"Liam, you just signed your own death warrant."

He had fallen more or less straight down, but the barge itself constantly shifted as it slid up and down on its perch on the front edge of the blockage. Duchesne and Liam and their dead friends sloshed around as if in a bathtub.

"All you do is kill people. Why can't you just let us go? We just want to be left alone."

Liam let himself be pulled with the water away from the ladder, while Duchesne had pushed his way through the dead to be closer to it. Liam was willing to let him climb again because he didn't think he had the energy to stop him. He knew he couldn't win a physical altercation.

Duchesne drew up the first few rungs of the ladder and turned back to Liam. "You're just a little kid. You have *no concept* what it means to control the fate of billions, so pardon me if I don't care about you or your opinion. I really wanted to keep the three of you together—see how valuable you are to HQ—but I think I've had enough of you and your girlfriend. All I need is your Grandma. You're going to die on this wreck."

The whole barge shifted considerably as he digested the words. Duchesne held on to the ladder while he went sloshing twenty or thirty feet sideways. He tried to see out of the hold to get a better sense of the wider disaster, but he could only see the tops of the pylons of the nearby bridge.

Duchesne reached the top lip despite all the movement.

"Liam, on second thought, I think I'll do some experimenting with Victoria, just for fun. Consider it a parting gift to for your antics back on the interstate."

He was so tired, he could only fight back with words. "You already paid me back for that one. Remember? You punched me!"

Instead of a witty rejoinder, Duchesne simply smiled and extended his middle finger.

Liam dug deep. If he was goading him to action—and Liam didn't care—it worked. He began pushing through the dead. He wished he'd been able to get some payback on the thugs who beat up Victoria back at the Arch. Now Duchesne claimed he was going to hurt her, too.

I can't allow that.

**

I am Victoria.

After jumping out of the barge to the nearby roof of a house, Victoria helped Grandma come down off the side of the barge as it dipped low. The wave action helped, though she still slammed down hard.

"Gotcha, Grandma," she said just after an "oomph" sound escaped.

"Thank you. Sorry for that."

Unlike the inside of the barge, the world out in the open of the massive river stoppage was in a deadly flux. They sat on the remains of a shingled rooftop. It had been pushed up and onto the debris pile. She had no clue how it held together.

"Grandma, I have to help Liam. He hasn't come over the top yet."

"Yes, dear. I'll be fine down here. Go!"

In the time it took for her to get Grandma settled on the roof, the barge had pushed up and then fallen back down. She could see a large group of loose barges heading their way from up the river. It looked like someone had deliberately let them all go at the same time. She estimated they had a couple minutes before the wave of iron came slamming in. She intended to use that time well.

First, she ran over some broken wooden beams that separated from the roof and grabbed a rope hanging over the edge of Liam's barge. It took incredible effort, as her upper body wasn't as strong as her leg muscles, but she gained purchase on the tilting top deck of the flat barge. She could see down into the hold. Duchesne hung from the top rung of the ladder, yelling back to Liam. Liam appeared tiny in the morass of bodies sloshing inside the gigantic hold.

She sized up her options and ran along the edge as she lined Duchesne up for a powerful body slam. He gave Liam the finger as she left her feet. She didn't believe it when he started to turn her way.

7

He was already on his way to try to stop Duchesne when he saw Victoria run up the deck from behind and push him so he fell backward off the ladder. She performed magnificently as she both grabbed him and pushed herself off the side of the deck. They went tumbling into the middle of the barge, and sloshing water carried them all the way out to the edge. He paddled toward them, beat down but not quite out.

Duchesne recovered quickly. He pulled himself onto the upriver side of the deck, which sat near the surface of the water, and kept himself steady. Liam watched as all kinds of small boats, shipping containers, and a million kinds of floating debris moved to and fro not far out in the river. Every last piece headed for the glorified beaver dam.

"Nice try, Victoria. I was hoping we'd get a chance to meet up close and personal, for Liam's sake, but I think I may just leave you both here." He wiped blood from under his nose, and angrily spit it from his mouth.

"You will never touch me, you sick sonofabitch. I'll hold you down and drown you myself before I ever let you take us again."

Liam reached her side, unsure on how she planned to execute that threat, but ready to help.

"Too funny. What are you two kids going to do from down there in all those dead bodies? You going to make them come back to life and jump out and kill me?"

Could we?

Liam looked around, wondering if any of these bodies *were* still alive. Zombie "alive" anyway.

"Maybe I'll just run around this vessel, grab Grandma, and leave you two here? Let the river take care of you." After a brief pause, he reconsidered. "No, that makes me sound inept. Maybe I'll come back and shoot you both from my helicopter. Hmm, how's that sound?"

Liam saw something approaching on the river. Heading his way, fast.

"Duchesne, what will it take for you to help us get out of here alive if we promise to help you with your experiments? I hate your guts, but the safety of that fortress sounds pretty good from where we sit."

"Liam, no! What are you saying? I'm not going with *him*, safety or not. You said we'd take our chances out in the world, together."

"Aww, how sweet. You two can argue about it all you want. I've already decided I can do this without you two." He pulled out a handgun from a holster just behind his hip. "Maybe a helicopter is too dramatic. Maybe I'll make sure it's done right and shoot you both myself, right now."

He knelt on lip of the barge, unable to stand up. He brought the gun to bear, even as the ups and downs of the wave action intensified. Only Liam knew why.

Liam watched the barge towboat—basically a huge tugboat designed to be the engine for dozens of linked floating cargo carriers—pushed a handful of barges directly for them. He heard a dull roar, suggesting great violence was approaching from out on the water.

He threw his last die.

"You *lose*, Duchesne. Hayes used fake blood on Grandma. She wasn't infected. She isn't the cure. Your men died for nothing. Now you'll die for nothing, too."

He looked at Liam for a long couple of seconds, calculating. He lowered his gun, just a little.

"So young and naive. I'd almost rather keep you alive just to watch your expressions over and over."

He seemed to think on it.

"Try this one for size. Are you ready? Hayes and I agreed to tell you that so you'd be inclined to leave him up in his ivory tower."

He found that very funny, giving a hearty laugh.

"So you see, she *was* infected. Checkmate, you little punk."

Liam didn't know how to respond. It was one of his rare moments where his reservoir of snark just spit out blanks. The boat began to lean upward, forcing Duchesne to grab on tighter to the lip of the hold. It didn't stop him from continuing to prod Liam.

"The best part is, you'll never know. You're going to die in there. So long." He laughed, and tried to raise his weapon, but he became distracted as the tipping accelerated. He managed to fire once before the end.

"What the...!"

The leading barge was on course to t-bone them. It pushed a rush of water in front of it. When the wave arrived, it first dropped the barge down in a great trough, and then raised the entire barge up and then down as the crest arrived. Duchesne fell backward over the side; he got sucked between both boats. The incoming barge hit the blockade almost exactly where Duchesne had been standing, and the violence of it warped the heavy steel frame of their hull. Liam and Victoria sloshed hard against the incoming wave and were thrown again toward the opposite side of their boat. The whole thing shifted under them as the captain of the towboat plowed his cargo into the blockage. It went right over the top of them.

Liam's final act was to pull Victoria directly in front of him, so that he had his arms and legs around her. She did the same in response. He had no time for words, but he looked directly into her beautiful emerald eyes and gave her a wink. It was the kind of thing Grandma liked to do when she was up to mischief. Now it felt like an appropriate remembrance of her.

She has no fear. I wonder if my eyes appear as strong to her?

The driving force of the rogue barge pushed theirs down into the undertow, and drained all the bodies, their own included, into the river, and then under the debris field.

He had just enough time to thank God for letting him die with his friend.

It never occurred to him to pray for a miracle. He'd long since assumed he'd used them all up.

TRIBULATION

Marty felt Victoria set her down on the smelly surface of the roof. She encouraged Victoria to run off and help Liam. After a short rest and a short crawl to somewhere a little safer, she felt a head rush as she passed out.

"Hello, Martinette." The entity using her late husband's identity was back. He stood in front of the open door of the strange room with the computer sitting on the table. "You've done it."

Marty stepped slowly toward the portal.

"What is all this? What will I find inside?"

"The end. And the beginning."

Marty reached her limit with his doublespeak. "I will not go in that room until you give me a straight answer."

Al smiled. "I have no doubt you'd stand here for eternity, my dear." He stepped into the room, and went to the other side of the 8088 computer sitting on the table. "This really is the end of the line for you, Marty. No one can get you across the river," he spoke faster, "but you can still save the kids. That's worth coming in here, isn't it?"

"I'm...dead?" She looked over her shoulder to see the stars above. "Oh dear Lord, the stars are going out." She struggled to keep her composure.

"Yes. I told you before, we're together inside that marvelous head of yours. But, this place *is* real. You can really save them. All you have to do is come to me."

She didn't want to surrender the vision of the starfield, though it darkened at an alarming rate.

"So you can help me save them?"

"Together, I think we can, though you may not like my methods."

That gave her pause. An image popped in her head of a pitchfork-wielding devil. A smooth-talking, dangerous being, full of seemingly good ideas that are actually traps for mankind. She was raised believing the Devil was real. Lately she'd seen the dead walking, the innocent die, and a too-good-to-be-true mirage of her husband whispering ideas to her in her mind. It wasn't a far reach to see evil at play.

"Marty, you know I'm not the Devil. Why do you think such horrible thoughts of me?"

"Because you've done nothing to help me all the times you've visited." But she halted again. That wasn't exactly true. "Well, I suppose some of what you said was useful. I just don't know who or what you are. That makes it hard to trust you."

"Fair statement. But your friends are out there now. Do you want to know who I really am, or would you prefer to save their lives?"

It wasn't a difficult choice, put in the starkest terms.

"Alright. As long as I don't have to sell my soul. I won't do that for any price."

"That's a deal. For now, let's see what your computer terminal will let us do." He motioned for her to come through the door.

Marty took a tentative step forward, and stood at the threshold. Many things swirled through her head, including thoughts of God, death, and the destruction she'd witnessed. But she also saw Al, the real Al, in her mind. She pictured him back at home, sitting on the couch reading his newspaper. He looked up and smiled at her. A small but significant symbol of his undying love, even as he neared his own passing. She also thought of Liam and Victoria...

"I see them. They fell in the water."

Trap or not, she charged through the doorway to be near the computer. "What do we do?"

"That's my girl," he said with the thick Jersey drawl he turned on when he wanted to impress her.

A spark of energy coursed through her and reached out to Al and to the ancient computer console. Rather than make any effort at working the ugly gray keyboard, "Al" just put data on the screen using a mix of voice commands and complex hand motions. An incredible amount of data displayed at first, but he pared it down at an impressive speed. What was left on the screen was a series of dots. Two blue dots marked Liam and Victoria—very close together but underneath the collapsed bridge. Beyond them was another blue light—her. She was almost directly above the other two. Appropriate, as they were even now slipping below her under the wreck. Elsewhere the screen was filled with red dots. Some were very close. Since she didn't see other people walking around the debris, she assumed they were zombies.

Now most of the red dots disappeared, leaving only a handful of yellow dots.

"OK, these are the ones we want. The swimmers. One is nearby."

"Are you saying this computer can control the zombies?"

"Wouldn't that be great? No, Martinette, I'm saying this terminal will allow us to project emotion to one particular zombie, much like you could sense the thoughts and emotions of Victoria and Liam on the rubber boat. Only this time, the link isn't with someone close to you, which is why we need this computer to focus it."

"But the zombies are dead. Right?"

"Unfortunately, yes. But they still have primitive functions requiring low-level activity in their brains. Motor control. Hand-eye coordination. Hunger. That sort of thing. They may look evil, but they're not possessed demons. They're more akin to rabid animals. Those animals are filled with primal needs. All we're going to do is give a nudge toward one of those needs."

He began entering a long sequence of characters, much too fast for Marty's tired eyes to follow. It took several minutes, leaving her itching to ask what was taking so long.

"I sense your concern, but time doesn't flow the same when the brain is near death. Trust me. Rest assured this little computer is merely symbolic. Your brain is the real engine I'm manipulating. I'm working as fast as your brain can process data."

"Oh dear. I'm afraid my old brain isn't much good for that. This is the first time I've used a computer." She gave a little chuckle despite the circumstances.

"Don't worry about that. Your brain is already a supercomputer, even if you don't use physical computers."

"OK, I think I've got everything lined up. Sadly, the element of chance cannot be factored out of my equations. This is, as you would say, a best guess."

"I guess you can't be a Devil or an Angel if you aren't all-powerful. I don't know if that makes me feel better or worse."

"Not even God would want to eliminate random chance. If that were true, nothing would be able to happen without His express consent. Why would a supreme being would want that kind of minutia to tend? To say nothing of free will."

"So you could still be a Devil. Oh my lands."

"I guess you'll just have to find out when you find out, Martinette. Are you ready to roll the dice?"

"I don't gamble."

"Fair enough. I'll do it."

He simulated a cup of dice being tossed. To Marty's dismay, more and more dice spilled from the cup. It was a never-ending stream of six-sided chance cubes coming out of an impossibly deep cup.

All she could do was pray.

2

Liam was in a dream world. He opened his eyes during his underwater journey, and was dismayed to look down into the greenest water he had ever seen. Light filtered down through holes in the pile up above, into the murky water, and it stretched down below them. His eyes burned in the dirty water, but he didn't figure he'd be needing them if he was dead.

From below, he saw something impossible.

I say that word a lot these days.

An impossible hand reached up to him.

The hand was attached to an arm, which was connected to a body. The thing's face was death itself. Black eyes. White skin. Nondescript black clothes.

Drowning and death by zombie. What a way to go.

He hoped Victoria had her eyes closed so she didn't have to meet her fate like this.

The zombie swam directly at them, even as the current pushed them downriver underneath the monstrous wreck. Liam imagined himself kicking it, but the current was too strong to move his legs.

The zombie rammed them. Instead of chomping a leg or hanging on to get a better place to bite them, it kept kicking upward. It changed their trajectory in the current. Instead of going down or sideways in the turbulence, they went up.

His head popped up in a cave of sorts. The zombie still pushed upward, even though they were now half out of the water.

"Victoria!"

"How did you do that?"

He had no time to respond. He wondered what he should do to the zombie swimming against him like a robot. They were all intertwined in some metal supports from the downed bridge. He grabbed on as best he could. The concrete deck was in pieces but the flat surface was just behind them.

Should I kick him away or say thanks?

It felt horrible but he kicked the zombie away. It lost contact with his body, squirted by Victoria—giving her a terrible fright—and fell under the surface going toward the back of the small cave. It kicked the whole way.

I'm so sorry. And thank you.

"We're still alive, Liam. This is a miracle."

Thinking of the mysterious zombie, he wanted to agree. It did seem like a miracle, or else really good luck.

Victoria responded, "Thank you, God!"

He didn't have time to solve it. Liam used the support beams to work himself around the tangled mess of crumpled superstructure, toward the opening up to the surface of the wreck. Victoria followed.

"You saw Duchesne die, right? That wasn't just a dream, was it?"

Liam replied to her. "He was—"

He paused. Duchesne definitely fell directly into the path of the incoming juggernaut, but he'd read enough books to know that didn't mean anything.

"He's most likely dead. Though I'd have told you we were *most likely* dead, too, if you had asked a minute ago. I think we're safe for the moment."

Inwardly, Liam knew that last bit was a stretch. None of them were safe in the post-collapse world, but more immediately, they were in mortal danger just for being on the shifting river wreck. They still needed to find a way off.

He reached the sunlit hole in the broken bridge deck above them. There was plenty of room for him to crawl through and slide onto the surface. He landed on the side of a flipped barge, floating as part of the mass of junk. More free-floating barges were crashing into the blockade. They needed to get off the drift.

He could see a way through to the nearby roof where he hoped Grandma was still waiting for them. "Come on, girlfriend." He was momentarily giddy at being alive; at being with her.

The grinding sound of all the shifting pieces of the bridge was unnaturally loud. He gained some height as he climbed the ribbing of a shipping container to get a better view of the whole wreck. He reached the top and figured out he was almost precisely at the point where he'd fallen in. The boat that saved him from Duchesne was directly ahead of him. It consisted of three barges in a row pushed by a burly tug that threw up huge rooster tails of propeller churn behind it. Like an icebreaker, it was intentionally pushing itself into the immovable object...

"Victoria, we don't have much time. Look!" He pointed to the ship as she joined him on the container's top, though it was impossible to miss.

Victoria took in the scene for a few moments, and seemed more concerned than Liam about the location of the roof—now in line to be run over. She didn't see Grandma where she'd left her.

For a panicked moment, he thought she was also sucked under by the big wave. Nothing could have survived the impact.

He took another quick look upriver. There were dozens of loose barges coming in their direction. They bounced off the piers of the bridges upriver like billiard balls redirecting after a powerful break. The huge logjam on which they stood couldn't last forever with such overwhelming weight bearing down on it.

"There she is!" Victoria screamed in joy. Grandma had moved from her roof to the inside of a partially crumpled shipping container. She was out of the direct path of the towboat. A zombie was sprawled on the debris nearby, though it wasn't moving very much. Victoria started to climb down. Liam took a few more seconds to get his bearings on Grandma before following. He also looked toward the Missouri side, hoping for an obvious escape route. The Illinois side was not an option because of the efforts of the powerful ship trying to cut open the blockade.

Back to St. Louis we go.

3

Victoria reached Grandma a few moments before him. They hugged each other like long lost friends. Liam was tempted to try to make it a three-person hug, but opted to save the celebration for terra firma.

"I saw you kids in a dream. You were swimming." She let out a weak laugh. "I thought I finally bought the farm."

Liam and Victoria traded concerned looks.

"Yeah, we *did* go for a dip." Liam wasn't ready to tell her how they were saved, though at some point he wanted to sit down with her and have a long, peaceful chat about everything he'd seen and done the past couple weeks. For now, the threats of the moment overshadowed any deeper discussion.

Liam let slip a bad curse word. He couldn't help himself once recognized the identity of the zombie on the ground at his feet. With a closer look, he determined he wasn't infected.

Duchesne wasn't a zombie, but his body was ruined and bloody like one. Apparently he'd been tossed up onto the wreckage by the same giant wave which sucked them under. Instructing Grandma to stay put, he and Victoria moved closer to the injured man; he was on his back staring at the sky very near the water's edge. As they arrived over him, his eyes focused. One of his hands was nearly severed and he had many lacerations along that side of his body. The wooden planks beneath him were stained red.

"Liam. Help me. You must. I can save your Grandma."

Liam was horrified to realize he wanted to help the broken man. Despite everything Duchesne had done. Despite the fact he *had* to be lying. He tore off his t-shirt and tried to staunch the bleeding.

He spoke to him in a strained voice. "Did you infect my Grandma? I have to know."

His only reply was a bloody-lipped smile. One of his eyes was swelled shut and he looked pale.

"Liam, no. You can't help him. We have to get Grandma to safety. You have to let him go. There *is* no cure."

Turning up to look at Victoria, he said, "But he'll die if I don't help him." Turning back, he continued, "He *has* to save her." He felt the tears welling up behind the anger.

"He's dead already. As much as I hate him, I wouldn't let him die if I could save him. Out here, on this floating nightmare, nobody can."

"She's right, Liam. She's honest. I like that about her." He tilted his head slightly in her direction, "And because you were honest, I'll be honest with you. Hayes put a tracking device in your phone and we've been tracking your movements all this time. Cool trick, huh?"

"I already told you it was always off. I was saving it for the day phone service returned so I could call my parents." She had a defiant look as she stood above him.

"We tracked you whether it was on or off."

"But when did you put it in? I never let it out of my sight."

Duchesne gave a wet laugh. "You'll have to ask Hayes. Not my concern."

He kept talking, with increasing difficulty. "Liam, listen. I need you."

Liam warily moved closer, still holding his bloody shirt on the man's side in a futile attempt to prolong his life.

"History will look unkindly on what we did for our country." He was glassy-eyed as he spoke. "It's up to you to set the record straight. We were building a better country so we could lead the world as we were meant to do. This was *your* country. *Your* tribe. Tell everyone the truth of it."

Liam was shocked at the audacity. His reply reflected his anger.

"You mean the truth about how you unleashed a plague so you could eliminate your political enemies? You did all this to kill women like my Grandma Rose. Are you nuts?"

Another wet giggle. "No, listen. We were making something better out of the world. People like your dad were the ones *ruining* it. You have to see that now..."

"Wait. What? My dad?"

"Oh." He coughed for twenty or thirty seconds, then tried to catch his breath for an equal amount of time. "I may have left that part out." Blood drained from the side of his mouth and he smacked his lips to clear it.

Liam felt himself walking the razor's edge between sobbing and stabbing the man in the heart. He did everything he could to stay in between the lines.

"Please. Tell me what my dad has to do with all this. Was he—"

The conspiracy gene activated.

"—NIS?"

Duchesne coughed out a spray of blood with his laugh, forcing Liam and Victoria to recoil. The bottom half of his face was splattered with it. Still, he motioned with one finger for Liam to get closer. He drew him in all the way to his face.

His voice became a whisper, "The NIS would never...take a *traitor* like your dad." He made a weak effort to spit on Liam, but he saw it coming. He moved back to safety.

"Traitor? You're the traitor. You betrayed the whole human race!" Liam pulled back his shirt, causing a slight whimper from the dying man.

"But I never betrayed the United States of..." He trailed off. His eyes rolled up into his head.

The situation reminded Liam of another death he'd witnessed back at Elk Meadow. Colonel McMurphy came to him after he was infected and just before his death asked him to consider finding another camp so they could test Grandma. He'd already resolved never to go near a government camp again—a decision which proved correct. At the time, Liam said nothing, not wanting to take a dump on the man's last words. This time however, he was ready to unload.

"Not only am I going to do everything I can to get the history books *correct*, I'm going to write my own book and tell mankind about *your* plague. I'm going to do everything I can to expose you to the world as the piece of filth you are. I'll kill all your NIS people for causing this. I'll destroy your fortresses. I'll raise an army. Your name will be synonymous with coward. Mankind will spit at the mere mention of the name Duchesne. I will—"

He went on for many seconds before Victoria interrupted him.

"Liam. He's gone."

He just stared. He had so much more to say. So much to unload on the man who, on the face of it, was directly responsible for every piece of this broken bridge, every zombie walking the Earth, and every dead person now fading from life's story. He could hardly accept the impossibility that *his* life would intersect with the one man responsible for bringing the fictional world of zombies to his own doorstep. It gave him some comfort to know whatever else happened today, at least this man was dead. He really was going to write a book someday. He willed himself to remember Duchesne's last words for the final chapter.

Grandma broke his introspection. "Liam, he's dead. You've got to go."

Liam looked up at Grandma and his eye caught sight of a small black drone many feet above her. He didn't linger on it.

"OK. We have to keep moving. This whole dam is about to collapse." He pointed over his back at the barge still assaulting the debris and the multitude of loose barges coming down the river behind it.

"I'm exhausted. I can't even move. Doctor would probably say I had a stroke." She laughed, but not convincingly. "I don't think I can make it to the shore from here." She pointed to the Illinois side.

"Sorry, Grandma. We have to go that way." He thumbed toward the Missouri side, which was twice as far.

"Oh dear. You two should go. Get to safety and I'll take my chances here."

He experienced deja vu. Almost two weeks ago, he was faced with a similar dilemma as he and Grandma talked about leaving the city or staying in her home. At the time, Liam had thought about leaving her, if only so he could run and get his dad to take care of her. Now, the notion of leaving her never crossed his mind. He wasn't going to sacrifice all the miracles that helped her survive this long.

"No, Grandma. You're always coming with us."

Rather than discuss it, he grabbed Grandma around the back, and motioned for Victoria to do the same. With a helper under each arm, she hobbled along the shifting debris. He couldn't help but feel the weight of the decision, once made. Looking ahead, it was daunting. He couldn't look behind now, but the chugging engines of the towboat, the overarching aroma of death, and the creaking and crunching sounds and vibrations of the garbage and debris under them was overpowering. As emphasis, the towboat captain began to lay on his air horns.

"My heavens, more sirens."

Liam was encouraged to make something happen. "Move up there. That beam looks like it reaches that other flipped barge. We can run along that if we can get up there."

They moved up, slowed to a crawl when they had to balance along the shaky beam. Some of the loose barges slammed into the blockage directly in front of them. Without a powerful tug behind them, they didn't have enough force to break the blockade, but as they piled up one after the other, they pushed the existing debris further and further upward toward them. It also increased the vibrations throughout the wreckage.

Victoria slipped as she reached the hull of the flipped barge. She stabilized herself and had a look of dismay at how close she'd come to falling over the side. The slimy bottom of the overturned barge was a considerable obstacle. They paused while trying to determine what to do.

Victoria asked, "Can we slide down it?"

It was canted slightly toward the downstream side of the mountain. Falling off the backside would put them back into the core of the wreckage, but there was no way to see what they'd be falling into. Victoria and Liam might get lucky, but Grandma probably couldn't handle such a ride.

"I have an idea. Grandma, I'm going to lay down and you're going to lay on my back. Hold onto my neck like a piggy back ride, OK?"

He figured she would argue as she was wont to do, but this time she said nothing. It took a minute to situate herself, but they got it worked out. Liam moved along the edge of the barge, using the angle of the bottom and side of the hull as a way to hang on as he moved from the front to the back end. Since his head and arms were higher than his feet as he slithered along, he was able to prevent himself from sliding down what was essentially a slimy piece of playground equipment. His bare chest and pants were a disaster, covered with slime and who-knows-what from the river, but at least they made progress. Victoria did the same, using her ruined white shirt and jeans to slide along.

When they reached the end of the barge, they saw what was beyond the hull. A large gap to the water below. There were a couple of zombies splashing down there. If they'd rushed their plan, they'd have slid off the edge and fallen twenty or more feet into the water.

Liam re-adjusted Grandma so she was next to him. Victoria dropped the ten feet over the side, to the deck of a small commercial fishing boat jammed in among the empty barges. It was covered in mud, as if it had been dredged from a mud bank before floating here.

"I'm sorry, Grandma, you're going to get messy."

"It's OK, I'm due for a washing anyway." She gave him her patented wink as she dropped over the side with his help. Victoria was on the bottom to grab her and make sure she reached the bottom safely. Together, they slipped on the muddy planks.

Liam was about to drop down himself when he saw the powerful tug start to push through the debris. In slow motion, he watched the towboat move faster and faster into the wreck, as if drilling inward. It broke through. The far pylon that once supported the bridge above fell over as everything broke loose. It made a huge splash downriver and threw water so high in the air he could see it over the wreckage pile.

The blockade runner blared his horn in triumph as he chugged through.

Knowing it was impossible for Grandma, he still said it.

"Run!"

4

They were very close to Missouri-side pier of the fallen bridge. Liam took some comfort the pier was still there, as it would hold some of the wreckage in place even if the rest of the dam cut loose. However, as more and more pieces of debris peeled off the blockage to follow the towboat, the middle would continue to get smaller. They wouldn't be safe until they were off the water.

There was no obvious path to get to solid ground. Most of what remained were various sizes and shapes of barges jammed together, but they shifted dangerously up and down with the wave action and impacts from arriving debris.

"Liam, I'm done. I can't cross that. Al said I wouldn't make it to safety."

"*Moses* is already ashore. You'll make it to the promised land of Missouri." He knew she wouldn't know he was talking about his rifle, which was laying somewhere near where they launched the motorboat.

Scanning the debris, he wondered if they could cross the variously spaced decks while they bumped and separated in the turbulence.

I'll die trying.

"All right, Grandma. No way Grandpa would tell you not to try. I need you to get on my back again. We're going to give it everything we've got."

"Oh Liam. You can't. It's too much."

"We have no choice." Victoria spoke quietly given the noises around them, but they heard her. "Liam has to try to run you across. I'll try to help where I can. I'll go first and be there when he has to jump with you. Please, just try?"

Liam looked back one more time. The barges spilled through the gap like curious cows heading for an open gate. It wouldn't be long before the barges on their part of the wreckage started to draw backward to seek their own freedom. Then he'd literally be stuck in the middle with no way out.

Grandma wasn't finished; she tried to use every option she had. "Maybe we could just get in one of these barges and ride out of here?"

Liam spoke as fast as he could. "Well, Grandma, I guess if we have no choice we can drop into one of them, but we have no assurance the barge won't flip or otherwise get damaged as it goes through the gap in the wreck. Also—," he surveyed the sky as if to add emphasis, "Duchesne's helpers are still out there. We'd be sitting ducks in a barge."

Victoria added, "We could also float all the way down to the Gulf of Mexico before we came ashore, if at all."

Grandma let herself be put on Liam's back.

"Hold on tight. Don't let go!"

His dad had often said that when he was on the swing set, the climbing wall at the playground, or learning to ride his bicycle. It seemed appropriate.

Victoria went ahead. The first jump was a difficult one. It was from a lower barge to a higher one. She had a rough landing as she hit her knees on the side, but she scrambled up and over. Liam used a similar running jump technique and also hit his knees as he tried to clear the deck. Victoria steadied Grandma at the very edge and helped them both up.

"I think she passed out on your back. Hold her tight."

They ran lengthwise down the next barge. They were 200 feet closer to shore. The next jump was onto a barge that was alternating between too high and too low. It was sideways relative to the one they were on.

"We have to time this just right."

It was easy for Victoria. She planted the landing perfectly, then crouched down to keep stable on the bouncing boat. She faced the hold for a long time before spinning back around with a chipper plea.

"OK, Liam. Come on over."

The gap widened as he ran with Grandma. The barge under him started heading backward to the hole in the debris field. He didn't dare stop. He landed as the other boat moved lower, but he was just a bit short again. He landed hard, tipping to his left side. Grandma somehow managed to hang on, even though her left side took some of the brunt of the fall.

The entire debris field was disintegrating. The barge they'd just left was already fifty feet away.

"Now or never, Liam!"

Victoria got up and ran a short way lengthwise along the walkway of the deck, then she turned and dashed across the front. Liam looked into the hold as he caught his breath—it was full of living zombies. They were packed in like sardines but someone tried to hide them by throwing a huge black tarp over them. The canvas moved up and down everywhere, and where it was torn there were heads and arms sticking out.

"You could have told me what was down there!" He shouted to Victoria, though he knew what she would say. They had no choice in any of it.

"I didn't want to scare you!"

He huffed while carrying Grandma, but made it to the far corner of the deck with Victoria. She lined up to jump to the last barge next to the shore. It pointed into the debris but began to turn as it and the barge they were on were called out into the river. Liam thought she'd jump to the final barge, then to shore, but she changed her angle to make a much longer jump to a section of fallen roadway that linked directly to shore. Victoria fell hard on the pavement with a loud grunt, but recovered quickly and looked up at Liam, beckoning him to follow.

Liam walked back a few steps to get in position to make his jump. His boat continued to drift.

Holding Grandma tightly, he ran with purpose toward the edge. As the boat moved, it settled in the front. Liam kept his footing as the nose dipped—it allowed him to make the jump at a much lower altitude relative to the pavement. He was going much faster than he intended—falling as much as jumping.

Hang on Grandma. This is going to be messy.

LOOKING UP

Liam landed on firm ground and immediately fell forward. Grandma lost her grip and slid right over the top of him. But Victoria was there. She anticipated the glide path and put herself in position to catch Grandma or, at the very least, absorb her fall.

Liam looked up to see Grandma on top of Victoria, who was on her back. They were hugging. Still alive.

Grandma blinked her eyes as if waking up. For many minutes, he thought she had passed out on his back. He even allowed that he was carrying a dead body...

But she made it. He helped them from the cobblestones.

Grandma came out of her daze, and recovered her faculties quickly. "Lord, watch over us and protect us as we try to restore the Light to this world. And Lord, if it's your will, please look after my angel Aloysius, too. Amen."

Liam and Victoria responded in kind. Grandma's only complaint after all that had happened may have been a joke. "I think I broke some ribs."

Liam's shirtless upper body was covered in abrasions, scratches, and other filth after surviving the crossing. Some blood trickled off his head, down the side of his face. He could see blood on his knees; they were raw under his jeans.

"You and I finally look like we're on the same adventure. You're almost as bruised and hurt as me!" Victoria giggled as she helped steady Grandma on her feet.

"And Grandma. You've done more than both of us combined and you still look as clean as the day we met."

Grandma laughed at the obvious falsehood, but countered, "Oh, you two never take things seriously. I may not look it, but I'm beat, bushed, kaput. And my clothes—they need to be burned."

"We'll get cleaned up as soon as we can, guys. For now, we have to get as far away from here as possible."

Liam urged the two women to get completely clear of the pavement of the bridge. They all limped as they exited the last bit of the collapsed bridge deck and returned to the cobblestone of the river landing. They were below the partially collapsed highway that formed a ramp up to the solid roadway above. It was where Liam and Victoria started their downtown adventure, much earlier in the day.

Victoria and Marty collapsed to the ground, stating they were content for the time being to simply be alive. Liam watched the amazing breakup. The last of the nearby barges slid out the ever-widening gap in the river blockage. A great portion of the middle section was gone, and most of the floating debris near shore was gone too. Portions of the highway were still wrapped around the near pier, but the disintegration of the blockage took nearly everything else away. The debris from upriver once again had a free and clear path to head south. Somewhere in that floating mess, heading downriver, was the man who destroyed the world.

Don't let the door hit ya!

Liam began to think about what came next, but was drawn back into the present. A helicopter made its way low from the north, veering in their direction as if they'd just been spotted.

He almost couldn't say the words, he was so beat down. "Up up! We have trouble heading this way."

Victoria turned her head to see if Liam was serious, and when he pointed to the helicopter, she slowly got up and helped pull Grandma off the ground. They trudged to the side of the ramp, where the debris of the fallen span provided some cover. Liam wanted to keep something solid between them and the helicopter.

The pilot was very good. The copter came in low and tight next to the downed highway. The craft rotated so the rear cargo door faced them. As it slid open, Liam saw Hayes with a large pair of headphones and a mic. His voice called out from a loudspeaker under the helicopter, "Liam, thank you for helping me get rid of him. You've taken the heat off me so I can continue my research."

"Not again." He had no energy for a fight, but knew he was once again going to be forced to surrender Grandma. It couldn't go on like this forever. He looked around for any kind of weapon. He might be able to use some rebar from the collapsed bridge, but against bullets it would be useless. They could run for it. They could swim for it. They could—

"Liam, Victoria, you two have to run now. You've really done an unbelievable job of saving me out on that wreckage. You've spent every last ounce of energy to get me to this shore. But now there is no chance against guns. Once they land and come down here, it's all over. Now is the time to let me go—no matter what implications that may entail."

Liam could see it all going down. Grandma captured once again. He and Victoria would plan another caper to save her. It had a certain symmetry to it.

Does our story just go on like this forever?

Victoria spoke up. "I don't want to. But..." She looked at him expectantly. He knew she was right. There was a point when even the best men had to sound the retreat, and leave their wounded on the field of battle. But he didn't want it to be like this. Not when they were so close to victory.

"Maybe we could make it to the Arch tunnel and hide there?"

"Maybe we could get back on the wreckage of the dam and hide there?"

"Maybe—"

"No, Liam. You've done all you can do. Your jobs now are to protect each other."

He hated to admit she was right, but he knew how this would end if he didn't listen to her. They would either all die in futile battle, or all be taken—and Grandma would be killed in testing. He had to choose the only path where they all had some hope. Live to fight another day, and all that.

He gave Grandma a long hug.

"I'm so sorry, Grandma. I'll never stop looking for you."

"I know. I know. And I'll never stop praying for you two out here. Now go."

Victoria gave her a quick hug and left without saying anything. The tears spoke volumes.

One last call from the underside of the highway, "Liam, you did great saving me. Never forget that."

He waved as the noise of the helicopter made it impossible to talk. It had floated closer.

Hayes' voice blared out on the speakers. "You don't have to run. I'm not going to take Grandma. I don't need her. I have what I require from her already."

Frozen in his spot, Liam searched for a trap. There was always a "but" in these situations.

When none were forthcoming, he looked up at Hayes and tried to yell something to him.

"I can't hear you. I'm sorry." And, after a hesitation, "I'm sorry for everything."

Liam had an inspiration. He made a very dramatic impression of someone injecting a shot into his arm. Then he pointed to Grandma. "Did you inject her?" he shouted.

The helicopter hung for a long time. Hayes keyed his mic, but didn't speak right away.

"Liam, your grandma is *very* special. You have to keep her alive. Find somewhere safe. I wish I could help, but you are looking at the extent of my resources now. It's just me and my wife against the world. If we look for you again, it will be as friends. Deal?"

Not knowing what else he could do, he gave Hayes a thumbs up sign. Better to have him go away than do anything more traditional like a shooting or a kidnapping.

Jane piloted the copter north up the river, then she banked left and went under the Arch and into the city, to points unknown.

"Good riddance!" Grandma's shout was surprisingly loud.

"Amen, Grandma. I hope we never see them again."

"Me too. Me—"

They both rushed to help as her head slumped to her chest.

2

"You did it, Marty. I knew you were a fighter."

"What did I do? I feel drained. Empty."

"That's to be expected. You operated the computer. You affected things in the real world using just your mind. You reached out and touched someone using nothing but thought."

"Hmm. Sounds like an ad for a phone book."

Al chuckled. He stood with her next to the closed door to the computer room.

"Well, take heart you are the only person who has figured it out as it relates to zombies, though many special people can sense this connection in each other. You've managed to weaponize it." He stopped himself. "Oh, such an ugly word. How about, harness it?"

"I forget everything you tell me once I leave here. Can you just explain it to me so I can understand what this place is, really. And do it so I'll remember it?"

He laughed heartily. "Ah, Martinette, that's what I love about you. Always seeking the answers to the important questions."

He walked her out to the bench overlooking the dark ocean. The stars in the sky had returned to their former brightness. As before, she was swept off her feet at the beauty and grandeur. "Please, sit down."

"I regret I can never reveal everything to you. I know you want answers. Trust me, I want to give them. But there are things even I'm not sure about."

He took a seat next to her, and spoke as they both looked out toward the green waters of the infinite sea. "We are in your mind. This place, all you see, is how your mind interprets the raw data."

"You said you were going to talk straight."

"I am talking straight. Listen, this is both in your head and real. You've developed a link with this place, and the only reason you have is because of the pathogen Hayes calls the Quantum Virus. He *did* inject you with it, yes. But Marty, you've carried the Quantum Virus since birth. You all have."

"We've all been infected? Who could do such a thing?"

"My dear, you haven't been infected. It was a gift. A wonderful gift." He paused for a long time.

"A gift? From whom?"

"Remember when I showed you the lights behind the planets?"

"Of course."

"Would it surprise you if I told you Earth now has a light behind it? Would you be surprised if I said it was by your hand the light came on?"

"Yes, I didn't know I was doing anything that magnificent. I mostly just rolled around in a wheelchair, rode in a bike trailer, or slept."

"Ah, Marty. Here's where you're wrong. You did much more than that. You drove your two young partners to do great things. You were there to inspire them. Advise them. Lead them to God, the Light, whatever you want to call the aura of goodness. But, they aren't the reasons the light was restored. *That* was all you."

He rubbed his hands in anticipation.

"Can you guess what it was? What made you special among the millions of Doris's, Agnes's and Ezra's now perishing in the Zombie Apocalypse, as Liam likes to call it? Do you think it was your strength, or your speed, or the fact you once ran over your own daughter?"

Marty winced at the painful memory, but Al was relentless. "Marty, none of that matters now. You established the link. When you walked into that computer room—that goofy 8088 computer—it was just a representation of what it really is. A link between your mind, and the minds of countless others. The Quantum Virus is very unusual in that it must..." He appeared to search for a word. "It must compile, for just over 100 earth-years. Only then can it start to interact directly with the mind of its host. Only then can it fight the abomination that is the zombie plague. Only then can that host begin to see the gift it was meant to see. A guidepost on the way to infinity. To God."

She froze at the word "God," unable to formulate her reply. She felt the warmth of her Savior all around her, and she truly and absolutely believed He was sitting on the bench with her. If this was God's work, then she had the revelation she'd been seeking her whole life.

"Or..." He paused for a few seconds.

"Such a curious word. Or." He stood from the bench and turned to look down at her. "*Or* this is all just in your head. A clever construction from the mind of a very clever woman as a way to process all the horrible things you've witnessed since Angie fell down those stairs two weeks ago."

"What? No." She shook her head emphatically to make her point. "I had visions. I saw memories from Victoria and Liam. From Phil's wife. I couldn't have made that up. That's impossible!"

She saw him smiling down at her. The light from the stars above was distracting. "My dear Marty. You're right of course, it is impossible. *Or* maybe you overheard Victoria on one of your nights together. You spend a lot of time awake when others are sleeping. What if you heard her dreaming and talking in her sleep about her terrible encounter with her fiancé in that dark forest? Who's to say Liam didn't leave his very favorite book lying out one day, and who's to say you didn't leaf through and read a few pages? Perhaps you read about a little green coupe on a bridge? He carries one of his copies with him everywhere these days."

"No. This had to be divine. You said you were an angel."

"I said I was like an angel. I never claimed to be a biblical angel."

"But Phil. I spoke to his wife. Gave him a message."

"Ah yes. A true miracle." He paused with drama once more.

"Or..." A smile to her.

"Is it possible you ran into someone at one of your weekly quilting groups up at the church? A certain grandmother who may have recently lost a granddaughter and a great-granddaughter? Maybe private words were shared? A photograph of the family was passed around. When you heard his men call his name, you remembered that innocent secret under high stress, and that helped you bond with Phil on that bridge in your darkest hour."

"Absolutely not! I would remember that."

"Would you? Is your memory *that* good? Have you forgotten nothing your whole life?"

Marty looked down at her hands. Often when she came here, or when she left here, her skin would appear rejuvenated and refreshed. She believed she was getting healthier somehow; that Al was making her younger. Now, she saw the same hands and arms she had back in her flat before the sirens.

"So none of this was real? I'm just an old worn out woman making up crazy scenes in my mind to help me cope?"

"No, not at all. Give yourself some credit. You played out those scenes in your head as a way to cope, yes. But you *did* cope. In fact, you used your imagination to strengthen yourself. You renewed your faith in God, you bolstered your faith in your great-grandson when he needed it most. Your beautiful mind created this place so you could contribute in a world where so many of your peers were tossed like trash. You came here so you could fight. Isn't that exactly what I—I mean, the real Aloysius—would have wanted?"

Her gaze fell to the ground just in front of the bench, content to accept what he was saying, but hating it nonetheless. She resigned herself to the notion she wasn't special. Al wasn't here. She had no miracle gifts to fight and survive in the zombie plague.

A bright light flared above her. She looked up. An illuminating pulse was directly behind Al, falling from the stars above. Then his world began to dim, and Marty felt herself returning to hers. Everything disappeared except Al. He wore a happy smile.

"Or..."

3

"Who do you think was driving that boat?"

Liam sat with Victoria in the shade of the remaining jumble of wreckage while Grandma indulged in a nap. They thought she died by the way she slumped over, but she'd only exhausted herself. She'd been swimming, running, jumping, and falling today. She earned a rest.

"I have no idea, but they sure arrived at the perfect time to take care of Duchesne for us."

"Do you think it was providence? The hand of God?"

Victoria gazed out over the water while she thought of an answer. "If it was God, He had to have set everything in motion hours or days ahead of time. That barge had to have come from somewhere upstream. Someone had to fire it up. They would have had to gather up the proper amount of barges so it could break through. Someone had to fuel it. Someone had to drive it down the river—through all the other junk floating by. And they had to arrive at the exact second Duchesne was getting ready to shoot us."

Liam followed her train of thought. "And He would have had to work in the other direction too. He would have had to put you and me together at the perfect time. He would have had to keep us walking around, hiding and fighting zombies in the county, and bring us back to the city at precisely the time needed to get us in front of that boat. There were an infinite number of variables along the way. I have a renewed belief in the divine, but that's impossible."

Grandma surprised them. She was awake. "Not impossible. Just improbable. It was *all* improbable."

They helped her sit up while she continued. "This disaster has awakened something in me. Al is in my head; he speaks to me. He's shown me incredible things. He's shown me my own memories I had forgotten. I see memories of those closest to me." She paused, thinking.

"Painful memories." She regrouped with more energy, "But if there's one thing I've come to appreciate through these weeks of—challenge— is that you two have been truly heroic. No matter if it was God, random chance, or some spaghetti monster floating in the sky, you two were responsible for getting me safely to this point. I honestly believe no one could have done it better."

A little book was in Grandma's hands. The travel Bible Liam had given to Victoria. She had given it to Grandma in turn. Now she handed it back to her. "I'm sorry dear, I couldn't keep it dry." They all laughed at the understatement of the year. "But it did bring me the comfort I needed during my stay."

Victoria took it and bent over to hug her. "I'm just so glad to get you out of that horrible place."

Liam watched. Grandma was a filthy mess. She was covered in mud and green slime from being in the water and out on the wreckage. But Liam only saw her bright eyes as his chest swelled with pride at taking care of her for so long. He and Victoria got her out. They were a great team.

"Well Grandma, we do have one more journey to make. And wouldn't you know it, we're back in St. Louis." He laughed, and he put on a brave face talking to Victoria, but he felt so tired and worn out he didn't think he had it in him to face more challenges like he'd just endured. Not only were they totally alone in the city filled with zombies, they were out of food, out of water, and most critically, they had no weapons. They were sitting in a little bowl of safety near the collapsed bridge, but once they went up the ramp and into the city—it would be hand-to-hand for thirty miles. Even the boats were swept away when the bridge pier tumbled in as the dam broke apart.

They rose to their feet and gathered themselves together for the climb up the ramp of the fallen bridge. It was the same path he and

Victoria had taken hours earlier. Maybe one of them could slide into the hotel and find some weapons. Going down to the waterfront by the Arch to get *Moses* would be suicide with all the zombies walking down there. He tried to think like a survivor. He *was* a survivor.

They crossed the threshold of rock and rebar at the bottom and began walking up the slope of the collapsed highway. Grandma was between them. She looked up and called for a halt. "Look up there."

A lone zombie stood at the top of the incline. He was on the flat surface of the raised highway. His clothes could have come from Liam's closet: blue jeans, a black t-shirt with a college logo, a red baseball cap. A few others drifted up from behind the first. In moments, there were a dozen.

Liam had been shielding himself from the truth. Something he'd ignored as best he could every minute of every day since he'd left with Grandma out her front door. He was never going to be able to avoid the zombies forever. He'd finally reached the moment he knew was coming. It eventually caught everyone.

I can't save her.

"Children, put me down," she whispered.

As one, they all got on their knees, willing the infected not to look down, but knowing it was inevitable.

"I'm so sorry, Grandma," was all that Victoria could get out while she teared up.

Liam gave her a quick hug. "Is this right? I don't want to leave you."

"Liam. Go. I love you. Go!" she shouted, forcing his hand.

The cries of the zombies above rose as they acquired their prey.

"It can't happen like this." But Liam had stepped away from her, resolved to run. Knowing this painful moment had finally caught up to him. The tiny form of his Grandma remained on her knees, though she hunched forward to hold herself up with her hands. Her knees were too frail to support her body.

Victoria grabbed his hand as he heard a familiar sound.

Buzzzzzzzzz.

He looked up the ramp to see several zombies get sliced in half.

Buzzzz. Buzzzz. Buzzzzzzzzzz.

Arms exploded. Heads were severed. Large holes appeared in the torsos of others. When nipped in the leg, they tipped over. Some tried to turn around to the new threat. Most never had the chance.

A final sweep eliminated the remaining infected. Body pieces were pushed by the powerful impacts of the chain gun; some went flying over their heads. Others rolled down the incline. A leg tumbled the fifty feet down the yellow dashed line on the pavement; it skidded sloppily to a stop just in front of Grandma. Liam spent a long minute soaking in the impossibility of it all.

Not impossible. Just improbable.

Grandma remained pragmatic, "I guess we should go up and thank our saviors. Whoever they are, they can't be worse than Duchesne and his people. We don't have much chance on our own with nothing but wet clothes on our backs."

Her words made sense. They had no weapons. No tools. No nothing. But he could think of people who would give Duchesne a run for his money on the evil scale. Gang bangers. Looters. Camo-clad predators. All those working to snuff civilization. They all made impressions on him these past weeks, though if one were to only compare death tolls, Duchesne won that contest hands-down. He directed people like Hayes to do great evil. No one person in history had caused as many deaths by their actions as him.

But, a *leg* just slid up to her.

"Grandma, does anything phase you? You didn't blink at the sight of that bloody leg."

From her knees, she turned around with a big smile. "Neither did you."

That was all they could say about another in a long line of miracles they'd experienced today.

Together they walked up the angled section of roadway. Liam had his hand behind Grandma's back, as did Victoria. He could feel his girlfriend as their arms rubbed together behind the frail little old lady between them. Their fates were now intertwined, symbolically as well as literally.

Liam laughed as they walked. He thought about being back in the city. Back where they started. "What have we accomplished so far? We're now heading back into the collapsed city we spent two weeks escaping. A hotel with thirty floors of mutant zombies is emptying nearby. We have the bosses of Duchesne to worry about. And who knows whether Hayes was telling the truth. Grandma may have been infected, but she appears OK. What does that mean? We have more problems now than we did back in the simple days of just running from zombies."

"Life is messy, Liam. It doesn't fit into neat compartments like those books you read. When you get to be my age you'll realize that. You just do the best you can when it splatters all over you. God never gives you more than you can handle. In your case, this all helped you find this pretty girl here. You found each other. I'd say that balances things out. Love is a precious resource."

He looked at Victoria and smiled. She gave a big smile back to him. Her necklace hung outside her stained, cropped, and soaked t-shirt. The cross was wet, but crisp and clean. It gave him comfort as it did when he first met her.

Grandma continued as they neared the top, "This bridge reminds me of a question for you, Liam. Your grandpa showed me a memory and he said it was from your favorite book. In it, I was standing on another bridge looking out over the water to the Golden Gate Bridge. I forget what he called it. There was a little green coupe sitting alone on the huge span, but it had been destroyed by nesting birds and other animals. Do you know what I'm talking about?"

"Of course. That's from one of my favorite books of all time— *Earth Abides*. The story ends when a plague survivor grows so old he gets a little senile, and during a big fire that burned the abandoned city of San Francisco, the younger generations in his tribe—his descendants —carry him across that bridge and by that car. He'd seen it many years earlier when it, and the bridge, were new. When he saw it again in his old age, it helped him come to the realization that though man and the works of man are destined to fall into the ocean, the Earth itself would survive. Thus the title, Earth *abides*."

"Thank you. That sounds like a wonderful story. Maybe I'd like to read it."

Though he wasn't yet an old man with a tribe of survivors to his credit like his hero in that book, he realized they'd done better than most during the present, real-life crisis now consuming his world. He'd heard about old people giving up and letting death take them because they were afraid of the unknown ahead of them. He'd seen parents abandon children. He'd seen the undead walk, and countless deaths by their teeth. It was more horrific than any book. Where so many had fallen, his group survived. If Grandma had been infected, and something in her had cured it, she could hold the key to the whole thing. It would help them retake the world from the darkness enveloping it. Not many people on Earth could claim to be doing so much. There were still many challenges ahead of them—including whatever was over the next rise.

All around him, the works of man were broken and defiled. This bridge had already tumbled into the water, though it was brought down by man, not nature. The Arch was scorched. The city was a husk. The river was coughing up hulls full of bodies. The worst of man was being purged.

It was true, the Earth *would* abide. But so would mankind. He was going to do everything in his power to make sure his own book didn't end with humans ceding all the advances of modern civilization to the zombies and to oblivion. If he was lucky enough to survive the day and live a long life, he was going to fight the zombies until his dying breath. He would also fight the Duchesne's of the world—all those men and women sitting in their comfy bunkers. They were waiting to restart society in their own perverted image. They would find *him* instead.

Grandma said, "If everyone waits for the perfect heroes to come along, the world dies waiting." Liam knew they were imperfect heroes extraordinaire, but he was willing to fight for the world. He would read every book on the apocalypse he could find. He would study military tactics. He would lead tribes of people from the Old World. The old would mentor the young. Anything it takes to rebuild. The pieces were all there for anyone willing to do the work.

He had faith they could pull it off.

Liam remembered his own memory. Something from that Old World he'd been dying to do since he first thought of it.

"Hold up guys. Victoria, will you hold Grandma? Grandma, can I have my phone back?"

"Of course dear." She pulled the phone out of her pants pocket. A small miracle it hadn't been lost.

Liam excitedly took a few steps back down the incline. When he turned around, he had his camera ready to go. "I've been wanting to take your pictures for days now." He gave them a big smile and then tried to slide his phone open. He stared at it for a long moment.

"Is it working, Liam? It did get very wet in Grandma's pocket." She laughed, letting him know it was OK.

"Yeah, I can't tell if it's broken or just needs to be recharged."

"Isn't that the way of the world?"

Grandma's response soothed him. He wore a real smile as he rejoined them. "I'll get your picture yet. Just you wait."

As they crested the collapsed highway, he could see the familiar outline of an MRAP parked fifty yards down the littered highway.

"Thank you, God, for helping us win one."

###

ACKNOWLEDGMENTS

This series has been a labor of love in so many ways. When I sat down at my keyboard and started the first book, I had no idea if I could even get through the first chapter, much less the whole book. Writing a novel was a difficult endeavor only "professional" authors could master. Or so I thought.

In the summer of 2014, on the day of the funeral for my 104-year-old grandmother, my sister mentioned she was writing a book. We discussed a few points about her challenges, when she planned to publish, and other details that at the time seemed innocuous. However, I was inspired by that conversation to spin up a short story based on an elderly woman living in a house with her nurse. I called it "104" because of the age of the protagonist. The story was a celebration of the spirit of my grandma and it helped me find something positive in that dark day.

But I wasn't done yet. I was so inspired I just kept writing. "104" became chapter one of book one. I dubbed it "CIV," which coincidentally was the Roman numeral for 104. It was the first of many coincidences I found while writing the stories, and the nature of coincidence fascinated me throughout the series. I didn't notice until well into book 2 that Aloysius used his nickname "Al" while inside Marty's head. His role with computers seems appropriate for a computer program, or AI if you prefer. Did that realization guide my writing down different pathways? You see, even an author doesn't always know where his creation will take him...

This series of books did take me into the publishing world, and for that I'm thankful my sister nudged me in the right direction. I'm also grateful for my grandmother and all the things she did to encourage generations of our family to seek the light. Maybe she is in a room somewhere with a rickety 8088 computer, making things happen in this corner of the multiverse? How many coincidences had to happen for me to be sitting there on that exact day, having a discussion about writing books with the exact person I needed, and then finding inspiration to write three books with a central character based loosely on her? Was it providence? Luck? Or was it always going to happen?

I want to thank every reader who came through the series, or just read this last book. As a writer there is no greater honor than knowing someone thought enough of my idea to take time out of their busy lives to step into my imagination for so many hours. It doesn't escape my notice that an author can get the near-undivided attention of a reader for periods far longer than many TV personalities and entertainers, including most politicians. This is what drives me to become a better writer, build more creative stories, and make my worlds as interesting and thought-provoking as possible. There are so many great authors out there—a multiverse of them! I'm eternally grateful you chose to visit my tiny waterfall.

Finally, a special thank you to my wife. As an indie author, you would think the pressures of writing and publishing would be reduced —I'm my own boss after all. But the opposite is true. I've spent a lot of late nights at the computer. She has never complained, has always been helpful with reading and correcting my drafts, and always encourages me to pursue my passion. I could not have done it without her.

E.E. Isherwood, Feb. 2016

ABOUT THE AUTHOR

E.E. Isherwood is the New York Times and USA Today bestselling author of the *Sirens of the Zombie Apocalypse* series. His long-time fascination with the end of the world blossomed decades ago after reading the 1949 classic *Earth Abides*. Zombies allow him to observe how society breaks down in the face of such withering calamity.

Isherwood lives in St. Louis, Missouri with his wife and family. He stays deep in a bunker with steepled fingers, always awaiting the arrival of the first wave of zombies.

Find him online at www.zombiebooks.net.

BOOKS BY E.E. ISHERWOOD

E.E. Isherwood currently has six books in the *Sirens of the Zombie Apocalypse* universe. Visit his website at www.zombiebooks.net to be informed when future titles are launched.

The *Sirens of the Zombie Apocalypse* series

Since the Sirens

Siren Songs

Stop the Sirens

Last Fight of the Valkyries

Zombies vs. Polar Bears

Zombies Ever After

Book 1: *Since the Sirens*

When fifteen-year-old Liam goes to stay with his ancient great-grandmother for the summer, he immediately becomes bored around the frail and elderly woman. He spends most of his time at the library texting friends or reading dark novels. But one morning stroll changes everything as the Zombie Apocalypse unloads itself directly into his life. Now he and his 104-year-old guardian must survive the journey out of the collapsing city of St. Louis while zombies, plague, and desperate survivors swirl around them.

Book 2: *Siren Songs*

After escaping the chaos of the collapsing city, teens Liam and Victoria are faced with a difficult choice. Do they try to find Liam's parents or defend their suburban home from refugees and the infected? They find new allies to hold things together, even as the government appears increasingly impotent in the face of a mutating virus. And why is a representative of the CDC trying to enlist Liam's 104-year-old grandma to his cause?

Book 3: *Stop the Sirens*

Liam and his parents are reunited at last, but the matriarch of their family has been taken to a covert CDC location for medical experiments. Liam wants to mount a rescue operation, but they must first reach a refuge, endure warring government agencies, and learn Grandma's location—not to mention survive a world awash in zombies. With Victoria at his side, Liam finds his fortitude bolstered by her faith. Together they begin to unravel the mystery of the zombie plague.

Book 4: *Last Fight of the Valkyries*

Liam, Marty, and Victoria are rescued from St. Louis. Now safely in the defenses of the town of Cairo, IL, they are once again free to look ahead—into the headwinds of the Zombie Apocalypse. Liam is separated from his parents, Mel and Phil are missing, and Grandma's status as a sane person is very much in doubt in their new town. But when Liam finally realizes what's on the chip given to him by Colonel McMurphy, he sees the way forward. Always with an eye toward saving civilization, he takes his first steps in that direction.

Made in United States
North Haven, CT
12 March 2024

49832664R00200